# STONESLAYER
## Book One

# Scandal

### Candace Lynn
# TALMADGE

Published by Wider Realities Media

www.candacelynntalmadge.com

Cover and Logo Design: Animella Agency

Interior Design: Stefan Merour


ISBN:

Paperback: 978-1-964293-00-4

Ebook: 978-1-964293-01-1

In loving memory of Marilyn Zuber,
who long ago encouraged a girl to write a novel.

# CHAPTER ONE
# (PREFACE)

"*Run, Mary! We sail or we perish. Now!*"

*Where mountains should stand tall, only a mountainous wall of water hurtles toward us. The noon sky blackens; the ground groans and roils. I try to move. My legs cannot master the wild beast bucking beneath my feet. I stumble to my knees. The relentless wave of doom rolls on, drowning everything.*

• • •

Gasping, my hands at my throat, I snap upright in my bunk. For a while all I do is breathe, in and out, over and over, relieved to be taking in air. *The nightmare of nearly dying returns.* Tears slide down my cheeks.

I fumble for a light-stick and flick it on. The privilege of a private cabin cannot cheer me. It is a cell jammed with a sleeping berth, a tiny desk, and one hard chair.

My home for the time being, an underwater vessel, is packed with things that are now useless, like the dead link on the metal tabletop close to my head. There is nothing to link to anymore; no one is at the other end, or anywhere else for that matter. The light-sticks may still work, yet they cannot be replaced. The secret to their fabrication died out in ages past.

*Will we who survive become as forgotten as the stonesmiths who forged these devices so long ago?*

I cannot stand even the thought of that prospect. I cannot bear it if those who come after this nightmare truly ends do not recall who and what preceded them. If they do not understand where we went wrong and learn the bitter lesson, they will repeat our fate, just as we now suffer the downfall our Toltec ancestors might have endured had it not been for Kronos the Deliverer.

I surrender to despair, crumble into sobs. *Damn you, Kronos! You did us no favor. You never should have rescued the Toltecs and brought them to the island where the Turanians lived. First the Turanians paid the price, and then we all did. Why? Why did you save them, Kronos?!*

"That is perilously close to what some might call blasphemy, Little Consort."

I shiver at the sound, reedy and echoing. In the gloom I can just make out the wall enclosing the foot of the bunk — it ripples and shimmers. A mist flows into the cabin and takes a stick-like shape. Soon the footless form floats before me, covered by a dark cowl and robe. Mercifully I cannot see the face. The voice is bad enough.

"Since when did the Mist-Weavers care about blasphemy, Maguari? And how did you get here? We must be a hundred fathoms below sea level. Should I inform the captain we have a stowaway?"

The cowl bobs from side to side. "I will not be staying long, Little Consort. And I have not the inclination to teach you fully about energy, so I cannot answer any of your questions."

My breath hisses through my teeth. It is a strange blessing to feel annoyed rather than devastated. Maybe that is his intent.

A disembodied smile pops into my mind. "I visit only to remind you that always there is hope, even in the darkest hour. Beyond destruction, love and life prevail. That is the way of energy."

"Did the Arkstone bring about the Toltecs' second devastation? Did we use it unwisely?"

The cowl swishes again. "No and yes, Little Consort. The stone's only property is to direct and magnify the energy of consciousness. The choices made by spirits exercising their free will brought you here. Some among you lusted for wealth and power, and made unwise use of the stone's capability."

I choke back tears. "No one will remember us, Maguari. We will be forgotten and lost."

He lifts one of his arms toward me. "Not so, Little Consort. You must tell the true story of the Arkstone and the Toltecs — and the Turanians. Through you and your tale those who are born into human-kind in later years will remember. You will stir their soul memories."

"I can't do it, Maguari. Where do I even begin? The entire story is so much bigger than I am. And it is full of the unspeakable. I don't even want to think so much about it. Some of the people involved did such wretched, despicable deeds."

"But speak you will, Little Consort." He pauses as though to think. "Yes, even of the being you came to call the Stoneslayer."

"Stop, Maguari! I hate it when you read my mind!"

"It is in your energy, Little Consort." He issues a sound between a snort and a sniff, his kind's version of a sigh. "As difficult as it may be for you, tell the story of the Stoneslayer.

"Begin with your dear friend, the Stonehealer. Was not she the one who inspired you to greatness? The greatness that helped you save from total annihilation those who chose to pay heed to your warnings."

He refers to Helen Andros. "She married the man of my childhood fantasies, Maguari. I probably should have hated her."

He emits a strangled cackle, the Mist-Weaver equivalent of laughter. "Choose to rise above pettiness of heart and spirit, Little Consort. I will leave you now to begin. I will not go far if you have need of me. Be at peace and relay the tale."

● ● ●

I find myself at the desk, in a seat that has no mercy on an old woman's backside. I stare at my withered hands. A Gridbook is also useless without the Grid. I will have to set this down the old-fashioned way, using a primitive sheaf of wordskin.

Yet I am at a standstill. The political and personal relationships (often the same) and the bases of power among the Toltecs in Azgard were complicated, to put it mildly. Perhaps if I provide a brief overview, it will jog my memory and make things clearer to anyone who reads this after I am gone.

# MAJOR POWER BASES IN AZGARD

THE KINGSHIP: Held by Kefren Poseidon.

THE PROTECTORSHIP: Held by Lord James Mordecai.

THE STEWARDSHIP: Held by Jacob Shinar.

THE CHANCELLORSHIP: Held by Griffin Mordecai.

THE TEMPLE OF KRONOS: Led by Ezekiel Malachi, the Supreme Lord.

# RULING, ROYAL,
# AND GREAT HOUSES IN AZGARD

RULING HOUSE OF POSEIDON: Kefren, Exalted Lord of the Kindred.

ROYAL HOUSE OF ATLAS: Enoch Atlas, Prince of Westar.

HOUSE OF MORDECAI: Lord James Mordecai, Duke of Alta.

HOUSE OF POLARIS: Lord Tarkon Polaris, Duke of Eden.

HOUSE OF PALLADIN: Lord Andrew Palladin.

# LESSER POWER BASES IN AZGARD

PRINCEDOM OF WESTAR: Prince Enoch Atlas.

PRINCEDOM OF ISTAR: Prince Seti Poseidon, Kefren's brother and heir.

THE STEWARDSHIP: Held by Jacon Shinar, Lord Matthew's father.

THE CHANCELLORSHIP: Held by Lord Tarkon.

DUKEDOM OF ATLANTA: Lord Sargon Poseidon, Prince Seti's heir.

DUKEDOM OF AVALON: Lord Nimrod Atlas, Prince Enoch's heir.

# UNOFFICIAL POWER BASE IN AZGARD

Consort of Azgard: Lady Naomi Palladin, Kefren's wife.

## Azgard Social Ranks

### 1) Toltec Royalty
**Ruling House of Poseidon**
**Royal House of Atlas**

### 2) Toltec Nobility
**Great Houses**
**Lesser Houses**

### 3) Toltec Commoners
**Business Owners**
**Professionals**
**Skilled Crafts/Merchants**
**Farmers**
**Laborers**

### 4) Turanian Subjects
**Mixed-Race with Royal/Noble Lineage**
**Turanians**
**Mixed-Race with No Royal/Noble Lineage**

There were also hundreds of Lesser Houses, all jockeying for recognition, advancement and, of course, more wealth. Painfully absent from my power bases list are the Turanians. Far more numerous than the Toltecs, they inhabited the island long before the Toltecs arrived. The Turanians had no power.

I have decided to fill out a glossary of people, places, and things that were in Azgard and put it at the end of each portion of my tale. I shall also draft a map of the island, which was large enough to pass for a small continent. I could put on it all manner of cities and other noteworthy landmarks, but I'll stick to the basics for simplicity.

I will outline family trees of the ruling, royal, and great houses, too. That should provide some idea of exactly how intertwined the power brokers and money-mongers of Azgard were.

* * *

I stare at my outline and quail again. Who am I to talk about the destinies of nations and of worlds? I am Lady Mary Atlas. I was once Consort of Azgard, heretofore the richest, most powerful nation on earth. Is that enough? Does that give me the right to proceed?

"If you do not have the right, then who does?"

"Confound it, Maguari! All right! All right! I'll do it."

Yes, I will write, although maybe not in peace. Not while I chronicle the monstrous deeds of the Stoneslayer. I will write to remember, no matter how painful. I will write, lest those who follow forget our legacy, flawed as it may be, because they did not live it as I did.

I will try to give the honor to Helen and our descendants that they richly deserve but so rarely receive. I will present truth as I know it. It may not be the truth, whatever that might be; even so, it is my truth, and the truth of those who shared their experiences with me.

May those who have passed beyond forgive my presumption in telling their story.

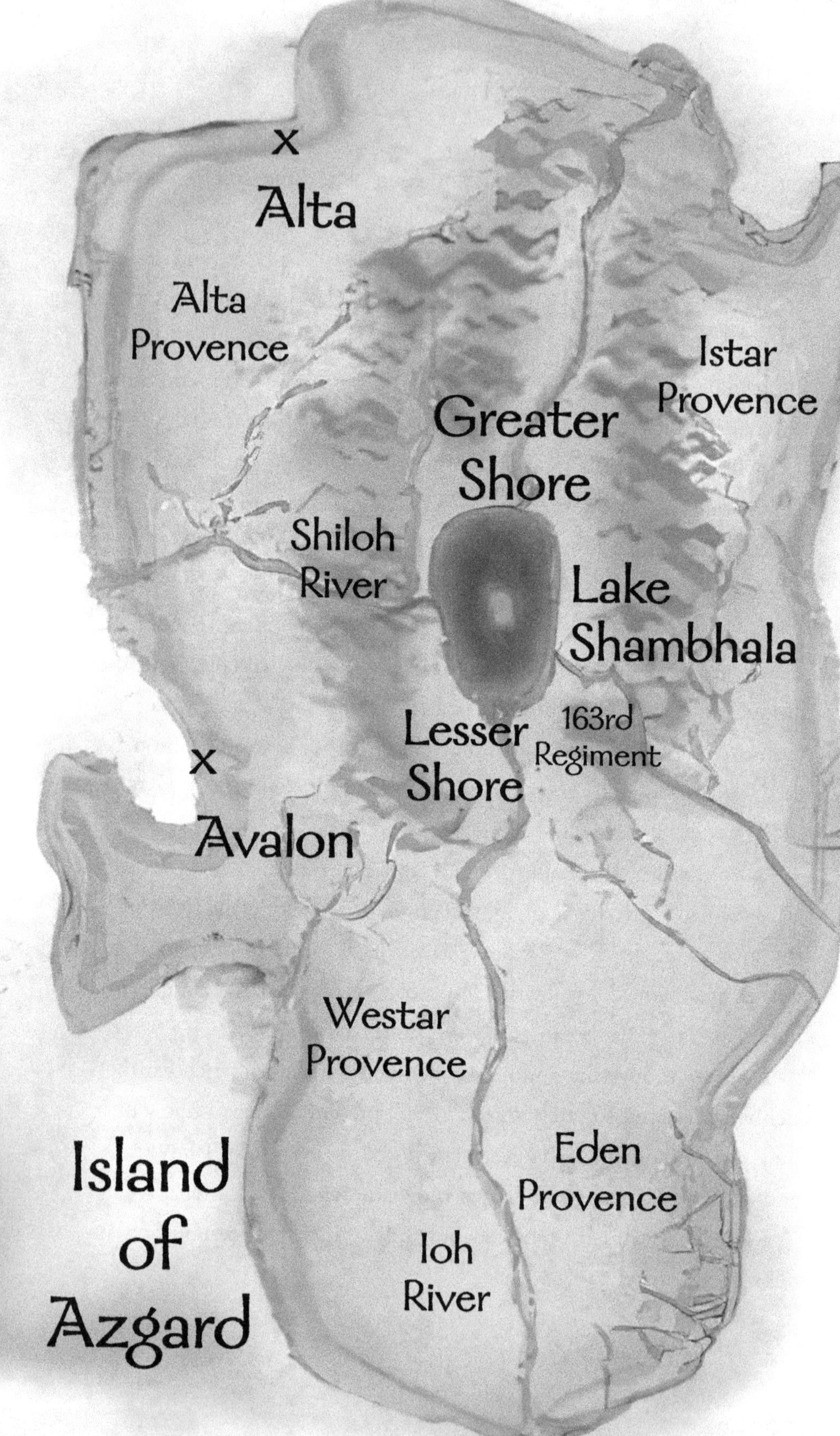

Alta
Alta Provence
Greater Shore
Istar Provence
Shiloh River
Lake Shambhala
Lesser Shore
163rd Regiment
Avalon
Westar Provence
Eden Provence
Ioh River
Island of Azgard

# CHAPTER TWO

The tissue sample results grieved Lieutenant Helen Andros, but did not surprise her. The sole medical officer for the 163rd Regiment pored over the conclusions and recommendations, reading and re-reading, searching for even a glimmer of good news, finding none.

Her throat constricted from a raging frustration. Helen covered her mouth with her hand, a habit when she was distressed, and swallowed hard to ease the discomfort.

She kept staring at the screen until a firm rap on the door claimed her attention. She glanced through the glass and stood up, hurrying around the desk to welcome her visitor with an embrace and a kiss on his copper-colored cheek.

"What on earth are you doing here, Isaac? Isn't this place just a little out of your way?"

The Grand Master of the Sacred Academy of Kronos was clad in the white robes of a high-ranking priest that also bore the green trimming of his healing office. His black hair, pulled back from his face, was held by a golden clasp at the top of his head, the braid trailing down his back.

He took Helen's hands in his. "I am delighted to see you, my dear. I'm in town for a private consultation."

She motioned him to a dilapidated chair and eased back down onto her own not-much-sturdier place to sit. "That must mean graduation exercises are done."

"They are. I'm surprised to find you still at work, Helen. Aren't you due for a holiday visit with your family?"

"Has Judith told the entire known world about this?"

The corners of his brown eyes creased in wry amusement. "Perhaps she just wants to make sure you show up."

Helen's empty stomach folded inward; she berated herself for her cowardice. "If you didn't expect to find me here, Isaac, why show up? Did you just get nostalgic for old times? I should have thought you relieved to see the last of me."

Isaac Sudras detoured around a touchy subject. Helen had managed to graduate from medical school and complete her professional internships and residencies by age twenty, nearly ten years younger than most students. Even a year later, she was still young to be practicing medicine as a fully qualified and credentialed physician.

"I couldn't help noticing that you have been keeping the lab students busy of late."

She suspected he was referring to the latest tissue samples she had sent in for analysis. Her smile was a little too sweet.

"Consider it their contribution to the military budget. Besides, a dose of real-world problems helps keep them on their toes."

"It's never easy to lose a patient, my dear," Sudras ventured.

"I haven't lost him yet, Isaac."

"It's a matter of time. We both know that. And this course of illness will be drawn out and painful."

Suddenly aware of her own fatigue and anguish, Helen fixed the Grand Master with a relentless gaze. "Years of study and exhaustive medical training, and all I have to offer is painkillers. Isaac, we *have* to do better than this."

It was their long-standing argument over the limitations of medical science.

"That is the entire point of research, my dear. One day we —"

"*One day* isn't good enough, Isaac. My patient is in dire need today, right now. *One day* just doesn't cut it."

Sudras tried to steer the conversation back to his primary reason for checking in on his former star student. "Have you told your patient?"

"That will be my last act as medical officer before the happy holiday."

The Grand Master chose his words with care. "May I make a suggestion, my dear?"

Helen tilted her head to the side, challenging him to continue.

"A hefty dose of professional detachment would be helpful. You do tend to become much too emotionally involved with your patients."

She exhaled sharply and lowered her face, saying nothing, too tired and overwhelmed to summon the energy to argue, much as part of her wanted to blast him.

The Grand Master scarcely knew what to make of Helen's uncharacteristic restraint. "What are you thinking, my dear?"

Her head popped up, eyes smoldering. "I'm thinking I don't much like this part of practicing medicine, Isaac. I'm thinking I don't much like not having more to offer a patient than, 'Sorry, fella. Here's a pain pill while you die'."

Sudras cleared his throat. "Aren't you being just a little harsh on your-self and our profession, Helen?"

"Harsh? I'm not the one under a death sentence here. How do you think he'll feel when I tell him?"

"I'm more concerned about how you'll feel when you tell him, my dear girl," he replied, getting to his feet. "You take too much to heart, Helen. You simply cannot save everyone. No one can."

He made his excuses and hurried out the door.

"I can try, Isaac! I can try!"

*　*　*

The 163$^{rd}$ Regiment's quartermaster knocked on the door to the lieu-tenant's office and did not wait for her reply before entering. Sergeant Miklaz Aran saw only the lieutenant's profile shadowed on the thin blan-kets hanging from a rope that stretched from wall to wall, separating the work space from the sleeping area. She seemed to be putting things into some sort of bag.

He watched her move, entranced as always. She was the tallest female he had ever seen; she almost looked him right in the eye when she spoke to him. And that figure was voluptuous enough to destroy a man's concentration entirely. He placed a sack on top of her desk, next to some brown bottles.

The curtain opened. Aran jumped to attention and exchanged a brief salute with the lieutenant.

"Good evening, Sergeant," Helen said. "What's that?"

He held the bag out to her. "A present for Lieutenant Angel. Something to eat on your journey."

She took it and put it back on the desk. "Wipe that damn grin off your face, Sergeant. A smiling Toltec is a contradiction in terms."

"You haven't eaten anything since morning. It's just some cheese and an apple."

"Do you look like my mother, Sergeant?"

"Someone has to look after you, Lieutenant Angel. You won't do it." His smile widened. "Marry me, Lieutenant Angel. I'll take care of you."

Helen didn't know whether to laugh or wring his neck. "For the millionth time, Sergeant. The answer is no."

He sank to his knees, repeated his proposal. She followed the path of his eyes, and noticed it didn't reach her face.

"Elevate your gaze, Sergeant, or lower your stripes. You are addressing a fellow officer."

"You don't look at all like a *fellow* officer."

"Off your knees, Sergeant, and sit. That's an order, damn it."

He slid onto the chair behind the desk.

"You are not making this any easier for me, Miklaz."

Helen paced for a while in the small area between the desk and the door. Having no idea how to tell him, she placed her hand on top of her uniform jacket, over her heart. Beneath her clothing she traced the hard oval contour of the green gem that she always wore, even on duty. It was the only possession of her mother's that remained with her. She loved it for that reason, and because it came from her unknown father.

Warmth soon radiated from the stone into her hand and her heart. It was so faint that Helen wasn't even aware of it. All she experienced was a vague sense of reassurance. Her confusion melted away and her chest was not as hard-pressed.

She had the strength to do it. She stopped walking and looked at him, her eyes bright. "You have stomach cancer, Miklaz."

He shrugged. "So, you'll cut it out of me or something. It's no big deal."

Helen shook her head, blinking back tears. "I can't, Miklaz. It's too widespread. It's also moved into your intestines. Surgery won't help. Any other treatment would destroy your stomach and other organs."

The real message started to sink in. "How long?"

She considered for a moment. "Six months, possibly longer. That is a very optimistic estimate."

She pointed to the mystery bottles one by one, explaining the differing herbal treatment each contained, when and how to use it. She repeated her words to make sure he grasped what she was telling him.

He took up one of the containers. "This isn't standard treatment, Lieutenant. I have never processed a purchase order for something like this."

"Of course not, Miklaz. It's not standard treatment because the regiment doesn't have the budget for standard treatment, or much of any other kind of medicines. I found these concoctions among a collection of ancient writings. They'll have to suffice. I am sorry I can't do more."

Aran's normally animated face was more pensive than she had ever seen it before. "What is it like to die, Doctor?"

His question caught her off guard. There was no answer for it in all of her medical training.

"Doctor?"

"I can't tell you, Miklaz. I don't know."

She leaned toward him, resting her palms on the edge of the desk. "But I can tell you this. You won't be alone. I will be with you. I promise."

"That's more than enough for me. You really are an angel."

* * *

Clad in full uniform, Helen strode toward the airstrip where the transport was preparing for flight. She shivered in a chill wind that heralded another snowstorm. She had no overcoat. She could not afford to buy a regulation garment out of her pay, made even more meager by spending her own money on herbs, and by having it docked regularly for insubordination. Not that she much cared; she didn't take this job for the money.

Her commanding officer, Colonel Jackson Orlando, walked beside her, carrying her satchel. She was irked by him. He didn't seem to care about the sergeant. The colonel asked only whether the man was fit for duty. Aran was, for the time being. Helen planned to monitor this patient closely in the coming months. She wasn't certain whether the sergeant's condition would deteriorate bit by bit or all at once.

Trailed by Aran, the two reached the bottom of the ramp leading into the hold of the transport. Troops were moving in and out, stowing supplies for the base on the far northern coast where the transport was headed, with one unscheduled stop at a farm on the journey there and back.

She took the travel bag from Orlando. "Tell me, Colonel. Do you always carry luggage for a lowly lieutenant? Or is this a special occasion?"

Orlando jerked his head toward the ramp. "Get going, Lieutenant. You'll be picked up in one week."

Helen slung the bag's strap over her shoulder. "I don't recall a transport scheduled for this time of the month, Colonel."

Behind them, Aran developed a cough, as did several other soldiers who overheard her.

Orlando ignored them. "They come and go when I say so, Lieutenant. So do you. Now move."

Helen rolled her eyes and climbed up the ramp. Aran close by, Orlando remained on the airstrip until after the transport took off, just to make sure she was on it.

He watched it disappear into the darkness, his heart aching for her. He probably should put her on report again for her insubordinate comments. He had no idea how much longer he could keep her unbecoming conduct a secret. She was a wretched soldier and so outstanding a physician that he did not have the heart to do what his duty demanded of him. It would take away the only decent medical care his men had received in years.

Satisfied she was gone, he turned and was face-to-face with the sergeant, alone on the pavement, under the glare of a torch-stick. He was very concerned about the quartermaster. He liked the man, as did almost everyone in the regiment. Furthermore, Aran was just about the best in the entire Army at stretching thin budgets by scrounging and finagling for supplies. Many men would be far worse off for his passing.

"What are you waiting for, Colonel? Why haven't you asked her?"

"Damn it, Aran! One insubordinate junior officer is more than enough in this outfit. Report to Major Tufts for extra duty."

Aran saluted and left. Orlando remained, the sergeant's question taunting him. He didn't ask because he didn't dare. His gut told him that she wasn't what she seemed. Even when she glared at him or disrespected him, as she had just a few minutes ago, he could swear she reminded him of someone very familiar, someone important. He just couldn't figure out whom. And until he did, prudence was the only safe course.

# CHAPTER THREE

Sudras poked his head into the dim bedchamber. Stepping across the threshold, he found a teen sprawled across faded, disheveled sheets. The youth's trim, muscular body was drenched in sweat. His skin was ashen-blue instead of its normal tawny shade. His dark eyes stared vacantly. Most worrisome was his labored breathing. He wheezed ominously when he inhaled and exhaled.

An older man beside the bed struggled to stand, leaning heavily on a cane. Sudras waved him back to his seat and moved closer, further assessing the boy's fragile condition.

Sudras felt the same kind of frustration that he imagined Helen must have experienced. Thanks to the Blood-Oath of the Brotherhood of Kronos, he could do little directly to avert this dangerous crisis, which had considerable political overtones.

"You take a big risk to visit us, Grand Master."

"I'm hardly the one most at risk here, Master Tuk." Sudras caught the old man's eye. "Let's focus on the emergency. How long has Prince Harnak been ill?"

Amal Tuk did his best to provide an accurate description of the prince's condition. "He seemed to have a minor cold just a couple of days ago. Instead of getting better, he has become sicker and sicker, as you see him now."

"Ambassador, if you can tear yourself away from your prince for a couple of hours, I think I know where we might find someone who can help you."

● ● ●

The Lord Steward of the *Kinshazen* admitted the unexpected visitors to his study despite the holiday and the early hour. His Chief Butler poured three glasses of pepper brandy and set them on a table, then departed, closing the doors behind him.

Directing his guests to well-padded armchairs, Jacob Shinar appeared incredulous as Tuk summed up his failed attempts to secure medical attention for Prince Harnak.

"What was the excuse the Lord Chancellor gave you?" Shinar asked.

Tuk swallowed hard. If the situation had not been so desperate, he would never have agreed to insert himself or his prince into the middle of the ongoing feud between the two most powerful factions that dominated politics in Azgard.

"The Lord Chancellor said he could not ask any priest of The Blood to violate his Oath of Purity. And with the holiday, it would be most difficult to secure anyone else," Tuk replied.

"Really." Shinar drained his glass and rose to get refills, pouring more dark liquid into all three goblets. He gazed at Sudras. "You're a priest of The Blood. Why are you involved?"

"I am interested in saving lives by not allowing the death of Prince Harnak, Lord Steward," Sudras replied. "As you know, such an avoidable tragedy most likely would provoke Kamut into another attempt at independence."

"Giving the Prince of Istar and the Lord Chancellor the excuse they need to clamp down completely and order the Lord Protector to station troops from Memfys all the way south along the Great River to the Nubian border," Shinar said. "Most likely that would start another war. What do you want me to do?"

Tuk deferred to Sudras, not daring to make such a request of the Lord Steward.

Sudras took the plunge. "Your son, Lord Matthew, was one of my best medical students at the Academy. Would you be willing to allow him to examine and treat Prince Harnak?"

Shinar, his hollow-cheeked face thoughtful, summoned the butler to fetch Lord Matthew and told him to include Tuk and Sudras for the morning meal. The two visitors departed the study to allow the Lord Steward privacy to confer with his son.

*　*　*

Lord Matthew stumbled into the room, catching his foot on the corner of a carpet. The young man, more than a decade older than Helen but her medical school peer nonetheless, had a stack of reports under his arm. The pockets of his wrinkled coat bulged with notes. He hadn't slept the entire night, working on an experiment.

Lord Matthew waited silently until the father he held in so much awe spoke to him.

Shinar outlined the situation of Prince Harnak's illness, relaying the urgent request of Tuk and Sudras. "The health and well-being of Prince Harnak have serious political repercussions, Matthew."

Lord Matthew faced a dilemma. "Sir, my experience is mostly theoretical and research oriented. It's one thing to work in a laboratory, and it's another thing entirely to treat a gravely ill patient. I do know someone I think is fully qualified for this task. One of my former classmates."

* * *

Lord Matthew's suggestion alarmed Sudras. He agreed to it over break-fast mostly because he did not want to explain to the Lord Steward that the physician was mixed-race and illegitimate.

Helen was the best possible choice for the assignment. Even so, Sudras had done everything he could imagine to avoid bringing her into a situation politically ambiguous and loaded with enormous risk, especially for a young woman as vulnerable as she. With Lord Matthew's refusal, there may have been no other options if Prince Harnak was to have any chance of surviving, but they were running out of time.

It was well past lunch by the time they nailed down all the details. Thanks to his excellent relationship with the Lord Protector, Shinar had little trouble persuading the realm's highest military commander to permit the medical officer for the 163$^{rd}$ Regiment to attend Prince Harnak. The Lord Protector even made one of his military aircraft and a pilot available to convey the lieutenant back to Shambhala.

The arrangement filled Lord Matthew with apprehension, guilt, and a desire to see Helen again. He insisted on going with Tuk to the Andros farm, despite his father's concerns and strenuous protests from his mother, Lady Siroma Poseidon.

Her silk skirt billowing in the sharp wind, she put her lips to her son's ear to be heard over the whine of the rotor's engines. "Why are you doing this? Why risk involvement?"

He kissed her on the forehead before turning to board the craft. "I'm already involved, Mother. I might as well make myself useful."

# CHAPTER FOUR

Too tired to think or move, Helen sat at the long table in the farmhouse kitchen, grateful to be in a seat that wasn't bouncing. The pale winter sun at last rose high enough above the horizon to shine through the windows, proclaiming the start of the holiday week known among Turanians as Kindling, the Lights of Passage.

Heartsick over the sergeant's fatal illness, Helen warmed her slender hands by wrapping them around a mug of steaming *kaf*. The cold managed to invade the large kitchen despite a healthy fire in the stone hearth directly behind her, and several ovens already sending out waves of heat along with the tantalizing buttery, yeasty, and meaty scents of a feast in the making.

Abigail Andros sat across from Helen. Every so often she paused to give directions to the serving girls and farmhands who busied themselves noisily with cooking, cleaning, and other holiday preparations. Trying, and failing, to be subtle, Abigail kept staring with kindly blue eyes at the young woman she met for the first time less than an hour ago.

Abigail thought Helen lovely in a remarkable way. Helen's long-waisted figure was evenly proportioned between legs and torso. She was well muscled and appeared strong, although Abigail believed her much too thin. Her wrist and collarbones protruded too far, covered by a smooth, unblemished skin that was too pale to pass for the earthen brown and red hues of the Toltecs, yet too dark to be entirely Turanian. It was the combination of the girl's hair and eyes that betrayed her mixed heritage, however. Her long, wavy tresses were the utter black of the Toltecs; her large orbs were luminescent blue with flecks of gray.

A mug clanged against the tiled countertop. Still half asleep, not quite steady on her slippered feet, Martha Galan poured herself some *kaf.* Her need to assure herself that her beloved niece had actually arrived safely prompted her to wake up unusually early. Martha sat at the head of the table between Helen and Abigail and brushed her wispy hair out of her eyes, downing the brew.

"John has taken Ariel and all the boys hunting," Abigail said. "The girls won't be back until late."

"On a wickedly cold morning like this?" Martha took another deep swallow, trying to collect her scattered thoughts into a coherent sentence. "It's insane. Surely we have food enough for an entire town. At least it smells that way."

"I suspect John and Ariel just wanted to get away to talk business," Abigail replied. "I threatened them with dire consequences if they do so within my hearing during this holiday."

Abigail looked at the newcomer to her home. "This is a time to be with family. I am very pleased you are here, Helen. It's a shame that we did not meet long ago."

Not knowing how to respond, Helen nodded. Her wrung-out physical and emotional state was evident in her tight, slumping shoulders
and moisture at the corners of her eyes.

Martha, the *kaf* kicking in, finally noticed. "How long has it been
since you slept or ate?"

"I can't remember, Aunt Martha. I'm fine, really. What may I do to
help, Abigail?"

"That's it. You're going to bed," Martha said.

"You need sleep if you are to look and feel your best for the First
Feast tonight," Abigail agreed. "I'll let Martha show you to one of the
spare bedrooms."

Too worn out even to pretend to argue, Helen grabbed the slipskin
satchel by her feet and allowed her aunt to lead her to a room on the
second floor of the rambling structure, which had been the Andros
family seat for untold generations.

She was asleep before her head hit the pillow.

● ● ●

Martha tiptoed into the bedroom; Helen still slumbered. She held
a new dress and a new pair of shoes. She hung the dress on a hook on
the outside of the closet door and put the shoes on the rug below it.

She gazed at her beloved niece, unsure of what to do, and put her
hand underneath her apron. Within the pocket was an unopened letter
addressed to Helen from her mother. That letter was with the child
when Helen, just ten, appeared at the Galan doorstep a little more than
a decade ago. Helen was homeless and presumed orphaned after fleeing
without her mother from the siege and sack of Memfys in the Second
Nubian War.

As she had, on many previous occasions, Martha was tempted to let Helen read her mother's letter. In a different letter addressed to her, however, Miriam had asked her younger sister to retain Helen's letter for the girl's thirty-fifth birthday. That was the age of her majority according to Toltec law and custom and was still many years away. Out of respect for her elder sister's wishes, Martha had kept that second letter secret from everyone. Not even her husband, Ariel, knew about it.

Helen awoke and Martha snatched her hand out from behind the apron. "Good evening, sleepyhead."

Helen sat up, rubbing her eyes and yawning. Martha stepped aside to show her niece the new clothes. "An early present from your uncle and me. Something special to wear tonight."

Helen saw that the gown was of the softest Upland wool, midnight blue, and had long, tight-fitting sleeves, and a close-fitting bodice with a full skirt. The neckline was just right to show off the green gemstone. The slipskin flats were of the same dark blue shade.

Helen was embarrassed by such a costly gift. "It's beautiful, Aunt Martha. But you—"

"Do you like it?"

"Of course. I've never had a dress this beautiful in my life."

"Then it's more than time."

Helen arose from bed and her aunt straightened the covers. "How are we to get you married if you don't look your best?"

Helen wrapped her shoulders in one of her aunt's shawls and sat back down on the quilted bedspread. "It seems to me we've had this discussion many times before, Aunt Martha. I'm not exactly prime marriage material. I have my work, and that's just going to have to be enough for me."

"Your work." Martha's disapproval and disappointment were undisguised. "It's no job for a respectable woman. You look like some sort of camp follower."

Disturbed as much by her aunt's tone as by her words, Helen arose and wandered to the windowsill. "Is that what you think of me?" Helen asked. "Is that what Cousin John and Abigail also think of me? That I'm some sort of whore? Just like—"

Helen clamped her lips shut to keep from adding, "my mother."

She folded her arms across her chest and stared outside. It was night and she could see little. Tears rolled from her eyes; she wanted to be any place except where she was at that moment, yet another household where, despite Abigail's welcome, she felt once again like an unwelcome burden.

After a few breaths, despising herself for indulging in self-pity, Helen tried to lighten the mood. "The soldiers I tend are mostly comatose, so they're no threat to my virtue, Aunt."

"Forgive me, dear girl. I simply worry about you among all those heavily armed soldiers who aren't in a coma," Martha murmured.

"We've already fallen off that bridge — only in a manner of speaking, Aunt," Helen added hastily, seeing Martha's alarm at the word 'fallen.' "A few of them tried to impose themselves on me, but Colonel Orlando made it very obvious they would be in big trouble if they took any liberties."

"Colonel Orlando?"

"Jackson Orlando. The regiment commander, although he won't be in that position much longer, I expect. He's now a part-time aide to the Lord Protector, and very young to be in such an important position of trust."

Helen pulled a hairbrush out of her satchel and sat down at the dresser to comb out the tangles. "I report directly to him. He made sure I had a ride out here."

That raised Martha's suspicions anew. "And how does *he* behave toward you?"

Helen stopped and laughed. "No liberties whatsoever, I assure you. We're all business."

She noticed her aunt's lingering skepticism and turned the swivel-stool toward her. "He's much too ambitious to allow personal feelings to get in his way, not that he has any for me. Getting involved with me would be a real career-killer for any officer. Which is why all of them pretty much leave me alone."

Helen returned to her task. Martha had never before heard her talk that much or that positively about any man not related to her. Since Helen seemed determined not to acknowledge her feelings for him, her aunt merely kissed her on the cheek.

"I'll leave you to wash up and get dressed, dear girl. Come downstairs and join us as soon as you're ready."

Descending the back stairs, Martha realized she had neglected to tell Helen about another much-anticipated guest who would be joining the Andros First Feast that evening. Perhaps it was a deliberate slip on her part, and perhaps it was just as well that this guest be a complete surprise to Helen. Martha feared that if her niece had known about his impending presence, she probably would not have agreed to visit, despite Abigail's persistent pleas and cajoling. And this was a guest whom Martha very much hoped her niece might someday marry.

# CHAPTER FIVE

Helen was scrubbed and clad in her new dress, her hair held out of her face by a nearly invisible headband and falling unbound almost to her waist. The green stone hung openly about her neck. Even though she usually kept it hidden beneath her shirt or dress bodice, she felt safe displaying the gem in front of a group of mostly Turanians. A wave of uncertainty hit her; she hesitated at the top of the front staircase and put a hand on the gem for comfort.

The common room below her glowed softly from light-sticks and was decorated with evergreen wreaths and vines. Two white candles stood on either side of the mantel. The one on the right was tall and unburned; the other was short and nearly spent. In the stone hearth an enormous log crackled and snapped as it blazed.

The Andros girls had returned, bringing friends and relations with them. More guests from nearby farms and the border town of Alton also had been invited. Everyone milled about, chatting and nibbling on savories from dishes on the sideboard, drinking mulled spice wine. The First Feast was nearly ready to serve; the smells of cooked food made Helen realize she was famished.

Her Uncle Ariel was waiting for her at the bottom of the stairs. Paying no heed to abruptly hushed conversations, he took his niece by the hand, planted a reassuring kiss on her cheek, and led Helen to her mother's cousin.

John Andros stood with his back to the mantel in the middle of a circle of neighboring farmers. "John, allow me to introduce Helen to you."

Ariel made no reference to Miriam. He was not yet certain whether Helen's mother could be named aloud again in this household, and he had no desire to open old wounds any further than necessary this night.

Uneasy, Helen curtsied to John and then rose, keeping her head bowed yet managing to look him straight in his eyes, which were blue-gray like hers and seemed as good-natured as his wife's. His blond hair was parted in the middle and reached to his shoulders; the pale skin on his prominent cheeks and square jaw was leathery and somewhat wind-burned from long hours working outdoors.

Despite Abigail's friendliness and her cousin's favorable appearance, Helen half expected to be ordered out of the house.

John instead took Helen's hand out of her uncle's and planted a brotherly kiss on her forehead, his eyes shining with amusement. "I see you have Miriam's willfulness."

At the casual mention of the name of Helen's mother, the entire room relaxed. People started talking to each other again and laughing.

John kept Helen's hand in his, looking her over. Abigail was right; the girl was stunning. Even so, as one of mixed-race descent, she was such an outcast that he could not imagine how she would ever find a husband. Good thing she had real skills with which to support herself.

"Ariel, you sly devil. You never told me what a beauty she is." He pressed Helen's hand to his lips and released it.

"You never asked, John. And a prudent man thinks twice before speaking too glowingly of any woman not his wife."

The group of men about them chuckled knowingly. Martha rolled her eyes.

It was time for Helen to meet the four Andros children. She was drawn instantly to Lillie, the youngest, who was shyly ready to welcome anyone who paid attention to her.

"Why are you so tall? Are you very old?"

Helen laughed right along with everyone who heard the child and scooped Lillie into her arms.

"Come up here, and we'll talk about it." She put her face close to Lillie's, mocked a scowl. "Why are you so short?"

Lillie giggled and tugged at one of the red ribbons in her hair, so pale it was nearly white. "Because I'm only four."

"I'm twenty-one, and I have no idea why I'm so tall. I guess I just got lucky. It's easier to reach the cookie jar."

To Lillie's delight, Helen held the little girl on her arm while being introduced to the neighbors and other guests.

The boys were the first to hear the sounds of the rotor.

"Cousin Justin's here!"

Eight-year-old Daryl Andros darted out the front door into the snow without a coat or boots. His mother followed him to the threshold and called after him to return, to no avail.

Lillie still in her arms, Helen was standing in a circle of women who included her Aunt Martha. No one had to explain to her who Daryl was talking about; she knew the name.

"Why didn't you tell me about this?" Helen whispered into her aunt's ear.

"I didn't want to make you more uncomfortable than you were already, dear girl," Martha replied. "Judith is with him, and you know her."

"I'm not sure I'm speaking to Judith right now," Helen retorted.

Lillie squirmed. Kissing the girl's forehead and setting her down, Helen retreated to the end of the common room farthest from the home's main entry.

Lord Justin Atlas, followed by Judith, entered. Daryl perched on his shoulders, Lord Justin had to maneuver carefully to keep the boy's head from hitting the top of the doorframe. Despite her anxiety, Helen put a hand over her mouth to keep from laughing out loud. Others didn't bother to stifle their amusement.

Also unable to keep from smiling, Lord Justin turned to Abigail. "I found this child wandering in the snow. May he stay here at least tonight?"

He reached up, lifted Daryl off his shoulders, and set him on the gleaming floor in front of his mother, who grabbed his shirt collar and suspenders and held on.

As the host of the First Feast and head of the household, John stepped forward to greet his highest-ranking guest. "You are always welcome in this house, my lord." He bowed.

Lord Justin shook his kinsman's hand and clasped him on the shoulder. "You honor me with your warm greeting, Uncle John."

Lord Justin's sincerity made him seem much less formidable to the guests, who now crowded round to be introduced to him and to greet Judith, who already knew most of them.

Although encouraged by John's open acceptance, Helen hung back. She was not eager to meet the son of a woman who held such an important rank, and who had so disapproved of Helen's mother that she refused to be in the same house as Miriam's daughter.

Helen thought about leaving the party to avoid Lord Justin altogether. She remained, fuming, because she did not want to insult or offend John and Abigail.

Observing Helen backed up against a wall, Judith made a point of going to her, taking her by the arm, and bringing her to Lord Justin, who was the tallest man in the room.

"My lord, this is your kinswoman, Helen Andros, Miriam's daughter."

When he saw her for the first time, the oddest thought fragment about his elder half-brother dropped from nowhere into Lord Justin's mind. *The woman for Nimrod—*

Startled, he quickly regained his composure. Helen did not comment on his momentary distraction. She gave a low, formal curtsey to her second cousin. Lord Justin touched her on the upper arm, signaling her to stand upright once more.

"I am very pleased to make your acquaintance, Mistress Andros," he said. "It isn't often you meet the student who graduates from the Academy first in her class."

Her cheeks stinging, Helen wondered how he knew. Judith must have said something to him.

"You are too kind, my lord. And it's not often a woman meets the man who has achieved the highest performance of any student in any class. You outrank us all."

She walked away. Another group of newly arrived guests claimed Lord Justin's attention at that moment, and when he finished with that round of introductions she was in the middle of a group of women, ignoring him, it appeared.

After John summoned the group into the great room for the feast, Lord Justin walked next to Judith. "Did I say something to offend her?"

Judith smiled. "I warned you she's not like any other woman you have ever met, my lord. You cannot buy her smiles and compliance with flattery, even if the words are true."

Judith paused to look up at him. "And yes, you may be correct. She could well be the woman for Lord Nimrod. She would do your brother good, and not put up with his nonsense. Whether he is the right man for her is highly questionable."

Lord Justin halted and gazed down at her. Judith swept by him, her smile serene. "You were thinking ever so loudly."

* * *

The great room had no illumination save for a fire in the hearth. Two long tables, side by side, were decorated with more wreaths and candleholders as well as laden with plates and cutlery.

As the guests entered the door of the hall, Abigail handed each child an unlit candle. Everyone stood in one large circle surrounding the tables, taking up the entire perimeter of the room. Helen's place was between her Aunt Martha and her Cousin Eli, Martha's and Ariel's son. She was intrigued, having never before witnessed a Turanian Kindling celebration.

John entered the room last, carrying the two candles that had sat on the common room mantel. The used candle was in his left hand, and the new tall white candle in his right. He walked to the fireplace and lit the short candle, then turned toward the room and stood in front of the hearth. The guests grew silent to hear him speak the Words of Passage.

He lifted his left hand. "This flame represents the waning year. What is done is done, and what is undone also remains so. Wisely or not, lovingly or otherwise, we have spent that time."

He then raised the new candle, used the old one to light it, and then tossed the spent candle into the fire to melt away.

"Here is the New Year, alight with possibilities and potentials yet unclaimed. Let us choose this day to light our way through this coming year with love, understanding, and peace."

"Amen," the crowd replied as one. Moved to tears, Helen was grateful for the darkness that obscured her face.

John lowered the newly lit candle, beckoned to the children. "It is time now to kindle light, even as the darkness of winter begins," he said, encouraging them with smiles and nods.

One by one each child came forward, touching the wick of his or her small candle to the burning wick of the tall white one. They then found a spot for every lit candle in one of the holders that were placed on the tables.

Lillie, making a point of choosing one near Helen, had trouble fitting the candle into it. Seeing the little girl struggle, Helen was not sure how to help her. Although ignorant of the precise meaning of each part of the ceremony, she realized there had to be a sacred reason the children were involved. No doubt it would be insulting to take the candle away from the child.

She sank to one knee by the table next to Lillie, and put her hand around the holder to keep it from sliding, since the little girl needed both hands to wrestle with the candle. Lillie then managed to secure the candle into the holder and scampered back to her mother's side.

"That was very well done," Martha whispered into Helen's ear. Other guests were also smiling at her.

John placed the new candle in a holder at the head of one of the tables and signaled to Judith, who stood directly across from him, beside Lord Justin.

"Mistress Altair, please do us the honor of the blessing."

Judith began. "Let us bow our heads and join hands." She gave the guests time to comply. John stepped into the healing circle between his wife and his eldest son, Jastred, and took their hands.

"Now let us close our eyes and open our hearts to the love of our Creator," Judith continued. "This love is all around us, even if we cannot see it with our physical eyes, or hear it with our ears, or perceive it with our other physical senses.

"Let us fill our hearts with this never-ending, all-embracing, unconditional love."

After a pause, Judith continued. "When your heart overflows with this love, share the excess and send it to the center of our circle."

Helen was lost and isolated, unable to participate with the rest of the group. She was outside the circle with no sense of any connection to a Creator, and no concept of what unconditional love might feel like. If any type of God had indeed created her, then that Deity had made a mistake too cruel to forgive.

The blessing completed, the circle dissolved into laughter and hugs. The guests needed no invitation to find their places at one of the tables. Abigail's cooking was legendary for its variety and flavor.

Helen saw that her hostess was occupied with making sure the many rounds of food came to the tables in the proper order, and offered to watch over Lillie during the meal. Helen put the little girl on her right to be able to help Lillie cut her food.

Once Helen's hunger abated, she realized she was still tired. She heard musicians tuning their instruments in the common room. Most of the children and some of the guests were close to finishing their meals. She helped Lillie off of her chair.

Abigail, accompanied by Martha, approached to reclaim the child, who yawned. Abigail lifted her sleepy little girl into her arms, intending to put Lillie down for the night.

Helen had an idea. "Why don't you let Lillie tuck me into bed and read me a story."

Abigail smoothed her daughter's hair and returned Helen's smile. Martha was crestfallen. "But surely you will want to dance with Lord Justin. The music will start soon."

Helen shook her head. "You're not very subtle, Aunt Martha. I'm bushed. There's no sense in Abigail leaving the guests when I'm already heading upstairs."

The mother handed her youngest, now fast asleep, over to Helen, who picked her way through the visitors now making for the common room. Many were dancing already to the merry sounds of a flute and fiddle playing a Turanian folk dance, accompanied by laughter and clapping. Helen recognized the melody; her mother had sung the words to her many times when she was a child.

Helen mounted the first step of the back staircase. The sadness and shame evoked earlier in the evening welled up within her. She closed her eyes, unable to go further, trying not to awaken the little girl in her arms.

Suddenly, the music and voices died away, replaced by a familiar whomping noise outside. Helen did an about-face and rushed into the common room, where the tension was palpable. Turanians lived under the ever-present shadow of their Toltec overlords. Unexpected nightly arrivals too often meant serious trouble for them.

Accompanied by Lord Justin and Ariel, John pushed through the guests to his wife, who was trembling. "Why would anyone sane be out in such weather, and flying," Abigail asked, one arm clutching her husband's waist, another around Daryl's shoulders.

"That's a military craft," Helen said. "I know the sound of that engine."

Lord Justin agreed. "Please, Uncle John. Allow me. I will find out what they want."

At John's assent, Lord Justin wasted no time, braving the cold without jacket or cloak to determine the visitors' object if possible before allowing them to enter the house.

John felt an enormous sense of relief and gratitude. Whatever the issue, he was certain that his nephew's presence would offer them some protection. He could not imagine what they had said or done to offend anyone or break the many laws that bound them, although even the law was no guarantee of safety from the anger of some petty Toltec official or nobleman.

The wait seemed interminable. Encumbered by her small burden, Helen nonetheless helped Abigail and Martha steer all of the children upstairs as a precaution.

Lillie stirred, sensed the fear, and began to cry. Leaving the other adults to supervise the older children, Helen carried the little girl to the bedroom she was sharing with her older sister, Joan, and her Cousin Kira, Martha's and Ariel's daughter. Helen placed Lillie on her tiny bed and spent a few minutes offering extra hugs, kisses, and calming words. The older girls appreciated her efforts to comfort them as well.

Her fatigue dispatched by an adrenaline rush, Helen was in the hall just outside the common room when the three newcomers entered the house. Briefed outside by Lord Justin, an officer in the uniform of the 163rd Regiment went straight to John and made a point of bowing politely to the master of the household. He explained his position as head of the regiment as well as his post as an aide to the Lord Protector.

"I am on a mission of utmost urgency and delicacy," Orlando added. "Where is Lieutenant Helen Andros?"

Helen walked into the common room but did not salute Orlando, since she was off duty and not in uniform. "You have found me, Colonel. How may I be of service?"

Before Orlando could reply, Lord Matthew stepped forward. He took both of Helen's hands in his, turned the palms upward, bowed his head slightly, and brought her palms to his lips. It was the greatest public display of deference a Toltec nobleman could make to a woman, and was usually reserved for the reigning Consort or a female of honor, such as a grown man's mother, or a highly beloved and respected wife.

Astonished at the mere sight of Lord Matthew, Helen needed every bit of inner strength she could muster not to lose her self-control entirely. Out of the corners of her eyes she could tell that Orlando and many others were regarding her as though seeing her for the first time.

A pained look in Lord Matthew's eyes warned her not to respond in haste, confirmed by his first words to her. "I am always honored to see you, Doctor Andros, and would be happier tonight if the circumstances were not so serious."

# CHAPTER SIX

Terrified of a uniformed Toltec soldier despite Orlando's attempts to display respect and tact, the guests made their excuses, gathered their children from upstairs, and departed.

Helen listened to Lord Matthew's explanation of the situation and then just stood, arms at her sides, gazing in Tuk's direction. Helen's family and the newcomers waited in the common room for her decision, to agree to treat Prince Harnak or to refuse.

But Helen was no longer in the room with them. She was a tall, gawky ten-year-old crouched in the back of a skimmer racing through winding streets filled with fire, choking smoke, debris, and roving gangs of heavily armed invaders. She parted unwillingly and without warning from her mother, the only person in the world whom she believed had truly loved her. She took charge of a four-year-old boy, and they and the child's guardian endured a long, harrowing flight from a war zone to an unknown destination.

Helen, her heart shredded, did her best to comfort and tend to the needs of the child, who wailed long and loudly enough for the both of them as they cowered in the cargo bay of a military transport. The soldiers leered at her and occasionally made rude comments about her. Only the protector fended them off of her and the young boy.

Helen stared at Tuk. The old man, his aged face pinched with worry, sat on a chair not far away. He did not recognize her, even though she knew he was that guardian, and was aware that the ailing prince was the same child, grown to his teen years as a state hostage. And now the prince needed her again, to carry him, not from one physical place to another, but from a life-threatening sickness into health.

At what price this time? The cost all those years ago had been to separate forever from her mother. Helen knew enough about Imperial politics to be fairly certain that this was no ordinary emergency. Tending Prince Harnak would not be easy. Most likely she would have little in the way of decent medical supplies or equipment.

Surviving the political consequences might be impossible. If he recovered, those who thought to deprive him of medical care might well take out their anger on her. And if he died, how convenient to blame her. She might even be executed.

And yet. And yet. This thankless, grueling, perilous task finally put her in the position of being able to repay the debt she owed the prince's family. It was only too appealing to refuse, and utterly shameful even to consider the notion of not answering this call.

She kept silent, struggling between the well-founded terror that tempted her to decline, and her abiding, deep-rooted sense of honor and obligation. She had no desire to explain her predicament to those who watched her, since that would raise more questions than she wanted to answer, even if she could.

Observing the indecisiveness that was so unusual for his outspoken, take-charge medical officer, Orlando decided he could wait no longer.

He approached Helen and reluctantly whispered a message from the Lord Protector, with its implied threat to her continued tenure as the 163$^{rd}$ Regiment's medical officer.

Helen's demeanor transformed. Her shoulders squared; she seemed to fill the room with her infuriated presence. She fixed Orlando with a gaze so hard he could have sworn she slapped him without lifting a finger. Her mouth tightened into a frown. Her mannerisms again reminded him of someone very familiar yet whose identity remained elusive. Orlando racked his brain. *I've seen that same expression before, but where? Whose?*

Abigail suppressed a gasp. Judith sat up straight. They also were put in mind sharply of another person — the very Lord Protector whose missive they did not hear but so incensed Helen. Abigail recalled that Miriam had never been willing to identify Helen's father but had worked for the Lord Protector for many months when his late wife was ill. Helen's reaction was simply another confirmation for Judith of a long-held suspicion that she never mentioned to anyone because she had not one shred of evidence.

Helen spoke up at last. "Please tell the Lord Protector, when next you speak to him, Colonel, that, all threats aside, my oath as a healer does not permit me to refuse to treat any wounded or ill person. Of course, I will attend Prince Harnak."

Orlando swallowed hard. "Those exact words, Lieutenant?" He implored her with his eyes to change or retract what she told him.

"Yes, Colonel. Those exact words. And now if you will excuse me, I must prepare."

Helen spun on her heel and stalked out of the common room, heading for the kitchen, intending to explore Abigail's pantry and root cellar. She hoped to find herbs and other substances that would be helpful in treating the prince.

Orlando let his breath out slowly and rubbed the back of his neck. He opted to delay a formal report to the Lord Protector until well after the flight back. He did have to check in with the base north of Avalon for a weather update and to file a return flight plan. He excused himself and hurried outside to the rotor.

* * *

Helen stomped around the kitchen, yanking cabinet doors open and flipping off the tops of canisters, peering inside for she hardly knew what. Betrayed. Set up for failure and its devastating aftermath. Stark terror churned in the pit of her stomach. No. That was cowardly. Suddenly she gave up trying to sort it out and collapsed onto one of the chairs at the table, her face in her hands.

Judith, Abigail, and Martha entered the kitchen, watching and waiting. Helen heard them whispering among themselves once her sobs subsided. Lifting her head, she sat up and wiped her cheeks with the back of her hand. Judith sat down next to Helen and passed her a handkerchief; Abigail and Martha sat across from her.

"I have such appealing options. Shit or go blind."

When Martha chided her mildly, Helen retorted, "If my language is rude, I think I have a right. Don't you understand, Aunt? Refuse, and I lose my job. The colonel made that very plain to me — straight from the Lord Protector, no less. If I agree to go, I do so on my own, not under orders. Should Prince Harnak die under my care, the blame falls squarely on me. How neat, tidy, and convenient for everyone, except me."

"Then I suggest a third option. Heal the prince," Judith replied. "It might work to your advantage, or it could if you didn't insist on defying the Lord Protector."

"I'm not sure I'm speaking to you right now," Helen said.

"No need to," Judith shot back. "You've spoken more than enough elsewhere. More than you should."

"What have you done, Helen?" Martha demanded. "Have you insulted this great lord?"

Judith sat back and put her hands in her lap. "Not quite, Martha, at least not yet. She will come close when the colonel makes his full report, as he no doubt will very soon."

Judith raised an eyebrow; Helen refused even to look at her.

Her cheery face pinched with alarm, Martha stood up and leaned toward her niece. "Take it back, dear girl. Tell the colonel you didn't mean it, whatever it was."

"No."

Judith sensed the finality in Helen's energy and knew it was pointless to continue arguing. "Martha, let's go upstairs and pack Helen's belongings for her."

Judith nearly had to drag Martha out of the kitchen, earning a grateful look from Helen, who was now calmer.

"Please send Master Tuk back," she called after them. "I want to ask him a few questions."

Tuk soon appeared in the kitchen, accompanied by Lord Matthew. When Tuk started to bow to her she shook her head, instead motioning for both of them to sit at the table. Helen rose and paced, questioning Tuk about the prince's symptoms. The old man did his best to provide the information she was seeking, although he did not fully understand her queries.

"Have faith, Master Tuk," Lord Matthew said. "Prince Harnak is in very good hands now."

"If he's still alive a week from now, I might agree with that, my lord," Helen replied.

She grabbed a pad of wordskin and wrote out a list. While she was writing, Orlando entered the kitchen, followed by Lord Justin, John, and Ariel.

"There is a storm beginning to the southeast, where we are headed," the colonel said, looking at Lord Matthew. "My lord, you've done enough already. I must beg you not to come with us. It's too dangerous."

"I can find you a ride back to Shambhala soon," Lord Justin interjected.

"It is not too dangerous for you, Colonel, or Master Tuk, or Doctor Andros," Lord Matthew said.

Helen kept her eyes on the instructions she was completing. "It's an old military term, my lord. Expendable. The colonel's superiors consider Master Tuk and me expendable, and even the good colonel himself, which of course must be a great comfort and honor to him."

Orlando tossed Helen a warning look, which she eventually acknowledged. "By all means, Colonel, put me on report. Again. If I'm still alive in a week, I'll gladly suffer the consequences."

She held out the list to Orlando. "Meanwhile, let us begin this mission even before we get off the ground. Can you relay this to someone who can take it to the prince's household?"

Orlando scanned the document. "Explain it to me."

"They must not allow him to lie flat," Helen answered. "Tell them to raise his upper body to at least a forty-five-degree angle and keep him that way, waking, sleeping, or unconscious. They should wrap his chest in cloths soaked in hot water, and keep large bowls by his bedside filled with water so hot it steams. Place these bowls as close to his mouth and nostrils as possible, so that he breathes in the steam.

"Above all, do nothing to hinder him if he starts coughing. We are trying to clear as much fluid out of his lungs as possible, or at least loosen it so he can breathe easier."

Orlando left for the rotor to send the message. Helen turned to Abigail. "Do you have any peanut oil? What about herbs?"

"All in the root cellar, dear girl. Come this way."

She led Helen to the mudroom, flicked on a light-stick, and pointed to a doorway in the far wall. "That leads down into the cellar. Don't hesitate to take anything you think you'll need."

Moved by Abigail's generosity, Helen bent to kiss her on the cheek. "Forgive me for spoiling your lovely evening."

Close to tears, Abigail threw her arms about Helen. "You did nothing of the sort, dear girl. May the Creator keep you safe," she whispered, turning back to the kitchen to prepare food and drink for her guests to eat now and to take with them.

In the root cellar, rows of shelves were packed with all manner of dried, canned, and cured foodstuffs; dried spices hung on overhead racks. Against the walls, bins held wheat, rye, and other grains. Helen worked on a table in the middle of two rows of shelves. She chose a tall clear jar of peanut oil, and used a mortar and pestle to grind dried mustard flowers, placing the crushed remains into a hemp sack. She moved rapidly, since every minute counted.

The stairs creaked. "Helen?"

They were alone now. "Shouldn't you be eating something with the others, Matthew? You must be starved."

He took her into his arms. "I don't have much appetite. I'm so sorry to put you into this position. I—"

She disengaged herself. "In good conscience, my lord, I could not leave the prince in your care. He would not stand any chance whatsoever. Not that he has all that much more hope for recovery with me."

Lord Matthew caught her face between his hands, placed his lips on hers, and slid his arms around her shoulders, wrapping his fingers in her long hair. There had never been much sexual passion in the few sweet kisses he had given her; for the moment, it was enough. Helen returned his embrace and his kiss, craving the warmth and comfort of another person's touch. She needed to feel it more than she had realized or wanted to acknowledge.

She finally broke away. "This is hardly helpful, my lord."

"I don't feel helpful. I feel like a heel."

She finished grinding the dried flowers. "Really? I did not notice you making any of these insane laws and rules about who can treat whom."

Lord Matthew stared at the peanut oil, open canister of mustard flowers, and the other herbs she had gathered. "Are you preparing to treat him, or fry him and serve him up for lunch?"

Helen burst out laughing. "I'm preparing to improvise, doofus. I'm betting there will be no standard treatment available. I am thus employing some ancient remedies I've been using on soldiers for almost a year now, since there seems to be scant funds for medicines in the military budget."

She handed him the jar of peanut oil to put back on the shelf. "Would you care to make yourself really useful, or do you prefer to confine yourself to criticizing the menu?"

"Anything. Just name it."

"How good are you at petty thievery?"

It was settled before they left the cellar. Lord Matthew would return to Shambhala to scrounge for the supplies Helen listed for him. Helen had no idea what condition the prince would be in when she finally reached him, provided he was even still alive.

They brought the oil and other items into the kitchen. Abigail had finished packing some of the holiday leftovers for them to eat on their journey. Helen put the oil and herbs into the food basket. Changing back into her uniform in a downstairs bathroom, she added a rolled-up apron borrowed from Abigail to her satchel.

Abigail insisted that Helen also take a gray, fur-lined cloak that had belonged to Helen's mother, to which Abigail added a change of fresh clothing and scarves for Helen to keep her hair out of her way as she worked.

Saying good-bye was painful. Lord Justin took her hands in his. "You are not entirely without friends, Mistress Andros. If he does not yet know about this, the Prince of Westar will before you reach Shambhala. He does have some influence."

Helen bowed her head. Her aunt sobbed; her uncle put the cloak around Helen's shoulders and took her arm to help her to the rotor.

Inside the craft, she insisted that Lord Matthew take the front seat next to Orlando. Helen and Master Tuk climbed into the back cabin. She strapped herself in, helping the old man secure his harness. She also showed him how to adjust the small headset, with its mouthpiece and ear covers, so that it would muffle the engine's noise and enable him to speak to the other occupants if he wished.

The rotor took flight, roiling and bucking in the wind. Helen closed her eyes and leaned against her seatback. She adjusted her headset so that her voice carried only to the man sitting next to her.

"Here we are once again, Master Tuk, you and I, flying through darkness into uncertainty. Odd how life sometimes seems to bring you right back to where you once were. That wretched journey all those years ago still haunts my dreams."

A soft gasp escaped Tuk's cold-chafed lips. He knew who she was now.

# CHAPTER SEVEN

Night shrouded the Sacred City. Orlando steered the rotor toward the base where the 163rd Regiment was stationed, just outside the city wall on the southeast corner of the great lake around which Azgard's capital city was built. They would travel by land to the small compound where the prince was housed.

When the rotor touched down, Sudras was waiting at the hangar next to a skimmer carrying medical supplies. The Grand Master helped Helen out of the rotor, then, like Lord Matthew, pressed the palms of her hands to his lips even as he guided her to the skimmer. Her courage humbled him.

Orlando assumed the driver's seat and Helen climbed into the skimmer beside him.

"Look at me, Helen," Sudras said, as if she were his student once more and had been sent to him to be lectured about her attitude or conduct. "Do not, under any circumstances whatsoever, venture outside the walls of the prince's dwelling. It is not safe for you anywhere in this city, but to be on the streets alone is especially perilous for you. Do you understand?"

"Yes, Isaac," Helen replied, letting go of his hands. "I'll be careful."

Lord Matthew made a muted scene about accompanying them. Sudras put his hand on the young man's shoulder. "My lord, our part for now is done."

The skimmer disappeared into the darkness. Sudras accompanied Lord Matthew to his father's estate to make certain he did not try to follow Helen. "If you value Helen's life, say absolutely nothing about this to anyone, even your father," the Grand Master admonished him.

* * *

As soon as she walked through the door of the house, Helen started to prepare, throwing her cloak onto a bench in the entryway, rolling up the sleeves of her blouse. Motioning to the manservant to fetch the boxes and bags from the skimmer, Tuk showed Helen to the bedchamber.

The prince, his upper body elevated, lay on the bed where his tutor had last seen him a day earlier. The youth was now unconscious, his breathing extremely labored, his skin drenched in sweat from a fever raging unchecked.

A maidservant was pouring more boiling water into a metal tub on the far side of the bed, as close as possible to the prince's chest as she could place it. As Helen was donning the borrowed apron, she smiled at the young girl.

"Her name is Nona," Tuk said.

He and Nona opened and placed the bags and boxes on a table so that Helen could get to their contents easily.

"Have you been keeping the tub filled with water, Nona?"

The thin, sad-eyed girl nodded shyly at Helen. "You've done well. Now I have more tasks for you."

Helen directed Nona to find a chafing dish in which to heat the oil. She also asked the serving girl to bring flannel or any other soft, strong material she could find, and a bowl.

Inside one of the boxes was a medical bag complete with all the instruments Helen needed to examine the prince thoroughly. She focused on his heart; the beat was faint and irregular. Without blood analysis or images Helen had to guess the cause of infection.

She chose a general-purpose antibiotic to mix with the fluids she would administer to him. Out of a box she pulled a metal stand with a hook on it. She unfolded it and placed it on the far side of the bed, next to the pot of water. Then she fished out a drip bag with tubing and catheter and hooked it to the patient. She filled a syringe with the antibiotic and injected it into the teen through the catheter in the prince's wrist.

Helen took more time to examine her patient. Asking Tuk and the manservant to help hold the prince's upper torso upright on the bed, she listened to his lungs with the scope. That task completed, she decided to put the youth's tutor to further use.

"Master Tuk, would you please go through all the boxes of supplies, and arrange them on that bench and the table? It will help greatly to see clearly what we have."

Tuk complied. Helen did not mention her biggest concern. The prince's heart might stop beating. She marveled that he was still alive and able to breathe on his own; her examination of his lungs hinted at the reason. Only one of them seemed to be infected and full of liquid. It was hard to be certain without an image, but the other had to be functioning, if not at full capacity.

She wandered about the tiny bedchamber. The problem sounded like the lung nearest the heart. If so, then the main source of infection most likely was centered in the heart rather than the lungs, and the resulting inflammation of the sac around the heart-lung cavity was backing up into the affected lung. If she could not bring the infection under control swiftly, it was only a matter of time before the other lung filled as well. Then the prince would either drown in his own body fluid, or die first of heart failure.

Nona returned with the flannel cloth and the chafing dish. Helen put it on the table, lit the candle in the center of the stand underneath the dish, and poured some of the peanut oil into the bowl. She asked Nona to test the oil and tell her when it became close to being too hot to touch.

She next reviewed the supplies Tuk had laid out very neatly, grouped together not so much by actual function as by similarity in shape or size. Helen had to smile; it was one way to arrange the unfamiliar. She was pleased to find plenty of bags of solution. There were enough antibiotics, and there were vials of heart stimulant, but no shocker for heart failure.

"The oil is getting hot now, Doctor Andros."

Helen found the sack of ground mustard flowers and the other herbs she had brought. She ripped the flannel cloth into long strips. She mixed some of the mustard powder into the peanut oil, adding several herbs that she knew were helpful in expelling fluid from the body. She took the hot mixture and smeared it on Prince Harnak's chest. She had Tuk and the manservant hold him upright a second time so that she could also spread it across his back. Nona helped Helen wrap the strips of flannel cloth completely around the prince's chest, covering the mixture. They eased him back against the pillows that supported him, and Helen pulled the covers over his shoulders.

"We want him to sweat the fluid out of his lungs, even as he takes in other fluid into his veins," she explained. "His heart is infected and not working properly, which is why the fluid does not stay in the blood where it belongs, but fills the lungs."

That was an accurate enough basic explanation. All Helen could do now was watch his progress by monitoring the drip solution and changing the bag when necessary, adding more antibiotic every few hours. She also planned to put more of the heated peanut oil/herb mixture on him at regular intervals.

With no further immediate action, Helen became aware of her own fatigue. To stay alert, she sat on a stool by the bed, placed on the side without the stand and the hot water pot, and spoke to the prince in his own tongue. Her words were halting at first. She had not uttered a syllable of Kadosh, the language of Kamut, since she was ten, and it took her some time to remember words and phrases.

Once she found her way, Helen was unstoppable. Something within her had needed to talk about this for a long time. She described Memfys, the capital, with its crowds, noise, and dusty, curving narrow streets lined with shops and open-air marketplaces. She talked about the Great River that wound its way down to the northern sea from deep in the southern desert.

"There are monstrous scaly creatures with sharp teeth in that river, Prince Harnak, so you do not want to swim in it. But the water birds are beautiful, especially the blue heron and the great white kingfisher."

Helen also told the prince about the mother he could not remember. If Tuk had any doubts about Helen's identity, even after her remark to him in the rotor, they vanished as she described a dark-eyed, black-haired young woman, short and plump, with a merry laugh, lively wit, and love of good company and food.

"Your lord father used to joke that he won her in a card game," Helen whispered to the unconscious youth. "But my Mama told me she had a hard time believing that."

Tuk laughed. Hekemtep had indeed played a hand of poker during a breakdown in the negotiations for his marriage to Princess Notufil. When he won the match, he asked only that her father sign the contract, and the rest of the debt would be forgiven. The man, a minor pasha from a border state, had wagered more than he could possibly repay, and agreed. Helen smiled while Tuk relayed the story, also using Kadosh, the language he and the prince often spoke to each other when they were alone.

Helen's eyes became sober recounting the fear that gripped Memfys in the weeks before it was captured during the Second Nubian War. Nubian and *Umarii* troops marched northward toward the capital city; most of Hekemtep's much smaller army was dead or scattered in the desert. Hekemtep had to accept Azgard's terms for protection. Helen recalled the moment he told the princess that their only son would be sent to Azgard to grow up as a hostage.

"I've never heard a scream like that. It carried all over the palace. I hope I never do again."

Helen took the prince's hand in hers and rubbed the top of it gently. "It was as though all the joy and spark and merriment were ripped out of her by some invisible force."

Tuk looked at her, his eyebrows raised, not happy with the turn of her tale. She shook her head vigorously at him and continued. "You must live, prince, and return to her. Only you can put that beautiful light back into her eyes. Stay with us. Live!"

Tuk finally understood. She was using every trick in her healer's bag to give the prince a reason to survive, although the old man wondered how much the boy could really hear in his condition. He asked her about it.

"No one knows for sure, Master Tuk," Helen replied. "My mother, who attended a lady in a coma for two years, was convinced that unconscious people are more aware than we realize. My own brief clinical experience has confirmed this for me. It certainly cannot hurt him to hear his native tongue."

Helen reheated the peanut oil, added more mustard flower to the mixture and, with Tuk's help, spread more of it on the prince's chest and back, replacing the soaked flannel with dry cloth. She checked the drip bag and replaced it, injecting more antibiotic.

Nona brought in a plate of cold herb chicken and dried apples, part of the food that Abigail had packed for them. As the two ate, Helen noticed the girl trying not to stare at the plate that held more pieces of the chicken, which was delicious, as was all of Abigail's cooking.

"Nona, are you hungry?"

The girl nodded wistfully, and Tuk sighed. "We are short of everything in this household, Doctor Andros, including food."

"That's absurd," Helen replied, taking a piece of chicken from the plate, wrapping it in a cloth and handing it to Nona, urging her to eat it and take some of the fruit, too.

Tuk thought about her intriguing comments. "You say your mother attended a lady in a coma. Who and where was that?"

"I do not know, Master Tuk. She would never say anything about it other than what I told you."

"What did your mother do for the lady, exactly?"

"She provided physical therapy to keep the bedridden woman's muscle tone from deteriorating. And she was very skilled in massage; that was what Princess Notufil hired her to do."

Tuk nodded, the memory coming back. He could picture the woman in his mind's eye. She was diminutive, blonde, and green-eyed, with an oval face that radiated character and purpose as much as it did beauty. And she was unmarried, although obviously some Toltec had fallen for her; the evidence of their union sat before him. He finished his mug of *kaf* in silence, grateful to the woman for bearing such a daughter.

Helen's cry of alarm yanked Tuk back to the present. The prince's labored breathing had stopped. She rushed to him, felt no pulse at his wrist, and put her ear to the cloth and could hear no heartbeat.

"Damn! Not on my watch you don't!"

She ripped off the cloth strips that covered his chest. On the table she found the heart stimulant, attached a needle to a syringe, filled it, and returned to the bed. She scattered on the floor the pillows that supported the youth, laid him flat on the bed, and plunged the needle into his chest.

She climbed onto the mattress and straddled his lifeless body with her knees. She laced her thumbs together and placed her hands just below his breastbone, pushing repeatedly on his chest. At her barked orders, Tuk tilted the prince's head back, held the youth's nose shut and breathed into his mouth after each series of chest compressions.

They worked for what seemed like an eternity. It didn't seem to help. The room blurred and darkened; Helen was moving fast inside a long tunnel. An echoing, reedy voice filled her head. *Put the green stone on his heart and place your palm on top of it. Ask for help and healing.*

Frantic, Helen did not question the intuitive prompting. She unbuttoned the collar of her blouse, pulled out the stone on its chain, and slapped it onto her patient's chest. She placed her palm with its long, slender fingers on top of the gem and bowed her head. *Help him, please!*

A gentle heat and vibration emanated from the jewel under Helen's hand. Suddenly the formerly lifeless teen gasped. His eyelids fluttered open and shut. His heart beat again and he was breathing, although still unconscious.

Slowly, never taking her eyes off the prince, Helen put the stone back on, slipped it under her shirt, and fastened the buttons. He continued to breathe on his own.

Not knowing what to make of the voice or what just happened, she slid off the bed and helped Tuk replace the pillows. She eased onto the stool and smiled ruefully at the old man, who was looking at her, respect and admiration on his lined face.

"That was sheer desperation rather than skill, Master Tuk. Sometimes you get lucky even though you have no idea how or why what you did worked."

The routine continued for another day. The youth began to breathe more easily. His fever also diminished. Helen and Tuk took turns at his bedside, since Helen determined that someone would have to listen constantly for any second sign of heart failure. When they weren't on watch, they slept on a bedroll on the floor of the room.

● ● ●

The second morning after her arrival, Helen awoke and sat up, rubbing kinks out of her neck and shoulders. Nona opened the shutters to the window that overlooked the walled courtyard of the compound; the bedchamber was filled with welcome sunlight. Since the room was located on an upper floor, Helen could see over the wall into the snow-laden woods and fields near the house, and even beyond them to Lake Shambhala itself, glinting in the light.

Tuk had fallen asleep on the stool, the side of his head resting against the stack of pillows that supported Prince Harnak. As Helen approached the bed to check the prince's vital signs, the youth's eyes opened. He moaned softly, trying to frame coherent words. The sound awakened his tutor, who could not hide his joy when he realized the prince was conscious once more, his skin color normal instead of ashen gray and his eyes much clearer, although his face was strained from pain and exhaustion.

"How long?"

There were tears in the old man's eyes. "Almost six days, my prince. It is so good to see you back with us again."

Helen wanted to examine him and make her own assessment before saying anything about the state of his health. She soon surmised he was much improved because his eyes examined her rudely while she checked his pulse rate and blood pressure. She was carefully pressing the tops of his shoulders and probing his neck for any signs of swollen glands when he turned to Tuk and smiled.

"Where did you find her?" He spoke in Kadosh, not realizing Helen could understand him. "She's got great breasts but she's a little too tall for my taste."

Mortified, Tuk could not even look at Helen. Nona giggled nervously.

Helen returned the volley. "And we've been in bed together, my prince. Too bad you're a little young and short for my liking. If you keep your mouth shut, maybe you'll live long enough to get bigger."

Answered in his native tongue, the prince was so shocked he flipped the coverlet over his face and lay still.

Helen laughed. "I'd say he's on the mend. I don't recommend that he leap out of bed any time soon to try his charm on other women. He needs a little practice in that department."

Prince Harnak remained silent under the blanket.

⦁ ⦁ ⦁

Having showered and donned the change of clothes Abigail provided for her, Helen was downstairs in the kitchen, getting a drink of water and sorting through the remaining herbs. Tuk approached her and started to apologize abjectly; she demurred, taking his hands in hers.

"Two days ago, he was dead for all intents and purposes, Master Tuk. As far as I'm concerned, he can make all the idiotic remarks teen boys are inclined to make about women as long as he just keeps breathing."

"Your point is well taken, Doctor."

Tuk now understood somewhat why both Lord Matthew and the Grand Master showed such high regard for her. He hastened upstairs to return to the prince.

Helen pondered her dwindling herb supply. Although the antibiotics were working, they would not drain his lungs fast enough to suit her. And his lungs had to be cleared as soon as possible, to avert re-infection.

She recalled seeing a field from the upstairs window. It was right across the lane connecting the compound to a broad paved road that wound along the entire perimeter of Lake Shambhala. She would have to dig beneath the snow and hope the ground was not frozen too solid, but she knew what root to seek. It would be there, waiting for the frost to melt so the plant could blossom again in the spring.

She investigated the mudroom and found a small trowel, dried mud clinging to it. Knocking it against the doorframe to get the dirt off, she threw it into the basket, grabbed her cloak, and headed out the kitchen door toward the garden. The lane was just on the other side of a small door set within the compound's whitewashed wall.

In her intense focus on the prince's needs, Helen forgot Sudras' warning. She unlatched the door and headed across the lane toward the field. She had not even reached the far side when four men appeared from nowhere. They seized her. Before she could even cry out, they gagged her and chained her arms behind her back. Two of them dragged her toward a skimmer waiting a few hundred yards away. They were clad in a dark brown uniform Helen did not recognize.

They did not find the going easy; she resisted ferociously, forcing them to spend seconds fighting her. That was just long enough. Nona happened to look outside and see one of them punch Helen in the face, knocking her out cold. The serving girl called out, grabbed Tuk's arm, and pointed beyond the window. They both watched, horrified and helpless. One of the men threw the limp form of the unconscious young woman over his shoulder and carried her the rest of the way to the vehicle, disappearing as the lane curved behind a thick stand of tall spruce trees.

# CHAPTER EIGHT

Not knowing whether to laugh or be incensed, Lord James Morde-cai cut the link to Colonel Orlando. Alone in his study, reasonably assured of being undisturbed, he had propped his booted feet on the one corner of his desk that wasn't covered by reports, spreadsheets, surveys, and other personal and official documents. He thought better in such a half-reclining position, although he did not like to compromise the dignity of the Protectorship by allowing anyone to see him this way except one or two very close aides and his best friend, Lord Nimrod Atlas.

Lord James had a lot to think about that afternoon. *I've just been told to go pound sand by a mere lieutenant.*

Not once, since he had come of age and assumed his hereditary post as Lord Protector, had any of his men, even his highest-ranking vice-generals, ever dared defy him in such a manner. The lieutenant surely understood what she risked by such a response. No wonder Orlando was so reluctant to make that report, and especially to relate her reply. At least she ultimately had complied. With any luck now the young prince would survive. Like everyone else who knew the stakes involved, Lord James would just have to wait and hope.

For many reasons, not least of which was the inevitable bloodshed, the Duke of Alta did not relish the prospect of how Azgard's vassal state most likely would react should Prince Harnak die. Lord James was a soldier. If he had to order his men to their deaths, he wanted what he considered a true necessity for doing so. He had no desire to provoke rebellion just to satisfy fanatics and ideologues. That seemed to be just what the Lord Chancellor and his allies were plotting.

Lord James also was aware that Azgard could ill afford any conflict that risked further destruction of certain ancient equipment and vehicles that could not be replaced. That was an absolute state secret known only to the Lord Protector and the Exalted Lord.

*Damn them all.*

He glanced out the window, saw the surf slamming against the shoreline at the bottom of the steep cliff below. He was spending the holiday in his ancestral manor north of Alta, the capital city of his province, catching up on the never-ending administration of two estates, one here and the other in Shambhala.

This private paperwork was simple compared with the far more cumbersome public burden of keeping the entire military machine of Azgard in a state of combat readiness. The Generals Council was some help in that task; he delegated various responsibilities to the officers who reported directly to him. Lord James still regarded himself as obligated to review their activities constantly, just as he had to keep up with a nonstop flow of reports from the managers of his estates.

It was proving far too much to read and take in all at once this afternoon. Trying to ease his fatigue and strain, he rubbed his eyes and ran a hand through his shoulder-length black hair, which he preferred loose instead of bound at the back of his neck like most Toltec noblemen.

He thought again about the lieutenant, who probably held more lives than just one young prince's in her hands, whether or not she knew it. Her whole situation was extraordinary if not downright unprecedented. Women occasionally served as nurses, especially during wartime. The Lord Protector, however, could not think of any other instance, either from his personal command experience or from the records, in which a woman had taken any kind of commission as a full-time medical officer.

The lieutenant's insolent reply fueling his curiosity, Lord James started to search the files for her service record. He wanted to know more about her in order to decide what, if any, discipline she should receive for her insubordination. He could not remember her name. He gave up and hit the link to signal Orlando.

"My lord?"

"What the hell is that woman lieutenant's name again? For some reason it always escapes me."

Orlando bowed to the inevitable. "Helen Andros, my lord. I can forward a copy of her file to you in perhaps a minute, if you care to review it."

The document appeared quickly on the screen before the duke. Intrigued even further by Helen's familiar last name, Lord James browsed first through her service record, growing more and more agitated the longer he read. It was completely unacceptable. How had Orlando managed to cover this up until now? Even more to the point, why? That was one of many questions Lord James intended to put to the colonel when he next met with him.

After seeing enough of the lieutenant's service record to put him in a foul mood, the Lord Protector turned to the basic personal information: date and place of birth, which was not Azgard but Memfys in Kamut. Interesting. As next of kin she had written in an uncle and aunt who lived in Avalon, and put no names for either of her parents, listing both as "whereabouts unknown." More interesting.

Then Helen's likeness filled the screen. It was obviously a copy of her Academy graduation portrait. When he saw her for the first time and realized she was mixed race, Lord James understood why she had accepted the post despite miserable pay and long hours. It was no doubt the only offer she had.

Having learned more than he thought he ever wanted to know about any junior officer, Lord James was about to store the file when something caught his eye. It was the unique necklace she was wearing. He swung his legs off the table and sat upright, peering hard into the screen at it. He enlarged the likeness, then highlighted the portion of the screen containing the image of the green gem and enlarged that again. He could scarcely believe what he saw.

※ ※ ※

*He feels the soft cloth covering on the box containing that very green gem. He is at the bottom of the stairs leading to her tiny loft apartment, in a modest neighborhood in Alta, near the wharf and fishing boat docks. He tastes the reek of sea salt in his mouth, smells it in his nostrils. He issued hundreds of orders daily to battle-toughened soldiers without a second thought; he had ridden straight into enemy gunfire without hesitation more times than he cared to remember. Yet as he toys with the jewel box in his pocket, he does not know if he has the courage to climb those stairs and knock on her door.*

*It had been four long months since he had seen her; the thought of her filled his mind and senses every day and every night as he slept alone, fitfully. Her healing services were no longer needed and she was gone once Lady Sabrina Poseidon, his wife, died after lingering in a coma for two years. She departed from his household without even saying good-bye to him. Odd, how he felt almost no sense of loss for his wife. Yet when she left his life, she took something important from him with her, and he wants it back. He wants her back. He does not want to live without her.*

● ● ●

*He had been wed only a few weeks when his bride fell off the horse she was riding. Her long skirt became caught in the sidesaddle, dragging her several hundred yards before he could stop the frightened animal. Lady Sabrina was unconscious and had lapsed into a coma even before he could summon medical help. The doctors suggested physical therapy to prevent his bedridden wife's condition from becoming worse. At Judith Altair's recommendation, Lord James chooses her. She is Turanian, and that might have stopped some, but he wants the best for his wife and he trusts Judith's judgment implicitly.*

*She proves to be every bit as talented as Judith had indicated. She is competent, energetic, quietly optimistic, and utterly discreet. Almost without being aware of what he is doing, he slips into a routine. In the evenings after his last meeting or appointment and before dinner, he drops by the suite transformed into a nursing ward to care for his wife. At first, he tries to remain unnoticed, standing in the room just outside the bedchamber, listening through the open door.*

*"How are you this evening, my lady?"*

*She speaks to Lady Sabrina all the time as she handles the comatose woman's body, massaging it or flexing the arms and legs to keep the muscles from going entirely slack. She sings as she works, or relates silly stories about the small domestic doings of the farm where she was brought up, just south of the border in Westar Province.*

*He laughs too loudly at one of her tales one evening because the talking stops, and then she appears, leaning against the door jam, looking him up and down. Her long golden hair is bound up in a striped cloth; she seemed to have some sort of oil on her hands and forearms, which were exposed because her sleeves were rolled up. He's never seen a woman with a waist that slender.*

*"My lord, why don't you come sit next to Lady Sabrina? She would welcome your company. You do no one any good standing out here all the time."*

*"You know?" is the only response he can make, feeling like a fool.*

*Although her green eyes flash with laughter, she simply turns away and returns to the bedchamber.*

*"Don't quit your desk job for stealth combat, my lord," she calls over her shoulder. "You'd endanger the whole squadron with the noise you make just breathing."*

*After that, when he is not in Shambhala on military business, attending the Kinshazen, or waiting upon the Exalted Lord, he sits in the evenings by his wife's bedside while she works. It seems strange to have a three-way discussion with only two of the parties contributing to it; she insists on including Lady Sabrina in their talks.*

*"A part of her knows we are here, my lord. I'm convinced of it," she tells him. "The sound of your voice certainly won't hurt her."*

*The days and weeks lengthen into months; a year passes and still the duchess lies comatose. During late summer evenings, when sunlight still casts a faint glow about the horizon while the sky straight up is deep blue and etched with stars, they walk together in the small walled garden or sit on a stone bench. It is just outside the double glass doors of Lady Sabrina's bedchamber.*

*Among the softly sweet scent of roses, and the dominant aroma of lavender, they talk and laugh about anything and everything. He marvels at the quickness of her mind; writhes when she skewers him with a gentle, pointed wit that she is just as likely to turn on herself. He is deeply and, he fears, hopelessly in love. He has no idea how she regards him or even if she has any desire for him. At all times she wears her professional demeanor like a cloak to obscure whatever she might think or feel.*

*One time as he sits looking at his wife, whose open eyes gazed out with unnerving vacancy, he feels overwhelmed by helplessness, frustration, and guilt. She must know something. She nods toward the glass doors, inviting him to step outside into the garden. She shuts the doors to keep their words private.*

*Seated beside her on the stone bench, he discusses it. He does not love Lady Sabrina and did not especially want to marry her, but the Exalted Lord, Lady Sabrina's elder brother, had insisted on it, over the objections of her other brother, Prince Seti Poseidon. The prince had always been jealous of the favor Kefren had shown him, and now is blaming him for their sister's condition.*

*No more than he blames himself. Lord James is accustomed to sizing up a situation, framing the problem, devising a solution, and then implementing it through a chain of command. It works just fine for the battlefield, but not here. This is a different kind of war. One of attrition, not action, and he can do nothing here, solve nothing.*

*He is honest enough with himself to realize he isn't visiting his wife out of a sense of duty or obligation anymore. He does not have the courage to tell her that, although perhaps she already knows it as well. He sees no judgment in her haunting green eyes, just simple acceptance.*

*Toward the close of his wife's second year as a comatose invalid, Lady Sabrina contracts a lung infection. The best doctors in Azgard descend on the bedchamber, and the physical therapist is thrust aside as they work diligently to save the duchess. As though making some final decision from wherever she is, Lady Sabrina does not recover.*

*He departs Alta Province with his wife's body for the week of official mourning, the funeral, and other state functions related to Lady Sabrina's death. He plays the part of the bereaved husband when he is in truth the relieved husband. She and her few belongings are gone and the bedchamber and suite neatly restored to their former condition the next time he returns from Shambhala.*

● ● ●

*Once again, she stands in a doorway, not surprised to see him. She moves aside so that he can enter the room and shuts the door behind her. Then she leans against it, hands behind her back, waiting for him to speak.*

*He clears his throat, hesitant. "The servants brought me the contents of Sabrina's jewelry case. I found a gem in it that belonged to my mother, and thought of you. I had it specially reset. It's known as a healthstone, and you have that healer's touch. I want you to have it."*

*She takes the box from his hand, opens it, and smiles. She places the chain around her neck, and he sees that the deep green of the jewel does indeed set off the brilliant color of her piercing eyes, just as he hoped.*

*"You are very kind, my lord. Thank you."*

*Awkward silence. She walks into the tiny kitchen to heat some water for tea. He is too nervous to sit down. "You're not going to make this any easier for me, are you, Miriam."*

*She drops the kettle onto the stovetop. "Do you think it's been easy for me, my lord? What do you want from me?"*

*"I want your love."*

*"You have that, and you must know it or you would not be here. What else do you want from me?"*

*He swallows hard. "I want you to live with me—"*

"As your lizun? Hidden away for your convenience, discarded when I'm not as young or pretty as I am now."

"No! As my wife."

She all but rolls her eyes. "Your grief has clouded your wits, my lord. Such a marriage is impossible. Surely there's another princess somewhere for you to wed after a decent interval."

"That's not fair."

"Fair? Who ever said any of this would be fair? Have you ever once imagined how I might feel? Seeing you every day, getting to know you, growing to love you despite my better judgment, my good sense and prudence, all the time knowing that I have no hope of you."

The kettle's whistle masks what might be a sob. She straightens her slender shoulders, then measures out tea leaves, places them into a pot, and pours the water into it. She looks up at him, an unbearable longing and pain in her eyes that she never before showed him.

"I never dared imagine how you might feel, Miriam. I never dared to hope for your love. To want it, need it, hunger for it, yes. To hope for it, no."

At his words, the anger and pain appear to drain from her. "You have never touched me, my lord. Am I so repulsive to you, then?"

His hand seemed to move on its own, the forefinger stroking her cheek, following the trace of a tear. She pressed the back of his hand to her lips, closing her eyes.

She is so small, so seemingly frail, she almost melts away within his arms. She returns his first kiss passionately. Joy and desire and a hundred other emotions and sensations that have been all jumbled up inside of him now spill forth unstoppable. He brushes his lips against her eyelids, her neck, her cheek, her chin. He runs his tongue lightly along her earlobe and is rewarded with a small gasp of pleasure from her. He lifts her and carries *her to the bed, lays her on it, and pauses, resting on his elbow just above her face, for a moment uncertain.*

*"Miriam, I—"*

*She raises her head and silences him with a kiss, then takes his hand, and puts it on her breast. "Sometimes, James, you talk too much."*

* * *

Lord James looked up with a start, his heart aching from emotions buried for more than twenty years. Realizing his face was wet, he wiped it with a rumpled handkerchief he found in a pocket. Afternoon had passed into early evening; the study was dark except for the glow of the screen on the desk in front of his chair. He sighed, flicked on a link to Orlando, intending to leave the colonel a message for the morning.

"Yes, my lord."

His throat felt tight. "What are you still doing there?"

"You have not yet dismissed me, my lord. I'm keeping an eye on certain situations, also."

Lord James recalled his years of waiting wearily on senior officers. "How long has it been since you had any sleep?"

"A while, my lord."

"That's what I thought. Here's another situation, but Orlando, this can wait until morning, and I mean it."

"Yes, my lord." The man didn't sound convinced.

"Find out everything you can about Lieutenant Andros. Talk to her teachers at the Academy, her family in Avalon, whatever. And do it in secret. We want as few of certain people as possible to know we are interested in her."

"Anything specific to look for, my lord?"

"I want to know who her parents are."

# CHAPTER NINE

Lady Mary Atlas sat across from the Consort, Lady Naomi Palladin, at a small dining table in the salon of the Consort's private suite. Floor-to-ceiling windows revealed a breathtaking southern exposure to the open water of Lake Shambhala, obscured under a blanket of ice.

The salons of all Royal or noble women were always luxurious; this one was especially well appointed. Two fireplaces were ablaze on either side of the windows, which angled outward to form an alcove lined by a large window seat, affording the best view in the entire room. Thick rugs of various shades of violet covered much of the white marble floor. A waterfall of bronze cunningly wrought into the shape of some large, exotic flower filled the room with an ever-changing, softly melodic tinkle of cascading liquid.

Lady Mary needed that soothing sound after a morning talk with her dead mother's brother, Lord Tarkon Polaris, the Duke of Eden. The Consort retired discreetly to her study next to the salon, still able to see both her guest and her visitor through the open door. Her young charge shrank against the seat on one side of the glass recess while the duke paced and gestured.

Lord Tarkon was a strange-looking man. His face was concave, almost like a spoon, with a heavy brow, jutting jaw, and skin that was a very dark reddish-brown, even for a Toltec. His manners were not much better than his looks, although his niece suspected her uncle could please and flatter when he cared to do so. That morning Lord Tarkon blustered and rambled, speaking at Lady Mary instead of to her. He seemed to have no notion of how to address an almost grown young woman.

"You are treated well in Avalon?"

"Yes, Uncle. Very well. Why would you doubt it?"

He sat down directly across from his niece on the other side of the window seat. "Because you're David's child, not his."

Although Lord Tarkon refused even to speak the name of Lady Mary's other uncle, the Prince of Westar, she knew whom he meant. She was three when her parents died, and hardly remembered them. Prince Enoch was the only real father she had ever known and his Turanian wife, the Princess of Westar, the only mother. Sensing that this would not be what Lord Tarkon would want to hear, Lady Mary waited for him to reveal the true reason for his visit.

"Has he mentioned your betrothal to Lord Sargon?"

Lady Mary's lips quivered. "The subject has come up once or twice. But don't you think I'm a little young for this, Uncle? I've not even been presented."

Lord Tarkon's eyes pinned Lady Mary with pitiless disapproval. "Not too young for childish fancies, and maybe even indiscretions. I hear your taste in men runs in an entirely unsuitable direction. Is this true?"

"I can't imagine what you mean, Uncle."

"Can you not? Good. See that it stays that way."

He rose and towered over his niece. "You are too close in kinship even to consider him, but most important, Mary, he is beneath you, despite his name. Remember that."

Lady Naomi chose that moment to return to the salon. Lord Tarkon paid his respects and departed.

Lady Mary was too dumbfounded to speak or make any type of gesture. It had never dawned on her that anyone would know her secret, or that anyone would care about it anyway. It was a rude awakening to her relative importance in the social food chain.

When the shock faded, Lady Mary found herself at the table, eyes downcast. The food probably was delicious; she could not smell it. The setting included a tablecloth and napkins of the finest linen from Kamut; she could not enjoy it. Not even the presence of Lady Mary's beloved *doma* could soothe her. Janel Mashim was sitting in a chair by one of the fireplaces, knitting and humming softly.

Lady Mary's stomach was in knots. To look as if she were eating, she tried rearranging the meat and vegetables on her plate.

The sharp-eyed Consort was not having any of it.

Lady Naomi was no longer young; at her temples, her carefully arranged hair was flecked with white, and there were fine lines on her forehead and at the corners of her mouth. Her curved nose, full lips, and high-boned cheeks were at once delicate in size yet gave the impression of strength and force of will. At all times she carried her diminutive figure erect and her almond-shaped brown eyes snapped with energy and cool, determined intelligence.

Much to Lady Mary's surprise, the Consort dismissed Janel and the butler who was waiting on them. She then turned to her young guest and patted her hand reassuringly.

"I have wanted to talk with you for some time now, dear girl. You and I have much in common."

"We do?"

"Yes. I am Consort of this island, and someday you will be. I speak to you now as one Consort to another. I rarely get that privilege, since there is not an overabundance of us."

"There is Lady Lydia," Lady Mary said, referring to the wife of Prince Seti, heir to the Kingship.

"She doesn't count. I do not think her tenure in this position will be very long or very distinguished."

Lady Naomi sliced another piece of black bread from the loaf, buttered it, and put it on Lady Mary's plate, indicating that she should eat it.

Lady Mary complied, and it seemed to ease her stomach. Or maybe it was simply the Consort's kind words. As she chewed, tears began to flow down Lady Mary's rounded face. She dropped the rest of the bread onto her plate, lowered her head into her hands, and sobbed, unable to repress her feelings any longer.

"I don't want to be Consort."

Lady Naomi caressed her arm, waiting until she was calmer. "Neither did I, dear girl. But here I am, and here you will be too, someday."

Lady Mary looked up at her, blinking back tears.

"No one in her right mind covets being Consort, which is why Lydia is such a question mark to me. She seems actually to want it. Silly, foolish woman."

Spellbound by the Consort's frankness, Lady Mary waited in eager silence for her to continue.

She smiled. "Good. You seem to know how to keep your mouth shut. Cultivate just that kind of ability. It is a lifesaving skill in a Consort."

She looked away, out the window, then fixed Lady Mary with her gaze once more. "No sane woman wants to be Consort, Mary, because it is the most dangerous position in all of Azgard. It demands duty and exacts great sacrifice, without bestowing any real power. Or at least direct power, the kind that men obey instantly and without question. And all the time, a Consort is constantly watched, her every word and gesture examined and replayed for any hidden meanings or political signals."

In the butler's absence, the Consort poured Lady Mary and herself cups of cinnamon-flavored *kaf* from a silver decanter on the table. "In case you are wondering, that is how your Uncle Tarkon knew to ask about certain subjects. You have been under scrutiny since your birth, if not before."

Lady Mary's fingers shook.

"On a personal level, Mary dear, I think your choice of men quaint. Though I'm not sure what a woman would find to talk about for very long with a mathematics theoretician."

Lady Mary tried to remain composed. "Cousin Justin doesn't speak much about his work, Lady Consort. We discuss music and poetry. He's so talented. He plays several instruments. He's just the kindest, gentlest person I've ever met. He's not beneath me. He—"

"Oh yes, he is, Mary. As a second son and a half-blood, he is far beneath you. Much as I hate admitting I agree with the Duke of Eden on anything, in this he is right. Remember, I am speaking to you now as Consort to future Consort. Get this through your head once and for all. Guard your heart and use much more discretion. You are bound to Lord Sargon and, like it or not, eventually you will wed him."

Lady Mary trembled and her eyes watered. The Consort's manner softened and she shook her head. "Let me explain it to you this way,

Mary dear. You have just enough power to put him in real and grave danger if you continue to show him any favor or regard above and beyond what you might properly display toward a cousin. And having enraged those who might despise him by your 'indiscretions,' as your uncle so delicately put it, you would then have no power to save him from their wrath. Is that what you want for him?"

Lady Mary pushed her chair back from the table and struggled to her feet. "Pray excuse me, Lady Consort. I am unwell."

She curtseyed as best she could with her eyes closed, then almost ran out the door of the salon, down a short hall to her bedchamber, where Janel was sitting, as if waiting for her young charge.

Lady Mary threw herself on the silk bedspread, dug her face into the satin pillows and cried so hard, she was almost screaming. Janel came and sat on the bed, stroking Lady Mary's head, hair, and back as she wept, trying to comfort her.

"A hard lesson in life today, my sweet lady-child," Janel said, sadness filling her voice.

● ● ●

Lady Naomi sat for a long time at the table, sipping another cup of *kaf*, wondering if she'd done the right thing, fearing she had been a little too harsh on the girl. *Better harsh now than disaster later. She has to realize there are consequences and repercussions to her smallest actions, and learn utter discretion if she is to survive. That is what I can teach her.*

The afternoon shadows were lengthening and the meal had been cleared away for some time. The butler entered the salon with a package and bowed. "A special weave with compliments from the cloth merchant Master Sheridan Ames, Lady Consort."

The Consort took the package and dismissed the servant. Once she was certain she was alone, she opened the wrapping and examined the fabric, searching for a coded message woven into the material itself. She ran her fingers back and forth across the warp and woof, reading the hidden letter by touch.

The Lord Steward was to hold a preliminary hearing late that afternoon. Indeed, she would barely have enough time if she planned to attend. The Consort had every intention of responding to Shinar's urgent plea. This had to be very serious indeed for the Lord Steward to risk contacting her in such a manner. Rumors were flying in the palace about a certain young state hostage's poor physical condition. She would find out soon enough.

# CHAPTER TEN

Helen had lost all sense of time in the frigid, windowless cell. She sat on a wooden chair, arms hanging behind her over the low back, wrists chained together. Her mouth was like sawdust, her muscles were screaming from long confinement, her bladder was ready to explode, and her head was still throbbing from the blow that knocked her out. One side of her upper face and forehead was swollen and felt like it was on fire. It hurt to shut that eye or open her mouth to speak. But she could tell that her jaw was not broken or dislocated. *I'll bet I've got a textbook shiner.*

Her mind was perversely clear. *All the better to feel every nuance of pain.*

First one of the officers and then another questioned her. Helen soon realized they did not know exactly what to ask her, or even what they were seeking from her. Unbelievably, they did not even search her. They obviously had no clear instructions and did not know who she was or why they were holding her prisoner. She was grateful for small advantages. Had they known her identity as a bastard, they would have been far less restrained in the way they treated her.

Helen stalled and delayed. She told them as little as possible, answering only direct questions, volunteering nothing. Name, age, place of birth. When they inquired about her family, she told them she was an orphan. It was true enough, as far as it went. Above all she did not want to bring the names of her aunt or uncle or her cousins to the attention of anyone, if she could help it. Until now she had not realized that the risk she assumed in treating Prince Harnak might also fall heavily on them. That possibility left her feeling sick as well as aching and cold.

Facing away from the door, she could not see at first who had entered the room. The two bored lieutenants and the captain posing another round of inane questions snapped to attention, surprised and fearful. The real interrogation was about to commence. Helen sighed. Worn out, she had no idea how long her strength would last.

The high-ranking official, a gold chain of office arrayed about his shoulders, sat down, a small table between him and Helen's chair. He unfolded a portfolio and pretended to review the notes he spread out on the table; he wanted time to take his prisoner's measure and to plot his next move. He was not pleased to find the prisoner in this physical condition, a point overlooked in the initial report on the interrogation.

At first glance, the new arrival seemed more comical than threatening. From the pudginess of his face and body, he obviously liked food and drink. His dark hairline formed a widow's peak at the center of his forehead; his eyebrows arched in a seemingly perpetual expression of innocent surprise. Once Helen looked into his brown eyes, however, she understood the other men's fear, and had to repress a shudder. *This must be how a bird with a broken wing feels when a snake approaches.*

He cleared his throat. "I am the Lord Chancellor of Azgard. You will answer a series of questions for me, Mistress Andros."

Helen's interrogator reviewed the basic questions the others had put to her. Then the tone of the interview changed.

"Tell me your father's name."

"I don't know."

He moved next to Helen's chair, sat on the edge of the table and lowered his face next to hers. She tried to turn away; he grabbed her jaw and yanked her head toward him, forcing her to look at him. She winced.

"How can you not know your father's name? Was your mother an alley cat?"

The men in the room snickered. Although angry, Helen realized he was trying to provoke her into revealing something.

"She was not inclined to kiss and tell."

His grip on her wounded jaw tightened. The pain was so excruciating her eyes filled with tears. She made no sound.

He leaned even closer, his lips just inches from her ear. "Then who was your mother, bitch?"

"A blacksmith's daughter."

"Her name, damn you!"

Helen said nothing.

"Do you want to feel my boot on your throat?"

She glanced at his feet. "Needs polishing."

He slammed the back of his hand across the already injured side of Helen's face and squeezed her jaw harder, like a vise.

She gasped. Blood trickled from the corner of her mouth.

"Well?"

"Miriam Andros."

He shoved her head away. "That's better. Where was the farm?"

When Helen again hesitated, he reached for her jaw and compressed it once more.

She cried out softly; the pain was too searing to resist any longer. "East of South Alton."

"Excellent."

At his nod toward the door, each of the lieutenants grabbed one of Helen's arms, hauled her out of the chair and dragged her along a dim passage to another cell. This one had a narrow cot for a bed, a crude table and stool, a sink, and a commode.

One of them dropped a comb and small mirror on the table and spoke to her. "Make yourself presentable."

"I didn't know you cared."

He hurled her against the wall and pinned her under her chin with his forearm. His strength was unnerving; the cuffs on her wrists were digging into her lower back.

"If it were up to me, *nahazi* scum, you would have found out long before now exactly how much I don't care."

He pressed her against the rough stone under her neck and groped her breasts and hips. Helen soon felt faint from lack of oxygen. The second soldier finally managed to pull her attacker off of her.

"Leave her be, man, or there will be hell to pay for both of us."

The second one removed the chains from Helen's wrists and the two left the cell. Panting for breath, rubbing her bruised skin, Helen sank to the stone floor. Why on earth did they care about her appearance?

● ● ●

Shinar took his time in his offices close to the hearing chamber. As Lord Steward of the *Kinshazen,* he was the presiding magistrate for the Sacred City. Any serious criminal, civil, or religious offenses were under his jurisdiction.

Having delayed as long as possible, the Lord Steward entered the somber courtroom. The Lord Chancellor was standing at the prosecutor's table before the bench. His prisoner was on her feet behind a table to the Lord Chancellor's side, flanked by two uniformed men, her arms bound behind her. The only others present were the Lord Steward's bailiff and Tuk, sitting in the front row of seats at the back of the chamber reserved for spectators or witnesses.

Shinar seated himself in the chair on the dais, scowled at the men beside Helen, again perused copies of the interrogation notes he had insisted on obtaining from the Lord Chancellor's secretary.

"Dismiss your officers, Lord Chancellor. And remove the restraining devices you have put on this girl. I won't have that in my courtroom."

"This prisoner stands accused of serious crimes, Lord Steward."

Shinar silenced the protest with a warning look. "One young woman armed with a garden trowel and a basket. Obviously, a national crisis."

Having freed Helen from the manacles, her guards were leaving the room when they dropped to one knee and bowed. An older woman, clad in costly silk and wearing a small fortune in glittering gems, passed them on her way into the chamber, preceded by a waiting woman.

Gratified and relieved that the message had reached her, Shinar rose to greet the Consort. Lady Naomi strolled to the bench and allowed the Lord Steward to take her hand, bow over it, and kiss it. The Lord Chancellor stumbled to rise and bow to her. Taking her cue from the Lord Steward, Helen curtseyed deeply.

The Lord Chancellor was rattled. "Lord Steward, this is highly irregular."

Lady Naomi sailed past him a second time on her way to the spectators' seats, where Tuk awaited her, head bowed, knee bent.

"My hearings are open to anyone who desires to attend, Lord Chancellor. Do you have a problem with this lady's presence?"

Griffin thought better of what he had planned to say. "Of course not."

Shinar turned to Helen, motioned for her to sit in one of the armchairs by the table where she was standing, and instructed the bailiff to bring her a glass of water. Helen drank it with alacrity, thanking him in a very subdued, hoarse voice. Her black eye and bruised cheek were obvious. Shinar also noted blood on her blouse and wondered why her voice was so strained. Lack of sleep, perhaps.

"What happened to your face, Mistress Andros?"

She swallowed several times, her words somewhat stronger. "Betrayed by my mouth, Lord Steward."

"How do you explain her face, Lord Chancellor?"

"My men had to use mild force when she resisted arrest, Lord Steward."

"Arrest?" Helen interjected, forcing the words out of a painful throat. "Is that what you call it? It seemed more like an abduction to me. Of course I resisted."

"Enough."

Shinar's voice was weary rather than angry. Using the interrogation report as a guide, he asked Helen a few questions not mentioned in it. The very lack of information in the notes told him that the Lord Chancellor already knew what she was doing in the Sacred City. Shinar wanted it inserted for the official record.

Helen briefly outlined her successful efforts to save Prince Harnak's life. The Consort's brow arched ever so slightly and Shinar saw it. *Yes, my queen. In return for your help, here is the opportunity you have awaited. Use it well.*

The Lord Steward also questioned Master Tuk, whose story essentially agreed with the girl's. The fact-finding phase was complete.

"It seems to me all you have here is a first offense, Lord Chancellor," Shinar said. "She is of Turanian extraction and was inside the Sacred City without proper authorization or papers. A fine would be in order, I think."

Tuk rose from his chair. "If it pleases the court. The government of Kamut assumes responsibility for this mistake and will gladly pay any fine charged to Doctor Andros."

Helen shot the old man a grateful look, a question in her eyes. He returned his own gratitude and added a thumbs-up to let her know Prince Harnak was continuing to improve.

Helen's relief was short-lived. The Lord Chancellor did not seem at all disturbed this time. "I suggest you read again the part of the report about the girl's birthplace, Lord Steward."

Shinar complied; it had not registered with him before. "You have said your place of birth is Memfys, Mistress Andros. Is this true? I remind you that you are still under oath."

"Yes, Lord Steward. That is my place of birth."

The Lord Chancellor snapped his portfolio together. "I intend to file capital charges, Lord Steward, and request that the prisoner be returned to my custody immediately to prepare for her trial before the *Kazil* at sundown in three days."

"Your request is denied, Lord Chancellor."

Shinar was grateful to throw at least this small kink into a smoothly laid, deadly trap. "The Prince of Westar will not be pleased when I inform him that you cannot seem to restrain your men from abusing a kinswoman of the Princess of Westar.

"I therefore remand Mistress Andros to the custody of the Consort, who has graciously consented to stand in the place of the Princess of Westar as guardian for this young woman while she awaits trial."

His cheeks more gaunt than usual, the Lord Steward fixed Helen in his gaze. "Do I have your solemn word that you will not try to escape, Doctor Andros? The guards have standing orders to shoot to kill any fleeing prisoner, no questions asked. Do I make myself clear?"

"Very, Lord Steward. You have my word."

# CHAPTER ELEVEN

Lady Mary hid in the Consort's study, watching and listening from behind the doorway. She was too consumed by curiosity about a kinswoman of her beloved cousin to fear Lady Naomi's ire.

Helen finally appeared in the salon, clad in a dressing gown that barely reached to the top of her calves. She was the tallest woman Lady Mary had ever seen or even imagined. Unusually short and constantly battling with her weight, Lady Mary at first found Helen's height and lean figure daunting and depressing.

The lights of Nighthall and various estates to the south of Agarthi were glittering. They drew Helen to the glass-walled alcove. She stood looking out, combing the tangles from hair that was still damp from a shower.

Lady Naomi carried an ice pack to Helen for her swollen cheek, along with a glass of ice water. She sent Janel on some errand and then took her favorite armchair by the largest fireplace, the one closest to the windows overlooking the lake, where she liked to sit to do her needlework.

The Consort at first did not permit Helen to sit. She pointed at a spot three paces before her chair; Helen left the alcove and knelt there, head bowed. Lady Mary could see their faces in profile.

"You are in very serious trouble, young woman."

"Yes, Lady Consort, I am well aware of it." Helen adjusted the ice pack over her face. "No one will tell me what crime I have committed."

"We won't know the precise charges until this time tomorrow, when the Lord Chancellor must file a writ with the Lord Steward, as custom dictates. You will be served with your copy here."

Helen dared to look up without being invited to do so. "I cannot thank you enough for your kindness, Lady Consort."

"Kindness had nothing to do with it. You have skills and training I need just now, and I intend to use you shamelessly, and expose you to greater danger."

"Get in line, Lady Consort," Helen replied. "Danger-filled usury seems to be a holiday pastime in this city."

The Consort stopped pretending to do her needlework. "I could have you whipped for such insolence, girl."

"Before or after you use me."

Lady Naomi laughed. "Our Lord Chancellor must have found you a pain in the ass. I should thank you for giving him even a little bit of hell."

She now motioned for Helen to be seated on the sofa opposite her armchair. Helen sank onto the cushions, removed the ice pack from her face and probed the swollen side, wincing occasionally.

"The hell part was mutual, Lady Consort."

Lady Naomi was silent for some minutes, still weighing something. Finally, she spoke. "Let me cut to the chase, girl. I want you to give the

Exalted Lord a thorough physical examination. He will be here for a visit tomorrow afternoon."

Helen was wary. "Why me? Surely the Exalted Lord has numerous physicians far better qualified than I to examine and treat him."

Lady Naomi stared straight into her blue-gray eyes. "And all are hand-picked by the Prince of Istar, his brother. I cannot always rely on their reports."

Helen returned the gaze. "If you want me to be able to help him, lay all of your cards on the table, Lady Consort. Better for me, better for you, and certainly better for the Exalted Lord. What do you suspect?"

The Consort fidgeted and then exhaled, her breath ragged. She spoke softly. "I suspect someone is poisoning him."

Lady Mary gasped and shrank back against the wall behind the door. The sound carried into the salon. Consternation on her face, Lady Naomi made for her study. She reached around the door and grabbed Lady Mary's arm, dragging the young woman into the salon.

The Consort almost threw Lady Mary onto the sofa next to Helen, who made no sound. Then she stood over Lady Mary, glowering.

"Perhaps I misjudged you, young lady. Perhaps you are already cunning in the devious ways of the court. Why were you eavesdropping on a conversation not meant for your ears? Who sent you?"

Lady Mary's eyes filled with tears. Although she was terrified, she had Helen's example to follow. She did not cringe before her interrogator.

"No one sent me, Lady Consort. It was very wrong of me to have listened, but I meant no harm, truly. I couldn't help myself. I was just so curious—"

Lady Mary glanced at Helen, who dipped her head.

The Consort dropped back into her chair, mollified. "Mary, do you have any idea how dangerous it is for you even to have heard what I suspect? I never wanted to put you in that position, dearest girl."

"Heard what, Lady Consort? I heard nothing. I thought I saw a spider on the carpet in the study and it so startled me I cried out."

Helen signaled her approval with a thumbs-up. "The quivering lower lip needs a bit of work, my lady, but otherwise I think you've got the hang of it."

The Consort laughed too, more relieved although still concerned. "Forgive my unpardonable manners. Mary, this is Mistress Helen Andros. Helen, meet Lady Mary Atlas."

When Helen started to rise to curtsey, Lady Mary extended her hand palm down, a sign to remain seated. "You are Lord Justin's cousin, are you not?"

"Second cousin, my lady. You, I believe, are closer kin. I had the privilege of meeting Lord Justin a few days ago, at the Andros family farm."

Although Lady Mary wanted desperately to ask Helen questions about Lord Justin, the painful memory of the Consort's words earlier that day restrained her.

It was soon settled. Helen explained what she would need to examine the monarch. Lady Naomi assured her she would have it.

Helen chose her next words with care. "To test for, shall I say, any unusual substances in the body, I will need certain tissue and blood samples analyzed. That presents a problem of confidentiality and I think I can solve it for you. Does the Exalted Lord's nephew Lord Matthew Shinar ever call on his uncle?"

Helen astonished the Consort again with her knowledge of the Ruling House's marital connections. "On occasion, yes, he does. He visits Kefren more than our daughter."

"Then let tomorrow be one of those occasions, Lady Consort. If you want as thorough a report as possible, do not let anyone veto this visit. He should be here after I have completed the examination. Above all, please don't reveal anything about why you have asked him. I'll explain what he's to do when he gets here."

"Why would anyone refuse to let him visit his uncle?"

"Because I am here, Lady Consort. That will be more than enough to displease some who are close to him."

Helen leaned against the sofa cushions, closed her eyes. She showed weariness for the first time. The Consort saw her exhaustion and decided to drill her later in more depth about her relationship with Lord Matthew. She pressed a button inside her armchair; servants appeared immediately with food, which they laid out on the small table where Lady Naomi and Lady Mary had sat.

"You must eat a little, Helen, and then get some sleep. I want you to feel your best tomorrow."

Lady Naomi looked at Helen's lower legs, exposed by the short dressing gown. "I must also find you some suitable clothing."

"Good luck, Lady Consort. I'm impossible to fit. No one makes dresses my size. I usually sew my own."

"You don't have the time or energy for that. I'm sure I can think of something," the Consort replied. She dismissed the servants again and then looked at Lady Mary. "And what are we going to do with you tomorrow afternoon?"

Lady Mary, looking innocent, shrugged her shoulders.

"I have thought of something to teach Lady Mary about the perils of eavesdropping," Helen said, winking at her. "She can assist me while I do my work."

Lady Mary was taken aback. "I can? How?"

"How good are you at small-talk?"

●　●　●

The medical attendants escorted the Exalted Lord into the Consort's salon the next afternoon. The Consort motioned for them to seat Kefren not in her high-backed armchair, but in a lower backed chair as Helen had requested, to make it easier to conduct certain portions of her examination.

As a ruse, the Consort had locked Helen in a guestroom next to Lady Mary's bedchamber. She now had to work fast and furiously to persuade Kefren's attendants to leave him alone in the salon with her and Lady Mary.

"You are harboring a suspected capital criminal, Lady Consort," the chief attendant said. "We must be vigilant for the Exalted Lord's safety."

The Consort indicated to him to accompany her down the hall. She unlocked the door to the room and permitted the man to enter and see Helen, who was seated on the bed and staring out the window.

After the chief attendant left the room, the Consort touched the door pad, securing the lock with her palm print. "The girl is in no position to disturb the Exalted Lord or anyone else."

They returned to the salon, where Lady Mary was already attempting to engage Kefren in conversation. The chief attendant would not yield. The Consort flashed a little Royal anger, arching one eyebrow slightly, pursing her lips.

"Your patient is my husband as well as my Exalted Lord. Are you daring to suggest that I am not concerned about his safety or welfare?"

He relented. The monarch could be left alone for two hours, no more.

The Consort herself locked the outer door that led into her apartments so that none could have access without warning. She then let Helen out of the guestroom, relocked the door, and led her back to the salon. Helen did not immediately approach Kefren, however. She asked the Consort to be seated next to her husband and to join Lady Mary in setting him at ease.

Helen observed the Exalted Lord, struggling to contain her astonishment at the similarity in appearance between him and Lord Matthew. Eventually she rolled up the sleeves of her blouse, and walked to within ten paces of Kefren's chair. She dropped to her knees, flattening her upper body to the floor and touching her forehead to the ground in an absolute submission, the obeisance due the sovereign from the humblest and lowest ranked of his subjects.

Helen rose to her feet. Kefren glanced at her and then looked at his wife. It was a good day because he could recognize the Consort. Often he did not know her.

"Now that's a pretty child. Have I met her before?"

Lady Naomi patted the king's hand, waved at Helen to approach. "No, my dearest lord. But she would like to visit with you, if that would not bother you."

Some of the confusion seemed to leave the king's eyes; his childlike shy smile was all the reply Helen needed to proceed.

Quickly, methodically, and gently she worked, examining him thoroughly. He nodded off. As soon as she heard his breathing deepen, Helen reached into the medical bag and brought out a syringe. When it was full of blood, she removed the needle and placed a gauze pad over the tiny entry wound. She asked Lady Mary to hold the pad in place for a few minutes.

Helen slipped the syringe into the bag, picked it up, and looked at the Consort. "In case they notice this needle wound on his arm, you had better come up with an explanation, Lady Consort. My guess? They won't know it's not one of their own making."

Lady Naomi's eyes widened.

"Oh yes, Lady Consort, they keep him heavily sedated. That's why he fell asleep. This blood test should tell us what drugs they are using. Some have worse side effects than others.

"I have done as much as I can without further equipment," Helen added. "Lock me back into the guestroom while I prepare these blood and tissue samples for transport and analysis. It must be fairly close to time for the attendants to come back."

Lord Matthew arrived just as his uncle was leaving. Lady Naomi asked him to enter the suite anyway. He took her arm as they walked back into the salon together. He apologized to her for being late, and she told him not to be concerned about it. When he saw Lady Mary, he smiled and greeted her as though he considered her an adult now and no longer a child. They exchanged pleasantries for a few minutes.

Helen entered the room, a black slipskin pouch in her hand. Lord Matthew fell silent and rose to his feet. They stood still, regarding each other. The Consort took Lady Mary's hand and they retreated to her study. Lady Mary assumed a position by the doorway once more. The Consort did not protest and eased onto the chair behind her desk.

Helen spoke first. "You really do look like your uncle. It's amazing."

"Yes. A likeness that's on all the coins. Fat lot of good it does me or him. You look like hell. What happened to your face?"

Helen placed the pouch on the table, right before him. "Call it a small token of the Lord Chancellor's high regard for me."

"Helen, I'm so sorry. I should have attended the prince myself. It's all—"

"Do stop apologizing to me every time we meet," she interjected. "You're becoming a bore. I want something from you. That's why you were summoned."

"Name it."

Helen touched the pouch. "Take these blood and tissue samples and analyze them. Do it in absolute, utter secrecy. The results are for the Consort alone. I suggest you memorize whatever you learn, then burn your notes and the samples."

"What does your examination suggest that I look for?"

Helen wandered about the room. "Mind altering drugs, for starters. I suspect his supposed mental condition has been induced by the wonders of modern chemistry. And those bastards have the nerve to call *me* unfit to practice medicine."

Helen was steamed. She either did not or pretended not to notice the tenderness and deep sadness on Lord Matthew's face.

"Test for any kind of poison you can think of as well."

Lord Matthew nodded. "My father knows, Helen. That's why I wasn't at the hearing."

He looked away, struggling to hold back strong emotion. "He knows about our relationship now. I'm surprised I have any ears left, the way he blistered them."

"Good," Helen said. "Someone has to get your attention. I've been trying for years. It's nice to have a little help at last."

He turned an utterly stricken expression on her. "Why are you acting like this, Helen? I thought you were my friend."

"Yes! I am your friend. The problem has always been your peculiar definition of that word. I can't ever be anything more than a friend to you. But you just refuse to get it."

"I don't want to get it."

He took her into his arms and tried to kiss her. Her injured mouth caused her pain; she turned her head aside and pushed away from him.

"Don't make this any harder on me than it has to be. I'm most likely living on borrowed time anyway."

"You are. Father explained it to me." His voice was almost hoarse. "It is a crime punishable by death for any non-subject to set foot within the Sacred City without permission from the Temple and the government. You were born in Memfys, which makes you a foreigner and a non-subject. There is no appeal."

Helen at last fully understood her peril. She drew in a deep breath. "You had best be on your way. The Consort will be looking for these results. I doubt we'll have a chance to meet again."

Her hands were clinched into fists at her sides and the tendons in her neck were taut.

Lord Matthew was hardly whispering. "How can I bear it? I can't live in this world without you, Helen."

"You bear it? If I can bear my part, you can live with yours." Helen whisked the pouch off the table, slapped it into his hand. "Now go! You have a job to do. So do I."

She turned her back on him and stared out the window, where the sun set in brilliant hues of gold and pink. He looked at her for another moment, tears rolling down his face, and departed.

The Consort and Lady ventured back into the salon. Lady Mary wanted to say something to Helen; the Consort shook her head and assumed her favorite chair. Lady Mary settled across from her. They waited.

Helen eventually slumped to her knees. "Damn you, Matthew," she gasped between sobs. "Damn your sweetness, your kindness, your disgusting sensitivity. Why couldn't you just be like the rest of them? Then I wouldn't have to feel any of this."

The Consort, wiping her own eyes, knelt next to Helen and put her arms around the distraught young woman, holding her and rocking her back and forth. Helen hid her face in the Consort's shoulder.

"You did what you had to, child. You did it because you love him." Lady Naomi glanced in Lady Mary's direction.

"Oh no, Lady Consort, that's just the problem. Of all the pain in this world, to me the hardest has been to know that I am loved by one truly good, decent man, and cannot return that love. The shame of it drives me to distraction. I never wanted to hurt him like I did just now. Matthew has always felt like a brother to me."

Sobbing anew, she allowed the Consort to help her up and onto the sofa next to Lady Mary. After a while Helen stopped weeping.

A servant announced the arrival of a messenger from the Lord Chancellor. Helen stood up almost coldly to receive the formal writ of charges, the Lord Chancellor's seal dangling from the gold band that encircled the rolled-up document. She waited until the messenger left, then placed the document, unopened, on the dining table, and stared at it.

"Finally. Some comic relief."

# CHAPTER TWELVE

Lady Naomi sat on her favorite chair in her salon, sifting through bolts of cloth that Sheridan Ames had brought with him at her special request. The cloth merchant, his blond, shoulder-length hair held out of his face by a leather band, advised her while his assistant measured Helen for her gown size. Helen found the not very subtle admiration they showed toward her annoying.

"This is a very serious occasion, Master Ames," the Consort explained. "No silk, no satin, no velvet, no lace, no gems or decoration of any kind on this dress."

She peered over the top of her spectacles at Helen. "It's a shame the law does not permit you to wear silk or satin, my dear. This fabric otherwise might be perfect for you," she said, patting a bolt of blueberry velvet she held on her lap.

Helen was uneasy at all the attention. "Lady Consort, why not a linen blouse and wool skirt? It's what I always wear."

"No, dear. It calls attention to your lack of rank."

"One look at me and that's obvious."

"Perhaps," the Consort replied, growing silent and thinking it through. She wanted Helen's appearance to convey an inoffensive air of mystery about her, a faint suggestion that she might just be more important than she seemed at first.

Ames coughed. He happened to have already made a dress in that deep blue velvet. The lady who first commissioned it decided not to take it. The skirt would be too short, of course, but it probably would fit the girl in the bodice.

"It will give us a chance to determine if this color and shade are appropriate, Lady Consort," he added with a conspiratorial smile.

She laughed. "And satisfy my vulgar curiosity. You are wicked, Master Ames."

The Consort did indeed want to have a look at Helen in a formal court gown, and insisted that she try on the dress. Helen disappeared from the salon for a few minutes, then returned and stood before the Consort's chair.

"Oh, my," was all Lady Naomi could manage. They were all astonished by the simple, natural loveliness they beheld that afternoon in Helen. The gown's neckline plunged so low it exposed her ample breasts almost to the nipples. The bodice fit Helen like a second skin, accentuating the curves of her waist and hips. Her lustrous black hair spilled over her pale, sculpted shoulders and down her back.

Ames unbuttoned the collar band of his tunic, as though his throat were somehow constricted. He leaned over to speak into the Consort's ear.

"Without even trying, Lady Consort, I can think of at least a dozen of the highest born in this land who would eagerly lay out a small fortune for her first night."

Lady Naomi's eyes rose in his direction. "Only a dozen, Master Ames? I should think any man in Azgard with a pulse and a large enough purse would be in that crowd." *And to whom would they apply for the pleasure?*

Helen's face became deeper and deeper shades of red as everyone continued to stare at her. She tried to conceal more of her chest by grabbing the fabric at the neckline and pulling it upward.

"Small wonder your client didn't want it, Master Ames. The top half of this dress is missing."

The Consort shook her head and stood up. She took hold of the skirt and pulled the bodice back down into place. Doing so, she noticed the green stone around Helen's neck. "May I have a look at this, my dear?"

Helen unfastened the chain and handed the gem to the Consort, then fled the room to change out of the offending garment.

The Consort returned to her chair, turning the jewel over in her hand. The more she considered it, the odder it was for a girl of Helen's impoverished background to possess such an expensive piece of jewelry. The stone, large and oval in shape, was a fascinating and unheard-of combination of teal sapphire and semi-precious rocks that the Consort did not recognize. Thin streaks of copper ran through it.

What made the piece so costly were the setting and the chain, both of which the Consort suspected were platinum, since neither displayed any hint of tarnish. The setting looped around the outside and fastened to the back of the stone; most of the setting did not show when looking directly at the gem. An extension of the setting band arced above the top of the stone, where two hand-cast platinum rivets attached it to the chain.

Between the rivets, under the curve of the band, a narrow oval of platinum perpendicular to the stone was also hand cast and bore an inscription that the Consort recognized as the ancient script of High Terzil from Southern Alta Province, although she could not decipher the word the letters formed. The chain itself was exquisite. Each link was hand forged, and all links went together in a loose weave that lay flat around the neck and chest, exposing either skin or the fabric beneath.

The high level of workmanship made the Consort suspicious. It seemed familiar. She fished a magnifying glass out of her embroidery case and hunted for the jeweler's mark on the back of the narrow oval platinum insert with the writing on it. What she saw unnerved her. The craftsman who set the gem worked on the Lesser Shore. For generations his family had served the Royal Houses and the highest-ranking of the nobility.

*No rank-and-file soldier could have afforded something like this for his lizun.*

Helen returned in a skirt and blouse, looking less ill at ease. The Consort set the gem aside for the moment. "On second thought, the dark blue makes you look too pale. We don't want to call attention to that, either."

"Why don't we just cover me from head to foot in an old flour sack, Lady Consort? They can guess what I look like if they are really hard up for a moment's diversion."

"Oh, shut up, girl," the Consort said. Lady Mary giggled.

Master Ames stepped forward. "May I suggest a color that highlights the subtle undertones in Mistress Andros' complexion?"

He unrolled a bolt of blood-red fabric, laying one end over Helen's shoulder and allowing the rest to fall down the front of her body. Somehow it suited her; the deep shade brought forth the darker hues in Helen's own mixed coloring.

Although she liked the effect, the Consort touched the fabric with a furrowed brow. "What is this, Master Ames? I don't recognize the feel of it."

"We are sliding around the law here, Lady Consort," he replied. "It is a lambswool-silk blend. I think we can get away with it because it looks like a woolen weave more than anything else. There is a certain amount of risk."

The Consort assented. "Nothing ventured, nothing gained. Let the morals guards bark at me if they wish." She smiled now. "And in deference to the occasion and to Mistress Andros, a high neckline is in order."

●  ●  ●

After the merchant and dressmaker departed, the Consort turned to quizzing Helen closely about her background while the three ate a late lunch. Lady Naomi told the two younger women that she needed the information to help Helen prepare for her trial. The butler poured steaming cups of mint tea and served up bowls of fresh Saba melon and other winter fruits for dessert.

The Consort knew that Turanians gave their children middle as well as first names. "What is your full name, girl?"

Helen had just explained about the lifelong strained relationship between her mother and her mother's cousin, the Princess of Westar.

"An interesting question, Lady Consort. It's Helen Elizabeth. I once asked my mother why my middle name is the same as that of the cousin who seemed to detest her so much. She just laughed and told me she chose my middle name after my father's mother."

"Indeed. Now what exactly did your mother do?"

Helen outlined how her mother trained at the Academy, specializing in physical therapy and massage. She also remarked that her mother once spent almost two years attending a lady in a coma.

That comment commanded the Consort's full if disguised attention. "Before or after you were born, dear?"

"Before, when Mama was still living in Azgard. She would never name the woman, but I suspect she was a very wealthy lady of considerable rank, because Mama was paid to attend her full time, and she had many other servants as well."

"Why did your mother leave Azgard?"

"I don't know, Lady Consort. That's something else she refused to discuss with me." Helen's eyes dropped. "I have always believed that she did not go of her own free will."

● ● ●

Asking Janel to accompany her, Lady Naomi left her apartments that afternoon, telling Lady Mary and Helen she was trying to obtain any intelligence she could about the coming trial. She also took one of her own pieces of jewelry for repair, and Helen's necklace, promising to return it that evening, although she would not say why she wanted it.

The Consort locked Lady Mary and Helen into Lady Mary's suite to protect the former's reputation and the latter's life. With Helen officially in her custody, the Consort had to make some sort of show of restraining her.

Lady Mary and Helen stood before the full-length looking glass, side by side. "You are truly beautiful." The words spilled out of Lady Mary's mouth.

"And you are much too kind, my lady."

Lady Mary cited the way the merchant and dressmaker salivated over her earlier that day. Helen looked disgusted.

"It's always open season on a woman like me, my lady. They wouldn't dare treat you in such a rude manner, even if they think it."

Then she smiled mischievously. "Besides, I'm a little too tall for most men." She placed her hand halfway between the top of Lady Mary's head and the top of hers. "Somewhere about here is the truly beautiful height for a woman, my lady. Or at least beautiful from a man's perspective."

Lady Mary took off her slippers and sat cross-legged on the mattress near the head of my bed. "Do you not like men, Mistress Andros?"

"Please call me Helen, when we're alone like this. All this formality is a pain, don't you think."

"If you'll agree to call me plain old Mary."

Helen removed her shoes and sat at the foot of the bed, facing Lady Mary. "All right then, plain old Mary. Somehow, I don't think it quite suits you. Definitely you are way beyond plain."

"I mean just Mary."

"Just Mary."

"The Consort's right," Lady Mary said. "You are a pain. And don't change the subject. Don't you like men?"

Helen lay back across the bed, hands behind her head. "I like some men just fine, Mary. Others aren't worth the time of day. The trick is sorting them out into the proper category. Some are obvious; others are not."

Helen lifted her head and smiled at Lady Mary's confusion. "How's that for a non-answer? I'm practicing for my command performance tomorrow evening. My first, last, and only."

Lady Mary shuddered, unable to repress a heartsick expression. "Are they really going —"

"To execute me? I believe that's the general idea."

Tears rolled down Lady Mary's face. "But why? What did you do? It's so unfair."

Helen got to her feet, found a handkerchief, and brought it to Lady Mary. She sat next to the younger woman and put her arms around her. Lady Mary tried to wipe her eyes and ended up sobbing even harder.

"Kronos, you are tender-hearted," Helen muttered, smoothing Lady Mary's hair and kissing the top of her head. "How did a sweet lamb like you fall into this nest of pit vipers?"

Lady Mary tried to pull herself together, ashamed of her tears when her companion was the one facing death. "Why? What did you do?"

"Mary, this really isn't about me or what I did, although I'm pretty sure the Lord Chancellor is none too happy that Prince Harnak still lives. I'm a pawn in the latest power play. It's an object lesson for you. A woman really should say no, frequently and loudly."

Helen walked to the window to watch as a few snowflakes drifted onto the gardens outside the Consort's apartments.

"Aren't you terrified?"

"I'm beyond terrified, Mary. I'm numb. This all has such an air of unreality about it. Which is why I propose to change the subject. You heard all about me this afternoon. What about you?"

Lady Mary shrugged her shoulders. "That's a short, dull story. I lead a boring and interminably proper life."

"So how did someone so short and dull, as you put it, manage a voice like yours?"

Lady Mary's gulp betrayed her acute discomfort. She was ashamed of her voice, deep and resonant. Everyone called it "mannish" and teased her about it, as if it were somehow unfitting for a female to speak in a voice with such depth.

Helen was instantly apologetic. "Mary, I'm so sorry. I did not mean to distress you. I'm just envious, that's all. With a little practice, you could pass for a drill sergeant. I know a few bonehead officers I'd love to use your voice on."

"It wouldn't sound so absurd coming from someone who looks like you."

Helen's eyebrow rose. "Think of it as a secret weapon. It will come in handy when you are Consort."

Lady Mary's eyes widened in astonishment that Helen seemed to know everything significant about her position in society, who she was related to, and even to whom Lady Mary was betrothed.

Helen returned to the bed, sat down beside Lady Mary, and put her arm around the younger woman's shoulders once again. Lady Mary returned her embrace, hugging Helen tightly. In that instant she had found a true friend, grieving in fear that Helen would be taken from her forever far too soon. They huddled together for some time.

"Mary, dear, you have about as much ability to hide your true feelings as I do," Helen said. "None at all, in other words. That's why I like you. I know exactly what I'm getting. Do yourself a big favor. Never make a wager when you play cards. Or at least, don't ever bet more than you can afford to pay!"

●  ●  ●

The master jeweler held the green stone close to a light stick, peering at it through his eyepiece. The gray-haired craftsman, his shoulders hunched from a lifetime of detail work, took his time studying the piece of jewelry. Tamaz Gideon recognized his own workmanship yet had to search his memory for some minutes to recall when he had set this stone. Once he had a better idea, he put the gem on the glass counter, nodded to the Consort, and then went into his office, where he kept his ledgers. The one that held the details of this particular transaction would be filed away, according to the year.

The Consort needed all of her self-control not to wander about the jeweler's showroom, especially once she realized that he knew the work was his. Her thoughts flipped to Helen's remark about her middle name. The Consort knew of only one man whose wife had been in a coma for two years and whose mother's name had been Elizabeth. She stretched her memory back to those unhappy days when she would head north to Alta periodically to visit her comatose sister-in-law. A tiny, blonde woman who attended Lady Sabrina appeared unbidden before her inner vision.

*She must have been the girl's mother.*

The jeweler returned carrying a dusty, faded journal. He put it on the counter next to the gem and thumbed through the pages. He found the entry at last and stared at it.

Watching him, the Consort wondered whether to let him know just how important this information might be. Surely her appearance there in person, asking about it, would be clue enough. She decided not to insult him by pretending otherwise.

"Master Gideon," she began. "I cannot tell you precisely why it is so important for me to know. I'm not even sure myself, yet. My heart tells me that what you have written down in your ledger might possibly help save a life, or at least prevent a miscarriage of justice. That is the only reason I am poking my nose into where it so obviously does not belong."

Gideon lifted the entire page out of the binder, turned it around so the Consort could read it, and placed it on the counter. He pointed to the item.

With all her years of masking her feelings and all of her current premonitions of trouble, the Consort still was not prepared for what she saw.

"Father of Kronos! No!"

   ◉ ◉ ◉

After returning with Janel to the Consort's apartments, the Consort unlocked the door to Lady Mary's rooms. Lady Mary was asleep on the bed, and Helen was in the rocking chair, singing softly in the twilight gloom. Helen followed the Consort back into the salon.

"Here is your gem, dear. It will look lovely with the red dress. I'm sorry to say I could find out nothing more about it."

Lady Naomi hated not relating the truth to Helen. Yet what truth could she tell the girl, really? All she had was circumstantial evidence and conjecture, along with her knowledge of the true identity of that lady in a coma. It did not make for ironclad proof. And even if such proof were to exist somewhere and were brought forth, it would only put the girl into an entirely new and different kind of danger. The Consort also did not want to distract Helen's focus just before her trial.

She assumed her chair; Helen sat across from her. First the Consort asked for a more complete description of Kefren's condition, which Helen provided to the best of her ability, given the lack of blood and tissue sample analyses and her inability to conduct more comprehensive testing. The Consort regretted that the girl probably would be in a prison cell or even dead before Lord Matthew would have the analyses fully prepared. She did not trust anyone except Helen to interpret the results for her. Lady Naomi was more determined than ever to pry her husband out of her brother-in-law's guardianship, if she could manage it.

After Helen completed her report, the Consort sat silent for some time before summoning the butler to order supper. Then she turned the conversation to the trial. She had a few tips to pass along to Helen on how to conduct herself during the proceeding. The Lord Chancellor was counting on the girl's ignorance, and the Consort was determined to make the field as level as possible.

# CHAPTER THIRTEEN

The trial awaiting Helen was known among the Toltecs as a *Kazil*, a special court convened to consider only those state crimes serious enough to be punished by death. It consisted of a joint session of the *Kinshazen* and the highest-ranking priests of the Temple of Kronos, who were referred to as the Host of the Faithful.

A *Kazil* was always conducted at Kindred House, the building where the members of the *Kinshazen* met. Its outer layer consisted of massive blocks of polished pink granite, which had a decidedly dark cast to it. Kindred House was closest to Lake Shambhala of all the structures in the Nighthall government complex.

Those summoned before a *Kazil* and convicted of the charges were invariably put to death within three days of the proceeding. And in only a few, very rare, instances had anyone been found innocent on trial before a *Kazil*.

● ● ●

Garbed again in his black robes of office, Shinar sat in the Lord Steward's place at the center of the dais, behind a table-sized lectern of green marble. The noise and commotion were unprecedented. Most of the lower ranking members clustered in small groups, speculating about the case. Many of them had been out of the Sacred City at their country manors and estates when they were summoned back to Shambhala. The proceeding was all the more remarkable for having been first called during the *Kindlemaz* holiday week just ended.

The Lord Steward picked up a gavel and pounded it on the lectern. At the sound, the Princes of Istar and Westar made their way to two chairs at the back of the dais behind Shinar and were seated. Lord Nimrod Atlas, Duke of Avalon, took his place next to the Lord Protector. Other high-ranking nobles also found their positions in the same section of benches that were on the side of the dais by the King's Chair. The Lord Chancellor sat at the prosecutor's table at the far end of the open space in front of the Lord Steward's dais.

In the Visitors' Gallery, Shinar's wife, Lady Siroma, and their son were next to the Consort, with Master Tuk on the Consort's other side. The Grand Master was next to Tuk. The Consort dressed especially elegantly and sported her best inscrutable face. Shinar noticed that the Consort was studying the Lord Protector a great deal.

The noise commanded Shinar's attention once more. The members would not stop talking. Even seated, they continued their conversations. Disbelieving, he glimpsed furtive exchanges of money. He was disgusted. A Toltec would bet on anything that wasn't nailed down. Someone apparently had offered odds as to how long the Andros girl could withstand the Lord Chancellor's interrogation before folding. Perhaps she would surprise them.

Shinar realized he sided with the accused. He did not think the girl should face death for an inadvertent transgression that happened only because she was trying to save one life and thus avert armed strife.

He brought the gavel down hard several times, as much to chase away his own self-doubts as to quiet the chamber. The noise did not subside. Shinar tried again with no success. Finally, he rose from his chair, swung the gavel downward with his entire arm and shoulder; it hit with a resounding crack. "One fool at a time!"

Silence. The Duke of Avalon stood up. The Lord Steward granted recognition and resumed his seat.

"An irresistible invitation, Lord Steward," Lord Nimrod said. "I request consideration of the petition to cancel this entire proceeding as unwarranted by the facts of the case."

"Petition denied, Lord Avalon," Shinar replied. "The facts of this case are actionable. The Kindred deserve the right to hear them and vote accordingly."

Lord Nimrod returned to the bench and Lord Tarkon asked for the floor. "I move to invite the Host of the Faithful to join us." He glanced along the bench toward Lord Nimrod. "Provided there are no more baseless petitions to consider."

The members voted to invite the Faithful, who entered the chamber via the East Doors directly opposite the Visitors' Gallery. The lower ranking priests walked to the benches and remained on their feet for the Supreme Lord of the Temple of Kronos. Everyone in the chamber and Visitors' Gallery rose to pay respects to Ezekiel Malachi, who paraded around the stands of benches to his chair. He sat down with a flourish and adjusted his white-and-gold robes. At his nod to the Lord Steward, the members and visitors sat once more.

Shinar read aloud the Lord Chancellor's formal writ of accusations. "The accused shall enter to face the charges."

● ● ●

Helen did not attend the start of her trial. Wrists chained behind her back, head bowed and eyes shut, she was on her knees before the altar of a small shrine located just inside the main entrance to Kindred House. The tiny place of contemplation was open to anyone, even a person of mixed-race descent. She begged for enough strength to endure the proceeding as well as her death, in whatever manner it would take place.

She was so deep in a meditative state she did not hear the *Valakim* approach. Two King's Guards took her, one holding each of her arms, and lifted her to her feet. They led her out of the shrine, into the noise of the main foyer, which was lined with spectators who did not have rank enough to be admitted to the Visitors' Gallery.

The onlookers whispered and pointed at Helen. She looked straight ahead, ignoring their disapproval. Her courage ebbed. It was just as well that the guards had a firm grasp on her arms. She could not have moved on her own even had she wanted to do so. They brought her to the doors that led to the inner chamber, stopped, and removed the chains from her wrists.

"You're on," one of her jailers whispered to her, giving her a shove forward.

Helen balked, unwilling to be rushed. She rubbed her wrists and arms, straightened her hair. She also took a few slow, deep breaths to try to calm and center herself. Since she was the object of this unseemly farce, she determined to give as good an account of her own performance as possible.

The Lord Chancellor ordered that Helen enter through the South Doors so that she had to walk the entire length of the chamber. The maneuver gave even the lower ranked members the chance for a close look at her.

Helen felt like some sort of exotic specimen under a microscope, or perhaps a filly on display before going up for auction. Every eye felt like it found a mark on her body; their hostile stares hit her like physical blows. Yet that was the challenge she needed in the moment to sharpen her focus and keep her wits about her. Had she detected any kindness or sympathy, she might have been undone.

Chin tipped upward, she focused her own eyes on a spot just above the Lord Steward's head. She moved down the aisle at a deliberate pace, neither too slow nor too fast. "Don't hurry through this part," the Consort had advised her. "Take your time to show them you refuse to be cowed."

To her surprise, Helen felt calm walking toward the Lord Steward's dais, despite more noises of astonishment and disdain from members who were seeing her for the first time. In the Visitors' Gallery, Lord Matthew's eyes glistened. The Consort covered the top of his hand with hers and offered a reassuring squeeze. Lady Siroma frowned.

Helen's ignorance of protocol could have gotten her into immediate trouble. Thanks to the Consort's coaching, she did not make the mistake of going directly to the Lord Steward's dais. Instead, she located the King's Chair and steered across the floor toward it. At ten paces from the chair, she dropped to her knees and offered another absolute submission to the symbol of the Exalted Lord of Azgard, her forehead and body resting on the granite floor. Some of the whispers of condemnation faded away.

Thus Lord James, seated perhaps twenty paces from the King's Chair, beheld in person for the first time the young woman he was certain was his only child. The duke needed every ounce of his self-control to betray nothing of the turmoil in his own heart. Her loveliness robbed him of breath.

When she got to her feet again and he glimpsed the familiar stone around her neck, he wanted to leap up in protest. He struggled to make no sound or gesture, anguished, knowing that he could do nothing for her in this moment. Such unaccustomed impotence tore at Lord James' heart.

Helen next crossed in front of the Lord Steward's dais to ten paces before the Supreme Lord, to whom she made a very deep curtsey, head bowed. He refused to acknowledge or even look in her direction, which angered Shinar, Lord James, and many others as an act of sheer pettiness. She turned to face Prince Seti, curtseyed, and bowed her head to him. He nodded slightly in her direction without looking directly at her. She saluted Prince Enoch, who acknowledged her obeisance with the appropriate response. Helen knelt last in front of the Lord Steward's dais, head lowered.

"On your feet."

Shinar signaled to his bailiff to bring the King's Seal forward and instructed Helen to place her right hand on it as the bailiff held it out to her. "Do you swear by the Covenant of the Kindred, and the Law of the Blood, to tell nothing but the truth throughout these proceedings?"

As briefed by the Consort, Helen took the seal from the bailiff in both of her hands, knelt and kissed it, then rose and gave it back to him, looking up at Shinar.

"I do so swear, Lord Steward."

More whispers from the nobles, this time of approval. Shinar could not refrain from taking a certain amount of pleasure in the Lord Chancellor's discomfiture at the girl's flawless performance. *You trained her well, my queen.*

The Lord Steward pointed to the armchair behind her. Helen turned and sat on it, shoulders squared, head up, hands in her lap.

"State your full name for the record."

"Helen Elizabeth Andros."

"Make your case, Lord Chancellor," Shinar said.

The state's prosecutor unrolled the sleeves of his brown robe of office. He circled Helen. She did not turn her head to follow him, refusing even to acknowledge his first attempt at intimidation.

"Andros. That's a name of significance to some among us. Is it your family name?"

"It is my mother's family name, Lord Chancellor."

"And your mother's full name?"

"Miriam Elinor Andros, Lord Chancellor."

"Where does her family live?"

Helen sat.

"You must answer the question, Mistress Andros," the Lord Steward admonished her.

"They farm land just east of South Alton, inside the northern border of Westar Province."

"Are they related to anyone in this room apart from you?" the Lord Chancellor asked. "Take a careful look in the Visitors' Gallery before answering this question."

She followed his outstretched arm, turned her upper body, and looked up. Although Helen had never before seen the Princess of Westar, she knew what the woman looked like, based on Judith's description.

Even so, Helen was not prepared for the identical physical resemblance to her own parent. She turned away again and closed her eyes, overwhelmed by her unresolved grief over her loss. Lord James was the only person in the chamber who entirely comprehended her reaction. The sight of Prince Enoch's second wife had always unnerved him, reminding him so sharply of his lost love.

"Well?"

She drew in a breath. "They are related to Elizabeth Andros, the Princess of Westar, Lord Chancellor. She is the sister of my mother's cousin, John Andros."

"You have a purpose to these questions, Lord Chancellor?" Shinar asked, commanding silence with his gavel.

"I seek only to establish this stranger's rather mysterious origins and family connections, Lord Steward."

In Terzil, the language of the Toltecs, stranger was another word for foreigner or non-subject.

"And your father's family name?"

"I have no idea, Lord Chancellor."

"No idea? How can you have no idea of your father's family name?"

"My mother never told me, Lord Chancellor."

"Perhaps she also had no idea."

Subdued laughter ran through the ranks of the Lord Chancellor's allies. Helen clung to her composure through sheer force of will. Lady Naomi fumed. This was every bit as vicious and disgusting as she feared. Lord James seethed in silence.

The prosecutor turned toward the back benches and spread his arms wide. "The mother has no idea, and the daughter hasn't either. Ignorance seems to run in the family."

More derisive noises. "Where is your mother now?"

"I cannot say with any certainty, Lord Chancellor."

"In other words, you have no idea?"

"No, Lord Chancellor, I don't. Any other answer would be sheer speculation on my part. I was under the impression this proceeding was to be an examination of facts."

Helen fixed her tormentor in a contemptuous gaze. "Perhaps the Lord Chancellor has no idea of the difference between speculation and fact."

The noises died away. Helen's presence and measured, lucid replies in the face of such relentless hostility earned her grudging respect. Lord James was filled with pride and the joy of certainty. Her courage alone confirmed for him that she was his child, even if no other evidence of her parentage existed.

Stung more than he cared to admit, the Lord Chancellor moved into the next phase of his questioning. He forced Helen to recount her life from her birth in Memfys through her admission to the Academy.

"And how did you manage to gain admission to the most prestigious institution of higher education in all of Azgard?"

"I passed the entrance examination after years of hard study, Lord Chancellor. You should try hard study yourself sometime. It might improve the quality of your prosecution."

His move to strike her was cut short by the Lord Steward's gavel.

"None of that in Kindred House, Lord Chancellor," Shinar said. "And you, Mistress Andros, keep your answers civil."

Helen bowed her head.

"And after all that hard study, did you actually graduate?"

"Yes, Lord Chancellor. I am fully trained in the healing arts and sciences."

He allowed that piece of information to sink in as well. "And where do you now practice your art, or science, or whatever you call it?"

Helen explained her role as medical officer for the 163rd Regiment. The chamber grew still. He stood before her now, his gaze boring down on the top of her head. He asked her to explain her presence in Shambhala. Helen felt her tension rise; this had to be the real focus of the whole miserable sham. She avoided mentioning Lord Matthew while explaining that she had been asked to treat Prince Harnak of Kamut, who was dangerously ill. Not widely known until that point, the news prompted another undercurrent of whispers.

"Who made this request of you?"

"Master Amal Tuk, the prince's tutor, I believe."

"Where were you at the time of this request?"

Helen's heart beat faster; she weighed each word. "At the Andros farm for the holiday, Lord Chancellor."

"How did you get from northern Westar Province to the Sacred City?"

She swallowed hard. "In a rotor, Lord Chancellor."

"A rotor? A half-blood and another foreigner in a rotor? Under whose authority?"

"The authority, Lord Chancellor, of my commanding officer, Colonel Jackson Orlando."

"And under whose orders was the colonel acting?"

Helen looked at him as if he had lost his mind. "My commanding officer does not make a habit of explaining his orders or his actions to a lowly lieutenant, Lord Chancellor," she replied. "Once again, any answer on my part would be sheer speculation. I prefer to stick with facts."

The Lord Chancellor made a prosecutor's one cardinal error. He asked the witness a question for which he did not know the answer. "Did anyone else accompany Master Tuk to put this request to you?"

Helen's hand flew to her mouth. She was utterly trapped and utterly miserable. *Not my sweet Matthew, too!*

He pushed her to respond and instantly regretted her answer. Confusion, astonishment, and outrage erupted among the members.

# CHAPTER FOURTEEN

Hearing her son's name, Lady Siroma leapt to her feet, cried out, and collapsed. Lord Matthew jumped up next to her and managed to catch and hold her, comforting her with soft words and caresses. King's Guards appeared in the Visitors' Gallery, summoning him to the private chambers reserved for the Lord Steward. Lady Naomi assured her nephew that she and Sudras would care for Lady Siroma while he was gone.

Having called a recess, Shinar waited in the reception room of his chambers. Also with him were Prince Seti, Lord Matthew's other uncle, and Malachi. Hands thrust in the pockets of his silk tunic, Prince Seti leaned against the wall near the door to Shinar's office, his pointed nose and chin seeming sharper than usual due to the storm of anger brewing in his expression. The Supreme Lord was a little too collected for Shinar's comfort. Prince Enoch was absent. The Lord Steward hoped he would not appear. The animosity between the two princes was too great to be contained in such a small space.

"I trust you are satisfied with the Lord Chancellor's line of questioning, my lord prince," Shinar said.

Before Prince Seti could respond, Lord Matthew knocked on the door to the chambers and entered after his father granted permission. Lord Matthew knelt to his uncle and the Supreme Lord and bowed to his father.

He stepped in front of the Lord Steward's desk. In his eagerness to protect Helen, he forgot his awe. "Swear me in, Sir. Let me testify. I can explain everything."

"No!" Prince Seti cut in. "I will not have any of the Exalted Lord's own bloodline demeaned thus in public. You are not on trial here, although, by Kronos, you will answer to me at least in this matter."

"I heartily approve, my lord prince," Malachi added. "The boy obviously is in need of more discipline than he has found so far at home."

"How can telling the truth be demeaning, my lord—"

"Silence!" the prince roared at Lord Matthew. "You will not speak again until I question you. Is that understood?"

Lord Matthew nodded. The corners of Prince Seti's mouth twitched and his dark eyes smoldered.

Shinar pleaded with Prince Seti, trying to spare his son the coming ordeal. The prince refused the father's entreaties. At Seti's signal, two *Valakim* shackled Lord Matthew's wrists behind his back and escorted him out of the chamber. The prince ordered them to take their prisoner to the same small jail within Nighthall where Griffin had interrogated Helen and hold him there until further instructions.

The Lord Steward hunched his shoulders, devastated. *How am I going to face his mother?*

● ● ●

During the first portion of the recess, Prince Enoch remained in his chair. The chamber was almost empty, except for a few lower-ranking nobles gathered at the far end, and the girl. The setting was perfect for the delicate query he was to make. He opened a secure link to Lord Justin, still at the Andros farm. It took a couple of minutes for his second son to respond.

Lord Justin was at dinner in the farmhouse kitchen when the link in his pocket emitted a signal that shocked him because he could not recall the prince ever making direct contact with him before. For privacy he answered in the mudroom, not realizing he had left the door ajar.

"You took your time, boy," Prince Enoch growled.

"I did not think the dinner table the best place to respond, my lord prince."

"Did Matthew accompany Master Tuk to the farmhouse?"

"Yes, my lord prince. He was here."

"You can swear to that if need be."

"Yes, my lord prince, I can swear to it. May I ask why this might be important?"

Prince Enoch sought additional information. "What kind of relationship was evident between Matthew and Helen?"

Lord Justin had so many mixed feelings he hardly knew how to respond. From what Lord Matthew said about her, he obviously had asked her to marry him many times. Perhaps Lord Matthew had pursued her so intently in order to avoid facing himself. Lord Justin understood that fear only too well.

"Let me put it this way," Prince Enoch pressed him. "Do you think they have slept together?"

"Lord Matthew displays great respect for her, my lord prince, and may well have sought her favors. My best speculation is she refused him."

Prince Enoch was not satisfied with his son's response, and made it clear he thought Lord Justin was not telling the truth.

To keep his anger in check, Lord Justin tried to change the subject. "May I ask, my lord prince, the status of the proceeding?"

"Not good. The girl will be convicted and sentenced to die shortly," Prince Enoch replied. "The officer who flew the rotor to and from the farm also faces arrest."

It was obvious to Lord Justin's unintended audience that he was speaking to his father. His formal mode of address revealed the strained relationship between the two.

Abigail leaned toward Judith. "He never talks about any of this."

"What can he say? It's between him and his father and they must sort it out in their own time and manner," Judith replied. "Spare what little pride he has left and say nothing of it when he returns."

● ● ●

The prince cut the link, returning the device to the inner pocket of his surcoat. He stepped off the dais and strolled toward the West Doors.

Hearing approaching footsteps, Helen looked up, saw the prince, and arose and sank to one knee in a deep curtsey. Aware that the nobles still in the chamber were watching, Prince Enoch took the girl's hand and helped her back to her seat as a display of respect for his wife's kinswoman. He saw that she had been weeping. He searched his pockets for a handkerchief and gave it to her.

"Thank you, my lord prince," Helen whispered, wiping her eyes. "Please tell them about Lord Matthew. He has done nothing wrong. Nothing at all," she repeated, and struggled to contain more tears.

Prince Enoch looked down at her without replying. He did not believe her; nor did he believe his son's interpretation of her relationship with Lord Matthew. Lord Justin no doubt was lying to protect his kinswoman. Lord Matthew must have taken her to bed, or there was something seriously amiss with the boy. She was simply the most gorgeous female the prince had ever laid eyes on.

He felt an almost overpowering lust for her. He wanted to smell her hair, to caress her smooth pale skin, to explore every part of her body with his fingers and his tongue, to mount her and take her a dozen different ways. What a waste to execute her.

Helen glanced about. Such a creepy-crawly sensation. Like someone was stalking her. The stone pinged against the fabric of her gown. Although she had no name for root energy, she had had similar experiences before, whenever men were thinking about sex with her. She usually was able to verify her intuitive impression with her eyes; something in their expressions or body postures invariably betrayed them.

This time, however, Helen's physical eyesight mistakenly assured her there was no threat nearby. Prince Enoch, his thin lips and receding jaw like stone, displayed none of his turmoil. Helen lowered her head into her hands once more.

"Compose and prepare yourself, Mistress Andros," the prince said. "Most likely this will only get much worse."

* * *

The Lord Steward brought the *Kazil* to order to reconvene the proceeding. "You are still under oath, Mistress Andros."

"Yes, Lord Steward. I am well aware of that."

Shinar nodded to the prosecutor, who once more walked to Helen's chair. She refused to meet his eyes; she was afraid her temper would get the better of her. He compelled her to recount her friendship with Lord Matthew during their years together at the Academy.

"You tutored him? In what? Body structure?"

Helen joined in the laughter that ran out through the inner chamber. "No, Lord Chancellor. Lord Matthew had that topic down cold long before we ever met. His problem was elementary calculus."

Her rejoinder caught the Lord Chancellor off guard. This wasn't going as planned. He changed focus. "Why did Lord Matthew accompany Master Tuk to the Andros farm?"

"I cannot speculate as to his motives, Lord Chancellor."

"Let me rephrase the question. What did he tell you about why he was with Master Tuk?"

Helen looked down at the floor for a moment, trying to recall everything Lord Matthew said to her at the farm and during their meeting in the Consort's salon. "He wanted to apologize to me, Lord Chancellor."

"Apologize? What possible reason on earth would the Exalted Lord's own nephew ever have to apologize to someone like you?"

Helen shot out of the chair, fists at her sides, eyes alight. She looked squarely into his eyes and took a step forward. "For refusing to attend Prince Harnak himself. He did not feel qualified to do so, Lord Chancellor."

She moved a step forward, forcing him to give way. "I agree. Lord Matthew's experience is in medical research. Mine is clinical.

"It's one thing to study the heart. It's another thing entirely to be faced with the reality of doing something about an actual heart attack. It made me wonder why on earth Prince Harnak was not treated long before I arrived. By all descriptions, he had been seriously ill for several days before I saw him."

Helen finally realized where she was and what she had done. She stepped back toward the chair and sat down. She had little idea that she had just earned a great deal more grudging respect, even from those who hated her most, for having forced the Lord Chancellor to back off, and exposing his attempt to kill the prince through neglect.

The Lord Steward saw an opening. "Are you saying Prince Harnak suffered a heart attack, Mistress Andros?"

"I am saying he lacked a pulse and stopped breathing for a few minutes, Lord Steward. How long, I have no idea. I was a tad busy for precise timing."

"What were you doing?" Shinar continued.

"I was administering what you might call a medical attitude adjustment, Lord Steward. His heart started beating again and he began to breathe once more. Fortunate, isn't it?"

Helen stared at the pattern in the floor, hardly aware of the appreciative laughter from many of the listeners.

Shinar brought the gavel down. "Let it be noted for the record that Prince Harnak continues to recover from his ailment."

He turned to the prosecutor, by this time slumped in the chair at his table, jaw grinding.

"Your witness, Lord Chancellor. Let's try to wrap this up soon."

Griffin remained seated. "How would you characterize your relationship with Lord Matthew?"

Helen looked over at him, on her guard again. "We have been good friends for many years, Lord Chancellor."

He rose and confronted her. Without warning he bent down and rested his hands on the edges of the chair's arms, forcing Helen backward. "How good? Did you ever touch him?"

"Yes, Lord Chancellor."

"In what way."

"In a friendly way, Lord Chancellor."

"How friendly? Did you ever hold his hand?"

"Yes—"

"Embrace him?"

"Yes—"

"Touch his hair?"

"Yes—"

"Kiss him?"

"Yes, but—"

"In other words, you seduced him."

"No! Never! It wasn't like that at all!"

Helen shut her eyes and tried to turn away from him. He stayed in her face. "That's not what he says."

Helen's eyes flew open.

"Yes, Lord Matthew repents of your so-called friendship, and says you seduced him many times. He has asked for and will receive the Holy One's restoration, after an appropriate discipline."

"Then he will suffer for something he never did, Lord Chancellor."

Griffin stood upright, turning to address the entire House. "My lords, let us review briefly the facts of this case. You have before you a stranger, a nameless half-blood of no rank who by some means managed to insinuate her way into one of our most respected institutions.

"What does she do there? She corrupts one of the Exalted Lord's own bloodline. Her way, perhaps, of expressing her gratitude for the opportunity of availing herself of a priceless and unsurpassed education."

Helen sat very straight.

"Then, to add insult to this grievous injury, she profanes the sacred soil of Shambhala by daring to enter it, although a stranger and non-subject, without seeking and receiving permission first.

"The law is clear, my lords. You must find her guilty."

The Lord Chancellor, if not entirely pleased with his performance, was at least fairly certain of the outcome.

The Lord Steward asked for a voice vote; it went overwhelmingly against Helen. Only Prince Enoch, Lord Nimrod, Lord James, and a handful of their allies voted not to find her guilty.

"Rise, Mistress Andros."

Helen found the strength to get to her feet.

"You have been found guilty of profaning the Sacred City, a capital crime," Shinar said. "Your punishment is death, the hour and manner of which to be determined by the Holy One, in consultation with the Host of the Faithful. Have you anything to say before you are remanded to their custody to await execution?"

Several white-robed priests approached Helen. They caught her arms and chained her wrists behind her. Holding her head high, she managed to catch her tormentor's eye. "Pray for a long, long life, Lord Chancellor. I'll be waiting for you in hell."

Her jailors cast a black hood over Helen's face. The eyes of the condemned were not allowed to gaze upon anything within the Sacred City. They steered her to the South Doors, then toward a dock where a skimmer was due to arrive to transport her to a prison cell. Lady Naomi hurried after them.

The members left the inner chamber, talking among themselves. Declining Lord Nimrod's invitation to a late supper, Lord James remained on the bench, his mind reeling, his heart exploding in grief and anguish. *Father of Kronos, help me! Miriam, our child is going to die.*

# CHAPTER FIFTEEN

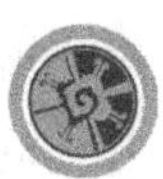

Ariel sat next to his wife on the bed in the room they always shared when they visited the farm. He had his arms around her, and was trying his best to talk her out of her hysterics. He feared that Helen's superior officer would hear Martha's screams. For some reason, the soldier had returned a few minutes earlier, bearing the news of Helen's death sentence that had driven Martha to the edge.

Scarcely less anguished than his wife, Ariel was also leery of Orlando. What more did this Toltec want from them, or with them? The colonel was looking for something and made a pointed reference to questioning Martha, who was in no condition to be helpful or even coherent.

He rocked his wailing wife in his arms for many minutes, smoothed her rumpled hair, kissed her forehead. When her screams died to whimpers, he laid her on her back, found a facecloth, dampened it, and placed it over her closed eyes and brow.

"Martha, compose yourself. We must not give this officer any reason to become angry with us. We must cooperate as much as possible with him. Come back down to the kitchen soon."

He stooped to kiss her cheek, and she managed to grasp his hand and press it, indicating that she understood him.

Ariel found Orlando at the kitchen table, consuming a mug of *kaf* and plate of food. Grateful for his first meal in almost a day, Orlando sensed the wariness in those around him. *They must really mistrust Toltecs, or soldiers, or both.*

Who could blame them? Orlando did not have to imagine their anguish at the news; he shared it himself. He tried not to dwell on the lieutenant's demise by focusing on this errand, which might yield information that could stop what seemed inevitable. It was the only thing that gave him any cause for hope.

Ariel took the chair beside the colonel and sat, dejected. Orlando finished the food and was unsure how to frame his request. Lord Justin touched him on the shoulder, nodded toward a door on the far side of the kitchen. Orlando followed him.

Lord Justin made sure the mudroom door was shut this time. "You are aware of the writ for your arrest, Colonel. I suspect they'll wait until you return to your base and pick you up there."

"No, I was not aware, my lord."

"The prince my father informed me of it just hours ago. That should be enough authority for you, Colonel. I am sorry. It will not be pleasant."

"It goes with the job, my lord."

"What exactly was the nature of the lieutenant's crime?"

As Orlando explained, something started taking shape in the farthest reaches of Lord Justin's awareness. It was too nebulous for him to make sense of it yet, but it had something to do with the definition of a subject. He knew himself better than to try to compel the insight to reveal itself. It would have to drop in on him in its own time and manner. He prayed fervently that it would not arrive too late to be of real help.

He continued in a different vein. "If you will tell me in more detail why you have returned, Colonel, perhaps I can be of some assistance. These are my kindred and they probably will trust me more than you."

Orlando outlined the Lord Protector's order to find out about Helen's background. "I have come straight from Princess Notufil of Kamut, my lord. She told me Miriam Andros wrote at least two letters that she gave to her daughter before putting the lieutenant onto a transport to Azgard."

They returned to the kitchen. Orlando allowed Lord Justin to explain the situation. As he was speaking, Martha descended the back stairs and entered the kitchen. Her eyes were red-rimmed with tears and glazed with pain, her gray-streaked hair and the scarf that bound it askew. She took the chair next to her husband, who put his arm around her shoulders and kissed her forehead.

"We know of no letters or other documents from Miriam, Colonel," John said. "At least Abigail and I do not." Ariel also shook his head; Martha sat and stared.

"Why do you want to know, Colonel?" Abigail asked.

"The Lord Protector suspects that Helen is his daughter, and is seeking anything that might provide word on this from her mother."

Most of those present were shocked into a long silence; Judith and Abigail exchanged knowing looks. "How would finding such a document help Helen, Colonel?" John ventured. "She's already been convicted."

"Most likely it will achieve nothing for her, Mistress Andros," Orlando conceded. "But if such a document exists, and names him as her father, the Lord Protector will do his utmost to save her life."

He sighed. "To be effective, he must have some kind of evidence beyond suspicion and circumstance. Hard evidence that he can present in a court of law."

Eyes closed, Martha reached into the pocket hidden behind the skirt of her apron. Unable to stifle a sob, she pulled out Miriam's letter to Helen and placed it before her on the table. She cringed when she heard the gasps from her family.

"Forgive me for never telling you — any of you," she added, looking from her husband to Abigail and John. "Miriam made it absolutely plain that this letter was to remain a secret until Helen reached her age of majority at thirty-five."

"There was another letter, then," Orlando interposed.

"Yes, Colonel. It was to me from my sister. I can assure you it had no word at all on a possible father for my niece, if that's your concern."

"Where is that letter now, Mistress Galan?"

"I burned it, as Miriam requested."

The colonel stood behind Martha's chair and retrieved the letter from the table. The bulging envelope was addressed to the lieutenant in what seemed to be a woman's handwriting. It also was sealed. That part relieved him immensely. He would have had no choice except to arrest the woman and take her for questioning before the Lord Steward if she had done something truly foolish, such as open it.

"You can swear an oath, Mistress Galan, that you have never seen the contents of this letter, and that it was indeed delivered to you eleven years ago?"

"Yes, Colonel. Why do you ask?"

"For possible future reference."

His eyes were full of pity. Judith knew exactly what Orlando risked by not placing Martha into custody.

"I must, of course, take this letter with me," Orlando added. "Since it is unopened, I see no need to involve you further at this time."

Ariel shot out of his chair. "Involve her? What are you talking about, Colonel? She's done nothing and given you precisely what you said you wanted. Have some pity, man. Can't you just leave us alone now to mourn our niece?"

Abigail cried out at his words, which seemed to distress everyone at the table. Orlando left the farmhouse for the rotor, to file a flight plan from the link, and to await Lord Justin and Judith, whom he agreed to take with him back to Shambhala because his errand was not official military business.

Judith bid the family farewell first and boarded the aircraft. She suggested to Orlando that she carry the letter, since he was likely to face the Lord Chancellor's police when he returned.

"My orders are to deliver it to either the Lord Protector, or failing that, the Lord Steward."

"So be it. I will make sure those orders are carried out. This is an exceptional circumstance, Jackson," she urged him. "We do not want this letter falling into the wrong hands."

"As always, Judith, your logic is annoyingly hard to ignore."

He handed the document over his shoulder to her. She secured it in a pocket deep inside her sheepskin cloak.

Having said good-bye to the other family members, Lord Justin stood with Abigail just outside the front door of the farmhouse. Although it was almost impossible for her to speak past the pain, Abigail felt compelled. Her voice trembled.

"Justin, dear. What will they do with her, when it's all over? I mean, would it be possible for us to, to claim her body? We want to bury her here, on the farm. Is that too much to ask?"

Lord Justin held her close for a moment, wiping the tears off her face with a handkerchief retrieved from his coat pocket.

"I plan to witness the proceeding and will file a claim for her remains on your behalf, Aunt Abigail," he said. "It is my right as her kinsman. I will bring her home to you. I promise."

# CHAPTER SIXTEEN

Lord Matthew spent two days in prison before several King's Guards delivered him, clad only in rumpled and stained shirt and trousers, to his uncle, who was in his private workout room. He faced the prince and waited, unwilling to beg the man for mercy Lord Matthew did not believe he deserved.

At the prince's signal, the guards descended on Lord Matthew. They stripped him and chained his wrists to a hook embedded in a tall post at one end of the rectangular room. Lord Matthew's bare feet dangled above the floor. He tipped his head back and kept his eyes on the ceiling, hoping he did not look as truly terrified or ashamed as he felt.

A rawhide whip coiled like a serpent under his arm, the prince approached his nephew. He jabbed the butt of the whip handle underneath the young man's jaw, compelling Lord Matthew to face him.

"You have a choice, Matthew. Confess your unlawful relationship with this *nahazi* whore, denounce her, promise to apologize publicly to the Holy One and seek restoration from him, and this can end before it ever starts."

"It's already started, my lord prince," Lord Matthew replied, and yanked his head to the side, away from his uncle.

The prince tossed the whip to the soldier standing ten paces behind his nephew, and held up two fingers. Nothing had ever prepared Lord Matthew for the searing, burning, tearing sensation he experienced as the lash raked across his back once, then twice. It felt as though red-hot knives with dull blades were scorching and stinging him.

He could not help moaning and gasping for air. He hung suspended in the chains, panting, his blood oozing toward the small of his back.

The prince put his mouth next to his nephew's ear. "How many times did you bed her?"

"Never, my lord prince. Not once."

"Impossible. We all saw her. Such unholy beauty would inflame the strongest of men. When did she first seduce you?"

"Never, my lord prince. We were friends. I wanted her to marry me and asked her for her hand."

Lord Matthew correctly predicted his uncle's response to that little piece of information, and endured ten more strokes. He began to feel lightheaded and nauseated; he had not eaten anything in more than a day.

"You asked her to wed you? You had no right to make such an offer without either the Exalted Lord's or my permission, and I can assure you such permission never would have been granted."

"That is what she said when she refused me, my lord prince."

Lord Matthew fought ever harder to breathe and to remain lucid enough to reply.

"You simply took her anyway, without her consent."

Lord Matthew dropped his voice to a whisper, so that his uncle had to put his ear right next to his nephew's lips. "Was that how it went between you and Lady Samantha, my lord prince? You forced yourself on your own daughter, didn't you? I would have thought you too proud for that."

The prince recoiled, struggling to maintain his composure against a tidal wave of panic. Matthew could not possibly know anything. He was just guessing. He could not prove anything; there were no witnesses, no physical evidence. The prince had always preserved her virginity, since so many other ways existed to take pleasure from a woman's body. And it had been years since he even touched her.

His panic took him over. He grabbed the whip from the soldier's hand and aimed blow after savage blow at his prisoner's back. Lord Matthew soon passed out, no longer able to endure the agony, in danger of bleeding to death.

* * *

From his office in The Citadel, the headquarters of the Temple of Kronos, Lucan Silenas, the Holy Deputy and the temple's second in command, used a series of spotters to observe the transfer of the prisoner from Kindred House to her cell deep in the bowels of the Temple's compound on an island in the middle of Lake Shambhala. Once she arrived, he cut the image feed, intending to return for further observation after she had been in confinement for a day or two and was feeling the effects of cold and starvation. He had plans for her.

* * *

Her face hooded, Helen saw nothing of her journey to The Citadel's prison. When her captors at last unchained her hands and uncovered her eyes, she was standing in a windowless cell. All except one thin-faced priestess-healer departed, locking the heavy door behind them.

The *koja's* eyes damned Helen without mercy. "Strip."

Helen did not respond.

"Do it yourself at once, or I will fetch others to do it for you."

Helen put her back to the woman and removed her dress.

"Everything," the *koja* ordered.

Helen took off her slip, shoes, stockings, and undergarments, placing them on the wooden stool next to her. Along with a crude sleeping board, without a blanket or even a mattress, the stool was one of the few objects in the stone room. A rope-handled bucket sat in the corner of the cell closest to Helen; its purpose was obvious to her. *They certainly don't believe in coddling the condemned.*

The ice-cold floor burning the soles of her feet, Helen remained facing the wall. She tried hard not to shiver even though the damp air was so frigid it stung her skin.

"Turn around."

She swallowed and shut her eyes, resolutely placing her hands at her sides. Helen did not want to give this woman the satisfaction of seeing her cringe. She opened her eyes and moved to face her tormentor.

The *koja* looked her up and down in contempt. "Be grateful the Holy One recognizes that your crime was unintentional, or we would shave your head as well."

"I'm overwhelmed with appreciation."

The *koja* darted toward Helen and slapped her across the face. The strong blow sent Helen reeling and she fell to the floor.

"Silence! The condemned may not speak unless asked a direct question."

The woman bent down and, as Helen lay disoriented, secured her ankles one at a time in steel manacles connected by a short chain. She dropped what looked like a long sack on the floor next to Helen's head.

"Cover your half-blood shame with this."

The *koja* gathered Helen's clothing, knocked on the iron door, and was released from the cell, leaving one feeble light-stick behind.

Helen waited until her vision stopped blurring before sitting up. She picked up the hemp cloth and discovered it was a crude robe with an opening for her head and ill-fitting sleeves. She pulled it over her face, got slowly to her feet, and found that at least it was long enough to reach to her ankles.

The thin garment was all that she had against the mind-numbing cold. Her chin resting on her knees, her arms wrapped around her calves and shins, Helen sat huddled, unable to stop shivering, on the board that kept her feet off of the icy floor. The shackles chilled her ankles.

Minutes dragged interminably into what had to be hours. Hours collected slowly into what must have been days. She knew only by her growling stomach that any significant time had elapsed. Every so often the door would open and a priestess would leave a cup of water on the floor for her, but never any food.

The relentless cold, her gnawing hunger, and her thoughts would not let her sleep or even rest. Helen's heart trembled when she focused on Lord Matthew. He was in a world of trouble thanks to what she was forced to reveal during the trial. She prayed fervently for his safety and welfare. She prayed that the colonel would not suffer overmuch for his role in her crime, not daring to examine her deeper feelings for him.

She also prayed that her family would not pay for her transgression. The more she thought about them, the more distressed she became; so much so that she soon forced them from her mind. She suspected there was at least one spotter hidden in the cell and did not want anyone to see her weep. She offered humble, silent thanks for the strength to endure the trial, and asked only that it remain with her through her death. She could not comprehend what might lie beyond that.

She hugged her bent knees to her chest to preserve what little body warmth she had in reserve. Helen slowly became aware of an unnerving red light. She lifted her head and looked around. The glow bounced off the cold stone walls and intensified quickly. It filled her with thoughts of despair and hopelessness. She tried to shake them off.

*You have what's mine! Where is it? I want it!*

Helen shuddered violently. She recalled the inner voice that urged her to use the stone to keep Prince Harnak from dying. That voice was comforting and encouraging. This voice was oppressive and angry and beat on her relentlessly.

"No!" she muttered. "Go away. I have nothing for you or anyone else, not even me."

The red light flickered out. Only the numbing cold and her utter isolation, cheerless companions, remained.

❂ ❂ ❂

While Helen suffered alone, Silenas hooked into the live spotter feed Horton Feril, the Chief *Shakti*. He was head of the *Shaktim*, a group of warrior-monks highly trained in the steps of the *kura*. Greatly feared, the *Shaktim* enforced Temple laws and punishments. Of all the Brotherhood of Kronos, the Chief *Shakti* was among those most skilled in using *kura*.

Silenas together with the Chief *Shakti* resumed observing Helen in her cell. Looking at the warrior monk's face on the link screen, Silenas could tell the man was impatient for his chance to test the half-blood. "Go ahead, Father *Shakti*, Let's find out about her abilities. But do not employ the higher energy levels on her. She can show no evidence of that kind of torture. Hers is to be a very public death."

The Chief *Shakti* frowned but obeyed the order, and started sending energy into Helen's cell. Unconsciously alert to the invisible invasion, Helen quickly became aware of something, almost like a presence in the space with her. In the gloom, perhaps her eyes were playing tricks on her. She could vaguely discern a black-robed form taking shape before her. When the form seemed to call out her name, she stood up as quickly as her hobbled feet would permit, grabbed the light-stick off the stool, and held it aloft to search the room. This presence was different and there was no red glow.

Silenas opened a voicelink to the Supreme Lord and added him to the image feed. He then asked the Chief *Shakti* to do another test. The head warrior-monk decided to play with the prisoner. He sent a finger of energy back into the cell, tapped her on a shoulder with it. He watched her brush that shoulder with her hand, looking at it in bewilderment. He next sent a ball of energy skittering like a rat across the stone floor. Sure enough, she sensed it, too. Even though her eyes saw nothing, they accurately traced the path of the energy.

The Chief *Shakti* smiled. He had driven hardened men insane with these simple tricks.

"That will be all, Father *Shakti*," Silenas said, and cut the feed to him, ending his participation in the meeting.

"She does not recognize what she perceives because she has not been trained, Holy One, but she is most sensitive to energy."

"This is terrible," Malachi rumbled, rubbing his ample jowl.

"Tell the Chief *Shakti* to pursue this no further, Lucan."

"As you wish, Holy One."

"This girl must die. Lucan, you are to represent the Temple at her execution and read the death sentence."

"As you wish, Holy One."

Malachi cut the link. After her arrest, the link monitors had informed him that she frequently researched the *Arkana,* seeking knowledge mostly of herbal treatments. Harmless enough. If she ever found her way past the locks into the secret sections of the ancient mystery texts, she might uncover and use highly guarded knowledge that could make her a formidable opponent, thanks to her considerable intellect and the training her mind received.

Malachi thought about the situation further. This natural sensitivity to energy seemed to be a direct result of blending the two races. Only half-bloods displayed the kind of awareness it took years for most Toltec adepts to achieve. It was the real reason the Temple forbade such unions. There could be no sharing of such potent knowledge without weakening the Temple's authority and power. And once the girl was dead, Malachi would turn his attention to the delicate yet imperative task of imposing the same fate on her half-blood kinsman.

* * *

Only half-conscious, dazed by repeated blows from the lash, Orlando started to sink to his knees and was caught and held upright by the chains that secured his wrists and pinned him facing the wall. The Lord Chancellor was interrogating him in the same small cell where he had first questioned Helen. Orlando refused to say anything beyond his name, rank, and service number.

"Don't be a fool, Colonel," his questioner said. "We know you would not have acted without direct orders from the Lord Protector. Say his name, tell us those orders, and all this will end instantly."

Orlando blinked hard to clear the sweat mingled with tears out of his eyes. In his fog of pain, his mind wandered to a time when he witnessed the Lord Protector closely questioning a vice-general. The man had clearly made a mistake, and was just as obviously unwilling to admit it. Enraged, the Lord Protector pinned him with the hardest gaze Orlando had ever seen one man show to another.

*Just like the Lieutenant gave me at the farm. Now I know where I've seen that expression before.*

He blinked again, looked up, realized it was not the Lord Protector speaking to him. It was the Lord Chancellor. It seemed impossible that this man could be related to Lord James, yet they shared the same family name. Orlando would die rather than provide this wretch with even the smallest scrap of evidence to use against the Lord Protector, or the Lord Protector's daughter, to whom he owed the same duty and loyalty he did his Supreme Commander.

"Well, Colonel?"

His mouth was so parched he could hardly speak. He moistened his lips to the best of his ability. "Orlando, Jackson. Colonel. Service number—"

The whip crashed down several times on his back. He gasped and writhed yet offered nothing more.

The Lord Chancellor raged with frustration. He took over the whip and applied it himself, giving Orlando twice the number of strokes prescribed as the maximum punishment for his role in the crime.

Orlando lost consciousness without revealing anything else.

# CHAPTER SEVENTEEN

Lady Naomi sat in front of the dressing table in her bedchamber, staring into the looking glass. One light-stick glowed on the table before her. She was unattended, having dismissed all of her servants and locked the door to her apartments.

The Consort had her reasons for seeking solitude. She picked up Helen's healthstone by the chain. The oval gem twisted and turned, gleaming in the light-stick's glow. Lady Naomi had bribed the priests guarding the girl to spend a few minutes with her, alone, before the skimmer took her to The Citadel. Bound and hooded, Helen had still possessed enough presence of mind to ask her to take the gem from her neck before the priests plundered it. The Consort was to deliver it to her aunt and uncle in Avalon.

"Please, Lady Consort, give them my love. Tell them I beg them on my knees to forgive me my many transgressions and all the trouble I have caused for them," the girl whispered, while the paid-off priests looked the other way.

The Consort's shoulders shook as she wept. *Transgressions? What could a girl that young know of sin?*

Finally, she reached for a handkerchief. Helen's demise was distressing, she realized, because it trod hard on her anxieties over her own daughter's safety. She was brooding as well over Lord Matthew, whom she had managed to see briefly late that afternoon, after he was returned to his father' house. She scarcely recognized the unconscious young man.

She could not hold back more tears. *What kind of people are we? We kill and maim our children in the name of morality and law and order.*

The wall panel slid open. She did not realize he was in the room with her until he came up behind her and placed his hands on her shoulders. Startled, she jumped, relaxing only when she saw his reflection.

"You're late, as usual."

"If I were ever on time, Mimi, would you recognize me?"

She smiled despite her fears and sorrow. He could always manage to amuse her. Perhaps that was one reason she took him to her bed all those years ago during Kefren's first incapacity.

He draped his cloak over a chair and took off his boots. Returning to stand behind her, he brushed his hands against her shoulders. The Consort put hers on top of his, felt the chill in the ducal signet ring he wore. Soon his fingers were removing the pins that held her hair in place. It spilled over her shoulders.

"Much better," he murmured, leaning down to kiss her face and noticing the moisture on it. "Mimi, what's wrong. Are you ill?"

Her eyebrow arched. "Just because I'm almost old enough to be your mother, Nimrod, doesn't mean I'm enfeebled."

She rose and wrapped her arms around his chest. "Kronos, how I want you tonight."

He made no objection when she unbuttoned his shirt and planted a kiss on his lips. Surrendering to her passion and her need, the Consort sank her teeth for an instant into his upper arm, then pushed him away. She was breathing heavily, the lace on the bodice of her dressing gown rising and falling.

Without taking his eyes off of her, Lord Nimrod ran a finger over the bite. She had actually drawn blood. A lustful, uncertain expression came over his face.

"Are you sure, Mimi?"

"Yes, damn you! If you're man enough!"

He came up behind her and stood for a moment; she trembled with anticipation. He grabbed her hair, yanked her head back, and forced her mouth open with his tongue. With his other hand he ripped off her dressing gown and groped her breasts, her hips, and her thighs. His kiss ended, he pulled her close and bit her in return, on her arm.

She moaned in pain and pleasure; this was exactly what she wanted — not to think about anything for a while. To feel instead his heat, his sweat, his mouth, his hands all over her body, to taste his scent and to hold him inside of her for as long as she could.

He picked her up and threw her onto the bed, stomach down, and was on top of her before she could move. Finding a silk cord in a night-stand drawer, he bound her wrists together behind her back. Straddling her with his knees, he finished undressing, turned her on her back, and assaulted her. He flipped her on her stomach again and lashed her with his belt. She cried out. The next instant he rolled her on her back, flicking his tongue across her nipples.

He continued to whipsaw her through an increasingly intense series of painful and then delicious sensations. She gasped, shuddered, sighed, whimpered, struggled against him and her bonds without success, giving up everything else to the feeling of the moment.

"Take me very, very hard, Nimrod," she whispered into his ear.

* * *

He lay on his back; she rested her head on his shoulder.

"I had no idea you went in for this sort of thing, Mimi. Not many women do. At least, not voluntarily."

He was referring to what Toltecs called *Sung-fei*, the Bloodlust. At its highest level, *Sung-fei* was an ancient, complex, aggressive mating rite believed to help conceive strong warriors and leaders. Most Toltec men lacked the skill and sensitivity to do it without inflicting serious injury on their partners. Most Toltec women were terrified of *Sung-fei*, which could last for several hours, depending on the participants' endurance and the man's dexterity.

"I had no idea, either, until tonight," the Consort replied. "It must have been the sight of you without a shirt."

He brushed a strand of hair out of her eyes. "Try again, Mimi. You've seen me dozens of times without a shirt or anything else on, and never reacted like this."

She lifted her head, her curls spilling onto his chest. She hardly knew where to start. "I have a confession, Nimrod. I don't much like my daughter."

He gazed back at her. "Allow me to enlighten you on this subject. No one likes Flora. She's a rude, selfish, insensitive, dictatorial bitch. And you want me to marry her."

She sat up. Sometimes he did not seem to understand just which one of them was in charge of this relationship. "Yes, but she's not bad looking, she's very rich, and has an impeccable family name."

"I'm not exactly hurting for money, and my family name's fairly acceptable as well," he countered, sitting up.

She offered a pleading expression. "Flora needs you, Nimrod. She needs the kind of protection only the House of Atlas can give her. Seti's faction has gone berserk. I'm so frightened for her."

She started crying. He put his arms about her and drew her close to him. He thought about the Andros girl's trial and condemnation and Lord Matthew's perilous condition. It was not hard to understand her distress. It was sobering for all of them, especially the thought of what might transpire once Kefren was dead and Prince Seti assumed the Kingship.

He held her until she was calmer, then laid her down again. She latched onto him like a child, her body quickly warming to his now gentle embrace and his deep kisses.

*   *   *

Lord Justin was aware he was dreaming. He could see himself as a first-year student at the Academy. He was in a mathematics class surrounded by rows of other pupils. The problem before him was a quadratic equation. His teacher came up and stood behind him, leaning over his shoulder. The man always seemed to single him out, push him hard. It took him years to realize that his professor was excited about his abilities in the subject and had high expectations for him.

"Well, Justin?" The teacher omitted his family honorifics. Not even the sons of Exalted Lords, if they were admitted to the Academy, were addressed by anything other than their first names. "How are you going to solve this one? Should you make an assumption about the value of X?"

Lord Justin tumbled out of the dream into waking reality. In the darkness of his bedroom, he groped for a light-stick and flicked it on. He gathered his thoughts and checked the time. His brother most likely was not asleep, even if he was in bed somewhere.

This could not wait. Lord Justin knew what could save Helen, provided that letter named Lord James as her father.

* * *

The Consort was on top of Lord Nimrod, covering his face, neck, and shoulders with kisses, nuzzling his ears with her tongue when the link emitted an insistent screech. She rolled off of him and lay back in the pillows.

"Another appointment? How kind of you to fit me into your busy social calendar."

Lord Nimrod removed a link from a pocket of his cloak and sat down on the edge of the bed to answer it. "This had better be really good, Justin."

"Is preventing Seti and Griffin from executing my kinswoman good enough for you, Nim?"

Lord Nimrod hit a switch on the link so that the Consort could hear his brother speak. "Repeat what you just said."

Lord Justin did so. The Consort bounced upright, eyes wide, hope in her face.

"You have my undivided attention, Shorty."

"It all boils down to assumptions, Nim," Lord Justin said. "We've all been assuming that the only way to be a subject is to be born on the soil of Azgard.

"But what if a person's father is a subject?" he continued. "Does that not naturally make the person a subject as well, from birth? Consider our grandfather, Prince Jared. If I recall correctly, he was also born in Kamut during a state visit. No one ever questioned whether he was a subject of Azgard."

After a silence, Lord Justin spoke again. "Nim, the law is your field, not mine. But it seems to me that if Helen has been a subject from birth, then she committed no capital crime by entering Shambhala."

"We still need hard evidence of her father's identity, Shorty," Lord Nimrod pointed out. "We can't stop this execution without convincing proof that her father was a subject."

He was not prepared for news about the letter to Helen from her mother, or about the Lord Protector's suspicions that he was the Andros girl's father.

"The letter has been in the Lord Steward's hands for the last two days, Nim," Lord Justin said. "He has promised to review it later this morning. He's been a bit preoccupied lately."

"Damn!" Lord Nimrod jumped up, grabbing his shirt, trousers, and belt. "I don't have much time."

"It all depends on what's in that letter, Nim. From what I have heard about Miriam, I'll bet she would have wanted Helen to know the full truth."

"Great. At least we'll be ready, thanks to you, Shorty."

"Leave me out of this, Nim. I'll be at the South Gate at sundown. Perhaps I'll see you there."

Before he cut the link, Lord Justin added, "Please convey my sincerest apologies to the lady."

❋ ❋ ❋

Throwing on his clothes, Lord Nimrod did not notice a strange look on his companion's face. The Consort walked to her dresser, picked up the healthstone and the ledger sheet that Tamaz Gideon had given her, and held both out to him. "Look familiar?"

Lord Nimrod recognized the gem the Andros girl wore at her trial. Lady Naomi explained how she got it. "I already suspected that James is the girl's father," she added.

He tried not to show alarm. If she had figured it out, others might also suspect it. This was a disaster in the making for the Duke of Alta — and the duke's allies.

The Consort understood more of his reaction than he realized, although she addressed only part of it. "James acted very out of character during the trial, but that was not what clued me in. I had some time to get to know the girl, and I just put two and two together."

She offered him the ledger sheet, kept the stone. "Take that with you. It's more 'hard evidence.' It shows the date James had the stone set for her mother. I believe it was months after poor Sabrina died. You may find it helpful in getting an adultery charge dropped."

Lord Nimrod secured the sheet in his cloak. He gave the Consort a quick kiss before departing the same secret way he had entered.

* * *

The Consort lay back down, unable to sleep. She intended to pay the Lord Steward another visit shortly to hear firsthand about the contents of that letter. She wanted to make sure that Kefren's favorite had genuine support from those who at least appeared to be his friends.

# CHAPTER EIGHTEEN

Bleary-eyed from lack of sleep, a mug of strong *kaf* by his elbow, Shinar sat at his desk and willed himself to put aside his fears for his ailing son to study the letter. The cover bore the full name of the Andros girl; the wordskin appeared to be from Kamut. It was faded and jagged at the edges, suggesting it was older than just a few years. It did not appear to have been tampered with in any way.

He opened the document, ignoring a legal technicality in order to give Lord James one final option, if necessary. The letter took him longer to complete than anticipated. He was hopeful until the very end.

* * *

The Lord Steward summoned Lord James to his study. Joining them were Lord Nimrod, the Consort, and Judith, who stood beside the Consort and stared out the window. A winter sunrise streaked the sky with pink-and-gold light. Judith wrestled with her anguish. *This is probably Helen's last sunrise, and she's no doubt in some stinking hole and cannot even see it.*

Lord James paid little heed to anyone else. All he saw was Miriam's face, her green eyes harsh with accusation. All he heard were her pleas. *Do something, James. Save her. Don't let her die.*

Thinking he had everyone's attention, Shinar got to the point. "It seems you have a daughter, James."

While not a complete surprise, the news hit hard.

"James is mentioned specifically by name in the letter to the girl?" Lord Nimrod asked.

Shinar nodded. "James, I have not yet entered this letter into formal evidence, although the law requires that I should have done so before reading it. I wanted to give you a choice."

Lord James looked up, startled. "A choice? Do explain. Can we save her?"

Thinking about Lord Matthew, Shinar swallowed hard, the circles under his eyes seeming to darken. "Unfortunately, no. For that reason, and others, I see no point to making this letter public. Let it simply vanish. It puts you at great risk, yet does nothing to help the girl."

Neither Lord James nor Lord Nimrod said anything. "This is far more than just a personal issue," Shinar explained. "As a father, I can sympathize. But I must urge you to think of your position as Lord Protector. Do you want to bring that into disrepute? Think of the consequences for national security."

Lord James recoiled as though Shinar had struck him. The Lord Protector had always maintained high ideals for the unique position to which he was born, even if he was keenly aware of his personal failings.

He got to his feet and wandered about the study. *Father of Kronos, help me! I could not stop myself from loving her.*

"Take the Lord Steward's advice, James," Lord Nimrod urged him. "I beg of you. Burn that letter. That would be in your best interest. It certainly is in the best interest of your office and of this realm. Let it all die here and now."

Lord James' strong features were pinched by pain and indecision. "You've said nothing, Naomi."

"They have valid arguments, James," she replied. "If Seti or his Lord Chancellor were to discover what's in that letter, they would have your hide nailed to a wall. That is, what's left of it after the Supreme Lord imposes one frightful discipline. And while you are suffering, this realm is vulnerable.

"I've always known Kefren doesn't just love you, James," she added. "He trusts you implicitly with the defense of this realm. Your integrity has always been our best shield."

"Integrity?" Lord James blurted out. "What kind of integrity does a man have who beds a woman without marrying her? Who fathers a child unknowingly and then corners her into her doom? If only the knowledge in this letter somehow could make a difference."

The Consort stared at Lord Nimrod. His silence told her clearly where his father, Prince Enoch, stood on the issue.

Shinar, well versed in the Consort's various expressions, realized something critical was not yet on the table and that the Duke of Avalon knew about it. "You have something to add to this discussion?"

Prodded by the grim set of the Consort's mouth, Lord Nimrod reluctantly explained about the complete definition of a subject of Azgard. The Lord Steward worked the link on his desk, summoning the applicable legal code and perusing the text.

Lord Nimrod waited until Shinar looked up. "Do you agree with my interpretation, Jacob?"

"I do," The Lord Steward said. "The law is very specific on this point. Interesting that none of us thought about it before."

His heart sagged anew. "You can save her life, James, but I have to urge you to think twice before doing so. The girl's survival most likely will be an even greater disaster than her death."

"I absolutely agree, Jacob," Lord Nimrod said. "Don't go public with this, James. There's too much at stake."

Lord James was unable to respond.

Judith usually refrained from scanning his energy. The Duke of Alta was more sensitive than most Toltecs and could easily detect an invasion of his aura. As he remained silent, however, she grew angrier and more fearful that he would yield to what she considered craven counsel. *How could he do this to Miriam's memory?*

She sent her energy into his. The response nearly knocked her over. Although he appeared calm, Lord James was a tidal wave of emotions. They threatened to smash him against every reef of guilt and regret, capsize him over every lost opportunity, and roll him through all of his doubts before depositing him and his vulnerabilities onto the shore for all to see.

Her insight fueling her fear, Judith asked and received the Lord Steward's permission to speak. She dropped anchor in front of the Lord Protector. "Where's your heart, James? You will let Miriam's child die for a crime she never committed?"

He turned away from her.

"Now, Judith, it's a little more complicated than that," Shinar offered.

"No, Lord Steward. It's really quite simple."

Judith could not contain her anger and anguish. "You failed Miriam once, my lord. Knowing now you can save her daughter, will you fail her again?"

"Damn you, woman! Damn you all!"

Lord James faced them, his back to the wall, his fists trembling, his breathing ragged. He did not bother to hide his tears.

Lady Naomi shut her eyes against her own surge of feelings. She thought furiously for something to say without revealing precisely what was on her mind. She recalled Lord Justin's words a few hours earlier.

"Surely there has to be a way to save the girl and keep the trouble for James to a minimum. Perhaps we are mistakenly assuming these are our only alternatives."

"By Kronos, Naomi, there is a way," the Lord Steward said. He mentioned the underground practice among Toltec nobles of selling bastard children into bondage as a way to avoid embarrassment, Temple discipline, and possible disputes over succession to titles or inheritances.

"It's not an ideal solution, but it's the best of any option available," the Consort agreed.

While the others discussed it, Lord James and Judith remained silent, sickened at the prospect of selling Helen into little more than sexual slavery yet also wanting her to survive.

"You will represent me, Nim?" Lord James ventured.

"For all the good in hell it will do you."

Lord James turned to Shinar. "Do whatever you have to, Jacob, but stop that execution. I acknowledge Helen Andros as my child. I can't live with any other decision."

"You may not be able to live with this one either, James," Lord Nimrod warned him.

Lady Naomi vacillated between relief and deep misgivings. She caught hold of the Duke of Alta's wrist as he walked past her to leave the study. "You will want to give this back to her, James."

She slipped the green stone into his hand.

● ● ●

Lord Nimrod spent the next few hours throwing together a case with Shinar's help and then arguing via link with the Lord Chancellor. After looking in on Lady Siroma and Lord Matthew, Lady Naomi contacted Master Ames to order a few more dresses for the girl. Helen would need clothes once she was out of custody.

Although the Consort did not say so, she intended to win any bidding for the girl. She had many uses for a trained healer, and should Helen be able to restore Kefren to health and full awareness, the Consort would give her to him. She remembered how stunning Helen looked in the blue velvet gown. *The girl may well end up in the silks and satins of an Exalted Lord's concubine.*

● ● ●

Lord James and Judith waited in the gallery for word on Helen's fate. He paced back and forth, feeling useless and apprehensive. It was plausible that the Lord Chancellor would simply have the girl killed privately since he now could not legally execute her in public. It was also possible his kinsman would not act that recklessly. Most likely the man would delay releasing Helen as long as he could. His cousin's petty cruelties were beyond comprehension to Lord James.

Most of Judith's anger with Lord James dissolved as soon as she heard him acknowledge Helen as his own daughter. That was a far greater act of courage than anything he had ever displayed on the battlefield, and his fearlessness was legendary even in his own lifetime.

She was still irate at the others. However well meaning, they were simply substituting one travesty for another, bondage for death. A girl of Helen's proud, independent spirit would not survive six months as a concubine.

Much about Helen's character, mannerisms, and behavior that were so curiously familiar before fell into place now for Judith. How ironic. A healer born of a house of warriors. Was Miriam aiming for that? Judith already knew the girl's existence was no accident; Miriam must have planned the pregnancy.

At least Judith wanted to believe that. She did not want to accept that Lord James had insisted on getting Miriam with child and then just walked away from her. If that was what happened, Judith did not think she could ever forgive him entirely.

Judith wanted a thorough review of the letter to Helen. She hoped it would provide some insight into what her friend was thinking when she permitted the child to be conceived. Judith's instincts told her that some very deep imperative was driving Miriam to behave as she did.

Lord James eventually realized his companion was not speaking. He could see the distress on Judith's face. "Do you want to hear my side of the story?"

"I've been waiting to hear someone's side for years now, James," she replied. "But first, I want to hear whether you plan to sell Helen. Do you?"

"Do you not know me, Judith?" he replied, his tone warning her to back off.

They stood next to each other in front of a huge window that over-looked the lake. He explained everything. When and how the affair started, Miriam's consistent refusal to wed him. She reminded him of the month Helen was born and he flinched.

"Kronos, she probably knew she was pregnant before I went east to direct the first Nubian campaign," he whispered. "She said nothing to me either, Judith. Nothing. I would never have left her without insist-ing we marry if I had known. Never."

He sat, head in his hands. Judith checked his energy, instantly reconfirming that his anguish, remorse, and deep regret were not feigned. The rest of her anger at Lord James faded, yet part of her still mistrusted him, recalling how he wavered.

Judith sat next to him and squeezed his hand. Then she closed her eyes, her own tears flowing.

"She was the love of my life, Judith. And I'm furious with her right now. Not for the child, but for never telling me anything about her."

"She was my dearest friend, James. And I'm angry, too."

* * *

They sat together for some time. He became aware of the stone in his hand. He would hardly know what to say to the girl, once she was in his household.

"What is she like, Judith? My own daughter is a total stranger to me."

Judith dabbed at her tears and smiled. "You saw her during the *Kazil*, James. She's you in a maid's body. What do you think she'll be like?"

"Father of Kronos! Help me!"

# CHAPTER NINETEEN

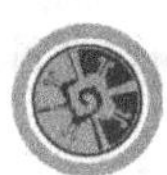

Helen saw nothing of her journey from The Citadel to the South Gates of Shambhala. Hooded once more, wrists and ankles shackled together, wearing the same garment now soiled and smelly, she was alone in the compartment except for the priest who presumably was on guard.

She endured in silent fury the disgusting touch of his fingers as he furtively explored her body, fondling her breasts, stroking her buttocks and thighs, reaching as far as he dared between her legs. Lightheaded from lack of food and sleep, she nonetheless almost laughed aloud when she heard his breathing deepen and become more rapid. *An upstanding man of faith, no doubt.*

As soon as the vehicle reached the South Gates and passed beyond the massive wall of the Sacred City, it stopped and descended to rest on the Ioh River. It was at the western edge of an enormous open-air market square that did not have any of the usual vendor stalls and booths this late afternoon. Only a hastily assembled platform stood several blocks away.

The door to the back compartment opened, slapping Helen with a rush of stinging air. Several priests hauled her outside, removed the hood, and pushed her into the back of a horse-drawn wagon. The vehicle lumbered through a narrow lane in the crowd, which was kept in line by *Valakim* spaced every few feet along either side of the route.

Shivering in the pitiless cold, Helen could identify no familiar faces among the throng. Although her garment covered her completely, she felt naked, raked without mercy by the gaze of all those present. She tried her best not to seem like she was shaking from fear.

The crowd was subdued. Most of those attending had been ordered to witness the execution, and could at least partially identify with the condemned. They were the Turanian or foreign-born servants of the noble houses. This was to be a lesson in the consequences of not obtaining proper authorization before entering the Sacred City.

Others were there by unhappy choice, including Lord Justin and Tuk. They stood together near the elevated spot where Helen was to die by firing squad. Underneath the wooden planks was a crate to hold the body of the condemned.

The cart halted at the stairs leading to the platform. Pulled from the wagon, Helen winced when her captors dumped her on the stone pavement. The ice burned the chafed soles of her feet. They pointed to the top of the platform. She worked her way up the steps one at a time, hampered as much by the hopelessness that undermined her spirit as by her fragile physical condition and the shackles that threw her off balance. Her feet left faint blood prints on the wood.

"Drown the bitch!" someone yelled. "Don't waste good bullets on her."

Resigned to the inevitable, Helen did not bother to respond. Instead, she begged in silence once more for just enough strength for the final minutes. Soon it would be over. Soon nothing would matter anymore for her. What a blessed relief. Death could not find her quickly enough.

At the top of the steps, more priests dragged her to a post at the far end of the platform and secured her to it. Six King's Guards, their weapons on their shoulders, climbed to the platform and stood at attention in a line toward the western end. They would turn to face her and fire only upon specific orders.

Acting on behalf of the Supreme Lord, the Holy Deputy stepped to the edge of the platform where the crowd was thickest. Silenas read the charges aloud and the writ of condemnation. He approached Helen, inspected the chains binding her to the post, and offered a blindfold that she refused.

"Do you have any final words?"

Helen summoned her last reserves. "Get on with it."

At their squad leader's order, the guards turned toward the prisoner, removed their weapons from their shoulders, and stood ready. Helen found it easy to look death in the eyes. Dying was effortless. It was living that had always been a struggle. Why had she, orphaned and despised, ever bothered to try so hard? What had been the point of battling every inch of the way for a medical degree? To this miserable end?

The strange red glow filled her inner vision. *Giving up! That's more like it. We will meet soon on the other side, and you will suffer for depriving me all these years of what is rightfully mine.*

Helen shook her head, unable to make any sense of what the red voice was saying to her. She stopped paying attention and looked beyond the soldiers at the sun, now almost below the horizon. It would not be long now.

The orders to aim and fire never came. The sun set; the torch-sticks upon the city wall flickered on automatically, as did ones lining the square. The cold turned ever more bitter. Starving, in the latter stages of freezing to death, Helen had no clear recollection of what happened next. The crowd seemed to grow much louder and restless. A military rotor landed not far from the platform.

Blinking hard, she watched two Toltec nobles disembark from the aircraft and rush up the steps. One of them argued with the priest who had proclaimed her death sentence. The taller of the two, wearing what she dimly registered as the uniform of the Generals Council, demanded the keys to her shackles.

Securing them, he walked behind the post. A curious mixture of anticipation and confusion filled Helen. Although she did not know him, a tenuous sense of hope stirred deep within her simply because he was there with her.

She turned her head from side to side, trying to watch him as he worked to free her. "Who are you, my lord? Why are you here?"

"You sent me a lecture not long ago about your duty as a healer, Lieutenant," he replied, on one knee behind her to unlock the manacles around her ankles. "I am your father."

His voice was rich and resonant. Not at all like the snarling red glow voice. By this time Helen was so confused she was not sure of anything.

He stood up and moved from behind the post to face her. Helen just gaped at him. Without the chains to hold her upright, her knees failed. She sank toward the platform, unable to comprehend his meaning, feeling the effects from her days of misery under the shadow of death.

Lord James caught her as she fell unconscious toward the planks. She did not see the tears in his eyes as he held her close, did not feel him kiss her brow, and was unaware that he removed his cloak and wrapped it around her before lifting her in his arms and carrying her to safety.

* * *

Tossing and turning, muttering and weeping, Helen lay on a canopied bed in Lord James' manor on Lake Shambhala. Sudras assessed her condition. She was dehydrated, even thinner than usual, and the wounds on her feet might need to be sealed. The circles under her eyes were most likely from lack of sleep although he could not rule out a head injury until she woke up and spoke with him. From the half-healed marks of blows to both sides of her face, it was clear she had been slapped hard if not punched several times over the past ten days.

A Turanian woman knocked on the open door to the bedchamber. Sudras waved at her to enter. She carried a tray of food; clothing hung over her arm. She placed the tray on a padded stool along the foot of the bed and curtseyed to him.

"I am Jean Farsil, the Lord Protector's chief housekeeper," she said. "May I assist you, Grand Master?"

He looked out the window while Jean removed the filthy garment Helen wore and dressed her in a nightgown. Sudras then lifted Helen to allow Jean to turn down the bedcovers and draw them over Helen's feet and lower legs.

The movement awoke Helen, who sat up and took in her unfamiliar surroundings. The bedchamber walls were paneled with warm wood inlays. Thick rugs covered the hardwood floor; a fire blazed in a polished stone hearth to one side of the bed.

Running her hands through her tangled hair, Helen noticed Sudras. "I can't be dead, so where on earth am I, Isaac?"

"In your father's keeping, Helen."

"My father? Impossible, Isaac. My father is dead."

"No so, my dear," Sudras said, explaining a little about her new circumstances. He then introduced Jean. Helen's eyes widened. A

Turanian woman holding such an important post in the household of a high-ranking Toltec noble was unheard of.

Nodding to the woman, Helen swung her legs over the edge of the bed. "Keeping? I don't need to be kept by anyone, thank you very much. Time for me to get up."

She tried to put her weight on her feet and felt sharp pain. She would have fallen had Sudras not caught her by the arms. "Damn you, girl!"

He almost shoved her back onto the mattress. "This is not the time or place for your pig-headedness. I am going to examine you, at your father's request."

Temporarily chastened, Helen leaned against the pillows. "No need for that, Isaac. I'm just fine. What's happened to Lord Matthew? And Colonel Orlando?"

The guarded look on his face alarmed her. She attempted once more to talk her way out of this examination. "Aren't you violating your oath as a priest by attending me, Isaac?"

"I am. But it's the least I can do for you, all things considered."

"You needn't bother on my account."

Unable to deter him, Helen sat unhappily, arms folded, refusing to cooperate. He listened to her heart and lungs, took her vital signs, and looked into her eyes.

After he finished and set his instruments on the nightstand by the bed, Sudras pointed to the mug of broth on the tray. "If you don't start eating and drinking, Helen, I'm going to hook you to a drip solution."

Throwing him a frosty look, she took the mug from the housekeeper and sipped from it. He cleaned the soles of her feet. The skin was cracked and had been bleeding in many places; the wounds fortunately were not deep. He applied an antiseptic and wrapped both in bandages.

"Would it do any good to suggest that you stay off your feet for the next couple of days?" Sudras asked.

She glanced toward the fire and did not reply.

"Of course not."

He placed his medical equipment back into his bag. Out of her sight, he filled a syringe with a small dose of a potent sedative.

"Isaac, you never answered my question. Why won't you tell me about Lord Matthew or Colonel Orlando?"

"We'll discuss that tomorrow, when you are more rested."

The voice from the platform. The uniformed man, just inside the door, walked closer to the bed. Shamed by her unkempt appearance and lack of proper clothing, Helen burrowed into the pillows and drew the blankets up to her neck. *I must look disgusting. I know I smell disgusting.*

Wary and confused, she stared at him. His face was determinedly masculine, with a square jaw, angular copper cheekbones, and black eyes that seemed gentle, although she suspected they could be stern and unyielding. She could not believe what he told her on the platform, even though the Grand Master confirmed it. The Lord Protector her father? Impossible. Her father was just a soldier who died in the First Nubian War.

Lord James backed off by going to the hearth and leaning against the mantel. He showed her the green stone and placed it on the mantel with the folded document he had carried in his other hand.

"These are for you, Helen, when you wake up. This is a letter to you from your mother. It will explain many things for you. I want you to sleep now."

Lord James looked at Sudras, who approached Helen, holding the syringe.

"No, Isaac, please," Helen protested. "That atrocious substance leaves my head spinning. I promise I'll get to sleep again."

"This will help you sleep much deeper," Sudras said. "You need the rest."

She shrank away from him, squirming.

"Keep still, and hold your arm out. That's an order, Lieutenant."

Helen froze. Anger flashed across her face. "Shall I stand at attention and salute, too, Lord Protector?"

Lord James ignored her remark and signaled to Sudras to proceed. The Grand Master rolled up a sleeve of Helen's nightgown and avoided her pleading eyes as he administered the contents of the syringe.

"Isaac, you know I consider this stuff—"

She slumped against the pillows, deeply asleep.

* * *

Sudras completed his report on Helen's condition in the billiards room, where Lord James and Lord Nimrod were monitoring the consequences of the Lord Protector's public admission of his relationship to the girl. Reaction was swifter and more virulent than even Lord Nimrod had warned. The Temple had already sent an ominous notice of its plans for a full investigation into Lord James' illicit relationship. Several of the Great Houses, led by the Duke of Eden, were angrily insisting that Lord James offer a public explanation before the *Kinshazen* at the earliest opportunity.

The Lord Chancellor was making new demands as well. Lord Nimrod took aim for a corner pocket. "Griffin insists on re-arresting the girl immediately on a morals charge, based on some presumed relationship with Matthew."

"He'll have to come through me to get her," Lord James replied, setting a large decanter full of pepper brandy on a side table and filling three glasses.

Sudras ventured a suggestion after a first taste of the liquor heated his throat. "My lords, I know a way to stop the Lord Chancellor in his tracks, at least as far as Helen is concerned."

Sudras advised the Lord Protector to have the girl undergo a physical examination to determine any signs of sexual activity. He offered to act on the Lord Protector's behalf; the Lord Chancellor would choose another priest-healer to participate and provide a separate report on the findings.

Lord Nimrod set his glass down. "It's risky, James."

"With all due respect, Lord Avalon, I've known Helen since she was eleven and first admitted to the Academy," Sudras answered. "I would never advise this course of action if I were not sure of the outcome. She is chaste."

Lord James recalled the girl's response when he entered the bedchamber. Her modesty pleased him greatly, and gave credence to the Grand Master's view of her character and behavior. He asked Sudras to arrange such an examination as soon as possible.

"Nim, please let Griffin know of our plans," Lord James said. "That should shut him up for a while."

Sudras faced Lord James. "My lord, your daughter has always had a sharp tongue and an unblinking eye for the truth. If you think you have a public fight on your hands, you also have a private one right here in your own home. I know from sobering experience that her respect is rarely and not easily won. I dare not vouch for her heart."

❋ ❋ ❋

The pepper brandy was low. Sudras had left several hours earlier, promising to send word of the time for the examination, and to check on Helen later that morning. Lord James and Lord Nimrod had their feet propped on the railing of the billiard table.

The Duke of Avalon could not focus his eyes. "What's it like to be in love, James? Never yet had the pleasure, myself."

The Duke of Alta stared right past him. "I'm not sure I would call it a pleasure, Nim. In the three years I knew Miriam, I always had the distinct impression she was at least ten steps ahead of me."

Lord James downed another shot of pepper brandy. "Kronos, she read me like a damned Gridbook. She knew me better than I knew myself. And all the while she was such a mystery to me — an utterly irresistible mystery. No woman should have the right to be that beautiful. A man could get completely lost in those huge green eyes. I did."

He wobbled to his feet. "I have no idea what being in love will be like for you, Nim. Happier, I hope. All I know is I fell in love and felt like a complete fool, and have proved it no doubt all over again."

Long after Lord James bid him good night, Lord Nimrod sat in the darkened room, polishing off the pepper brandy, pondering his friend's words.

# CHAPTER TWENTY

Thinking she heard someone calling her name, Helen awoke abruptly. Throwing off the covers, she made the mistake of trying to sit up quickly. Sharp pains shot through her skull.

*Damn you, Isaac. I hate this stuff. And damn the man who claims to be my father.*

Momentarily defeated, Helen lay back down, panting, rubbing her eyes and temples, her mind like cotton wool. She recalled the green stone and her mother's letter, waiting for her on the mantel. That motivated her to try to sit up again. She took it much slower and succeeded.

Feeling around the night table, she found a light-stick and flicked it on. Helen compelled herself to get out of bed just as slowly as she sat up. On tender feet she shuffled over to the fireplace, snatched the gem off the mantel, and pressed it to her heart, rocked by a wave of loss and pain. It was the only thing her mother had given her before they parted, and she never expected to see it again. She slipped the chain around her neck. Ah. Such a deep sense of comfort and support. What a relief.

Helen thought about her mother's letter and her heart quailed. Did she have the courage to read it? Maybe. Maybe not. But she could wait no longer. She had to know. Spotting an iron poker, she ignored her throbbing head and nausea to stir the embers. Despite sore muscles and feet, she managed to put more wood onto the embers in the fireplace. Soon it was burning brightly again.

Helen retrieved the letter and returned to the bed to read it. It was a copy; she was uneasy wondering what had happened to the original. She recognized her mother's handwriting, which was a unique mixture of ornate and flowing.

*Dearest Helen:*

*It is my deepest hope and prayer that you are reading this because it is your thirty-fifth birthday, the age of your majority, and your Aunt Martha has given this letter to you at my request. I write it now because I will not be with you, except in spirit, at that time, and you deserve answers at long last to the questions I know will have dogged, if not haunted you all your life.*

*I met your father nearly four years before you were born. I was hired to attend his wife, who was in a coma after a terrible fall from a horse. You have heard me mention this a few times. We grew to know each other because he would visit his wife most evenings, provided his many duties did not demand that he be elsewhere. We would talk. I could tell he thought me rather odd for including a comatose woman in our conversations, but I was and remain convinced she knew we were there with her, and our presence was important to her.*

*Somewhere, someplace, somehow, amid the philosophy, politics, military strategy, history and the dozens of other serious and comical topics we discussed over many months, I fell deeply and forever in love with him. Even worse, I could tell he had similar feelings for me. I write 'even worse' as though love between two people is some sort of sin. Well, love between* two such as your father and I has always been a sin to his proud people, the Toltecs, and dangerous for a woman such as I, a Turanian of no rank or importance.

I wrestled for many months with my feelings, determined not to betray them to him or anyone else by word, look, or deed. My common sense warned me it was the most foolish thing I could possibly get myself into. And at the time, he was not free to make any sort of respectable offer to me.

When I first realized he was interested in me, I was alarmed and on my guard. I kept expecting him to proposition me. Until I got to know him better, I wondered if he might not simply force himself on me. That would hardly have been a first in the history of our two peoples, and who would have stopped him or even cared? I was at his mercy, and we both knew it. He never said or did one thing that could not be regarded as completely proper. I did my best to match his blameless conduct.

His wife died after almost two years. My reason for remaining in the household no longer existed, and I left, never expecting to see him again. Despite all the very lean and hard times you and I have endured together, my dearest child, I was never lonelier than during the months between the poor woman's death, and the day he appeared on my doorstep.

He gave me the healthstone I will soon pass on to you, my precious child. Keep it safely tucked away, just as your father asked of me when he gave it to me. Your father also asked me to marry him. Had I not wanted children, I might have agreed to do so. But he needed an heir, and any half-Toltec half-Turanian son of ours would face enormous obstacles in claiming his rightful legacy.

I refused his offer of marriage, but not his offer of love. Creator help me, dearest Helen, I could not stop myself from loving him, even if it was indeed the most foolish thing I could have gotten myself into. If I had to do it over *again, I would make the same foolish choice. I will never repent of the sin of honoring my heart, if sin it was.*

*The months we spent together were the happiest of my life. We met in great secrecy, for obvious reasons. The only real argument we ever had was the issue of marriage. Your father has a confounded sense of honor and decency. He kept asking to do what he considered the right thing by me, which was to marry and live openly with me.*

*I kept refusing because I knew that such a course of action would materially weaken his position among his people. And my people needed and continue to need him as strong as possible. He has proved just and fair toward them, even though too many Toltecs, especially among the powerful, revile Turanians. Your father is not like most of his people, Helen.*

*Reluctantly, over many months, I finally admitted to myself that our relationship would have to end before it became a disaster for both of us. He had the most to lose, and my desire was to protect him at all costs. Selfishly, I also wanted something of him in my life after we parted. The only thing I could think to do was to conceive a child by him, and that is how you came to be.*

*Be careful what you ask for, Helen. With you I did indeed get something of your father, more than something. I got a virtual duplicate of him in a female's body. As you grew from an infant to a child and toward your teen years, I never stopped being amazed at how like your father you are, although you have not ever met him or even heard his name spoken. You and he are one of a kind: in the words you use, your hand gestures, your complete inability to suffer fools lightly, your extremely annoying, pig-headed stubbornness, your fierce warrior's courage, your sense of honor and justice. It took all the strength and effort I had to make even the smallest impression on you. I regret deeply that you did not have him in your life as a little girl, when you very much needed his strength and integrity to guide you.*

*Although your parents never married, Helen, you are not some after-thought or accident. I wanted and love you very much. I am aware you have felt that you have been a burden on me, and that I would have been much better off without you. That is utter nonsense. You have been the only light in my life, once your father and I parted.*

*And I want that light to go on and shine for others, which is why I am sending you away from this city, to escape the carnage about to overwhelm us. I know you will not understand why I cannot come with you back to Azgard, and that has to do with the final reason that divided your father and me.*

*Right after I knew for certain I was pregnant, your father left Azgard to take part in the First Nubian War. I returned for a time to the family farm, and my condition soon became known because I was violently sick every morning. When my Uncle Ethan learned I was carrying a mixed-race child and yet not wed to the father, he literally threw me out of the Andros household and forbade me ever to return.*

*He did this over the objections of my Cousin John, and my grandmother, Gilreth. They and my dearest friend, Judith, whom you have met, helped me make my way to Shambhala, where a new position awaited me in another household.*

*I was running an errand one late afternoon on the Lesser Shore. Suddenly, there was a huge red flash. Multiple retail and commercial buildings simply collapsed, killing and maiming scores of people trapped inside under the rubble, and on the streets when falling wreckage hit them. I stopped to render what aid I could to those who were wounded, and was arrested and charged with being part of some sort of Turanian conspiracy to bring down the government.*

*It was not true. My whole life and being have been dedicated to healing, not hurting people, and I see signs that you also will walk the healer's path, which gladdens my heart, dearest child. Once again, I got what I asked for in spirit. And that was the means by which to force me to leave my beloved for good.*

*I was given a choice. I could choose exile, or wait in prison, possibly for months, for a trial. By that time my condition would have been obvious. I had no desire to be forced under oath to reveal the name of my baby's father, so I took exile. I was sent East in a troop transport ship to Kamut, and dumped on the street, almost penniless and certainly very much alone, except for the little girl growing in my womb. It was not a time I recall with any pleasure, I can assure you.*

*And on the street you might have been born, my child, had it not been for the kindness of certain ladies of the evening, who took me in, starving and nearing delivery, and cared for me until well after you arrived. You had many doting mothers when you were a newborn and very young child.*

*They urged me to take up, shall we say, their line of work. Instead, I offered to provide an additional service, massage and physical therapy, to their clients, who included several advisors to Hekemtep, Faro of Kamut, along with many courtiers and a lot of the more prominent businessmen. One of the courtiers who had benefited from my services happened to mention me to Princess Notufil, who suffered from severe headaches and neck aches due to an injury she received at birth. She tried me out and was so delighted with the results that she hired me full time. That is when you and I went to live at court and times got a little easier for us.*

*Now Azgard has demanded the young prince as a hostage in return for its help in rescuing Kamut, and his parents have no option except to agree or watch their people perish. I volunteered to have you care for the little boy during the journey because not many in Memfys will survive in the coming days, and as I said before, your light must go on, Helen. And yet I cannot return to Azgard with you. If I do and am discovered, I will be put to death with no appeal. I do not send you away from me, Helen, because I do not want you. I send you to the only future I can now provide for you. I pray you will in time forgive me for that as well.*

*Although you are very young to be left in the world with no parents, your light must not die out, Helen, because you have special abilities. When I say 'abilities,' recall the games we would play when you were a very young child. You would think of something but not tell me, yet I could relate what it was. Or I would picture something in my mind and say nothing about it, yet you could describe it to me very accurately. Do not make the mistake of thinking you can do this only with me. You can do it with anyone.*

*Such abilities are the true gifts of the spirit, my daughter. They are inherent in every soul that walks in physical form on this earth, having been given freely to all of us by a loving Creator. These abilities were once unusually strong among the Toltecs, who used them to develop a high technology. They also apparently misused these gifts for conquest and domination. Over time, these gifts have atrophied in the Toltecs, while the Turanians, as a conquered people, have relinquished the power they need to implement them fully.*

*As I grew to know and love your father, I wondered more and more about what might happen to these latent abilities in a mixed-race child. That was as much a motivation for my conceiving you as anything else. Once you were born and began to grow up, and we played our games, I wondered no more. It was clear that for some reason, mixing the two races rekindled the strength of these gifts and abilities. At least such was the case with you.*

*If our two peoples are ever to live in true harmony and peace with each other, we need to reclaim these abilities, these gifts of the spirit, and stop trying to live solely out of half of who we truly are. Your light, Helen, is to show both peoples the enormous healing possibilities and potentials of the path of love instead of judgment and hatred. You do this simply by being who you are — a bridge of hope, dearest child.*

*You do not yet have any idea of who and whose you truly are. I urge you to consult Judith and learn from her. She will know what to do and how to help you find your way. Others I know you can trust include your Aunt Martha and Uncle Ariel, and your Cousin John. Curiously enough, on that short list you may include the Consort, whom I met and observed several times when she visited her comatose sister-in-law. My heart tells me the two of you will also meet at some point, although under what circumstances I can scarcely imagine.*

*My time for letter writing draws to an end. Having learned the name of at least one of that unfortunate lady's relations, you could find out for yourself the name of your father, so I will tell you now. But before I do, I must warn you in the strongest possible language never to seek him out. Do not approach him ever, I beg of you. Mixed-race bastard children of noble houses tend to meet with extremely unkind fates. If they are underage and male, they are simply killed. The females usually are sold as concubines. He will want to protect you, but if your relationship is revealed he may not have the ability to do so.*

*That is why I waited to tell you this until you came of age and would have at least the thinnest of legal protections against any such action. But it is still very thin. And in high places are many others who will despise and fear you, not because they know you, but simply because of who you are. These are the ones who have chosen the path of judgment and hatred, who have abused and then denied the gifts of the spirit.*

*Do not give them any cause to pursue you, child, by insisting on pro-claiming the truth of your parentage. Your true identity is far more than the sum total of your parents' flesh or names. Show this letter to Judith, commit whatever portion of it you want to memory, and then burn it, and say no more to anyone. You have no idea and do not want to know the trouble this knowledge will cause should it ever be made public.*

*Instead, be wary and completely discreet, but be also proud. You are the daughter and firstborn of the Lord Protector, Lord James Mordecai, lord of a Great House among the noblest of all in Azgard. In my heart I married your father long before I ever took him to my bed. And while he lives and I also still draw breath, I can have eyes for no other man.*

*Go now and live, in joy and peace, quietly sharing your hope and light with those who have the eyes to see it, my dearest child. You have my love and blessings evermore.*

*Your loving and proud mother —*

*Miriam Elinor Andros*

● ● ●

Helen was numb. She could not see through the tears that streamed down her face. She collapsed onto the pillows and sobbed, her heart, soul, and entire body racked by shame, pain, guilt, and a fear that she could scarcely dare acknowledge.

*You always told me he was a soldier. Mama, you had a true gift for understatement.*

● ● ●

Judith stared out the windows of the Supreme Lord's study. The light waned over Lake Shambhala. She gazed toward the Lord Protector's estate, where she hoped and prayed Helen was now safe, at least temporarily.

Almost as soon as Miriam's letter was entered into evidence, the Supreme Lord issued a writ of inquiry with her name on it. Judith had no choice except to answer the formal summons immediately, or be imprisoned for contempt. She had a brief chance to peruse a copy of Miriam's letter, so she knew her name was in it. She very much wanted more time to reread it slowly and think about it.

Malachi entered the room and stood behind Judith. She felt the hard, angry, disappointed edge in his energy. That alone told her Helen was not to die, at least not that night. Her relief did not last long. He slid his arms around her, one hand on her breast, the other stroking her hips and thighs. Her muscles tensed involuntarily, betraying her revulsion and rejection. He started to breathe harder, kissing her neck and running his tongue over her ear.

"After all these years, you are still beautiful, Judith," he murmured. "Take the Blood-Oath, come to me willingly. Together we will rule this island."

She closed her eyes and willed herself to relax, shielding her thoughts from him with a veil of energy. *I'd sooner kiss a snake.*

"You wanted to question me, Holy One," she said. "What may I tell you?"

His hands dropped to his sides. He walked to his desk and retrieved the official copy of Miriam's letter from the Grid. Then he opened a drawer and pulled out a sheaf of wordskin with more writing on it. He motioned her to the chair. "Sit, and compare the handwriting of these two documents."

Judith complied. She knew Miriam's handwriting on the link screen, and scanned the physical letter on the desk. It was not long:

*My dearest friend:*

*War now is inevitable. Come to me at once and take the child back with you before this city is besieged and falls. This child very much needs your help and guidance to reclaim the full power of the spirit's abilities and gifts.*

*Once you come to know the child, you will know how best to proceed. I suggest you go to the hill people of Alta for help. You must promise to do this for me without fail. Far more is at stake here than just me or even this one child, but the future of our two peoples. Again, once you know the child, you will perceive the extent of the child's real power and understand more of my meaning.*

*Yours in haste —*
*Your dearest friend*

Judith was stunned. The short letter was also Miriam's handwriting. "What does this have to do with me, Holy One?"

"Don't play games with me, woman, or by Kronos and the Covenant, I'll have you stripped and whip you myself."

He moved behind her once more. "This letter was addressed to you." He jabbed the physical document.

"I've never seen either letter before this day, Holy One," Judith protested, her heart pounding. The anger and fear in his energy beat on her every bit as hard as physical blows.

He grabbed her under each arm and hauled her roughly out of the chair, turned her toward him, and squeezed her face between both hands, forcing her to look up into his eyes, which were so narrowed with rage they appeared as black slits. Judith could not raise even a finger to resist him; to do so would be considered sacrilege and punishable by death.

"Are these two letters written by the same woman?"

Judith steeled herself. "I believe so, Holy One."

"And is the child mentioned in both letters the same child?"

"I cannot know that for certain," she hedged.

His grip on her jaw tightened. "Horse shit. Did that Andros woman have any other half-blood spawn? Any sons, perhaps?"

"Not that I am aware of, Holy One."

He released her. "What exactly have you been teaching this *nahazi* bitch all these years?"

His voice was all the more menacing precisely because it was so soft and low. "Any other pupils? The Prince of Westar's half-blood second son, perhaps?"

"No, Holy One," she replied. "I have taught neither of them anything. Their training is strictly orthodox, from the Academy."

He made a derisive sound. "How orthodox can those scientists be if they permit half-bloods to train? But they will soon feel my wrath. I shall bring them back into line with the One True Faith."

His agitation assuaged for the moment, Malachi again attempted to woo the woman he fell in love with decades earlier, when they both were attending the Academy as seminary students. As always, Judith evaded his clumsy advances, never rejecting him outright, never intending to yield. She might also have taken the Blood-Oath, except her instincts long ago warned her that his boundless ambition would one day put him in a position of ultimate authority, and she had no desire to answer to Malachi for the condition of her soul, or her body.

The Supreme Lord insisted that Judith spend the night in meditation and prayer, to reflect on his stern warning against interfering on behalf of any mixed-race person. Judith instead mourned over the letter that the Temple somehow purloined all those years ago.

Her one issue with her friend had always been that Miriam would never ask for help, even when she needed it most. Never one to trust others completely, Miriam kept all of her pain and problems inside, and Judith always had to pry out of her whatever she could sense was troubling her friend.

Finally, Miriam did ask for her help, at a time when she must have been desperate with fear for the survival of her precious child. What could Miriam have thought when she never got an answer because the letter never arrived? That Judith didn't care? That likelihood pained Judith almost too much to bear: that she, even inadvertently and unknowingly, had let her friend down. She was always telling Miriam that she could trust her at the very least, and yet when Miriam finally reached out to her, all she got was nothing.

On her knees in a row of priestesses before an altar, Judith stifled her sobs with the back of her hand. In her heart she called out to Miriam, hoping to meet with her in spirit, since Miriam was surely dead. Judith longed more than anything in the world to be able to explain her lack of action to her beloved friend.

Ultimately Judith had to focus on other thoughts to maintain any semblance of equanimity, yet nothing brought her any comfort. When she attempted to recall the contents of the longer letter more fully, Judith suddenly understood the source of Malachi's fear. Miriam had mentioned the gifts of the spirit, and that Helen had greatly enhanced abilities. Obviously, Miriam was alluding to energy discernment, and possibly even higher abilities of true *kura* manipulation and energy healing.

That reference to energy, however guarded, would send the Temple into a panic. The priests regarded the steps of the *kura* as theirs alone to dispense, and would certainly be repulsed as well as terrified by anyone of Turanian extraction who displayed such abilities or gifts. And where did the stone come into play in all of this? Why had Miriam in the letter suggested that Helen keep it safely out of sight? Possible answers to these questions made Judith nervous.

Far from being safe now, Helen was in much worse peril. No doubt Lord Justin shared that danger. He thought his father was his greatest threat. Their differences seemed tame by comparison to the covert and deadly hostility of the Temple. Judith's blood ran as cold as the stone floor that tormented her shins.

●  ●  ●

The skimmer headed away from the gloomy island, racing over the ice. Judith threw back the hood of her sheepskin cloak, letting the wind blow through her hair. She reconsidered all that she had learned, bitter tears sliding down her cheeks. She dissolved into sobs, her hands hiding her face.

*I swear Miriam: I would have found a way into Kamut to take the child, if only I had known.*

# CHAPTER TWENTY-ONE

Still clutching the copy of her mother's letter, Helen looked up from the pillow. Sunrise was soon. It was a dawn she was not meant to have seen. The first streaks of light in the sky evoked an almost overwhelming series of emotions in her. Profound gratitude to be alive still, in one piece, still healthy.

Also, deep apprehension and confusion. Everything she had believed about herself — her mother, her missing father, how she came to be, and even the purpose of her life — seemed true no longer. Helen had always been certain that her life's work was to be a healer, and she clung fiercely to that conviction to complete her training in the face of mostly unrelenting hostility. Now she was no longer sure of her purpose in the world. It all seemed to be shattered, and she had no inkling about what was to replace it.

Wrung out with trying to sort everything through, she spotted the door to a walk-in closet and decided to investigate. Hanging inside were several unfamiliar dresses that looked like they might fit her. There also was her mother's gray cloak, lost in her struggle with the soldiers who first kidnapped her, along with the clothes she had brought with her when she treated Prince Harnak, and her uniform. All were cleaned and neatly pressed. On the closet floor were her military boots and a pair of suede shoes. She rummaged through a stack of drawers inside the closet and found undergarments, slips, and stockings.

Disgusted at her tangled hair and filthy body, Helen headed for the shower. She stood under the luxuriantly warm water for a long time, hoping it would cleanse away her degradation along with the grime. She dried her hair under the heat lamp and dressed as rapidly as her tender feet would allow.

Her mother's cape over her arm and her boots in hand, Helen tested the door to her bedchamber. It was not locked. She made her way down the servants' stairs and along several long halls before locating the kitchen. Only one cook was on duty. Helen did not realize someone was following her.

She guessed correctly that the huge pantry on the far side of the kitchen would have outside access. Once out of sight of anyone in the kitchen, she stopped to put on her boots, wincing a little over the painful protests of her sore feet. Wrapping her cloak around her shoulders, she made her way outdoors, down through meandering garden paths to the icy shore, where she found a wooden bench. Her tracker was still behind her, keeping a discreet distance.

More tears on her cheeks, Helen sat and watched the sun ignite a golden fire on the snowcapped tips of the Mountains of Mourning, filling the sky first with purple and red hues that then faded into blue. Wiping her eyes with the handkerchief, she bowed her head, pressed her hands together against her chest, and offered one prayer of heartfelt gratitude, and another for guidance.

Now what? She and her father were total strangers. What could they possibly say to each other? She dreaded facing him or anyone else; she was mortified to learn she had been born in a brothel. She was also dismayed and burdened with guilt over her mother almost having been forced into prostitution for them to survive. Almost? Perhaps she really had taken up that line of work, as she put it, and simply was trying to spare her daughter's feelings.

Helen considered what she knew about her mother. With the one glaring exception of telling her that her father was dead, her mother generally had been honest, the very few times she had volunteered any details. Helen wanted to think her mother was being truthful on this subject as well. She suspected no one else would believe what her mother wrote, especially not the man her mother named as her father. And no doubt certain people would be only too eager to cite this letter as proof that her mother was indeed a whore.

*Whatever did you see in him, Mama? Why did you love him so?*

She thought about her aunt and uncle, now probably back at the shop in Avalon, and her Andros cousins, and grimaced, ashamed and embarrassed. More than likely they would regret their kinship to her, once they read that letter. Her mind skipped to Lord Matthew and Colonel Orlando. Something dreadful must have happened to them both or Isaac would have answered her questions last night. She did not yet understand why she had escaped death, but if for some reason her capital crime had been invalidated, then they both had suffered wrongfully. She bristled over that possibility and at being away from active duty. She was neglecting the very men who so desperately needed and certainly deserved skilled medical care.

Sergeant Aran's predicament especially preyed on her. He most of all would need her help over the coming months as he suffered through the final stages of his fatal cancer and faced his death. Would she be allowed to return to her post? She had not been expressly forbidden to do so, yet she was not hopeful.

And where on earth was Judith? Helen had never needed her mother's wise friend more than she did now. *I guess I am speaking to her again.*

Helen did not notice a huge black-and-brown dog that had come up to the bench and was standing next to her, regarding her with dark eyes. Finally, the beast sat on its haunches and laid its head on her lap, issuing what sounded like a sigh. She looked around and then down, laughed, and stroked the top of its head and ears. It was an enormous, thick-furred wolfhound, a hunting breed native to the southern mountainous region of Alta Province that was feared and respected for its courage, strength, loyalty, and tenacious ferocity. This beast seemed to be in its prime and belonged to some household. It was well groomed and fed and wore a braided leather collar.

"Aren't you supposed to growl at strangers? Flash some teeth?" Helen asked, continuing to scratch the dog's ears. "I could have stolen the family silver, after all."

She stood up, stretched, and decided she needed something hot to drink. The beast accompanied her to the door of the pantry but would not enter with her. A few more members of the serving staff were now awake and busy preparing break-fast; it was still early. Hanging her cloak on a hook, Helen located a pot of *kaf*, found a mug, and poured herself some.

A young serving girl approached her and dropped a hurried curtsey. "Please Mistress, may I have a word with you?"

She directed Helen out of the kitchen into a wide hallway that connected the entire servants' wing to the rest of the manor. Asleep on a bench was a Toltec whom Helen assumed to be of considerable rank and consequence based on his attire of dark blue silk and the heavy platinum ring with an enormous sapphire on his hand.

The serving girl was extremely agitated. "Please, Mistress," she whispered. "It's not proper for this lord to be in this part of the house."

She pointed to a bucket of water she had placed near the bench. "I must scrub this entire hallway. Can you wake him for me? Is he ill?"

Helen bent over the man, who was heavily asleep, and tried to rouse him. He simply muttered and rolled over on his side, facing toward the front of the bench. His breath gave him away.

"He's not ill," she told the serving girl. "But he certainly won't feel all that great when he does wake up."

Helen motioned the girl back to the kitchen and asked her to fetch a towel. After poking around one of the pantries for a few minutes, Helen found the ingredients she needed. Tomato juice, an egg, some common household herbs that would help counteract the dehydrating effects of too much alcohol, as well as soothe a severe headache. She mixed it all in a large glass and added a dash of a savory sauce to make the blend at least palatable. Picking up the glass, she took the towel from the serving girl and went back into the hallway.

He was still on the bench. Placing the glass and the towel on the part of the bench he did not occupy, Helen picked up the bucket. "What's in here?"

"Just some lukewarm water, Mistress."

"Perfect."

Helen dumped the contents of the bucket over his head. The serving girl cried out in dismay and fled down the hallway to the kitchen.

"Son of a bitch!"

Lord Nimrod was awake, gasping and swearing. He jerked into an upright position and then fell back against the bench, head pounding mercilessly, tongue thick and dry. Dazed, he tried to wipe the water out of his eyes and focus on the blurred figure now standing in front of him.

A woman's voice spoke coldly. "Use this, my lord." A towel dropped on his head.

He blotted his face and hair and glared at her, too unsteady to do much of anything except fume and curse. He now at least recognized her. *She's a menace to all mankind. James should sell her quickly and be done with it.*

Ignoring his rude remarks, Helen returned his gaze. When Lord Nimrod stopped speaking, she held out the glass to him.

He looked at it suspiciously. "What's in it? Poison?"

"There's a thought, my lord. Alas, no. It's a simple but effective home remedy for too much indulgence."

She set the glass down on the bench next to him and left the hallway. As angry as he was with her, Lord Nimrod could not help admiring her figure and her long, waving hair. She was beautiful, he conceded, but overall, a menace. *Why did James ever do something as foolhardy as acknowledge her?*

He looked at the glass, realized he was extremely thirsty, and decided to try it. The concoction didn't taste all that bad. He sat for some time. His head seemed to ache less and he felt steadier. The home remedy at work? He wrote it off to the power of suggestion. He got to his feet and found his way to the guest bedchamber where he was to have spent the night, had he not passed out first.

● ● ●

Lord James preferred to take his morning meal in a sunroom that overlooked the lake. Having located Helen in the library, he had to issue an order to induce her to join him. Then he almost had to arm wrestle her into eating even just a few bites. She went through the entire meal without saying a word.

*Kronos! You are one stubborn girl.*

Lord James decided to outwait her. A servant removed the plate in front of him. He set a link on the table, activated it, and perused the daily intelligence digests and troop readiness summaries that appeared within seconds before him.

After watching him for a few minutes, Helen arose, curtseyed, and walked toward the door.

"Sit down," he said. "I have not given you permission to leave."

Helen returned to the chair, yanked it away from the table, and dropped onto it. "And will you issue me daily marching orders like one of your soldiers, Lord Protector?"

"You are one of my soldiers, Lieutenant, or have you forgotten?"

She refused to respond.

"Even more to the point, your entire situation is still very perilous," Lord James continued. "The Lord Chancellor is demanding that you be returned to custody to face a morals charge."

A servant admitted Sudras to the morning room. He bowed to the duke. "The examination has been agreed upon, my lord. A *koja* is on her way here from The Citadel, even as we speak."

"What examination, Isaac?"

The Grand Master's silence ignited Helen's fury. She closed her eyes and took several deep breaths to try to calm down.

Lord James stood by her chair. "Look at me, Lieutenant."

She opened her eyes and met his.

"I am going to ask you some questions. Before I do, let me make one thing clear. I want none of the remarks that seem to land you on report constantly. I'm in no mood for it. Your freedom, not to mention Lord Matthew's survival, depends on it. Do I make myself understood?"

"Perfectly, Lord Protector."

"Are you chaste?"

"Yes, Lord Protector. I am chaste."

"I am not referring just to Lord Matthew. You have denied under oath any relationship with him other than friendship, and I believe you, as far as that goes. What about other men?"

"There have been no men whatsoever, Lord Protector. I am chaste."

He gave permission for Helen and Sudras to leave the room.

Now that Helen realized how the examination might help her dear friend, her anger diminished, even if she remained indignant at the prospect of being vetted like livestock before an auction.

They awaited the *koja* in the main reception hall. Helen almost laughed when she saw the woman. Sure enough, the *koja* was her same sour-faced pitiless jailer.

Sudras insisted on taking Helen's arm to escort her upstairs.

"You'll have to do some quick catching up with her," Helen teased, climbing beside him. "She's already seen just about the best I have to offer."

# CHAPTER TWENTY-TWO

After the examination Helen refused to get dressed, come out, or eat lunch. She spent the rest of the day in the bedchamber, rereading her mother's letter, concerned about Lord Matthew, Colonel Orlando, and Judith. Where were they? How were they faring?

She slumped over the dressing table, tears on her face. She had forgotten how uncomfortable a pelvic examination could be. She felt queasy to realize the result of this examination was public by now. She clutched at her stomach, her guts churning. Nothing came up.

"Humiliating, isn't it."

Recognizing the voice, Helen stood up, turned, and curtseyed, holding her stomach. Lady Naomi closed the bedchamber door and took the girl into her arms. Helen returned the Consort's embrace and they held each other for some minutes, weeping.

The Consort took Helen by the hands and looked her in the eye. "They did the same thing to me right before I married Kefren. Exalted Lords insist on marrying virgins." *And they prefer to bed a virgin concubine.*

She turned away from Helen to open the closet door, not noticing the expression on the girl's face. In her head Helen heard the Consort's thoughts. She complied without comment when the Consort cheerily ordered her to sit on the stool in front of the dressing table.

The Consort sorted through the clothes, selected a light gray wool-silk blend dress with billowing white muslin sleeves and a narrow black suede belt at the waist.

"How did you face anyone afterward, Lady Consort?"

The Consort stood behind Helen, took the hairbrush, and worked through the girl's tresses. "If you had not passed this little test, you would have every reason to be miserable. And you can still choose to act insulted and humiliated.

"Or, you can consider this your triumph. I extracted a rather large ruby from my father after passing my test."

She showed Helen a ring she wore. The square-cut gem flashed in the glow of the light-sticks.

"I want nothing from him."

The Consort took the girl's chin between her fingers and forced Helen to look up at her. "Mind your manners, young woman," she said. "Some very important people will be gathering here tonight. If you shame your father, you'll answer to me as well as to him, and you won't like it. You have no idea what he is risking on your behalf."

She let go and the girl's head drooped. "Yes, Lady Consort."

Lady Naomi decided Helen's hair looked best the way she always wore it, unbound and held back from her face.

She left Helen to get dressed, and found Lord James at the bottom of the main staircase. Clad in a semi-formal uniform that consisted of a deep red, gold-trimmed tunic, black trousers, and boots, he paced like an expectant father.

The Consort could not help smiling. She took the duke's arm and patted his hand. "She'll be here in a few minutes, dear. Go easy on her. She's terrified."

"That makes two of us, Naomi."

The Consort stood with him, breezily making small talk until Helen appeared at the top of the staircase. Then she slipped away to join the growing crowd in the gallery awaiting the Lord Protector and his newly acknowledged daughter.

Helen caught sight of the duke and for a moment lost her nerve. She paused, uncertain of her next move. Lord James beckoned to her with his index finger, pointed to a spot a few feet away from him. Taking a deep breath, she descended the stairs, reached the place he had indicated, and dropped to her knees. She remained on her knees before him, head bowed.

Lord James helped her to her feet. He raised her hand to his lips and kissed the back of it, smiling. "You have spoken truthfully, Helen. I am very pleased."

She looked away, unprepared to return the familiarity he offered to her in using her first name. And yet, his opinion of her was somehow important to her. That made her uneasy, angry, and filled her with a grief that she did not fully understand. *I don't even know him. How can I possibly trust him, much less love him?*

"It seems ridiculous to be complimented for something I did not do, my lord," was all she could manage.

Lord James laughed, took her arm, and walked by her side into the gallery.

● ● ●

Several familiar faces were among the group. Helen caught sight of Judith and Lord Justin, seated together on a bench next to a window. Sudras was also in the room, smiling at her encouragingly. Orlando stood at attention not far from a door connecting the gallery and another room. Something about the colonel alarmed Helen. Her instincts told her he was not well.

Lord James led his daughter first to Prince Enoch, by far the high-est-ranked and thus the most important visitor. Helen curtseyed in silence, rising only when he acknowledged her.

The prince pressed the back of her hand to his lips, his dark eyes devouring her. "Virtuous as well as beautiful. A rare combination, Mistress Andros."

Helen did her best to smile. "You are most gracious, my lord prince."

Prince Enoch did not relinquish Helen's hand fast enough to suit Lady Naomi, on full alert for possible competitors in bidding for the girl. The Consort made a point of being next to welcome Helen. She caused more than a few heads to turn by treating the girl as she would any other familiar and favored noblewoman, refusing to allow her to kneel, and instead taking her hands in her own and kissing her on each cheek.

"You do look lovely, my dear," she said in a normal tone. She leaned toward Helen and murmured into her ear, "Smile more. You're not at a funeral."

The Consort held one of Helen's hands and spoke to several of the men close by them. Judith rose from the bench and took Helen's other hand. Helen surveyed the gathering, noting that the only women present were the Consort, Judith, and herself.

She turned her head toward Judith. "I guess they don't bring their wives or daughters when they are inspecting the merchandise."

"We'll speak more about this later, dear girl," Judith whispered in return.

Having read the end of her mother's letter several times, Helen assumed the Lord Protector was putting her on display as a prelude to selling her.

Taking Helen's arm once more, Lord James steered her to a circle of men engaged in heated speculation about Prince Seti's and the Lord Chancellor's policy for Kamut. During a pause in the conversation, he tapped the shoulder of the lord whose back was turned toward them.

"Nim, allow me to introduce to you my daughter, Helen Andros. Helen, this is Lord Nimrod Atlas, Prince Enoch's heir, and my best friend."

Lord Nimrod turned toward her. Helen stifled a gasp. It took every bit of her self-control not to betray any expression while curtseying to him. He took her hand and bowed over it, but did not kiss it as he greeted her with no compliment or remark.

Helen was heartsick; she had not meant to insult her father's best friend. She paid scant attention while Lord James introduced her to the others in the circle, including the Consort's nephew, Lord Andrew Palladin.

A servant announced the arrival of Tuk, who was on a formal visit on behalf of the government of Kamut. He entered the gallery and paid his respects to the ranking visitors. Tuk next approached Helen, and caused another minor stir by honoring her in the Toltec custom, taking her hands and turning the palms upward before kissing them.

"Hekemtep, Princess Notufil, Prince Harnak, and the people of Kamut are forever in your debt, Doctor Andros."

He offered a leather purse weighed down by coins. "Please accept this token of our deepest appreciation, along with our earnest wishes for your full recovery from your ordeal."

"The government and people of Kamut are far too generous, Master Tuk," Helen replied. "My action was merely a long overdue repayment of the debt I owed Hekemtep and Princess Notufil. Please return this handsome gift to them with my deepest thanks. Beg them, please, to bestow it on whatever cause they deem worthy or fit. I ask this in the name of she who once served them, my mother, Miriam Andros."

The room fell silent. Tuk looked a long time at the young woman who stood before him, her eyes displaying sadness, pain, and pride. All he could do, without seeming venal or petty by comparison, was grant her request.

"Prince Harnak continues to recover, Master Tuk?" Helen ventured.

"Yes, Doctor Andros. Slowly but surely."

Helen's eyes now hinted at mischief. "Very good. I would hate to think we've had all this fun for nothing."

Lord James laughed along with many of his guests. He took Helen's arm and escorted her into the dining room. He glanced at her as they walked together. "You realize you just gave up a tidy sum, young woman."

Helen shrugged her shoulders. "Who needs such incidentals, Lord Protector, when she can live it up on Army pay?"

● ● ●

Sitting at Lord James' left hand during the meal, Helen ate little and talked even less. When Prince Enoch asked her about the debt she mentioned, she deferred to Master Tuk. He relayed a story that matched much of what Helen's mother said in her letter. This was significant because as a foreigner, Tuk did not have Grid access. His words confirmed the truth for many in what Miriam had written.

Lady Naomi was reluctant to leave the table. At last, she rose to her feet; everyone also stood up. She motioned to Helen and to Judith. "Let us leave the men to their small talk and lesser vices."

Before exiting the room, the Consort brushed by the Lord Protector, stopping to whisper into his ear. "I'll top any bid you get, James."

Helen curtseyed to her father and followed the Consort and Judith out of the dining room into a formal drawing room, where a pot of *kaf* was ready. At a nod from Lord James, the colonel joined the women and stood at attention just inside the door.

Not long after the three were seated and making small talk, Lord Justin appeared, bowing low to the Consort, who acknowledged him politely although without any warmth.

Helen made up for the Consort's coolness. Tears in her eyes, she rushed to her kinsman and held him tightly.

He returned her embrace, stooping to kiss her forehead like a brother. "I have informed your aunt and uncle, and Uncle John and Aunt Abigail, that you are safe and unharmed."

Emotions that Helen had spent days repressing now burst forth. She almost collapsed. Lord Justin helped her to the sofa across from the Consort and Judith, sat next to her, and put his arm about her shoulders. She rested her head on his chest, continuing to weep. Offering her a handkerchief, he stroked her hair, trying to calm and reassure her.

"Thank you, my lord," she whispered. "They are well?"

She sat up, dried her eyes, and turned to look at him. His mouth curved upward even if his eyes, a curious mixture of green, gray and blue, were sad. "They are well now that they know you are safe."

Helen continued to study him. Lord Justin was taller than anyone she knew, with a slim, wiry build: all bones, lines, and angles. His hair was several shades too dark to be blond like the Turanians' yet much lighter than the black manes of the Toltecs. Beyond his physical appearance, her kinsman was troubled about something, although she yet had no intuitive hint about what it might be.

Helen got to her feet and walked to the floor-to-ceiling window, drawn by the light of the full moon. He joined her, and they stood side by side. Their hands met and clasped together in a gesture of support and comfort.

They heard a thump behind them.

"Oh, dear," the Consort said.

Orlando, slumped to the floor, gasped for breath, his chest heaving. "Kronos!"

Rushing to the ailing man and kneeling next to him, Helen turned him on his back. She felt for his pulse. It was very faint and rapid. "Please bring me Isaac's medical bag," she asked Judith.

While Judith hurried to find it, Helen scoured the room, deciding to place the colonel on the rug before the hearth. Lord Justin and a manservant whom Judith had sent to the drawing room carried the colonel to the spot she indicated.

Helen kicked off her shoes and knelt beside him. She checked the back of his head for signs of injury. *What else did those bastards do to him besides beat him?*

Orlando opened his eyes. "I'm on duty, Lieutenant."

She thrust him back down onto the rug. "You're on fire, Colonel, and as of now you are relieved from duty. You're in no damn shape to do anything but expire."

Judith returned with the bag. She opened it and set it next to Helen, who was unfastening the buttons of Orlando's tunic and of the collar of his shirt. Her attention absorbed, Helen did not notice the room beginning to fill with other guests from the dinner party, Lord James among them.

Orlando was aware of them. His breath ever more labored, he put his hand on her wrist to try to stop her. "Lieutenant, this is unseemly."

"Unseemly?" She removed his hand from her wrist and put it back on the rug. "I'll tell you what's unseemly, Colonel. And that's any man dying of wounds from punishment for his role in a crime that never occurred. Now that's unseemly."

She hunted in the medical bag for antibiotics and a heart stimulant. "Do you have any idea how much money the government has invested in your training, Colonel? Look at it that way, if you must."

He did not respond; he had stopped breathing. He also had no pulse. She let out a rather pungent oath. "Did you have to take me literally when I said expire?"

Helen plunged her hand into the bag, retrieved a syringe and a vial. She filled the syringe, then ripped open the colonel's shirt. Popping the protective cap off the needle, she plunged it straight into his heart. Replacing the cap, she tossed the empty syringe aside.

Nothing. Helen straddled the colonel's chest with her knees and started pressing on his heart. Sudras assisted her by adding the breathing portion of the resuscitation. They worked for what seemed like hours instead of quick minutes, and still Orlando did not respond.

Sudras sat back, stood up, and shook his head, his forehead even more creased than usual.

"No!" Helen grabbed the colonel by the collar of his tunic, yanked his chest upward, and thrust her face next to his.

"Damn it, Orlando! Wake up! Breathe! Do you hear me? That's a damned order, Soldier. Now!"

Helen slapped him hard across the face and lowered his upper body to the rug. He moaned and coughed, remaining unconscious.

Helen caressed his brow. "It's a damn good thing one of us knows how to obey orders, Colonel, and an even better thing in this case that it's you."

His pulse was stronger and more regular, the effect of the heart stimulant. She had to get some antibiotic into him right away. Helen located the bottle, found another syringe, and hunted for a vein in his forearm. Something almost like an invisible hand stopped her and the encouraging voice spoke. *Allergies.*

She scanned the service tag on a chain around his neck. Sure enough, Orlando was allergic to the drug she planned to use, the latest and most potent. The voice again in her mind. *Use the stone. Keep it hidden.*

She put her hand on the stone. It was unusually warm, almost hot. Keeping her eyes on her patient, she slipped off the stone and covered it and the chain with her fingers. She placed it over Orlando's heart, hidden completely by her hand. She held it until it stopped pulsing and the heat was gone. Then she covertly put it back on and slid it underneath the top of her gown.

At last, she looked up. Realizing that she had an audience, including the Lord Protector, Helen straightened the bodice of her dress. She repacked the medical bag. It could not be changed now, and she could not have done anything differently even had she known. She would have found the colonel's death far more unbearable than being punished for unseemly behavior.

# CHAPTER TWENTY-THREE

Several footmen carried Orlando to a bedroom near the servants' quarters. Helen accompanied him, happy to have a legitimate excuse for leaving the drawing room. Lord Justin went with her, also wanting to escape notice and to be helpful.

After they departed, Prince Enoch turned to Sudras. "Why did you not intervene earlier, Grand Master?"

"My lord prince, if I am ever in the same condition as that unfortunate young officer, I hope the person treating me is Doctor Andros," Sudras replied. "Her abilities as a physician far exceed those of anyone I have ever witnessed, including my own."

He located the empty syringe, stooped down, retrieved it, and stood up again. "My lords, Lady Consort, Judith, I don't use this word very often, and certainly not lightly. All of you just witnessed a miracle. That man was a corpse; there's no doubt in my mind. I gave up on him, but not Doctor Andros. There's no rational explanation for how she did it, yet she brought him back."

Sudras took a glass of pepper brandy offered by a servant and swallowed the contents in one gulp. "To answer your question, my lord prince, the best thing I could do for the colonel was stay out of her way until I could provide very specific assistance, which I was honored to do."

●  ●  ●

Helen directed Lord Justin and the servants to remove Orlando's shirt and place him on his stomach so she could get a good look at his back. Just as she suspected, some of the welts were oozing fluid and pus.

"Infection," she murmured. "What a surprise."

She would have to lance, clean, and close the contaminated wounds. She wondered how much of his body was covered with welts. Two weeks ago, she would have simply looked for herself and no one would have cared. Things were different now.

"If you wouldn't mind," she said to Lord Justin. She explained what to look for and then turned away. Her kinsman did as she asked.

"There's one infected welt on his upper left thigh," he said.

She had Lord Justin turn the colonel on his back to make it easier to insert the catheter into his wrist. As they were preparing, Orlando opened his eyes and blinked, trying to focus.

Having taped the catheter in place, Helen stopped and smiled. She moistened a cloth and used it to wipe the sweat from his face and neck.

"Welcome back, Jackson."

She spoke as if she were addressing Lillie or some other young child.

"What happened?"

She poured the water into a glass and offered it to him, placing her arm behind his head to hold it upright so that he could drink more easily.

"You died, Colonel," she replied. "But you cannot get away from me that easily. So, man up. You're stuck with me, the medical officer from hell. Which, come to think of it, is somewhere I almost got to visit earlier this week."

Helen put the glass back on the table after he had consumed the entire contents.

Orlando tried to sit up. "I'm on duty, Lieutenant."

She put her hands on top of his shoulders, pressed him back down onto the bed. "We've already had this argument, Colonel. You lost."

He gave her another warning look. He was close to putting her on report, again. "Do I have to remind you that I outrank you, Lieutenant?"

"That's not much of an accomplishment, Colonel. Everybody and his dog outranks me."

Lord Justin could not help smiling. He was in a chair on the other side of the bed, his long legs stretched in front of him.

Helen retrieved a fluid bag and hung it on the stand she had set up. "And may I remind you, Colonel? Any medical officer may remove any officer of any rank from active duty, if, in that medical officer's professional opinion, the aforesaid officer is unfit or too ill."

He scowled, pretending, as usual, that he was angry with her. All he really wanted to do, even in this miserably afflicted condition, was take her in his arms and kiss her.

"I know you may find it hard to believe, Colonel, but I have read every volume of the military code of conduct, and all the officer regulations handbooks."

"Indeed, Lieutenant. Very hard to believe."

She searched in the box of medical supplies for a syringe and an anesthetic. "I just tend to ignore the really stupid rules, which leaves out ninety-five percent of everything written."

"A soldier simply cannot pick and choose which rules to obey, Lieutenant, and which to ignore."

"How boringly consistent, Colonel."

She filled the syringe with the anesthetic. She did not want to risk putting him under; he might not wake up from it. She would have to numb the areas around the infected welts to work on them.

He saw the needle. "What are you doing, Lieutenant?"

"Taking full advantage of the situation, Colonel. After all, not many lowly lieutenants ever get the chance to stick it to their CO."

Lord Justin guffawed. Orlando did not trust himself to speak.

Helen decided to go for the shoulder wounds first, until the slow-acting sedative that she had mixed in with the solution had a chance to take effect. After Orlando turned on his stomach and they arranged the drip stand, Helen studied the locations of the infected welts to know where to inject the anesthetic. She inserted the needle so skillfully he did not feel it.

The wounds were essentially untended; she opened and cleaned most of them, even some of the uninfected ones that looked especially deep. She used the sealer she found in the medical bag to close them to minimize scarring.

She worked from the top of his back to the welt on his thigh. By the time she was finished, the sedative had put her patient to sleep. Lord Justin placed the colonel on his back, removing the rest of his outer clothing, dressing him in a nightshirt.

Before leaving, Helen sat next to the bed for a few minutes, holding Orlando's hand in hers, feeling the anger and gratitude she had held in check to be able to treat him. She was incensed over his unnecessary suffering and thankful he had refused to reveal anything.

She kissed his forehead. "Get better soon, Jackson. I don't know who I'm going to torment until you do."

*   *   *

During the time Helen spent tending to Orlando's wounds, most of the guests had left. Only the Consort, Judith, Lord Nimrod, and Sudras remained when Helen and her kinsman returned to the drawing room.

Helen poured Lord Justin a cup of *kaf* and then one for herself. She took a sip, then sank onto the chair next to Judith, and shut her eyes.

"What is the Colonel's outlook, Helen?"

"He'll recover in time, my lord. He needs at least five days of bed rest. Good luck keeping him there more than one."

"I recall suggesting something similar to you just last night," Sudras said.

"I don't have a life-threatening infection, Isaac," Helen retorted. "Just a few cuts and bruises."

She took another sip of *kaf*. "But if it will make you feel any better, Doctor Sudras, the very next time I go into full-blown heart failure, I'll stay off my feet for a few days and think kindly of you."

"Mistress Andros, have you always been this pleasant, not to mention well dressed, in company?" Lord Nimrod inquired.

Helen saw she had forgotten to remove the apron that she used to work on the colonel. She took it off, rolled it up, and handed it to a servant. "No, Lord Avalon. I've mellowed considerably. I used to be a lot more pleasant."

The Lord Steward's arrival cut short their exchange. Helen stood up, alarmed by the very troubled expression on Shinar's face. *Please don't let Matthew be hurt badly.*

Shinar apologized to Lord James for his absence earlier that evening, explaining that his son's condition was still extremely serious. Helen was introduced formally to him and curtseyed deeply to her beloved friend's father.

Shinar put her hand to his lips and kissed it. "I beg of you, Doctor Andros. If you feel up to it, would you examine my son tonight? You have been through a terrible ordeal yourself. I would not ask but my son has been calling for you in his stupor, and I am desperate."

He sat next to Lady Naomi, who covered his hand with her own and tried her best to cheer him.

Helen finally learned the extent of Lord Matthew's injuries. She was as appalled and infuriated as she had been over Orlando. It seemed to her that Lord Justin was also distressed, although he was trying hard not to show it.

Helen silently implored Lord James' permission, resenting that she no longer could make such choices for herself.

The duke was uncertain. It was late already and very risky to permit her to leave his house. Shinar had stuck his neck out for him, however, and Lord James wanted to return the favor. He agreed, with the provision that he accompany Helen. He sent an aide to prepare a skimmer.

Helen requested a link and sent for her medical bag, which had been delivered from the base to the Mordecai manor.

She caught Lord Justin's attention. "If you don't mind, my lord, you were most helpful with the colonel, and I will probably need your assistance with Lord Matthew."

He bestowed a brief look of gratitude on her, indicated his assent, and turned away. Helen began to have an idea about the exact nature of her kinsman's relationship to her dearest friend.

Once she had a link, Helen searched for medical records, not sure her authorization would still be valid. She obtained Grid access. "Not dead yet," she muttered.

As she worked, she leaned back and twisted sideways in her chair, her skirt-covered legs draped over the arms, ankles crossed. Lord James' eyes widened at her display of mannerisms so like his own.

Scrolling to Lord Matthew's medical history, she opened the file on his current condition and found it empty. She checked to make sure she had the correct file. "Isaac, surely we have not changed medical records protocol since about ten days ago."

"Not that I'm aware of, my dear."

That was truly odd. There was no indication anywhere of any medical activity related to Lord Matthew's present condition. She continued working the screen. "How long has Lord Matthew been unconscious, Lord Steward?"

Slightly more than two days, Shinar told her. Helen was not happy to find out that Prince Seti's personal *kojei* had been tending Lord Matthew until that afternoon, when the results of her examination went public. At that point the Lord Steward summoned the nerve to dismiss the *kojei*, who had been keeping everyone away from his son.

Lord Matthew needed a blood transfusion. The problem was his blood type. It was the rarest. Helen could donate to him, and Lord Justin also probably could donate. It would not bother Lord Matthew one jot and probably not his father, either. His mother and her family no doubt would object. Those of The Blood often refused transfusions from anyone not also of pure Toltec ancestry. Such considerations invariably complicated the logistics of even the simplest of medical procedures, since there were so many more

Turanians in Azgard than Toltecs, and thus a far greater supply of blood from them available.

Helen limited her donor search to high-ranking (and therefore Toltec) active and reserve military officers. With any luck, the Lord Protector could always apply the same kind of arm-twisting he had tried on her a few days past to get the man to agree to provide blood.

The name of the blood type match, a colonel in the reserves, appeared on the screen before her. Helen almost groaned. She explained the situation to Shinar.

"You have found a match, Doctor Andros?"

"Lord Avalon is an exact match, Lord Steward. Perhaps he will consent to help Lord Matthew."

Lord Nimrod sprang up from his reclining position. Helen thought it best that Lord Matthew's father plead his son's case.

A servant set her own medical bag on the table next to the screen. She opened it and sorted through the bottles containing various herbal tinctures she prepared to treat ailing veterans. She heard Lord Nimrod agree.

"This is an extremely rare match, my lords," Helen remarked. "I wonder what the odds are against having two people with this same blood type in a room together."

"Off the top of my head, I'd say about one million, two hundred thousand fifty-four to one," Lord Justin replied, smiling.

Helen placed bottles from the medical bag on the table before her. "What, my lord? No decimal point calculation?"

"I rounded up."

"Numeric exaggeration. How quaint. Is that anything akin to poetic license, my lord?"

"Don't let her get away with this nonsense, Shorty," Lord Nimrod growled.

"You call him 'Shorty' my lord?" Helen shot back. "Perhaps I should adjust the medical portion of your service record to note severe visual impairment."

She picked up different bottles of the various tinctures, smelling the contents of each to ascertain its potency. The Lord Steward looking at her, puzzled, and she explained how the various tinctures would work to help Lord Matthew.

"Of course, Lord Steward, the taste will probably knock him into next week," she added. "Then again, it does take quite a bit to get Lord Matthew's attention."

# CHAPTER TWENTY-FOUR

Unwilling to risk revealing his feelings for Lord Matthew, Lord Justin went with most of the group to the drawing room of the Shinar manor. For the moment, this suited his purpose. He had made a promise to his aunt and had to ask Helen's father to allow his kinswoman a visit to the Andros farm for a family reunion.

Helen, Sudras, and Lord Nimrod were shown to the sickroom. Sudras lifted the blood-streaked sheets draped across Lord Matthew's body, holding them to shield the boy's back, and his own face, from anyone's view. It took every bit of the Grand Master's self-possession not to gasp out loud. He blinked back tears, needing some minutes before he could even think about examining Lord Matthew's ghastly wounds.

His silence did not fool Helen, who was preparing Lord Nimrod for the blood transfusion. "That bad, Isaac?"

She busied herself setting up a direct transfer of blood from Lord Nimrod to Lord Matthew, noting the time and pressure rate so she would know when to end the procedure.

Focused on the Grand Master, Lord Nimrod glanced down and jerked his head in surprise. Helen had already inserted a catheter into his arm and was taping it to keep it from slipping. "Are you sure it's in place, Mistress Andros? I didn't feel anything."

"I'm somewhat better with needles than with buckets, my lord," Helen replied. "To answer your question, yes. You are literally stuck here for some time. Boredom is the blood donor's only compensation, I'm afraid."

That task completed, Helen steeled herself with several deep breaths and stepped beside Sudras for her first look at Lord Matthew. She cried out and averted her eyes. Sudras put his free arm around her shoulders and drew her close; she pressed her face into his chest. *What kind of butcher does this to so sweet and gentle a soul?*

Eventually they began assessing the extent and nature of Lord Matthew's injuries. The worst of the wounds were on his lower back, buttocks, and upper thighs. Near the base of his spine and across his buttocks, the flesh had been shredded so severely that even the muscle tissue clearly was destroyed, leaving only tattered flaps of skin beginning to rot due to lack of blood supply. None of the welts had been cleaned or sealed. Why he had not bled to death was inexplicable.

"You're a tougher bird than I thought, dear, sweet Matthew," Helen murmured. Sudras nodded.

At the sound of Helen's voice, Lord Matthew moaned and uttered her name. Helen stroked the back of his head and bent close to his ear. "Matthew, this is Helen. I'm alive, and I'll be very cross with you if you don't snap out of it and wake up."

The Grand Master could not help laughing, especially at Lord Nimrod's shock at the familiarity with which Helen treated Lord Matthew.

The two commenced their healing work. Sudras first hunted down the supplies they needed while Helen monitored the transfusion and the patient. Then together the two went over all of Lord Matthew's injuries slowly, cleaning them carefully, doing their best to seal the wounds, which in some cases was almost impossible because little to no healthy skin remained. To cover those gaps, they used a temporary artificial skin. His condition remained serious.

Helen finally ended the transfusion, replacing the blood-filled line to the large vein in Lord Matthew's leg with one attached to a bag of fluids and antibiotics. She removed the catheter from Lord Nimrod's arm and bandaged the small entry wound.

Lord Nimrod pretended not to notice. She might be a menace, but by Kronos, at the very least she was exotic. He had never seen a girl with eyes so large or lips so naturally red and sensual. He wondered what it would be like to taste them, and if the nipples of her gorgeous breasts were just as red. He wanted to taste those, too.

"My lord, please tell Lord Matthew's father we'll know more when he wakes up," Helen said, letting go of him.

Lord Nimrod started to get to his feet and grabbed the bed rail, disoriented. "I took a bit more blood out of you than usual, my lord. All in a good cause," Helen explained. "No strenuous physical activity for the next day or so, and lay off the pepper brandy. Some food right now will help, too."

* * *

Just as Helen and Sudras were wrapping up their initial treatment, Lord Justin appeared in the doorway. Helen suggested her kinsman remain with Lord Matthew to notify them when the patient regained consciousness. She received another brief look of gratitude. She popped off her gloves, removed her surgical gown, and left with Sudras to join the group.

Helen deferred to the Grand Master to explain the basics of Lord Matthew's condition. She poured her own cup of *kaf* and took a place next to Judith, across from the Consort.

"With your approval, Lord Steward, we will prepare for skin grafts," the Grand Master said. He turned to Lord James. "If you will permit Helen to assist me with this procedure, Lord Protector, I think it will help Lord Matthew's frame of mind. He trusts her."

"Provided the procedure is not in the next few days, Grand Master, I agree," Lord James replied. "I need a brief time to make security arrangements."

Sudras outlined a very basic description of the purpose of grafts. Helen rose to pour herself another cup of *kaf*. She was gratified by Sudras's invitation and infuriated that she now had to await someone's permission to do that for which she trained long and hard over many years.

After Sudras completed his explanation, Helen spoke. "Skin grafts won't be enough."

"That is by no means certain, Helen," Sudras countered. "We truly won't know anything until Lord Matthew recovers enough so that we can conduct mobility tests."

Helen returned to her seat. "As if he hasn't been tortured enough already."

"Why not enough, Helen?" the Consort asked.

A servant burst into the room. "Forgive me, Lord Steward, but Lord Matthew is conscious now, and there's a problem."

They could hear for themselves. Lord Matthew's cries resounded down the stairway and through the ground floor of the manor house. Helen ran out of the room, mounting the steps to the bedchamber two at a time.

Lord Justin was next to the bed. Helen took the other side, slid her arm under Lord Matthew's shoulders, and put her other hand on his head.

"Matthew," she said. "This is Helen. I'm fine. I'm here with you now. Can you understand me? Look at me."

He turned toward the sound, trying to focus his eyes. Beads of pain-induced sweat dotted his forehead. He shifted one of his legs and screamed in agony again.

Helen pointed to the table next to Lord Justin. He saw the syringe, uncapped it, and passed it to her. She administered the painkiller.

The rest of the group reached the landing outside the bedchamber. The double doors were open. They could see and hear what was going on without having to enter the room. Only Shinar approached the bed, his eyes bright.

Lord Matthew tried to turn in the direction of his father and shrieked. Helen tightened her grip. "Damn it, you moron! Quit moving. At least until the painkiller starts working."

He swallowed hard, panting. Lord Justin held a glass of water to Lord Matthew's lips, and he drank with alacrity.

"Thank you," he said. "I thought you were dead, Helen."

She ran her fingers through his hair, struggling with guilt, anguish, and remorse. "Apparently I'm hard to kill."

Lord Matthew grimaced; the pain was now bearable. "Do not blame yourself. This is my doing, not yours."

Unable to repress a sob, Helen saw that Lord Matthew's mother had joined the group, standing near the bed next to the Lord Steward, who had his arm about her. Helen disengaged from Lord Matthew and curtseyed to Lady Siroma, whose hostility was palpable.

Helen and Lord Justin left the room, closing the doors behind them so that the parents could be alone with their son.

# CHAPTER TWENTY-FIVE

Lord Justin sat in his father's study before an enormous ebony wood desk with platinum inlays. He was on trial for the umpteenth time, and wondered what his crime was now. The prince had summoned his second son as soon as Lord Justin, his brother, and Judith had returned to the Atlas manor after their visit to Lord Matthew.

Fatigued, Lord Nimrod had retired immediately. In his elder son's absence, Prince Enoch did not hesitate to unleash his latest displeasure on his younger son. Resenting the need to look up to speak with Lord Justin, the prince ordered the young man to sit whenever he planned to question or lecture him.

The prince stood over Lord Justin. "Your meddling has only made matters much worse, boy."

Lord Justin shot a glance at Judith, seated on a small sofa next to the wall. Her eyebrow rose almost imperceptibly.

He did his best to keep any anger out of his voice. "If you would please explain, my lord prince. I have no idea what you are talking about."

Prince Enoch glared. "No idea? James has declared he will not sell the girl. This is the worst of all possible outcomes. Better she should have died than this."

Lord Justin thought he now understood the source of his father's ire and his brother's gloom that past evening.

"Better she should have died or been sold, my lord prince? Why is that?"

"Are you stupid as well as insolent, boy?" Prince Enoch replied. "This decision leaves the Lord Protector extremely vulnerable to his enemies. And since the House of Atlas is counted as one of his allies, it leaves us vulnerable as well."

The prince walked about the room, muttering. "The last thing I need on my hands is yet another half-blood to undermine the position of this House."

The full meaning of his father's words was not lost on Lord Justin. "What have I to do with the Lord Protector's decision, my lord prince?"

Prince Enoch searched the pocket of the smoking jacket he wore in his study late at night. He found his favorite pipe, thrust the stem in his son's direction. "Don't insult my intelligence, boy. You interceded on her behalf."

Lord Justin was unable to contain his indignation. "I did no such thing, my lord prince. It was not my place to ask and I would never presume to interfere in a decision of such importance."

"Not your place? It seems to me you frequently forget your place, boy."

"Never, my lord prince. You are always here to remind me."

The prince slammed the back of his hand across Lord Justin's face. "Consider that another reminder."

The salty taste of blood in his mouth, Lord Justin closed his eyes. He pulled out a handkerchief and wiped his lips.

The prince returned to the chair behind his desk, sat, and filled his pipe. "I watched you last evening, Justin. You tried to approach James several times and then spoke to him. You must have asked him something. What was it?"

Mustering all of his self-control, Lord Justin explained his promise to his aunt and the visit to the Andros farm he had requested of Lord James for Helen. He lowered his gaze, fully expecting his father to explode with more anger.

Prince Enoch drew deeply on his pipe and was silent for such a long time that Judith went on full alert. She projected a sliver of her own energy toward him, immediately picking up his anger, disgust, and raging desire. The almost total disconnect between his highly agitated aura and his calm comportment filled her with foreboding. What on earth was he plotting? She had no clear idea. He was too well defended for her to probe deeper into his energy for more specific information without making herself far too obvious to him.

"Possibly such a visit might be useful at some point," the prince said.

He studied his second son, whose expression was difficult to interpret. Was he truly submitting or simply trying to hide his feelings?

"Look at me, boy."

Lord Justin raised his head again.

"I will not tolerate any further defiance or insolence from you, Justin. I am your father and the lord of your House. You owe me your duty and unquestioning obedience. I trust I make myself clear."

"Yes, my lord prince."

Judith lingered after Prince Enoch dismissed his second son. The prince opened a link; she coughed gently.

He did not look up at her. "I don't recall inviting you to my study."

Judith rose from the sofa, her gray *keftan* flowing in long folds by her sides, and walked toward his desk. She took several timed breaths, moving her anger and deep misgivings away from the surface of her energy field, so that the prince would not readily be aware of them. She clasped her hands in front of her and raised them, keeping her energy and her body language conciliatory. *If this keeps up, I'll be on my knees groveling soon.*

"It was very wrong of Justin to have spoken the way he did a few minutes ago."

"Criticism from his chief apologist?"

She sank into the chair Lord Justin had vacated, her hands still together. "Enoch, I have never condoned that kind of behavior and have told him so."

"Nonsense, woman. You have done nothing but defend him ever since he was a willful and disobedient child."

"How do you expect him to behave? He feels as though his pride and dignity are constantly insulted and demeaned."

"Justin has no pride or dignity, except what I decide to bestow on him. And he will have neither from me unless and until he submits to my authority and reverses his attitude."

He focused again on the screen. "This conversation is ended."

Judith arose. "Enoch, please."

She stopped when she saw the prince's mouth compress into a curl of fury. She curtseyed and hastily departed the study before she made things even worse for the young man whom she loved like the son she would never have.

# CHAPTER TWENTY-SIX

The letter from Helen's mother prompted a hastily called regular meeting of the *Kinshazen* the next evening. Unable to persuade the duke to sell his daughter, Lady Naomi recognized that the altered circumstances called for down-and-dirty street fighting. She warned both Prince Enoch and Lord James that Prince Seti would try to embarrass his political foes, and devised contingency plans to implement if the situation deteriorated as much as she feared.

As part of her maneuvers, the Consort chose to take Helen to Kindred House to sit next to her in the Visitors' Gallery to watch the session. Concerned about his daughter's safety, Lord James at first refused his permission. They discussed it with a great deal of heat and in the hearing of Lady Mary, whom the Consort had taken under her protection to mentor.

Unlike some of his peers, Lord James respected Lady Naomi, who had deeply compelling reasons for wanting Helen to witness the proceeding firsthand. The Consort was brutal, effectively countering every one of Lord James' arguments against Helen's presence in Kindred House. She also offered very specific advice about his attire that day and would not allow him to refuse her in that as well.

He made one final effort at resistance. "I can't wear all of my medals and awards, Naomi. There's no room for them. Everyone knows about all that nonsense anyway. No one cares."

The Consort's dark eyes crackled. "They don't? You should. James, tonight is entirely about appearances. This is far from nonsense. Your medals will help remind those ungrateful jackals just exactly how much they do owe you. Wear the really important ones at least."

The Lord Protector knew when to concede defeat, which the Consort accepted most graciously. She then went to work on Helen, who was terrified of returning to the place where she had been condemned to death less than a week earlier. In a not very subtle jab at Prince Seti and his Lord Chancellor, the Consort insisted that Helen wear another red dress that the Consort had made up for her in the exact style and fabric of the gown Helen wore at her trial. Curiously, blood red was the color of the House of Mordecai.

* * *

Lady Naomi made sure the Lord Steward was in his place and that most of the Kindred were at least on the floor of the inner chamber before she orchestrated an unusually ostentatious entrance into the Visitors' Gallery. Threading her way down the tiers of seats, she took her time and allowed other visitors to approach and kiss her hand. She chose the very front row, so that the members would be able to look up and see her and her companions with little effort.

Trying not to tremble, Helen followed the Consort, and was in turn trailed by Judith, who knew Helen needed as much moral support as possible, and whom Lady Naomi had asked to accompany them. The Consort finally chose her place, signaling to her companions to do likewise. Assuming her chair between the Consort and Judith, Helen suspected someone else was to join them by the way the Consort kept a surreptitious watch over the gallery entrance.

In a few minutes, Lord Justin hurried through the double doors, made his way to the Consort, and knelt before her, taking her hand to kiss it and offering an apology for being delayed. Knowing they were being observed, the Consort smiled warmly at him, pointing to one of the chairs. Judith moved over one seat so that Lord Justin could be next to his kinswoman.

Sensing Helen's deep trepidation, he covered her hand, cold and unsteady, with his, warm and unwavering. Turning her head as though looking around the chamber, she studied him. He was attired formally if very humbly, especially for one of Royal blood. With the exception of an Academy graduation ring on the third finger of his right hand, he wore no gems or adornment either on his person or his clothing.

"What happened to your mouth?"

"I got careless inserting my foot into it late last night."

"Is this an Andros family tendency, my lord? I thought I was the only one whose mouth gets her into trouble."

"Hush, girl," the Consort said, pretending to frown.

Ready to call the session to order, Shinar looked up from the notes and records on the lectern before him. He glanced at the Visitors' Gallery and needed all his experience as Lord Steward not to laugh out loud or betray any expression when he saw the girl and her kinsman next to the Consort. *How did you persuade her father to cut loose of her, my queen? Or Prince Enoch to permit his second son such visibility? You have more nerve than all the peers of the* Kinshazen *put together.*

Shinar became aware that the members were unusually quiet. He realized that Lord James was not yet in the inner chamber. At the sound of the gavel, the two princes moved toward their chairs. The other heads of the Great and Lesser Houses also were on their way to their seats when the Lord Protector finally appeared in the West Doors.

No sooner had Lord James stepped onto the floor than a chorus of cat-calls, hoots, whistles, and insults arose from members of Houses known to be loyal to Prince Seti. Other lords sat, not knowing what to do or say, stunned by the revelations concerning the Lord Protector and by the blatant display of disrespect for the conventions of Kindred House.

Lord James strode to his seat next to Lord Nimrod, on the banks of benches nearest the King's Chair that were reserved for the high-est-ranking nobility. After several minutes of repeated attempts, the Lord Steward gave up trying to call the members to order. Chaos was the only order. The gavel's ringing was overwhelmed by the members' noise, which did not die down even after the Lord Protector was seated.

Lord James put his lips to Lord Nimrod's ear in order to be heard. "Don't you think they're overdoing it just a bit, Nim? Next thing you know I'll be single-handedly responsible for all death, pestilence, and misery known to man."

Lord Nimrod inclined his head. "Surely you didn't expect anyone to pin another medal on you over this, James?"

"Certainly not. Just a few knives in the back."

"Then you won't be disappointed."

The Consort shot a look at the Prince of Istar, who was making no effort to refrain from gloating over Lord James' disgrace. She scoured the chamber for the Lord Chancellor, found him seated toward the front of the benches reserved for the Lesser Houses. His head was bowed and arms folded across his chest. Such circumspection was highly unlike Griffin. She rubbed her chin, pondering the situation. Was there some sort of rift between the prince and his Lord Chancellor? Or was this all part of the setup? She intended to find out for sure.

While the Consort plotted her next moves, Helen withdrew into herself, devastated. As the tumult and insults continued, a deeply buried part of her became more convinced than ever that she was not worthy of and therefore did not deserve her father's open acknowledgement or support, much less his approval or love. The price to him was obviously way too high. *Why on earth do you simply not sell me?*

Helen barely managed not to writhe in agony, yet could not stop herself from whimpering once or twice. She dropped her head and covered her lips with her fingers.

Aware of his kinswoman's increasing distress, Lord Justin squeezed her hand with his, then put his arm about her shoulders and drew her upper body closer. Not even when she was slowly freezing and starving in a prison cell, waiting in solitude to be executed, had Helen ever needed another person's support more than she did in that moment. She turned away from the spectacle below, resting her head against the side of his chest, within the comforting protection of his strong arm.

"Thank you once again, my lord," she whispered.

Fed up at last with the unending commotion, Lord Nimrod stood up and faced the Lord Steward. Several other members of the Great Houses, among them Prince Enoch and the Consort's nephew, Lord Andrew, did the same. Frustrated beyond patience, Shinar acknowledged their silent pleas for order.

Reluctantly, he walked over to Prince Seti's chair and bowed. It was obvious the prince meant to humiliate him as a warning to any others who might consider supporting the Lord Protector in this matter. The Lord Steward raised his eyebrow, leaning forward to put his lips to the prince's ear.

"You have more than made your point, my lord prince."

Prince Seti smiled icily, stared straight ahead, appearing to ignore the Lord Steward. Permitting an insulting amount of time to pass, he at last lifted his hand and complete silence followed. The prince found this an even more satisfying display of power and influence than the girl's execution, had it occurred.

It was also a major miscalculation. While inside Kindred House, members of the *Kinshazen* were honor-bound to obey the Lord Steward's authority and to accede to his commands. Within that building, the Lord Steward's word was inviolate in matters of conduct on the floor and procedural issues. The willingness of Prince Seti and his faction to trample on that principle frightened many nobles. It even gave pause to some who were extremely angry with Lord James and wanted him to be punished severely, precisely for his violation of a different time-honored tradition of not mingling the blood of the Kindred with what they regarded as a lesser race.

Shinar sat once more in the Lord Steward's chair; the members who were standing resumed their seats. A hum of whispers subsided. Lord Tarkon stood up. Although reluctant to give any more time to Prince Seti's supporters, the Lord Steward had little choice except to recognize the duke.

"My lords," Lord Tarkon began, "we have been most ignobly betrayed."

He paused to allow Prince Seti's faction to pound on the backs of their benches for several minutes. This time, however, they stopped when the Lord Steward brought the gavel down.

"The very man charged with the defense and protection of this realm has been revealed as an adulterer, a fornicator, a *kufir*-lover."

Before Lord Nimrod could stop him, Lord James shot out of his seat, restraining his anger long enough to be recognized by the Lord Steward. He fixed the Duke of Eden with a rock-hard stare.

"Brave words indeed, my lord, since the undeserving object of so base a slander is in no position to defend herself."

Lord Nimrod tugged hard on the sleeve of Lord James' jacket. "Sit down, and shut up," he hissed just loud enough for his client alone to hear. The Lord Protector reluctantly took his legal counsel's advice.

"Kronos, James," Lord Nimrod whispered. "They're obviously trying to provoke you into saying something that can be used against you later. Don't give them any help."

"I intend to say something, Nim."

Most members, including Prince Seti, were horrified and insulted at the open use of such vulgar language on the floor of Kindred House.

Unaware, Lord Tarkon continued. "We have been so ignobly betrayed, my lords, that I can see no other recourse but for the Lord Protector to step down from office, at least until this whole disgraceful business is resolved."

Taken aback by the Duke of Eden's unprecedented suggestion, the members became engrossed in animated debate. The Lord Steward had to pound hard with the gavel for several minutes.

Prying Lord Nimrod's fingers from his sleeve, Lord James stood again. "My lords, I cannot resign the Protectorship any more than Lord Eden can resign his dukedom. Or our gracious Exalted Lord can resign the Kingship. As long as I draw breath, the Protectorship is mine, with its many and heavy responsibilities. Nothing and no one has ever prevented me from fulfilling those responsibilities. I am well aware of my duty.

"As to certain accusations made against me tonight, this is neither the time nor place to respond to them. I will answer to the Kindred fully and completely if and when any formal charges are brought against me."

Lord Nimrod found nothing to fault from a legal perspective. His relief was temporary.

"And as for any accusation or formal charge of adultery, my lords, I flatly deny it," Lord James concluded.

Lord Nimrod rubbed his temples in extreme exasperation. He opted not to risk talking about it in public.

Lord James, sitting down, sensed his advocate's agitation. "I had to say it, Nim. I'm not thinking too clearly right now. Sorry."

"So am I, James."

Lord Andrew rose from his bench to seek recognition. "This is your maiden speech, is it not, my lord?" Shinar asked.

"Indeed, it is, my Lord Steward," Lord Andrew replied. "And I would give a great deal to make this a happier time for a first discourse before this august body."

Always curious when a member of a Great House made his formal debut into open politics, the members grew quiet and still. His position as the Consort's nephew made Lord Andrew's opinions even more important and interesting.

Only too aware of the extent of the Duke of Eden's offense, Lord Andrew set out to observe all the conventions and niceties of public debate. He paused for some moments, fighting a case of nerves, and trying to collect his thoughts.

"Forgive my slowness, my lords," he began. "Ever since the death of my honored father, I have sat many times in this very chamber, listening and trying to learn. Tonight, and the preceding session have been especially instructive."

"Hear, hear," many voices called out in unison. Other members nodded.

He found his stride. "I stand before you tonight disappointed and uneasy, although perhaps not for the reasons you might think."

Lord Andrew looked over at Lord James, who returned his gaze.

"Frankly, I'm disappointed in a man of integrity I thought I knew. But I agree. This is not the time or place to discuss these matters of law, and I for one want to hear both sides before I pass judgment. I owe the Lord Protector, myself, and especially the Kindred, that much at least."

He had to stop. Many members pounded their benches. It was an unusual gesture for an unusual first speech, which generally garnered little notice because inexperienced members tended to keep their initial efforts as brief and as inoffensive as possible. Lord Andrew was making a very bold move.

The speaker glanced toward Griffin. "And I am uneasy because I am not certain I can rely on this Lord Chancellor to make a competent case against anyone about anything. Think about it, my lords."

Lord Andrew looked around the entire chamber, locking eyes briefly with many of the members. Then he directed his gaze upward toward the Visitors' Gallery, taking their attention with him.

Helen sat up straight and looked down at him.

"I voted to send to her death a guiltless, virtuous young woman whose considerable medical skills saved Prince Harnak's life and thus may have prevented much bloodshed."

He acknowledged Helen with a nod that she returned. "I did so because I thought it was the law, based on what the Lord Chancellor told all of us."

Lord Andrew returned his focus to the chamber. "Not so next time, my lords. When this Lord Chancellor makes any kind of case, I intend to scrutinize his legal rationales most closely. Again, I owe this to any accused, myself, and to the Kindred."

After he sat down, Prince Seti sought permission to address the members. The Lord Steward waited some time before yielding the floor.

"Let us not be sidetracked from the real issue before us, my lords." The prince folded his arms across his chest. "The Protectorship is not the same as an indisputably hereditary noble title or the Kingship. The Protectorship was bestowed on Mordecai by Kronos Himself. The Lord Protector serves at the Exalted Lord's pleasure."

He glanced at Lord James, who returned the prince's contemptuous stare without wavering. "Somehow, I cannot imagine my brother taking any pleasure in knowing that this Lord Protector committed adultery while married to our sister."

"That's a lie!"

The words ripped out of Lord James, bounding to his feet.

He sank back onto the bench. The Lord Steward used the gavel vigorously. Never had the members seen the two long-standing opponents feud with each other so openly. It terrified them all, especially the lords of the Lesser Houses.

"That remains to be determined," Prince Seti continued. "In the meantime, my lords, we now have a formal motion on the floor to order the Lord Protector to surrender his position at least until the questions about his conduct have been settled."

One of Lord Tarkon's followers seconded the motion. The Lord Steward had no choice except to take a vote. Shinar was painstaking in his count, checking and rechecking the final tally. He had been certain that this motion would be defeated soundly on the first round because it was so utterly unprecedented, not to mention foolish as well as dangerous. Instead, the results were, effectively, a victory for Prince Seti.

With a heavy heart, the Lord Steward announced the tally: two hundred thirty members voted in support of the motion, the same number against. Forty members abstained.

The session could not adjourn with a motion undecided. Shinar was hoping a bit of persuasion and arm-twisting among the abstaining members might give Lord James the edge. He ordered a recess, after which there would ensue a second vote.

The members dispersed from the chamber. It threatened to be a long evening, with the Lord Protector hanging on to his power and most likely his life by the slimmest of threads.

# CHAPTER TWENTY-SEVEN

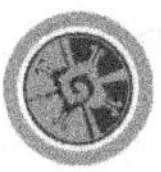

Signaling to Judith to come with her, Lady Naomi hurried out of the Visitors' Gallery. Correctly guessing that the Prince of Westar would lobby some of the abstaining lords who were economically dependent on the House of Atlas, she caught up with him as he walked the hallway outside the West Doors. The Consort slipped her arm under the prince's elbow. Judith tagged behind them at a discreet distance.

"Your heir is his advocate, my lord prince," the Consort said. "Your second son escorts his daughter. It's a suitable role for one who is distantly kin to her, and might even be closer one day."

She paused, still smiling, still matching his stride. "What shall I tell Kefren that you did personally to support James in his hour of need?"

Prince Enoch slowed his pace and glanced down at the Consort.

"May I make a suggestion, my lord prince?"

He quit moving and leaned his head toward her. She rose onto her toes to whisper into his ear. A dozen or so paces behind them, Judith knew by the way Prince Enoch had to stop himself from recoiling that the Consort must have said something to him that was truly outrageous.

●●●

Despite Lord Nimrod's urgent pleas, Lord James would not move from his seat in the inner chamber until he had made a quick voice link to his estate to arrange for his daughter's security. Lord Nimrod then dragged his client to the Lord Steward's private chambers, all but ordering Lord James not to leave until the session resumed.

Shinar arrived as Lord Nimrod was heading out the door on his own campaign to influence the next vote. The Lord Steward was glad to see Lord James, and wryly amused by the duke's frustration at his inability to influence the evening's events. Kindred House rules prevented Lord James from lobbying members on a motion that directly involved him.

Shinar pulled a bottle of pepper brandy out of his desk and found glasses on a bookshelf. He filled two and passed one to his guest. "Well, James, now you know how my job feels. I rarely get to vote and never can lobby anyone on anything."

Lord James nodded and pulled his link out of a pocket of his uniform jacket. "I need to check something, Jacob. Do you mind if I use your office for a minute?"

Shinar waved a hand. "Of course not."

Lord James walked into the office, sat on a chair in front of the Lord Steward's desk, opened his link, and was soon engrossed.

Lord Andrew entered the chamber and slumped onto a seat, his unusually dark-skinned face a study in aggravation. His expression changed to curiosity when he heard Lord James mutter an oath.

"What on earth are you doing, James?"

"My job as Lord Protector, while I still have it," the duke replied. "I just saw something that probably will keep me awake the rest of the night trying to sort out another screw-up."

He cut the link, grabbed his glass, and returned to the reception room.

Lord Andrew looked ill at ease as well as exasperated. "James, what will you do if the vote goes against you?"

He shrugged his shoulders. "Take my daughter, go home, and get my first night in decades of uninterrupted sleep."

"Do you really think Seti will leave you to sleep in peace if you are forced to surrender the Protectorship?"

"Jacob, do I look like someone who gives a damn what Seti thinks or does?"

Shinar located a third glass, filled it with pepper brandy, and handed it to Lord Andrew. "Allow me to congratulate you on an outstanding first speech. It was just what we needed, shall we say, to help elevate the tone of the discussion."

"I second that thought," Lord James agreed. Lord Andrew's eyes glazed over with wariness. The duke laughed. "Relax, Andrew. I'm following my advocate's orders not to say anything about certain issues to any member. You need not fear any arm twisting from this quarter, at least."

"Kronos, James. Too bad you waited until now to take your advocate's advice. Had you done so earlier, we might not be in this untenable position."

Shinar could not resist nodding in agreement.

Lord James became thoughtful. "Andrew, how long now until Lady Sarah delivers?"

"Three months or so."

"This will be your firstborn, will it not?"

"Yes."

He rose from his chair, poured another shot of pepper brandy into his glass, walked to the window, and stared out at the frozen winter landscape. "I don't know when this will happen to you, Andrew, once you are a father.

"But I promise you this. There will come a moment when you will look at your child, your firstborn, and realize there isn't anything you would not do, would not suffer, would not sacrifice, for that child's well-being."

Lord Andrew did not reply. Lord James heard Shinar clear his throat and turned to face the Lord Steward, eyes full of compassion and concern. "How is Matthew today?"

Shinar rubbed his forehead. "Surviving from injection to injection. The pain is completely unbearable without the medication."

Overcome by his own emotions, Shinar felt a hand grip the top of his shoulder, and looked up to find Lord James standing over him.

"Hang tight, Jacob. Helen spent most of the morning and afternoon researching possible treatments. If anyone can find a way to help Matthew, she can and she will. If she's anything, she's one single-minded medical warrior."

Shinar managed a small smile, his eyes glistening. "I wonder where she gets that from, James."

"Her mother, of course."

● ● ●

Sitting beside Helen in the gallery, Lord Justin could not help comparing her father's behavior toward her with his father's treatment of him. Lord James scarcely knew his child, yet was willing to risk everything for her. The duke so obviously loved her, even if Helen was too confused or scared or whatever to feel that love and return it. Lord Justin could hardly blame his kinswoman. Helen was so vulnerable, and did not yet know whom, if anyone, she could trust in the dangerous world she now inhabited.

In sharp contrast, his own father was willing to risk nothing on his behalf. Lord Justin started to understand at a deeper level why everything had changed so painfully when Uncle David died. Judith had often told him it had little to do with him, and never before had he believed her until last night. He always thought he had done or said something terribly wrong for his father to have so abruptly withdrawn his affection and approval.

Lord Justin still believed that part of the issue was his father's suspicions about his sexuality. He could now recognize, however, that his loss of his father's love and affection and the mistreatment he endured were caused primarily by the prince's fear of his enemies. Had Lord James feared his foes, he could have averted their wrath by selling Helen.

Lord Justin was filled with sadness, this time not for himself. His grief was for his father, whose weakness and lack of principles he finally was able to acknowledge. It was not the easiest thing for a son to admit, yet it was also freeing for him. He no longer regretted losing or felt compelled to fight to regain the regard or approval of a man without inner strength or honor.

A strange sense of peace along with profound sorrow settled into his heart; he also knew this was not something he could ever mention to his brother, who all but worshipped their father. Lord Nimrod would probably always regard the prince as the principled and honorable man he pretended to be to the world.

Having encountered genuine courage and principles in Lord James, however, Lord Justin was wise enough to perceive the difference, and honest enough to admit it. He wanted very much to get to know the Duke of Alta better, yet was extremely leery of appearing to insert himself into the friendship between his brother and the Duke of Alta. He sighed.

"Does something trouble you, my lord?"

Helen put her hand in his once again. He smiled at her, and asked her to call him by his first name when they were alone together. She agreed, provided he did the same for her.

Another thought popped into his head. "This is neither the time nor the place, but I'm going to ask anyway. What is going on between you and Nimrod? He doesn't usually snarl at beautiful women."

Helen reluctantly explained about their highly unusual first meeting over a bucket of cold water. She was on the verge of apologizing when, to her amazement, she realized Lord Justin was laughing.

"It's not funny, Justin."

"Yes. It is."

The more Lord Justin thought about it, the harder he laughed. Perhaps there was some justice in this world after all, and she was the angel sent to dispense it.

He stood up. "Let's get some fresh air while we still can."

Arm in arm, conscious of the many stares directed at them, they picked their way through the crowd in the main hallway outside the South Doors.

Orlando entered the foyer. He rapidly scanned the room, spotted Helen, and moved to her, obeying the Lord Protector's explicit orders. Clad in the black and silver uniform of the Generals Council, his usually deep copper skin was pallid and he seemed to struggle to move and stand.

"What are you doing out of bed, Colonel?" Helen hissed at him. "You are still ill. You have no business here."

Orlando nodded at Lord Justin. "I'm here on the Lord Protector's business, Lieutenant. You've been overruled."

Helen fumed. The Consort and Judith caught up with them and Lord Tarkon reappeared, accompanied by several of Prince Seti's other supporters. He bowed to the Consort, who, offended by his language earlier that evening, nodded curtly in his direction.

Helen turned her head away from him, refusing to acknowledge him.

Lord Tarkon came up behind Helen, speaking loudly over her shoulder. "Those who attend you seem somewhat lacking in manners these days, Lady Consort."

The conversations died away; everyone turned to watch the confrontation. By this time, Prince Seti was at one end of the foyer, while Prince Enoch, Lord James, Lord Nimrod, Shinar, and Lord Andrew had arrived at the other.

Unaware of her father's presence, Helen pivoted on her heel to face Lord Tarkon. "You would not recognize manners, Lord Eden, if you tripped over them."

"How dare you!"

Lord Tarkon swung the back of his hand hard across her face. Helen withstood the force of the blow and, while the duke was off his guard, returned the favor. Her fist slammed an uppercut into the side of his jaw; caught off guard, he fell to the floor.

Lord Justin pulled her aside. Orlando put himself between Helen and the Duke of Eden, who refused the colonel's offer of help in getting to his feet and was preparing to strike her again. Lord James hurried through the onlookers and stood beside the colonel.

The two together prompted the duke to reconsider; he backed away and left. Lord James knew there would be no calls for Helen to be punished when he saw heads nodding and heard murmurs of approval from many of the witnesses.

The Consort led her party back to the Visitors' Gallery, with Orlando bringing up the rear. His orders were to stand guard over Helen, just inside the gallery entrance. His arm remaining about her shoulders, helping her up the steps, Lord Justin offered Helen a handkerchief. She pressed it to the gash on her lower lip.

"How symmetrical, my lord," she said, eyes directed at the cut on his upper lip. "Now we have something else in common."

"First a bucket of cold water, now a fist," he teased her. "Remind me never to get on your bad side, kinswoman."

# CHAPTER TWENTY-EIGHT

Upon reconvening the *Kinshazen*, the Lord Steward called for another vote on the motion to remove Lord James from his office as Lord Protector. The results were the same as the first round, compelling Shinar to open the floor to further debate.

Assuming the attack-dog role previously filled by Lord Tarkon, the Lord Chancellor sought permission to speak. In far more restrained language than the Duke of Eden had used, Griffin repeated Prince Seti's contention that the Protectorship was not a hereditary position, and could be withheld or reassigned at the Exalted Lord's pleasure.

"Where's the Exalted Lord, Lord Chancellor?"

The question came from Lord Nimrod, who was leaning back in his bench, legs in front of him, arms folded across his chest, eyes shut.

"Are you crippled, Lord Avalon, or do you merely have trouble thinking on your feet?"

"Sometimes it's difficult to stand under the weight of all I know, Lord Chancellor."

Laughter rang out; Lord Nimrod jumped upright. "I ask again. Where is the Exalted Lord?"

He glanced around the chamber. "We have heard people all evening putting words into the Exalted Lord's mouth and making assumptions about what pleases or displeases our gracious sovereign," he continued. "Until he himself tells me or indicates otherwise, I will vote based on what I have heard him actually say. He is well pleased with this Lord Protector."

Lord Nimrod sat down. Lord James leaned toward his friend. "I hope no one holds you strictly accountable for every one of those words of kingly praise, Nim."

Lord Andrew stood. "I hate to throw the cold water of practicality over this lofty theoretical discussion, my lords.

"One question is nagging at me. If we insist the Lord Protector relinquish his office, who among us would be able to take his place? We know our enemies are re-arming. We have heard reports of new threats further to the East. Is it prudent or wise to leave the defense of this realm so vulnerable by, in effect, depriving us of our most seasoned and experienced military commander? Frankly, that prospect scares me and I hope it does all of you."

The members talked quietly while Lord Andrew sat down.

Impatient with the pace of the debate, the Consort directed her focus at Prince Enoch, subtly at first.

Sensing an opportunity to make more points, Prince Seti rose.

"Lord Andrew has a valid concern, my lords. And if my long-standing proposal to fortify our position in Kamut had been approved and implemented, we could act as we choose on this motion and not be vulnerable."

"Nonsense, my lords," Lord James interjected.

"This motion pertains to you, my lord. You may not speak," Prince Seti countered.

"I speak not to tonight's motion, but then, neither do you, my lord prince," Lord James replied. "I speak to your earlier motion. We would already be at war with the Nubians and possibly many others if we were so foolish as to fortify our presence in Kamut beyond its current level."

"You do not know that for certain, my lord," Prince Seti said.

"Yes, I do, my lord prince," Lord James said. "Arming Kamut any further is tantamount to declaring war, and our enemies will respond in kind. My long experience on the battlefield has taught me that much, if nothing more."

Shinar pounded the gavel. Lord James sat down in disgust, while Prince Seti remained standing.

"Be that as it may, my lords, we can still require this Lord Protector to step down for a time and fill the post. There is, after all, another of the House of Mordecai on the floor of this chamber."

Helen needed every ounce of her self-possession not to gasp as she saw all eyes turn toward the Lord Chancellor, who bowed briefly to Prince Seti. Until that point Helen did not know about her kinship to Griffin. The tips of her fingers covering her mouth, she drew in her breath sharply; the pit of her stomach sagged.

"Are you ill, Cousin?" Lord Justin whispered.

She was unable to reply. Judith covered her hand and pressed it, sensing that Helen at last was beginning to understand the danger that losing her anonymity posed.

"I'm confused, my lord prince," Lord Nimrod said. "First, you contend that the Protectorship is not hereditary. Then you suggest we bestow the post on Griffin Mordecai, whose military expertise must be vast indeed because it's way beyond my comprehension."

Nervous, hushed sounds of amusement circulated throughout the floor. Griffin had no military experience, yet none of the lords had dared bring up the point.

Lord Nimrod was going for the throat. "Besides, should the Lord Chancellor assume the additional heavy burden of the Protectorship? When would he have time to sleep, or eat?"

Griffin arose and bowed again. "Lord Avalon's tender concern for my well-being is touching, my lords. But we must all make sacrifices when the welfare of this realm is at stake."

The Consort continued to stare at Prince Enoch. When she finally had his attention, she raised an eyebrow ever so slightly. The Prince of Westar finally stood up and sought recognition. All noise died away instantly. Most of the members could not even recall the last time this prince had addressed the *Kinshazen.*

Prince Enoch inclined his head in Lord James' direction and paused, making direct eye contact with many of the members. "The security and welfare of this realm, my lords, is best left in the hands of one who has proven his ability to defend it with an unbroken record of victories.

"I have given those victories and Lord James' many years of devoted service a good deal of thought under the present circumstances," the prince continued. "Far from asking him to relinquish his position, I intend to seek a binding contract with the Lord Protector for the marriage of his daughter, Mistress Helen Andros, to my son Lord Justin Atlas."

He might as well have lit the fuse on a bomb. Kindred House members sat unmoving, their mouths agape. All at once, the chamber exploded, the peers arguing among themselves the merits or faults of the proposed union. Most of them thought it a suitable match, given that both parties were mixed race. Some had reservations about wedding a bastard female to any lord of Royal blood. Others did not at all care for the thought of half-blood couples marrying and reproducing.

As astonished as almost everyone else in the chamber, Lord James was torn. He had only just found his daughter and was not at all ready to send her away to live with any man; he scarcely knew her himself. Glancing up at the Visitors' Gallery, Lord James noticed the Consort's expression. She was behind Prince Enoch's announcement.

He leaned toward his advocate. "Never a dull moment, Nim."

Lord Nimrod nodded, his own shock giving way to jealousy at the thought of his younger brother bedding the most beautiful girl in Azgard.

Judith was alarmed. Clearly the Consort somehow forced Prince Enoch to this gesture, and Judith knew that Helen and Lord Justin would pay for the prince's displeasure.

Helen was simply numb. Too many conflicting emotions were stirring within her to make sense of much of anything. She could only hope that the marriage negotiations would take a long time.

Lord Justin brushed her shoulder. "We have to talk later."

"This is an outrage, my lords," Prince Seti called out.

The members regarded each other nervously, fearing the rogue waves of animosity between the two princes would swamp them all.

His muscles taut and movements awkward, the Prince of Istar blasted the Prince of Westar with a hostile glare. "How dare you presume to propose marriage for anyone of Royal blood without seeking permission first."

Prince Enoch looked unfazed. "I am lord of the House of Atlas, my lord prince. I will dispose of my own children in marriage as I see fit. Unless I hear the Exalted Lord's objection to this marriage contract, I will proceed with it."

Prince Enoch decided to raise the stakes. "In fact, while this contract is in the making, my lords, I invite Mistress Andros to wait upon Lady Mary Atlas."

Helen's heart beat fast. Glancing to her side, she saw the Consort smile regally while motioning furtively to her to stand. She obeyed, dreading to be once more the center of attention.

"Curtsey and lower your head, girl." The Consort managed to instruct her without appearing to move her lips. Helen was relieved when the Consort told her to be seated. Close to overwhelmed, she wished fervently for an end to the proceedings.

As though others reached the same conclusion, scattered calls for a third vote began to ring out. The chorus grew steadily louder. The Lord Steward acknowledged the cries, and asked for additional comment. When there was none, he painstakingly counted another vote. The numbers were the same: two hundred thirty for the motion, two hundred thirty against, forty abstaining. Although many lords groaned in frustration, for the first time that evening, Shinar felt cheerful.

He swung the gavel down once again. "My lords, since this House has taken three rounds of votes and is unable to reach a decision on this motion, I invoke my right as Lord Steward to break the deadlock."

The members didn't move. With the news of Lord Matthew's condition not widely known, many were uncertain as to how the Lord Steward would vote. Shinar could not resist turning to look at Prince Seti before he spoke.

"This motion is defeated, my lords, and the session adjourned."

● ● ●

Helen said nothing during the departure from Kindred House. She was in a skimmer heading across the lake toward the Mordecai estate when suddenly she laughed.

Sitting next to his kinswoman, Lord Justin raised an eyebrow.

"Do you suppose my match-making Aunt Martha knew something we didn't?"

# CHAPTER TWENTY-NINE

During a late supper at the Mordecai manor after the end of the *Kinshazen* session, Helen sat across from Lord Nimrod, separated from her father by Lady Naomi. She nibbled at her food, unhappy that Lord James appeared to have ignored Orlando's illness in summoning him to duty during the session. *He damn near died on your behalf, Lord Protector. Does that mean nothing to you?*

At the end of the meal, the Consort delayed leaving the table. Prince Enoch, impatient to review the evening's political events with the men, resorted to prodding her into action by signaling to Lord Justin to pour a round of pepper brandy. Lord Andrew, the next youngest and lowest ranking male, located a silver box of *sigras* on the sideboard and offered it to each of the men.

The Consort finally nodded to Helen and Judith to retire to the drawing room. As they were leaving the table, Lord Justin served the dark golden liquor first to Lord James as host and master of the house, then filled a glass and set it before his father.

Prince Enoch clamped his hand around his second son's wrist and squeezed to the point of discomfort. His dark eyes searched Lord

Justin's face carefully for any signs of defiance. "When you are done, go sit where you belong, with the women."

Lord Justin inclined his head and pulled his wrist out of his father's grip. Engrossed in a joke Lord Nimrod was relating, Shinar and Lord Andrew paid no attention. The Consort, Judith, and Helen heard the prince, however, and so did Lord James.

Walking behind Helen, Judith saw her stop and start to turn around. She closed the gap between them, took Helen's elbow, and dragged the girl out the door and into the drawing room. Indignant and frustrated, Helen pulled away from her and slumped onto a sofa across from the Consort. "You heard what he said."

"There's nothing any of us can do about it except make it worse if we intervene," Judith replied. "Trust that I speak from experience in this, or you, and Lord Justin, both will regret it."

Judith accepted a cup of *kaf* from a servant, and sat down next to Helen. The Consort regarded them, her bejeweled fingers wrapped around another cup of the fragrant spiced liquid.

"It does seem somewhat odd," she offered, lapsing into a frustrated silence of her own. She scarcely noticed Lord Justin enter the drawing room and bow to her.

He sat next to Helen and put his arm around her shoulders, drew her close to him and kissed her on the forehead. Too full of emotions to say anything, she closed her eyes and rested her head against his shoulder.

"I don't care if we are intended for each other, I claim a cousin's right of familiarity and companionship," he teased her.

An especially loud wave of laughter erupted from the room where the men were discussing the evening's events. Lady Naomi stood up and asked Judith to go with her. Helen and Lord Justin stared first at them and then at each other as the two departed. Not long afterward the merriment faded away.

Realizing they could be alone for some time, Lord Justin dismissed the servant and closed the door after him. "There are a few things you should know about me, Helen, before any contract is signed. Not one of them is good."

He ran his fingers through his hair and walked around the room. "I guess I'll start with money. I haven't got any. I have a title and even a Royal family name, but any woman bound to me will be sorely disappointed if she expects luxury and ease."

"Surely your mother has some sort of dowry," Helen said. "Even if he was a Turanian, Ethan Andros was a man of substance."

"She does. The prince forbids me access to it," Lord Justin said.

"But it is yours by right, by law. You are of age. How can he do that?" Helen protested.

"The prince can do as he pleases within Westar Province."

Lord Justin sat next to her and took her hands in his. "Which brings me to my second point. My relationship with my father is undoubtedly the cause of my money problems."

Lord Justin explained the situation as he now realized his father perceived it. The prince thought he could manage to appease the enemies of Westar while not alienating the province's numerous Turanian subjects.

"So that justifies treating you like dirt?"

"Only in front of important Toltecs. I don't really understand or like it. All I know is that my wife most likely will share in my estrangement from a very powerful lord."

Helen was so incensed she arose and stalked about the room. "If you're trying to discourage me or put me off, you have not succeeded."

"You have not yet heard my third point."

Having no idea how to put what he wanted to say into words, Lord Justin sat, staring. He looked so miserable and uncomfortable that Helen took pity on him.

She sat beside him and put her hand on top of his. "I think I know your third point already. You do not find me physically attractive. You do not find any woman attractive in that way. You are drawn to men instead." *And I bet I can even tell you which man.*

"You must despise me. Is it that obvious?"

"I most certainly do not. And no, not at all. Not without a reason for looking closely. I have done so over the past couple of days to try to get to know you better."

She caressed the side of his face. He did not bother to hide his tears. "The man I've come to know I very much respect and admire for his honesty, his courage, his gentleness, and his kindness. These are the wealth I value."

"Enough to be bound for life to that man? I cannot be with you as a lover, Helen."

She pulled a handkerchief out of a pocket and wiped his chin. "I know that."

He closed his hand over hers. "You must believe me when I tell you that if I could be with a woman in such a manner, I would choose you freely over any other. I understand completely now why Matthew always spoke more highly of you than anyone else."

Helen's smile dimmed; she did not know what to feel or to say in return.

He mistook her silence. "I tell you this so that you may inform your father and put a quick end to the contract negotiations. I will not be a party to such a travesty."

She shook her head. "Travesty? The only travesty I perceive is the possibility of what might happen to you if anyone such as your father were to find out. And I won't be a party to that."

"My father will find out anyway, if he doesn't already know. I should warn you as well about the Atlas intelligence network. It's probably as good as your father's, and you will now be spied on as well, if you have not been already, given your kinship to my mother.

"You deserve so much better than I can ever hope to offer you," he added.

"Better? I was born in a brothel, if you recall."

"We all have to be born somewhere."

Helen kneeled next to him. "Listen to me, Justin. I once never dared hope for any legitimate offer of marriage, and without marriage I refuse to consider children. I know only too well what it's like to be a bastard, and I won't do that to any child. Yet I want babies so much I can almost taste it."

The bewilderment on his face made his question plain. She took his hands into hers. "Remember my training. It's more than possible to impregnate me with your sperm without sexual relations. That will be the least of our concerns."

Lord Justin frowned, as though he tasted something bitter. "There's something not quite fair about that, somehow."

She shrugged her shoulders. "If we agree to it, it's no one else's business."

He thought for a while. "I can agree to it, provided you take a lover, Helen. Father of Kronos knows that's what I hope to do."

She could not respond right away. She suspected by the way her heart seemed to sink as he spoke that she might not find it possible to break her marriage vows, even as she also realized she would not hold him to his, especially since she was now certain who that lover would be. She did not think this the best time to bring up his relationship with Lord Matthew, however. That could wait for another day.

"Without a contract, this is all pure speculation. If we do marry, I ask only one thing of you as a husband, Justin. I beg you to allow me to continue my work as a healer. I trained so long and so hard to do it, and my idleness now is driving me to distraction."

He laughed and pulled her onto the sofa beside him. "Allow you? Woman, didn't you hear what I said about money? One of us has to earn a living, and there's not much market demand for math theoreticians."

"But surely the Academy would hire you as a mathematics professor in a heartbeat. Chairman of the entire mathematics department more likely."

Lord Justin sighed. "My father forbids it. He does not want me to have an independent income and thus be less easy to control."

❀ ❀ ❀

Lord James paid little heed to the others while they rehashed the twists and turns of the evening's session at Kindred House. Adept at mimicry, Lord Nimrod entertained the group with his cruelly accurate caricatures of their opponents. He had kept them laughing while disposing of Lord Tarkon and Griffin, and was portraying Prince Seti in a fit of inarticulate rage when the door to the room opened and the Consort entered, Judith behind her. Her arms folded, she stood next to the wall until each man noticed her and fell silent.

Prince Enoch frowned. "Aren't you in the wrong room, Naomi? This is no place for a woman. We are having a serious discussion here."

The Consort circled the table. "Indeed, Enoch. We can hear just how serious all the way down the hall."

"You can hardly blame us for celebrating our winning strategy," the prince countered.

"*Our* winning strategy?"

Lord James had the grace to be embarrassed. He caught the Consort's hand as she walked by his chair, stood up, lifted her off her feet in an expansive embrace, and kissed her on the forehead.

She straightened her skirts and composed herself when he set her back on her feet.

"Smooth your ruffled feathers, Lady Consort," Lord James said, eyes glinting with mischief and affection. "In all fairness, I have to admit it. You're the one who out-foxed Seti tonight."

Shinar and Lord Andrew nodded in agreement; Lord Nimrod avoided any response.

"Then you at least of this company admit you owe me one, Lord Protector?"

"Yes, Lady Consort, I do," Lord James replied without thinking, returning to his chair.

She stepped up behind him, put her hands on his shoulders. "Then I am more than satisfied, my lords."

She leaned down, put her mouth next to Lord James' ear, and spoke for his benefit alone. "I'll keep that in mind."

He swallowed hard, almost choking on his pepper brandy. Lord James realized he had just promised something to her and suspected he would not at all like it when she finally chose to tell him what it was.

# CHAPTER THIRTY

Before sunrise the next morning, Helen went to the kitchen to prepare an herbal treatment for Orlando. She was still incensed over what she thought were the orders that brought him to Kindred House the prior evening. She also prepared a pot of *kaf* and brought two mugs along with the tincture and her medical bag to the colonel's bedchamber.

Orlando shook his head when she entered, recalling that she was now a subject of a pending marriage contract. He tried to suppress another round of the coughing that had kept him awake a good deal of the night. "What are you doing here, Lieutenant? This is not proper."

Helen set the tray and medical bag down on the table next to the bed and measured several droppers of the blend into a glass of water.

"Good morning to you, too, Colonel," she replied. "You certainly know how to make a girl feel welcome."

She held out the glass and pointed to the mugs on the tray. "How about a deal? Drink this; then you can have some *kaf*. I made it myself."

He closed his eyes wearily, nodded, and swallowed the foul-tasting contents of the glass in one gulp.

She did make outstanding *kaf*. The taste reminded Orlando of the many times he had watched Helen at work. There seemed to be a sacred light around her and her patients. The only other place or time he had ever felt so close to the presence of the Divine was when he stood at the crest of the treeless, cloud-shrouded mountain peaks that surrounded his father's farm in Southern Alta Province. She had a gift like none other he had ever seen, not even his own mother, who was well known among the hill folk for her exceptional skills as a healer.

Helen took the empty glass out of his hand. "Jackson, are you all right? After all you've endured, I would hate to have you scald yourself with a hot mug of *kaf*."

He opened his eyes. "A deal's a deal, Lieutenant. I drank your damn potion and probably won't live to regret it. Where's my *kaf*?"

He hoped he sounded stern and intimidating, not that he had ever made much of an impression on her.

She laughed and handed him one of the mugs. "Spoken like a true addict."

Her brew was as smooth as ever. He was savoring the taste until he remembered that he had not even the dimmest prospect of her now.

Oblivious to Orlando's deep feelings for her and ignoring her own for him, Helen pulled her medical instruments out of the bag and took hold of his wrist to check his pulse.

He coughed again. "Lieutenant, this is unseemly."

She continued to count out his heartbeat. "Relax, Colonel. Your virtue, or what's left of it, is perfectly safe with me."

His eyes widened. She laughed and hooked the earpieces of her scope around her neck. She wanted to listen to the sound of his lungs as well as his heart. At least his cough was productive, which indicated that the fluid was draining.

"Your men have thoroughly apprised me of your, shall we put this delicately, exploits. Yes, Colonel, I've heard all about your 'saber' and how it has cut a wide swath among the ladies of the evening. I think they were trying to see if they could shock me. Didn't work."

Acutely uncomfortable, he leaned back against the pillows and made no further objection. She placed the head of the scope against his chest. His heart beat strong and regular once more; his lungs were clearer and the welts she could see peering down his back under his nightshirt were healing.

"You're on the mend, Colonel, but not as far along as I'd like," she added. "Stop trying to suppress your cough. You need to clear your lungs completely. You're still not getting enough oxygen with each breath, which was why you were so exhausted and disoriented after last night's tour of duty, and probably are still a bit that way this morning.

"And if you keep getting ordered out of your sickbed, it will take you just that much longer to recover."

He understood and caught her wrist in his hand. "He did not order me specifically to Kindred House last night, Lieutenant, if that's what you think."

The colonel did not have to explain who 'he' was. They both knew.

"Look at me, Lieutenant."

She met his eyes. "Your safety was in great jeopardy. He ordered me to find someone trustworthy to stand guard over you. I chose myself in part to save time, and also because I owe you for saving my life. Thank you."

"You owe me no thanks for doing my job, Colonel."

When she spoke in that soft way, there was little in this world he would not give to her, do for her, concede in her favor. He was toughened in battle and from long years of consuming, thankless military service, yet she conquered him every time with gentleness.

Orlando realized he still held her wrist, and that she made no move to free herself. He let go of her. She would never be his to hold, to keep, to cherish, or to protect. Somewhere deep within him, a part of his heart wept in desolation. He lay back on the pillows, turned away from her, and covered his face with a hand, not wanting her to see him struggle with his emotions.

Freed from his grasp, Helen packed her medical bag. She refilled the carafe with water, set it and the bottle of blended tincture on the table by the bed.

"Three full droppers in a glass of water, three times a day. Think you can handle those orders, Colonel?"

"What are you doing here, Lieutenant?"

Lord James stood just inside the door. Orlando sat up much too quickly and felt like his head was spinning.

"My duty as a medical officer, Lord Protector," Helen replied. "One of *your* aides was severely wounded in the line of duty, if you recall."

Orlando swallowed hard. She was already in trouble for her previous insubordination and here she was doing it all over again. Did she truly have no idea or did she simply not care?

Helen curtseyed to Lord James, slung the medical bag over her shoulder, and headed out of the room.

"You will join Judith and me for break-fast in half an hour, Lieutenant," he said.

"I don't usually eat that meal, Lord Protector."

"You do in this household, Lieutenant."

She registered her anger in the loud stomp of her boots on the tiled floor in the hallway. The Lord Protector was not pleased when he noticed her wearing them. He would deal with that later.

Turning to the most pressing matter, he looked at Orlando, who was coughing hard after trying to get to his feet and collapsing back onto the bed.

"At ease, Colonel," Lord James said, pulling a chair next to the bed and sitting down on it. "What am I going to do about you, Jackson?"

"My lord?"

"You present me with an unhappy dilemma."

The colonel did not understand his Supreme Commander.

"I should discipline you for covering up the lieutenant's service record. It's a damned disgrace. She joined exactly one year ago, and she's been on report fifty times. That's almost once a week. I cannot condone such a dismal performance from any soldier, much less my own daughter."

Orlando felt wretched. "My lord, I know I should have disciplined her and then revoked her commission months ago. But she's damn good at what she does, and the enlisted men and their families had gone without medical care for too long. I could not bring myself to deprive them again. I tried to keep it quiet."

The argument only made Lord James suspicious. "What exactly is the nature of your relationship with Helen?"

Orlando went on full alert. "She is the medical officer for the 163$^{rd}$ Regiment, my lord. I am her commanding officer. Other than that, there has been no relationship."

"Let me rephrase the question. Are you in love with Helen? Yes or no."

Orlando rubbed the back of his neck and fidgeted. He took a deep breath and stared at the ceiling. He closed his eyes and tapped his fingers on the coverlet.

"Well?"

"Yes, my lord. I am."

"That only makes my dilemma even worse."

Orlando looked over at him. "Even worse, my lord?"

"Yes. I should discipline you severely for allowing your personal feelings to get in the way of your duty as a senior officer. You know better. I'm disappointed in your performance in this matter."

Orlando gulped. He knew months ago he was taking a big risk over the lieutenant.

Lord James folded his arms across his chest. "But I cannot bring myself to do it. You have already suffered for your role in a crime that never existed. I am inclined to consider that sufficient punishment, and allow the matter to drop."

"I don't know what to say, my lord."

"I do."

Lord James leaned closer to the bed, covered Orlando's hand as it lay on the coverlet with his own.

Orlando's eyes widened; he dared not respond in kind.

"Son," Lord James said, "I am fully aware of just how much I owe you, the hell you went through on my behalf. Your strength, determination, and just plain grit have spared me a great deal of additional trouble and embarrassment. Thank you."

"You owe me no thanks for doing my job, my lord."

"Yes, I do. And a mere 'thank you' is hardly adequate in this case."

A thought occurred to Lord James. "Why did you never act on your feelings for my daughter?"

"I ordered the entire regiment, on threat of severe punishment, to leave Lieutenant Andros in peace to do her job. She was not to be pestered, annoyed, or harassed in any manner or the offender would answer to me personally. How could I then do what I had forbidden to my men?"

His reassuring answer helped Lord James make a tough decision. "Jackson, I am offering you a position in my household as Helen's bodyguard. To be frank, it will remove you from active consideration for promotion. You have the right to refuse this offer without prejudice. Given the nature of your feelings for Helen, you may wish to do so."

Orlando accepted without hesitation. His career was not his priority anymore. She was, and with this job she would be his, at least to protect, at least for a time. That was all he really cared about.

● ● ●

The Lord Protector walked to the sunroom, thinking about his daughter. He placed Helen on inactive duty status as of early that morning and ordered Orlando to say nothing about it to her. Lord James was in no frame of mind to deal with her anger over it just now. He was tempted to revoke her commission entirely, except such action would deprive him of the only leverage he seemed to have over her. For whatever reasons, she refused to acknowledge him as her father or yield to his authority. She could not ignore him as her Supreme Commander. So be it. That was how he would deal with her for the time being.

Putting Helen on inactive duty also bought Lord James a bit more breathing room to decide about her service record. His heart quailed at the prospect of subjecting her to the humiliation of a full military discipline, which was nothing short of torture and would scar her body.

Yet he already knew it would come to that. She did not seem willing to give him any other choice. In that regard she was just like her mother.

And when the time arrived, he already knew that he would be the one to put the whip to her; he could not allow any other man to do it.

*Why? Why does my daughter have to be a stubborn, willful, pig-headed girl hell-bent on self-destruction?*

* * *

Helen stared at the plate before her, reluctantly sampling the food. She was seated across from Judith, her father to her side. The rising morning sun flooded the room with warmth and light. All Helen could feel in her heart was winter's chill.

She paid scant attention while Lord James outlined her first encounter with Lord Nimrod to Judith. Lord James had finally learned about it the night before, when he asked Lord Nimrod to explain his hostility toward Helen.

"Decking my enemies and dunking my friends," he said. "Striking a fellow officer, bringing him back from death, and performing emergency surgery on the Exalted Lord's nephew. All that, Helen, and we've known each other for less than three days. Any more surprises up your sleeves?"

"If I told you, Lord Protector, it would scarcely be a surprise."

"Let me put it to you this way," Lord James tried again. "Do you do anything at all womanly?"

"You've already had that examined and certified, Lord Protector," Helen replied. "The answer is no, or at least, not yet. I thought perhaps one member of the family might wait until marriage."

He slammed his cup down on the table; Helen flinched. She sat with shoulders squared, eyes forward, chin defiant.

"I've had just about enough of your lip, Lieutenant."

He was barely able to contain his own anger and pain. "I have another crucial decision to make, and I want truthful answers from you, not insolence or defiance. Think you can handle that for a few minutes?"

"Yes, Lord Protector."

Lord James walked to the window, glanced out at the lake. "Speaking of marriage, do you have any objections to Lord Justin as a husband?"

Helen thought back to her conversation with her kinsman the previous night. She understood fully that Lord Justin had handed her information she could now use to destroy him.

"I had no idea that my opinions about anything mattered, Lord Protector." Helen was stalling; Judith could sense her mixed feelings.

"I'm not quite the unfeeling tyrant you must think me, Helen," he said.

*Amen to that*, Judith agreed.

"I will not bind you in this or any marriage if you have objections. Do you? Yes or no."

She took a deep breath. "No, Lord Protector. I have no objections."

"Very well."

Lord James checked the time; he was late for the first of an endless day of interminable staff meetings. As he left the sunroom, he caught Judith's eye; she nodded at him.

At the door he paused. "One more thing, Lieutenant. Do not ever again wear your boots with anything but your uniform. It's not regulation and I won't have it. If you need shoes, ask for them."

Helen bristled. "I am accustomed to earning my way, Lord Protector, not sitting idle with my hand out."

"Things are different for you now. Get accustomed to that."

● ● ●

Judith gave Helen some space by vacating her chair, moving to the window, and turning away from her. At first Helen sat still and silent, tears streaming down her face.

Thump. Judith looked back toward the table. One of Helen's boots was on the carpet, and she was pulling off the other one. After she dropped it as well, she burst into violent sobbing, face in hands, elbows on the edge of the table. A serving girl who entered the sunroom took one look at Helen and swiveled on her feet, closing the door behind her.

Judith slipped into the chair next to Helen. She sent her heart energy to the girl, trying to comfort her, also to assess her emotional state. Helen's wails of anguish were genuine and deeply felt; her sorrow greatly distressed Judith.

Gradually Helen's sobs diminished. She sat up and drew in several ragged breaths. She removed a handkerchief from a skirt pocket and wiped her face.

"Why didn't he just leave me on that platform?"

"After the crack you made a few minutes ago, I'm sure he's wondering that himself."

Helen flinched once more. "I didn't mean it, Judith. I don't want to hurt him. I'm just so confused and so terribly angry. I don't know where all this rage is coming from. It frightens me. I just can't seem to stop it."

She wept anew. Judith stroked her head and offered a quick prayer for insight. Then, perceiving the rare opportunity in Helen's wide-open energy field, she sent more of her own love straight into Helen's heart. She had to know what was transpiring at the deeper levels of the girl's being.

Always sensitive to energy, Helen felt Judith's gentle invasion, raised her head and turned toward her, eyes glistening with pain and puzzlement.

Judith smiled sadly at her. "I'm just trying to find answers to your questions, dear."

Insights flowed instantly back to Judith and took shape in her conscious awareness. "You've been angry for a long time, Helen, angry at least since I met you when you were a little girl. Probably long before that."

Helen was now standing at the window and staring at the frozen lake. It would be glorious simply to ice skate away to freedom.

Judith went on. "You have always been terribly angry with the father who you believed had abandoned you and your mother, haven't you?"

Helen gasped; Judith knew she was on track. "Your confusion now comes from your mother's letter, which makes it plain he was not the one who did the abandoning."

Helen whimpered, crossing her arms over her stomach in a defensive posture.

Judith stood by Helen's side, reached up to put a hand about the girl's shoulder. "You have a right to be angry. Things are very different for you now and yes, you have lost your freedom. Forever, I'm afraid."

Helen shook her head. "Reading my mind. That is so disconcerting." She leaned down and kissed Judith on the forehead.

"I'll take that as a compliment," Judith replied, giving Helen a quick squeeze about the waist. "And I'll leave you with a couple of things I want you to think over very carefully in the next few days."

Helen regarded her expectantly.

"First, the anger you direct at your father is, perhaps, misplaced."

Judith considered the situation. She did not believe that Helen was truly angry with her father; he was simply the only target available. Instead, the real focus of Helen's fury was surely the mother who had robbed her of her father.

She continued. "You have no idea of the consideration he showed you just now in bothering to consult you before undertaking to bind you in a marriage. That is almost unheard-of from a lord of a Great House."

Helen exhaled sharply. Maybe Judith's perspective was valid, but it hurt too much to consider — at least for now. "And second?"

"If he had left you on that platform, Colonel Orlando would now be dead, and Lord Matthew would have no hope of anything except probably a very brief life of unbearable pain."

Judith released Helen's shoulder and faced her. "Stop demeaning yourself, young woman. It's very tiresome and not true. You and your life have far greater value and meaning than you yet realize. Your mother saw it, I can see it very clearly, and so can others. You are worth loving and are loved deeply by many of us, even if you cannot yet feel it or admit it."

Helen stood a long time in front of the window after Judith left the room. She had a great deal to think over, and of all she had experienced that morning, Judith's final words were the most unnerving to her.

# CHAPTER THIRTY-ONE

Lord Matthew lay prone, his hair sprawling in stark contrast to the pale silk pillowcase. Helen held his hand in hers, watching the medical technicians. They were nearly finished with their task of removing additional patches of his skin from his calves and lower thighs. Almost a month had passed since Lord Matthew's discipline; the time for the grafts was drawing near. The procedure would take place at the small hospital inside the palace. A medical team from the Academy led by Sudras was making final preparations.

"You would think they all have pared or peeled enough flesh from my hide."

"We're going to return it to you this time, my lord, in far better condition than you gave it to us," Helen said, letting go of his hand.

Having completed their task, the technicians bowed to Lord Matthew and departed.

Before allowing Helen to close the door, Orlando walked through the bedchamber and adjoining rooms, to make sure no one else was present and that all doors and windows were secure. Once the door was shut, the colonel stood next to it on the landing, to hear any disturbance in the bedchamber.

Helen pulled a chair next to the bed and sat on it. She again took her dear friend's hand in hers. "Matthew, what on earth did you say to Prince Seti? Did you by any chance mention anything about the samples I asked you to analyze?"

"I would never say anything about that. Ever," he insisted. "I was insolent and have paid for my folly."

"Why would your uncle try to kill you for rudeness?"

"He has a very short temper."

That was true enough. Lord Matthew dared not discuss his suspicions about the sinister nature of the relationship between his uncle and his cousin, Lady Samantha Poseidon, the prince's daughter.

Tears of guilt and exasperation moistened Helen's eyes. *This is getting tiresome. All I ever seem to do these days is cry.*

He lifted his hand out of hers and with his finger wiped a lone tear that spilled down her cheek. "I'm so sorry. Please forgive me." Helen covered her face with her hands.

"Why do you insist on blaming yourself, Helen?"

"You would not be in this wretched condition but for our friendship and your kindness toward me," she said.

Lord Matthew swallowed hard. "Kindness? Is that what you call it? I used you, Helen."

She wiped her eyes on a handkerchief. He licked his lips. She reached over to the table beside the bed, poured him a glass of ice water from a glass carafe, held it for him so he could drink it.

"That was a nice delaying tactic. Thank you," he teased her in return.

He became serious again. "I pursued you to hide my real self from everyone. From my parents, my teachers, the rest of my family, and most especially from myself."

Helen's suspicions were confirmed. "Hide what, dearest Matthew? What is your 'real self,' as you put it?"

This time tears slid down his face. Too fearful of her judgment to explain further, he could not force any words out of his mouth.

As with Lord Justin, Helen decided to help him. "You think your real self is defined solely by your sexual desire for men, don't you?"

His wide-eyed expression was so endearing that she might have laughed except she had no desire to wound him further.

"How long have you known?"

"It depends on how you define 'known'," she answered. "You were about the only student who paid attention to me and didn't make any attempt whatsoever to get me into bed."

"I told myself it was because I respected you."

"I should hope so."

She rumpled his hair. "You never felt like a lover to me, dearest Matthew. At first it grieved me deeply that I could not return any of the desire you seemed to feel for me. I was so ashamed. How could I not desire such a sweet, decent, honorable man? That's the real Matthew I've always known."

The love and acceptance behind her words were too hard for him to bear. "How can you call me decent and honorable? I'm despicable, perverted. A *kudik*."

Helen snapped upright, jerking back from the bed as though he had punched her. "Stop that! How dare you? I won't have anyone say something like that about my best and dearest friend. Not now, not ever. Got that through your vacant, fuzzy head?"

He smiled through his tears. "Well, woman, what's it to be? A bucket of cold water or a fist? Your avenging angel reputation precedes you."

That silenced her. Her expression turned much too sweet for Lord Matthew's liking. He knew what it signified.

"None of the above," Helen said. "It will be my surprise."

"Don't hurry it up on my account."

Unable to remain upset with him for very long, she bent over and kissed his forehead. He brought her hand to his mouth and brushed it with his lips.

"Only of late have I come to understand why you have always felt like a brother to me," she continued. "And if you supposedly used me, then I used you in return. Once you made our friendship abundantly clear to our classmates, most of them backed off and decided to leave me alone. It was such a blessing and relief."

He was surprised. It had not occurred to him that she also might have found some practical benefit in their relationship.

"I should have been stronger," Helen added. "I should have ended our relationship years ago, while we were still students. You would not be in this condition if I had been more careful of your welfare. It's just that I was very lonely. I was selfish. I'm sorry."

She looked so sad that he could not bear it. "Damn it, Helen. At least grant me the dignity of having thoroughly screwed up my own life. Don't take that away from me."

She was perplexed.

"Do you have any idea how tired I am of bedpans?"

She shook her head.

"What a production it is for me just to take a piss or a shit? Physically I'm a helpless child again, and believe me, it's beyond humiliating. It's mortifying."

She opened her mouth; he cut in. "But it's *my* doing. *I'm* the one responsible, not you. And that awareness is the only dignity I have right now. Got that through your stubborn, half-blood head?"

"You needn't bring my forebears into this, thank you very much."

He was the only person in the world she permitted to tease her on that topic. He mentioned it so rarely that she knew he truly meant what he was saying.

They sat in silence for some time. Then he told her where he had hidden the results from the first batch of the king's tissue samples. She explained that if her father granted his permission for her to continue her secret investigation into the king's condition, she would need his laboratory to conduct additional analyses over an extended timeframe. He readily agreed.

"Using me again, woman?"

"You have no idea."

⊛ ⊛ ⊛

Helen wandered about Lord Matthew's laboratory, shaking her head. *No wonder his mind is vacant. He had a total brain dump, and this is where all the clutter landed.*

Next to the sink was the closet where Helen found Lord Matthew's lab coat with the test results crammed into the pocket. She cleared off a small length of countertop and placed the readout in front of her. Sitting on a rolling stool, she smoothed the wrinkled sheets and studied them.

She found the results disquieting and discouraging. It was clear that the *kojei* were rotating drug combinations, perhaps in a random sequence, perhaps in a defined pattern. It was not going to be at all simple to figure out what the priest-healers were dosing the Exalted Lord with, as well as the sequence of drug use and interaction. Devising an effective and fast-acting counteragent would also be dicey. She would need a series of tissue sample results, not just this one set. That, of course, only made the danger greater.

"How does he ever find anything in this place?"

Lord Justin was standing in the doorway. Helen beckoned to him to come in and shut the door.

"Matthew has his own unique system."

She offered him a stool close to hers. "Father of Kronos alone knows how, but it seems to work for him."

Lord Justin glanced at the readout on the countertop, realized it did not seem to have much to do with Matthew's condition. Since she was ignoring it, he decided to make no mention of it, either.

Instead, He sat and looked around the room. "If someone were to bring order to this place, Matthew probably would never find anything again."

"I have a much better plan to get even with him than cleaning his laboratory. I'm going to play matchmaker for him."

Helen rested her elbows on the countertop. "Any suggestions?"

"No one I can think of."

"Really? I seem to recall you saying you hoped to take a lover."

"If this is your idea of a joke, Helen–"

She stood before him. "I would never trifle with feelings such as these, Justin. It seems obvious to me that you love Matthew very much. Am I that mistaken?"

He shook his head. "I have loved him since we were both very young."

"Excellent taste in men. Have you ever told him?"

He shook his head again.

"What are you waiting for? An engraved invitation?"

"Matthew might not even welcome such attention from me."

"Yes, he would. Trust me on that one."

He took her hands in his. "It's not that simple, Helen. If I act on my love for him, I put him in mortal danger. I'm not sure I have the right to ask him to risk it."

"I put him in mortal danger simply by being his friend," Helen replied. "And it seems to me you risk equally as much as he."

"I'm just flat frightened, Helen," he whispered.

Her hands gripped his tighter for a moment, her eyes fierce. "You would be an utter fool if you weren't."

Helen released him and walked next to the countertop, running her fingers along the tops of stacks of documents, searching for something to help move Lord Justin past his fear.

"Do you really want to help Matthew?"

"Of course, I do."

"Then let him know how you feel about him. He desperately needs to hear it from you. You're the only one in this world who can offer him something to recover for, to make all the horrible pain and struggle worth it."

"What about the skin grafts?"

"Between you and me, they won't be enough. He's going to need something else."

"Such as?"

She looked deeply unhappy, almost haunted. "I have an idea, Justin, but it's strictly experimental. I'm not sure they'll allow me to try it on him."

"And if they don't?"

"Then it won't be a pretty sight."

# CHAPTER THIRTY-TWO

Lady Naomi first advocated a marriage between Helen and Lord Justin as a purely political countermeasure to support Lord James against Prince Seti. Once formally proposed, such unions had a way of taking on a life of their own. The signals Prince Enoch and Lord James received suggested there would be little opposition to the match. The Kindred generally regarded Helen as the sole female even remotely suitable for Lord Justin.

In a situation most unusual for any son of a Royal House, Lord Justin was not betrothed despite having attained his majority. The marriages of Royal children usually were contracted at birth or by their early years through a betrothal, a written pledge to execute a binding accord at a later date. Lord Matthew was another exception to this because his father, who was not a member of a noble house, did not believe in betrothals. The obvious reason for Lord Justin's unattached status was his mixed-race parentage. Members of the Kindred avoided him when seeking husbands for their daughters.

Lord Justin's mother, Elizabeth Andros, the Princess of Westar, was in high denial over the Kindred's rejection of her son and of her. She chose to believe that because the Consort (and the Exalted Lord, when his mind was present) publicly treated her with cordiality, (for political considerations only) she was accepted when, in fact, she was despised.

On her denial was founded the princess' indignation over the proposed match. To her, it was the worst possible outrage to wed her son to a bastard, even if the proposed bride was the acknowledged child of a Great House. It soon became clear to Lady Mary, even with a young person's limited understanding, that her aunt by marriage was ashamed of her Turanian heritage. Lord Justin never shared his mother's denial of the true precariousness of their position, and felt very close to his Turanian kin.

On top of her anger over the proposed marriage, the princess also objected strenuously to Lady Mary meeting again with Helen. Since it was a significant yet relatively cost-free gesture of support, Prince Enoch overruled his wife and ordered the princess to accompany Lady Mary at least on the initial visit. The prince thus forced his wife into what she swore she would never do. And that was acknowledging Helen by meeting her in person.

* * *

Helen and her father invariably found the sight of the princess a sharp, uncomfortable reminder of the woman both had loved in their own ways and lost. Helen moreover already knew how much the princess despised her, and was reserved in her manner and speech toward her prospective mother-in-law. The unrelenting hostility the princess directed at his daughter was a rude awakening for Lord James. If not for Lady Naomi's common sense and graciousness, that first encounter between the Princess of Westar and Helen in the Consort's apartments at Agarthi would have been far more awkward than it was.

After the introductions and formal greetings, Lady Mary stood opposite Helen in the Consort's salon, and had a chance to observe her friend. Learning the truth about her father appeared to have brought Helen little joy. Helen now seemed as imprisoned by her new identity as Lady Mary felt she had always been ensnared in hers as a member of a Royal House and future Consort.

To the deep pain and sorrow Lady Mary saw in Helen's eyes the day they first met, there was now added a trapped look that broke Lady Mary's heart, probably because she could empathize with it. In that instant, Lady Mary felt as though her dream of freedom died also, even if she could not have put it into words at the time because she did not understand it until much later.

Lady Mary burst into tears and threw her arms around Helen's waist. While the Consort and the princess regarded the emotional display with disapproval, and Lord James with surprise, Helen was instantly tender. She leaned down and gave Lady Mary a reassuring hug.

Her friend only wept harder. Helen kissed the top of her head. "This is supposed to be a happy ending, my lady."

Then Helen took her hand, made their excuses, and led Lady Mary down the hall to the same bedroom she had occupied when they met. Closing the door for some semblance of privacy, Helen helped Lady Mary onto the bed and sat beside her. Eventually her companion's tears subsided.

"Keep this up, Mary, and you're going to give everyone the distinct impression you're sorry to see me."

Helen put her arm around her friend's shoulder and squeezed. "Mary, spill the beans. Why are you so upset? Is it something I've done or said?"

Lady Mary finally confessed to the only part of her distress that she could acknowledge. She haltingly related a jumbled, incoherent tale of a little girl's foolish crush on a much older man. She expected Helen to scoff at what everyone else seemed to consider nonsense.

Helen did not. She pressed Lady Mary's shoulders again. "I honor your choice in men, sweet lamb. The fact that you love Justin tells me a great deal about you, and all of it is highly positive."

Lady Mary was astounded. "The Consort does not approve of my choice. Somehow Uncle Tarkon found out about it and he doesn't like it, either."

"Of course not, silly." Helen threw her head back and laughed. "He's a half-blood, and he's also your first cousin. Need I say more?"

She did. She told Lady Mary about her first meeting with Lord Nimrod, and how Lord Tarkon had insulted her mother on the floor of Kindred House, and what she did about it.

The gray flecks in Helen's eyes sparkled. "Perhaps I should apologize to the Duke of Avalon's cousin, and the Duke of Eden's niece, for my behavior."

Lady Mary tried to pretend she was insulted, and collapsed on the bed in a fit of laughter.

Helen waited until her companion regained her composure before continuing. "I'm sorry, Mary, if the thought of my wedding Justin causes you such pain. It's only a proposal right now. It might not ever happen, you know."

Lady Mary sensed it would eventually. Sooner or later, Helen would marry the only man Lady Mary had ever loved. She wiped more tears out of her eyes and summoned the courage to ask something very important to her.

"How do you feel about him, Helen?"

Helen did not say anything right away. She comprehended that her friend was asking far more than the words alone said.

"A wife is honor-bound to obey her husband, and I don't have to tell you that obedience is not my strong suit.

"This was not of my choosing, either, or of his," Helen went on. "But if I do marry him, I will try my hardest to be a good wife for him, not simply out of duty. He's worth loving and honoring, Mary. He has more courage and integrity in his little finger than almost all of the Kindred combined."

Lady Mary could not stay angry with or distant from her companion after such a reply. She put her arms around Helen. They clung to each other once more, united in friendship by their shared regard for each other and for one man, and their shared position of powerlessness as women in a land run by and for the benefit of a few men only.

* * *

Not long after Lady Mary and Helen left the salon, the Princess of Westar also departed, leaving Janel to accompany Lord James when he escorted Lady Mary back to the Atlas manor in a couple of hours. The Consort became even more agitated, pacing in front of the fireplace closest to her favorite chair. She asked Janel to leave the salon.

"Sit down, James, please."

The duke complied and the Consort assumed her chair. "You do recall what you said to me all those weeks ago, after supper following that dreadful session of the *Kinshazen*."

Lord James remembered. It was time for her to reveal to him precisely how she wanted him to repay the debt he owed her.

She told him of her plan to have Helen examine and possibly treat the king. Lord James did not dare respond for some minutes. The Consort used that time to summon Janel and ask her to retrieve Lady Mary and Helen from the bedroom.

Helen entered the salon and knew right away from her father's stunned expression that the Consort must have told him something. She remained silent and standing; Lady Mary did as well.

"I do not make this request frivolously, James."

"Frivolous is about the last word I would associate with you, Naomi," he replied ruefully. "I have to assume you have extremely serious reasons for asking me to put my daughter in mortal danger."

"Your daughter is in danger already, and if you are defeated, she will be in dire peril. You need Kefren well and whole before you go on trial. You need his open support. It's about the only thing that will back some of those jackals down."

He experienced an unaccustomed sensation of extreme vulnerability. "And your other serious reasons?"

The Consort looked at Helen, who shook her head. "The test results are inconclusive, Lady Consort. I need a series of several such tests in order to be able to say anything more than what I have told you already."

Lord James looked from Helen to the Consort in growing consternation. "You have examined him already?"

"Yes, Lord Protector. When I was in the Consort's custody awaiting trial."

He leapt off the sofa. "Damn it, Naomi! How could you?"

The Consort seemed to expect such a response. "How could I? James, I had no idea about Helen at the time. None of us did. And I was desperate, too. I still am."

Lord James stood next to Helen, waiting for the Consort to continue. "I have long suspected that someone is trying to poison Kefren."

"Mentioning no names, of course," Lord James replied in disgust. The prime suspect was Prince Seti, who stood to inherit everything upon his elder brother's death.

"Of course."

The duke scrambled for a different option. "Can we not simply go to the Kindred and demand openly that the Exalted Lord be tested for poison?"

"We will not find any known poison in his body, Lord Protector," Helen said. "The first test results have confirmed my initial suspicions. The *kojei* are poisoning him by combining different drugs and allowing the toxic interactions to take their toll over a number of years. Slow, yet ultimately lethal, unless it can be stopped in time."

"I would not have thought he had that kind of patience," the Consort said.

"It's the cautious way to murder, Lady Consort," Helen answered. "It leaves no evidence that can be cited in a court of law. The Exalted Lord's vital organs simply will fail over time, as though from age or a long illness. It will seem so natural that most likely there will appear to be no reason for an after-death examination of his remains."

Lord James took Helen's hands. His regard for her was so tender and full of concern that Lady Mary's eyes filled with tears. He had good reason to fear. She was already guilty of this capital crime. If her past actions were brought to the attention of the Lord Chancellor, she could be put to death on the spot. No need even for a sham trial.

Lord James told Helen for the first time why it was that his acknowledging her spared her life, by establishing that she had always been a subject of Azgard and thus had committed no capital crime when she entered the Sacred City without permission.

"I cannot protect you from the consequences of being discovered for this crime, Helen," he said. "How can I ask you to take such a risk?"

"How can you ask, my lord?" she finally replied, her voice unsteady. "How can I ask you to risk on my behalf what you do now?"

He smiled. "You never asked me. I chose to do so willingly."

Tears flowed down Helen's face. She released herself from her father's grasp. "No need to ask me now. I have already chosen this risk of my own free will."

Lord James could not yet make the decision.

Helen saw him sizing Lady Mary up and smiled. "Lady Mary is a fellow conspirator, my lord. She's known about our project since its inception, and obviously has not said a word to anyone."

Lady Mary offered her very best so-innocent face. "Known what?"

Helen just snickered. "Lady Mary, when you're a Consort bouncing your grandchildren in your lap, you'll have to think of something else. Sweet innocence won't cut it any longer."

Lady Mary feigned Royal indifference to her teasing. In truth, the young woman was terrified on Helen's behalf, and had no trouble identifying with Lord James' fears and hesitation.

"What exactly will you be doing, Helen?" Lord James asked.

Her efforts would be threefold. First, she would conduct a series of exams and take samples from the Exalted Lord at regular intervals. She would analyze the tissues to determine which drugs and drug combinations the *kojei* were using.

Once she had that knowledge, the second part would be to administer what she called an antagonist, a counteragent drug to bring Kefren rapidly out of his stupor and permit him to reign once more. Third, when he was fully in charge of his faculties, Helen would devise tonics to cleanse his body of any residual medications.

Helen also outlined what she needed to do her job. The Consort would have to arrange for the Exalted Lord's visits to coincide with their meetings in her salon. Helen would use the cover of attending to

Lord Matthew to analyze the samples she took from the king in Lord Matthew's laboratory. At that point she had to confess to her father Lord Matthew's part in the first examination.

"He might have said something about it to Seti. Maybe that was the cause of the severity of his discipline," Lord James said.

Helen shook her head. "He didn't, my lord. I have asked him that question already. He has said nothing about this to anyone."

Lord James finally yielded.

Helen's life became a dangerous routine. She alternated between visits to the Consort ostensibly to meet with Lady Mary, covertly to examine the Exalted Lord, and visits to Lord Matthew to examine him and to work on his recovery and the king's tissue samples.

How she kept her wits about her was beyond Lady Mary's understanding. The peril to all of them was so great that Lady Mary put it out of her mind entirely, except those times she was in the Consort's salon, watching Helen at work. Lady Mary prayed every night for their safety and success with a fervor she never knew she had.

# CHAPTER THIRTY-THREE

The Consort could not help wandering about her salon, tense and distracted. She was hosting Griffin for dinner that evening. Fiercely determined to sweet-talk him into revealing Prince Seti's strategy, she had taken great pains with her appearance. Her hair was held on the top of her head in a jewel-covered knot. Her lips were painted, the almond shape of her dark eyes was accented, and the fine lines in her face smoothed away by copper-colored powder. The bodice of her gown exposed most of her cleavage. She had covered the insides of her wrists and the skin between her breasts and behind her ears with a cheap scent her spies told her Griffin liked.

Lady Naomi had insisted that Judith join her. Her counselor sat close to the fire, irritated. The cold wind was taking its toll on the hip that had been arthritic since Judith's youth. "You look and smell like a Lesser Shore trollop, Naomi."

The Consort glared at her. "One has to lace the hook with the right bait."

Judith grimaced. "Best to throw this one back in the water."

"Not until I pick its puny little brain of every morsel of intelligence I can find."

"Intelligence?" Judith grumped. "You'd starve before you'd glean even a mouthful from that source."

Judith crossed and uncrossed her legs; she shifted her weight; she could not get comfortable. "Oh hell, Naomi. I'm just in no mood for this farce."

"Then get in the mood, fast," the Consort retorted, eyes glinting. "You will take part tonight and you will not laugh, damn it. I've never needed your insight more than I do now."

* * *

The Consort, steering the Lord Chancellor to one end of the table, motioned to Judith to take the seat opposite him. She placed herself between the two so that she could touch Griffin as she talked to him, as well as angle her body to provide him with stimulating scenery. The position also enabled her to keep his goblet filled with wine.

Griffin gave to the butler a black velvet cloak that was threadbare in many places and needed hemming. He bowed and presented the Consort with a single red rose.

"For me? How lovely."

She snatched it from him and pressed it to her nose as though the scent was the sweetest she had ever encountered. She passed the flower to the butler with instructions to put it into a small vase and set it in the middle of the table.

*How cheap*, Judith thought, approaching her chair. *He could have brought her at least a dozen, considering how much she's spending on food and drink tonight.*

Griffin kissed the hand the Consort extended to him, his eyes glued on Judith. He did not look happy. Granting them permission to be seated, the Consort acted fast to turn a negative into a positive.

"You must forgive me for making this a threesome, Lord Chancellor."

She nodded to the butler to fill his and her goblets with wine. "Judith's here to keep me honest."

She reached out as though to caress Griffin's arm, then snatched her hand back, turning her face away as if overcome and embarrassed. "I just can't trust myself alone with you."

Judith choked on her watered-down wine.

"Lady Consort is too kind," he said, his smile effusive.

"Too kind to you, Lord Chancellor? Impossible. I just wish I could be kinder."

She twisted her upper body, watched his eyes follow the gap between her dress and her breasts. Although it wasn't quite enough to reveal the nipples, it showed him the possibilities. He gulped and reached for his goblet.

The Consort made small talk during the first part of the meal, until she was certain he had consumed at least one entire bottle of wine. Satiated for the moment, Griffin pushed his chair back and faced in the Consort's direction.

The Consort reached over to refill his goblet, this time bending far enough to expose one of her breasts. Taking advantage of his shock and curiosity, she rose and stepped toward him. She straddled his legs with hers and leaned forward, massaging his temples with her fingertips. She displayed her aromatic chest to him in its entirety, just inches away.

"Affairs of state keep you so busy, I'm surprised you have any time at all to visit a mere Consort," she murmured, working her fingers back into his hairline and shifting her weight, knowing he was riveted on her naked breasts.

She leaned closer, as though to kiss him. Before their lips met, Judith cleared her throat. Pretending to be flustered, the Consort backed away and returned to her seat. She sat down and fanned herself with her gold-trimmed napkin.

She blinked and smiled. "Prince Seti must find you absolutely indispensable to the welfare of the realm, Lord Chancellor. I surely do."

The Consort knew precisely which buttons to push. Taking a long swallow of wine, Griffin started to talk. Once he warmed up to the subject, the Consort could only steer him subtly in the direction she wanted him to take.

"Surely the prince always consults you on policy decisions, Lord Chancellor."

He stared at her. "It's very foolish to base policy on childish resentments, Lady Consort." He slurred his words.

She returned a dutifully admiring gaze. "You are so wise, Lord Chancellor, that I must confess, you're talking way over my head."

Judith spluttered again. The Consort shot her a warning glance.

Griffin swayed in his chair. "I warned him not to piss off his allies."

"Really."

"*Nahazi* bitch," Griffin rambled on almost incoherently. He drained his goblet and set it down. She refilled it. "Must have something to do with getting rid of Lord Virtue's little moral lapse," he added. "Silenas thinks so."

Despite her annoyance, Judith started paying very close attention at the mention of Helen.

"I just hope Prince Seti fully understands your true value, Lord Chancellor," the Consort prompted. "Please assure me that he's not taking credit for some of your accomplishments."

He finally disclosed what she was seeking. The prosecution's strategy was to focus on the most serious charge, adultery. He leaned toward her conspiratorially. "Even if we lose that one, we win, Naomi."

His use of her first name infuriated her. "You are so clever, Griffin. Whatever do you mean?"

He winked at her. "*Kojei*," he replied. "More than one way to kill a cat after you've skinned it."

*   *   *

The Consort held her head in her hands. Griffin had mercifully departed, almost too drunk to move on his own. She glanced over at Judith, raised an eyebrow.

"It's fairly certain that Seti has quarreled with the Holy One over the timing of filing these charges against James," Judith replied.
"Yes. The longer this issue goes unresolved, the more it undermines James. Just what Seti would want."

"But not necessarily what the Temple would want," Judith said. "It's also clear that Seti is hatching some sort of plot against James."

"Another poisoning?" The Consort's tone was bitter. "Is there anyone he's not planning to murder?"

The part of the puzzle that troubled Judith the most was the hint at possible moves by the Supreme Lord against Helen. She decided to say nothing of this unless and until she could get a better idea of what it involved.

"Let me meditate on it all again tonight, Naomi, and we'll compare notes in the morning," Judith said. "I need a little time to sift all the kernels of truth from his self-congratulatory chaff."

"Not only do I look and smell like a Lesser Shore trollop, Judith, I now feel like one," the Consort confessed.

Judith picked up right away on her shame, tried to offer comfort that her companion merely shrugged off. Judith understood the

Consort's emotions and predicament, which she shared. As a woman, the Consort had no power to command men in authority. That left her only subterfuge and seduction. Her position was degrading and demeaning yet she could not change it.

Setting those gloomy thoughts aside, Judith tried again to lighten the mood. "You should have been an actress, my dear. Your performance tonight was magnificent."

The Consort stared back at her, smiling sardonically. "Who says I'm not? I've been playing the part of Consort for more years than I like to admit. And in my performance is my only real power."

# CHAPTER THIRTY-FOUR

Pipe and *sigra* smoke always filled the dim common room of the Golden Plume, a tavern on the Lesser Shore that was popular with the politically well connected. Salazar Cain, Prince Enoch's spymaster, made his way to a booth at the back of the large room. He sank down onto one of the benches; his limp was worse than usual. Cold, damp wind always abused his war wound.

Ordering a mug of ale, he sipped the brew, waiting for the precise time for the meeting, pondering his next moves. He heard the rustle of a skirt. Standing beside his bench was one of his favorite prostitutes. Although she appeared to be of Turanian extraction, the deep copper tinge to her complexion betrayed her mixed descent. Her long, fiery red hair was secured at the top of her head; her gown fitted her like a second skin.

She hooked her arm over the top of the booth divider and leaned toward him.

He patted her breast. "Simka, my dear. You look especially bewitching tonight."

"You've gone without too long, that's why, Commodore," she teased him in return.

He lowered his voice. "Are you available?"

She pretended to hesitate. "I've been busy, and I was headed upstairs to sleep. But for you, Commodore—"

She bent lower and brushed the base of his neck with her tongue. He caught her head in his hands and put his mouth on hers. She yielded willingly.

He bought a flask of wine before they went upstairs, arm in arm. As soon as she closed and locked the door to her room, he wrapped his arms around her, covering her face and neck with kisses, steering her toward the bed.

She giggled. "You planning on holding the bottle along with me?"

He set the flask on the table next to the bed. He also flicked off the light-stick, allowing moonlight to filter into the room through shuttered doors that led to a balcony.

His hands seemed to take on a life of their own; her gown slipped off so easily, crumpling around her ankles. Her body was a delightful mixture of softness and firmness beneath his touch; she undressed him and they wrestled on the sheets.

Afterward he sat up and opened the flask. She brought him two glasses and disappeared into the bathroom. While she was unable to see him, he mixed into her glass a packet of white powder retrieved from the pocket of his jacket.

She entered the bedroom again, her hair combed. He held out the spiked glass. "A performance like that deserves an extra reward, my dear. Drink up."

She downed the wine and returned to bed next to him. He kissed her and ran his hands over her breasts, waiting for the drug to take effect. After she passed out, he shut off the light-stick, pulled on his trousers, tapped on one of the door panels in a repeating pattern.

The door opened and shut. Cain stared at the dark figure of a master of disguise and deception. He did not know Ibrihim Akkad's true appearance despite having used the man's services over several decades. He did not know the man's true name. And he did not want to know either, certain that would be a death sentence. All he knew was the distinctive voice. Too smooth and honeyed, like he used it to conceal murderous intent. Not someone to be trifled with or double-crossed.

Akkad slumped onto the shabby chair near the doors; Cain sat on the trunk at the foot of the bed. The newcomer looked beyond him at the sleeping woman.

"I had forgotten how chilly it is in Azgard this time of year, Commodore," he said in Kadosh, a language he presumed the slut would not be able to comprehend were she to awaken too soon.

"We don't have much time," Cain responded, also in Kadosh. "How deep are your contacts among the *Umarii?*"

"Deep enough. Who do you want me to find?"

When Cain told him, even Akkad was taken aback. "That will require some time and a lot of cash, Commodore."

Cain pulled a leather pouch stuffed with currency from his jacket pocket and tossed it to Akkad. "That should get you started. Do it, and keep me apprised of your progress. We want to open a dialog as soon as possible."

Unknown to the men, Simka was awake once more. The dosage was not high enough to keep her unconscious for as long as Cain had planned. Her instincts warned her not to let them know she was awake and could understand their conversation. Her flesh crawled. A malevolent power hung about the man meeting with her customer. How could anyone stand to be near him? She struggled to make no sound and keep her breathing rate steady, grateful the darkness hid her silent shivering.

"Can you supply me with an assassination team?" Cain asked Akkad.

"I usually work those assignments alone," Akkad replied.

"It won't be necessary immediately," Cain said. "I'll let you know who and where when the time arrives."

Since Kadosh had no word for what he was about to discuss, Cain switched to Terzil. "What do you know about half-bloods?"

Simka drew on all of her self-control to pretend she still slumbered.

"Enough," Akkad answered. "Why do you ask?"

"I want everything there is to know about them. And I do mean everything, even knowledge that is well guarded. With your background, you should be able to provide it. Can you?"

"Have I ever failed you before?"

Simka lay still, kept her eyes closed, and continued to breathe slowly, evenly. Silence and deception were her only protection.

"Not so far. See that it stays that way."

Cain nodded toward the glass door. Akkad rose as if to leave. He paused, looked at the naked form on the bed, and grinned anew. "Mixing a little pleasure with business, Commodore. You must be mellowing in your old age."

Before Cain could respond, he was gone.

Knowing she would not be able to hide her alarm from her client, Simka decided to continue her pretense in the hope he would simply leave. Cain finished dressing, placed the payment for her services on the table next to the bed, and departed.

Only when she no longer heard footsteps in the hall did Simka sit up, heart pounding, head throbbing from the drug. Anger and fear assailed her. Fully aware of the great prince Cain served, Simka realized certain people should know about this meeting right away. For now, she was far too frightened to do anything except keep her mouth shut. If that terrifying stranger found out she knew anything, he would return to kill her.

* * *

Prince Enoch tried to open the door that separated his bedroom suite from his wife's. He had not been with her for several months. To his surprise and extreme annoyance, the door was locked. He pounded on it. "Elizabeth, open this door. At once, woman!"

The princess was on a sofa in her bedchamber. A nearly empty bottle and glass were on the table close by. He kept repeating his demand to be let in.

Furious with him, she did not move. "No! Stick it elsewhere. You usually do."

Her defiance ignited her husband's smoldering anger with her into a firestorm. He decided to teach her a lesson. He put several pieces of cord in the pocket of his smoking jacket, to which he added paper currency in about the amount it would cost to secure an hour or so with a Lesser Shore harlot. Under his arm he carried a riding crop. He stalked out of his bedroom and down the hallway to the entrance to hers. It was not secured. Cold with rage, he jerked it open, stepped inside, and locked it.

She folded her arms across her chest. Seeing the bottle and glass, he was contemptuous. "You're drunk."

"It helps make you tolerable," she answered in the same tone.

He grabbed her arm and yanked her off the sofa. She tried to slap him and he returned the favor several times. She cried out and offered no further resistance. He ripped her gown from her. He dragged her by her hair, naked, to the edge of the bed, forced her to her knees, and pushed her stomach down onto the velvet bedspread.

Using the crop, he beat her. As the brutal blows ripped into her skin and pounded her back, buttocks, thighs, and legs, Elizabeth screamed in pain, burst into tears, and begged him to stop. He ignored her pleas. She slid off the mattress and curled into a ball on the rug beside the bed, her arms wrapped around her head to shield her face.

He quit at last. He dropped the crop on the floor, bent over, pulled her up to her feet again by her hair, and forced her onto the bed, on her injured back. Elizabeth gasped and groaned as the weight of her body collided with her bruised and bleeding flesh. He produced the cord to hog-tie her, right wrist to right ankle, left wrist to left ankle. The bonds were cruelly tight.

Throwing off his smoking jacket he mounted her, rammed his tongue into her mouth, and pawed at her breasts, hips, and thighs. The sight of any woman naked and bound always aroused him; it was especially stimulating and pleasurable to see his haughty Turanian wife stripped of all her ludicrous pretensions to status and respect. She had always been completely at his mercy; perhaps now she understood that just a little bit better.

He took his time reaching his climax. He wanted her to experience her own inconsequence and powerlessness for as long as possible. When he was finished, he put his smoking jacket back on and removed the currency from the pocket. Rolling it into a tube, he reached down to stuff it into her cunt.

"Do not ever again lock your door against me, woman. You won't live to regret it."

He departed through the now unlocked door between the two bedchambers.

* * *

Stunned beyond any reaction, in shock from her wounds, Elizabeth lay on the bed, the pain in her wrists, hips, knees, and ankles growing worse by the minute. Mercifully, she had drunk enough wine that she soon passed out.

When the princess did not appear later for break-fast with Lady Mary, Janel went looking for her. Her instincts on high alert, Janel asked the housekeeper to unlock the door to the princess' bedchamber, dismissing the servant before the woman could catch a glimpse inside the room. Elizabeth was lying semi-conscious in her own blood and urine.

# CHAPTER THIRTY-FIVE

The Lord Steward sat between the Lord Protector and Lord Justin in the observation gallery of the operating room. They understood little of the procedure unfolding before them, except at a simple level.

The medical team was preparing. In their masks, gloves, and surgical gowns, their hair covered, the team members were difficult to distinguish except by voice. Lord Matthew lay prone on the operating table, his entire body covered, except for his lower back and buttocks.

"So, when are you going to stick that damn needle in me?" Lord Matthew asked Helen. "I've been looking forward to it for days now."

Helen looked up from the tray of replacement skin she was examining. "Already done, my lord."

"Already? I felt nothing."

"Very clever, my lord. You're not supposed to feel anything," she replied. "If you're disappointed, I can always stick another in your ear. That might make an impression even on you."

"That's one of your better ideas, *Doctor* Andros," he retorted. "I'll soon be deaf to all your nagging."

"Soon be, my lord? Since when have you ever listened to me or anyone else?"

At that point, the Consort entered the gallery, along with Lord Andrew. After exchanging greetings with the three already there, the new arrivals became engrossed in the procedure.

Helen and Sudras removed portions of the newly grown skin and then assessed how they would lay in and secure it to their patient's existing skin. They wanted the natural growth pattern of the grafts to conform to the shapes of the areas on Lord Matthew's body that were missing skin. That way they would need to do minimal cutting on flesh that had already endured too much abuse. It was like fitting pieces into a puzzle.

They paused to discuss a particularly challenging section, where the size of the gap concerned them both. It was over Lord Matthew's hip. With the temporary skin removed, Helen could see bone; the muscle tissue and fat had not grown back. By the alarm in Sudras' eyes, Helen knew that her mentor was aware of the problem.

Lord Matthew waded right into the debate. "Andros, you are one opinionated cuss. Has anyone ever told you?"

Rotating a sheet of grafted skin at various angles to fit it into the gap, she did not even glance at him. "Not until now, my lord; it *was* a very well-kept secret."

She finally found the right position for a close fit, and wedged the patch of skin into place.

He tried to bait her again. "Find anything interesting?"

"Not without a microscope, my lord."

Lord Justin and Lord Andrew laughed, the Consort shook her head, and Lord James winced.

Once the graft was where she wanted it, Helen secured it with a protein string that would be readily absorbed as the new skin grew and spread. They could not use a sealer to bind the new to the existing skin. The device would bruise or destroy too many new cells, not to mention the delicate blood vessels critical to the survival of the grafts.

Helen smiled behind her surgical mask at the notion of sewing on Matthew as though he were a sheet.

He seemed to sense her thoughts. "Don't forget to make a tidy knot when you're finished, Andros."

"Keep talking, my lord. I'll leave a tidy little message to amuse your wife."

He jerked a finger in Helen's direction.

Helen caught the rude gesture even though she kept her eyes on the task before her. "No thank you, my lord. I'm not *that* fond of you."

Lord Andrew and Lord Justin laughed louder. Mortified, Shinar had no idea how he would face Lord James at the reception he was hosting that afternoon.

● ● ●

Lord James did not know whether to feel proud of his daughter or throttle her. He had managed to collar her quietly among the guests at the Shinar manor, and they were alone together in the Lord Steward's library.

He ordered her to a sofa in front of a ceiling-high bookcase. Helen heard the same hard quality in his voice that she had perceived the first time they spoke together. She swallowed hard. He was not in a mood to be trifled with or flouted.

"You dress and behave modestly enough, Lieutenant," he said. "But your language earlier today was utterly appalling. You sounded like a Lesser Shore whore, not a proper young woman, or a professional healer. I simply won't have it."

"Two out of three is a start, Lord —"

He brought the back of his hand down across her face. She leapt to her feet, not wounded so much as angry. "Is force your answer for everything, Lord Protector?"

"Are sarcasm and insubordination yours, Lieutenant?"

He put a hand on her shoulder and pushed her back onto the sofa. He had scarcely used any of the strength in just that one arm, yet her unwilling knees buckled beneath his touch as though she were a rag doll. That was downright unnerving.

She gulped again. "No, Lord Protector. I apologize for having offended you with my language."

"What about the future, Lieutenant? Will you promise to continue to behave and speak as befits a woman of your station?"

"In all honesty, I cannot make any such assurance, Lord Protector." Helen's voice quavered. "No doubt my ignorance of propriety will offend you and others again."

Lord James gave her credit for candor, his heart aching because he agreed with her. He was not sure there was any way to avert it, either, unless she had a change of attitude and stopped fighting his authority as her father.

He studied the top of her head. He loved how her long, full black tresses flowed in waves down her back and streamed over her shoulders. She had the hair and the height of the Kindred, with the eyes and skin of her mother's people.

He decided to act on the agreement he made weeks ago with Lord Justin. Perhaps a change of scenery would lift her spirits. And it was long past time for him to say his thanks to Miriam's family for caring for Helen all those years when her true parentage was hidden.

* * *

Lord Justin was elated at finally being able to keep his word to his Aunt Abigail and the rest of the family. His happy mood vanished upon returning to the Atlas manor that evening.

He insisted on seeing his mother; Elizabeth was napping atop her silken coverlet, a light blanket over her lower body to ward off any chill. The evidence of the previous night's violence and degradation that he could see were the bruises on her face and the rope burns on her wrists and ankles.

Lord Justin sat on the edge of the mattress and kissed her on her forehead. She awoke and put her arms around his neck. Not knowing where she was hurt and not wanting to cause her any additional pain, he stroked her head. She smiled as much as her bruised lips would permit her and closed her eyes under his reassuring touch.

"Kronos, Mother. I'm so sorry," he whispered.

She opened her eyes. "Let it go, Justin. I'll be fine. I need more sleep, that's all."

Judith tapped his shoulder; he reluctantly allowed her to lead him down the hall into the princess' salon. After he entered the room she followed him, shut the door, and stood in front of it.

She did not have to encourage him to express his emotions. Lord Justin ranted and raved, swearing at his father, and calling him every nasty name she had ever heard of, along with a few she had not. In a while he quit stalking about the room and stared in her direction. He was behaving a little too calmly for Judith's liking, especially since his energy was so agitated. She had never felt him this distressed.

"Justin, what are you thinking?"

She stepped backwards until the palms of her hands could feel the carved patterns in the door behind her.

"I'm thinking I need to have a talk with him."

She shook her head. "Did your mother ask for your help?"

"No."

"She told you to 'let it go,' didn't she?"

"Yes."

"Then follow her advice, and your own."

He blinked and raised an eyebrow.

"It seems to me you have told your brother more than once not to intervene on your behalf," Judith continued. "That your issue was between you and your father and the two of you would settle it in your own way."

He sighed and nodded, rubbing his forehead.

"The same thing applies here, Justin. This is between your parents and they must sort it out between themselves."

He sank down onto an armchair and covered his face with his hands. "How could he do this to her? She's so tiny and fragile."

Judith knelt on the carpet and wrapped her arms around him. "Perhaps she's a little more resilient than you think. After all, she survived bringing you into the world."

Sensing the guilt her words evoked in him, she instantly regretted that remark.

"I have to say something to him, Judith."

He started to his feet and she held onto him, making him lift her weight as well as his own. "Are you prepared to kill him?" she whispered into his ear. That was not something she wanted a spotter to capture.

He sat back down.

"If you confront him over this in any manner, either by word, deed, or even by facial expression, you must be prepared to make an end to him," Judith continued to whisper. "Otherwise, he will surely make an end to you, and then go right on treating your mother even worse for the sin of bearing him a treasonous son."

Lord Justin conceded defeat. As usual, Judith was right.

"I despise him, Judith."

"Join the crowd."

Judith decided to ask the prince to allow Lord Justin to go with her tomorrow to the Andros farm. He needed a chance to regain some sort of emotional equilibrium. She wanted the opportunity to prepare Helen's family, too. Just as Helen's life had changed completely once her father's name became known, Judith suspected her Andros kin also would feel the effects in far-reaching ways.

# CHAPTER THIRTY-SIX

Silenas plodded down the dim hallway toward his bedchamber. The hour was late and he was worn out, at least mentally. He had spent yet another long, frustrating day trying to broker some sort of agreement between his master, the Holy One, and Prince Seti over what, if any, charges were to be levied against Lord James and the precise timing to file these indictments.

The Holy Deputy reached the door, opened it, stepped inside the sitting room, flicked on a lightstick in a wall sconce, and shut the door. He put a hand on the door jamb and leaned against it, running the situation over in his mind.

The prince, of course, wanted the most severe charges — but not for a while. Maybe not ever. Prince Seti obviously got perverse pleasure, not to mention political points, in leaving his enemy publicly wounded but without any chance to clear his name. The Holy One, on the other hand, was champing at the bit to string Lord James up as soon as possible. The Duke of Alta was a longtime Temple opponent, always first to resist Malachi's harsh policies toward the Turanians. Malachi was all but drooling at the prospect of payback.

"Well, well. Aren't we deep in thought."

A familiar, unwelcome voice. Silenas jumped back from the doorway and spun around, breathing hard. A figure in a dark cloak and cowl reclined in one of the two sitting chairs in front of the fireplace, where a small blaze flickered and crackled softly. Thankfully the window was shuttered.

"You are such a bundle of nerves."

"Wha-what are you d-doing here, of all places?" Silenas sputtered. "You are crazy to come back here. Malachi will roast you on a spit if he finds out!"

"Are *you* going to tell him?"

Silenas shook his head.

"Then we should be just fine. I am here to give you some intelligence." He pointed a gloved finger toward the armchair next to his. "You annoy me hovering like that. Sit down and listen up."

Silenas slid onto the seat cushion, never taking his eyes off his unwanted visitor, who explained about his future assassination assignment from Salazar Cain.

The Holy Deputy was puzzled. "Who would the Prince of Westar want dead?"

The murky figure snorted. "You really are a dimwit. Think about it. If the prince wants more power than he has already, who would be the one man standing in his way?"

The understanding came. "Why should I care about that?"

"Because, Dimwit, the prince has also asked for any hidden information about half-bloods I can find. Both of us should care about that. Anyone else knowing too much about half-bloods poses a direct threat to our plans."

The skin on the top of Silenas' shoulders prickled. "You aren't going to give him any, are you?"

"Of course, I am," his visitor countered. "I could buy a small eastern state for the cash he's paying me to fork it over."

Silenas opened his mouth but the dark figure held up a gloved finger, stopping him. "I will provide you with the originals I can find, and I won't give my customer anything vital. It will just look like I did."

Silenas nodded, swallowing hard. His uninvited visitor continued. "It isn't just payback Malachi wants, you know."

"It isn't?"

"He wants the girl. The half-blood. He can't get at her until and unless her father is either dead or incapacitated. Don't let that happen, Lucan. He wants her dead, but half-bloods are the linchpin of our strategy. Keep her alive. By any means."

Silenas rubbed his forehead, nodding. "You really should go now."

"What's the hurry? I have more information for you."

Silenas clasped his hands together and just looked at him.

"Your Chief Healer is in Prince Seti's pocket."

It was Silenas' turn to scoff. "I know that already. I do have other intelligence sources, you know."

"Well, did you know that one of your newly promoted *kojei*, Brother Shem Sutfin, has a *lizun* tucked away on the Lesser Shore? Complete with three, soon-to-be four little bastards."

Silenas drew in a sharp breath but made no reply. The figure got to his booted feet. "Check it out if you don't believe me. This little nugget will come in handy someday. Probably sooner than later.

"And do be more concerned about your Chief Healer's relationship with Prince Seti. That could put the Temple in a real bind if Kefren ever regains his faculties."

"That's not likely," Silenas argued.

"Keep believing that if it brings you comfort."

Before Silenas could do or say anything else, a red flame lit up the chamber for an instant and then shut off. His unnerving guest was gone.

●  ●  ●

Alone in one of the rooms of the Atlas manor's guest quarters, Judith tossed and turned. She finally gave up on sleep and sat up, smoothing the blankets and sheets over her legs. She fumbled for her pipe and tobacco pouch, filled the bowl with leaf, and lit it, drawing deep.

She let her mind ramble. Prince Enoch, she decided, probably did Lord Justin an inadvertent favor by hitting him and then following that with his brutality against Elizabeth. The first action only too literally drove home her longstanding advice to Lord Justin about his relationship with his father. Judith was filled with disgust and sadness. It always pained her to witness the disparity between the ways the prince treated his two children.

Judith had little regard for the elder Atlas son, a spoiled, indulged, not very intelligent playboy with far too much time and money on his hands. Lord Nimrod had no real, useful employment or purpose in life, other than to wait for his shot at power mongering. *What a prime waste of time.*

In sorrow she turned to her unresolved issues with Miriam. Judith closed her eyes and, in her heart, called out in desperation, praying for resolution between her dear friend and herself. She was not hopeful. She had sent out the same urgent plea almost every night since she learned in the Supreme Lord's study about the letter from Miriam she never received. Miriam had never responded, and Judith grieved for her and their relationship.

*Miriam, Miriam, I do understand, even if I have been angry with you.*

There. She had sent out her feelings in the energy; she did her part. Whether such resolution could come to pass was no longer up to her.

To help herself let go of her anguish and longing, Judith put as much of her attention as she could on inhaling and exhaling pipe smoke. The tobacco scent always reminded her of her childhood in the hills of Southern Alta Province. Seated on rough wooden chairs on the wide front porch of the ancient Altair farmhouse, her father and her uncle would light up at sunset after a long day's toil in the fields.

Unnoticed, Judith would sit quietly underneath the porch, listening as the men talked politics. Her Uncle Jason knew much about such matters. He had been a high-ranking soldier and aide to Lord Jess Mordecai, the father of Lord James. She watched many a summer evening fade into darkness to the sounds of their animated and sometimes heated discussions.

Memories of the lingering twilight, the cool breezes of summer in the higher elevations, and the dry-sweet odors from their pipes helped relieve Judith's sorrow and tension. She felt calmer, if not yet altogether ready to sleep. She placed her pipe on the table next to the bed, and rested her head again on the pillow.

She began a simple series of breathing exercises, designed to induce a light meditative state. Perhaps some insight into Prince Enoch's deepening anger and his plans would come to her. She had to find out.

Somehow, she knew it was critical and did not bode well either for Lord Justin, Helen, or any Turanian related to him by marriage to his wife, Elizabeth.

Suddenly Judith's consciousness split in two. Her physical body and a portion of her awareness were still in the Atlas manor in Shambhala. The rest of her hovered over a ring of tall evergreens like the ones that flourished in Southern Alta Province.

That part of her floating above a stone obelisk in the center of the circle knew of this place, even if she had never set foot near it before. It was sacred to the *Oonakim*, or Mist-Weavers. The flesh crawled on the physical body that lay in bed. The sensation was remote, as though it came from a great distance. She was astounded. *How did I get here?*

Then she saw the eyes. The round pools of yellow-green luminescence without pupils or lids, like the surface of eternity. The familiar reedy voice echoed within her consciousness as though her physical ears heard it.

"You enjoy our method of travel, my friend?"

"Maguari!"

"Of course. And our method of travel?"

The Mist-Weaver could be irritatingly single-minded. Some of Judith's amazement faded. "I prefer more conventional means, thank you."

She detected what seemed like an indignant sniff. "Your methods are very slow and cumbersome, my friend. I have my reasons for fetching you as I did."

"Reasons? Maguari, I don't understand. I haven't thought about you for ages."

"Perhaps you should. You have been praying earnestly of late. Anyone with any sensitivity to energy can detect your heart's desire."

Tears formed in Judith's eyes.

"I have brought you that which you have asked for, my friend. Go in peace."

The Mist-Weaver's powerful presence faded away. Judith now found herself in a dim, misty, ill-defined space. A form took shape before her. It was almost indistinguishable from the haze, yet Judith had the impression this being was standing as though leaning against something that Judith could not distinguish.

Through her keen sense of spiritual feeling rather than her inner vision, Judith could make out the form's appearance. Green eyes and long blonde hair bound up in a brightly colored scarf. The being also had sleeves that were rolled up, and wore an apron, as though ready to start work. Judith's nostrils detected the pungent scent of massage oil.

"Miriam!"

"Hello, Snoop. It's been a long time."

"Why did you never come to me when I called for you?"

The lightness of Miriam's energy faded and folded inward. "Why did you never come to me when I wrote you?"

Judith related how someone stole the letter and it ended up in the possession of the Supreme Lord, who kept it secret for more than ten years. "I finally read your letter less than three months ago."

Miriam's energy became still, as though she was considering the explanation with care.

Judith's own pain and searing regret propelled her to continue. "Confound it, Miriam. I tried to help you so many times, but your own damned pride would not allow you to accept it from me, or anyone. Certainly not from James."

Miriam's shock slammed into Judith.

"Oh yes. I know all about your relationship with James, and his relationship to Helen. Everyone does. The Kindred have read the letter you wrote to her."

"No! Oh, please heaven, no!"

The energy of Miriam's tiny frame trembled. Judith's heart responded in kind; both were unable to continue for some time. After they calmed down, Judith explained the full circumstances surrounding the document being made public.

"It does not feel as though he sold her." Miriam's thoughts were the softest of whispers inside Judith's head.

"As it happens, dear heart, he refused to put her up for bid," Judith replied. "But that doesn't matter anymore. Keep Helen or sell her, James is a dead man. Most of us know it, you know it, and at some level he knows it as well."

"Snoop, please," Miriam said with great effort. "Do what you can to save Helen."

"You thought you had to ask?"

"This is more important than you realize. I don't ask this simply for the sake of our friendship or even my daughter. The very survival of our peoples is at stake."

Miriam directed waves of intense feelings toward Judith, whose inner vision exploded with horrifying images. They were tiny, as though viewed across a great expanse of space or time, yet very sharp. She saw Toltecs marching across the island, engaged in armed combat that was destroying the countryside. Large groups of terrified Turanians were being rounded up and slaughtered or enslaved. Famine and disease ravaged the land and the people.

As the vision faded, the entire island exploded, splitting asunder straight along the mountains that divided the land in two halves, both of which then sank rapidly beneath the waves, forever lost.

Miriam gave Judith time to digest the unspoken understandings that accompanied the images. At some point early in her life, Miriam had previewed the utter destruction of Azgard. Its apparent cause was the Toltecs' internal power struggles.

"Snoop, have you ever heard of the Arkstone?"

Judith gasped. The existence of the Arkstone was one of the Temple's deepest secrets. How did Miriam know about it? She lay stunned.

Miriam continued. "I know you know what a Resonator is, Snoop."

Judith's eyes popped open; she shut them gently. How could Miriam have learned about this as well as the Arkstone? The Resonator was another of the Temple's closest secrets. Every Supreme Lord had ordered his underlings to experiment with such a machine for hundreds of years now, trying to learn how to control the dispersal of the energy. Not all the chants and rituals undertaken at The Citadel were purely spiritual.

"A Resonator is not a physical device, Snoop. It is a group of people. And one person, the anchor, must use a fragment of the original Arkstone — just like the green stone that I gave to Helen. It was part of the original Arkstone."

Judith inhaled sharply, then lay motionless while Miriam filled in more understanding of the vision. The ancient Toltecs of the era of Kronos had the capability and knowledge to activate and harness the power of a resonator, provided they had a piece of the Arkstone, most of which were now hidden or lost.

Those abilities atrophied, however, because they used the resulting energy solely for conquest and domination rather than for loving, healing, and nurturing. They accelerated the decline of their abilities by judging against emotions as weak, and by denying their hearts in favor of their intellects and raw power over others.

Once the specific heart vibration was diminished or missing altogether from their auras, the Toltecs could no longer activate a Resonator and even forgot what it was. Turanians still had heart energy, yet lacked any ability to implement the design because they had judged themselves powerless since the day of their final military defeat by the Toltecs. As a result of these judgments, Turanians by and large were lacking in personal power.

"Imagine it, Snoop." Miriam's energy was filled with awe and hope. "The lost intuitive abilities and raw power of the Toltecs married to the heart of the Turanians. The mixed-race children of such unions would have the ability to bring peace and restore prosperity to all in Azgard. They could even hold off any external or internal force if necessary. All by blending mental toughness with heart love, then accelerated and enhanced by a green stone."

"How, Miriam? I don't understand it fully."

"By setting up a Resonator and using the energy," she replied. "Just one person, properly trained and using an Arkstone fragment, like the green stone, can raise the vibration sufficiently to draw and focus enormous amounts of power. Four or five is better."

Another part of the vision unfolded before Judith. Helen stood in the center of a small group, arms reaching out, palms upward as in an act of supplication. Her long black hair was waving and full-length skirt billowing in what could have been mistaken for a brisk wind, yet was wave after wave of powerful, pulsating energy.

Dumbfounded, Judith realized that the energy was forming a barrier. Bombs were exploding all around it; bullets were hitting it; nothing was affecting it. All those surrounded by that energy were completely safe.

Even more shocking, Helen used no physical device except the green stone hanging over her heart. It seemed to be much larger than its usual size and glowed brilliantly. The resonator generating the energy waves consisted of Helen, flanked and supported by Judith herself, Lord Justin, Jackson, and, of all people, Lord Matthew.

Miriam smiled at Judith's reaction to Lord Matthew's presence in the group. "The House of Poseidon is no longer of pure Toltec ancestry."

Judith was still confused. "What's the method? Exactly how do we generate this energy field?"

The heart was the primary key. Energy summoned from the Divine Source through the aura's power center also had to flow through the heart to add the personal love that made it healing, nurturing, and protective. Energy summoned without the heart and flowing solely through the power center could be only destructive. This was the kind of energy that formed the essence of and emanated from most present-day Toltecs. It was judgmental, violent, punitive, and loveless.

The process also needed one person with one stone as the focus. Miriam seemed to speak directly into her beloved friend's ear. "Look into Helen's heart, Judith. She is the anchor you seek for your Resonator. She has that raw power that somehow, she must learn to harness."

Judith saw Helen again at the core of the energy field. She understood. The stone could help magnify and focus any energy Helen and the others of the group summoned. It was no substitute for the ability or the energy itself, but when both were present, the stone could enhance the effects considerably and make the buildup of power much more rapid.

"You begin to know why the ancients revered the original giant Arkstone, Snoop," Miriam said. "It is a very powerful tool for healing and for protection, provided the energy is loving. That is why I asked Helen to keep it hidden. If such a stone falls into the wrong hands, and is used to magnify unloving energy for power or control, the outcome could be disastrous."

"Then we will just have to keep that from happening," Judith murmured.

Miriam's energy filled with a heavy dread. "The Stoneslayer also has a piece of the Arkstone and is looking for more. Snoop, you must keep Helen and the green stone safe from him."

Judith was confused. "Who is the Stoneslayer, Miriam?"

"An evil entity that has already caused much death and destruction, like the mysterious building collapses that separated me from James. A man right now is under his thrall. If, through that man, that evil being gets his hands on another part of the Arkstone, it will be impossible to stop."

Judith groaned silently. So much bad news.

"Don't give up, Snoop," Miriam urged softly. "There is hope. The chain that surrounds Helen's gem is also important and can help counteract the Stoneslayer. Ask Maguari about it sometime."

"Maguari?"

"Yes. Maguari supplied James with the design for the chain. James had no conscious idea of the deeper reasons Maguari encouraged him to give me the stone and chain. He thought he did it because the stone matched the color of my eyes, silly man."

Miriam's energy was so wistful, so full of longing that Judith could hardly stand to feel it.

"I had this vision long before I became involved with James," she added. "And had we not loved each other, Snoop, I still would have sought him out to father my mixed-race child once I got to know him. He is the most principled, most honorable, and the kindest of any Toltec I ever met."

Judith nodded in heartfelt agreement. So, there were many layers of causation behind the meeting of Lord James and Miriam. At the conscious level, he needed someone to provide specific care for an ailing wife. And at another, far deeper level, she needed someone to provide a very specific contribution toward helping her fulfill the obviously strong commitment she had made to this portent-laden vision.

Now what? Judith acknowledged with tremendous sadness that there was little she could do for Lord James in his hour of peril, other than offering advice that he was not likely to take. She did have something specific to offer Helen, who more than ever desperately needed such help. Judith had no idea how much assistance she would be permitted to provide. Lord James was not likely to want to part with his daughter. Helen might not recognize the imperative of *kura* training, which was the best way to impart the energy manipulation skills needed to activate a Resonator. If only Miriam had not waited so long to send for her.

"I was selfish, Snoop," Miriam said. "Just as I did with James, I kept Helen with me for as long as I could, until so-called circumstances forced me to part with her."

More tears streamed down Judith's face. "I still feel like I failed you, dear heart. I didn't come in time to get you or the child. I would have found a way, if I had just gotten that letter."

She sensed Miriam shaking her head. "I know now you did not fail me. I could not and would not have come back with you anyway, my dearest friend. There was no safe place for me in Azgard anymore. Maybe there never really was such a place, especially after I fell in love with James, and it just took me a while to come to understand and accept it."

Overcome by unresolved feelings of loss and regret, Judith sobbed. "Forgive me," she said. "I do understand some of your feelings, Miriam, especially why you did not want to marry James."

Slowly, and then more quickly, her heart filled with love coming from Miriam's spirit. She was shocked. Her dear friend was giving her a hug, enfolding her physical body with her soul energy. Judith opened her heart to return the embrace.

"It feels so real, Miriam."

Laughter. "Of course it does, Snoop. It is real. Love does not depend on physical existence. It's the other way around. Love never dies. It's the only thing that's real. The rest is just window dressing."

Judith's tears spilled into her ears. This time they were cleansing and healing instead of painful. She could tell Miriam was weeping right along with her.

"Why do you cry, dear heart?" Judith asked.

"I need your forgiveness, too, my dearest and true friend. I accused you of failing me, and I hurt you, and I never wanted that. Never."

Judith lay happily enfolded in Miriam's gentle spiritual embrace, relishing the presence of her beloved friend's energy. Once again, she felt just how deeply she had missed Miriam all these many years. She also realized that before she truly could forgive Miriam, she very much needed another answer. Then she sensed what had to have been a chuckle.

"Now what do you want to ask me, Snoop? This time you'll have to tell me, because I have refrained from reading your energy."

"Why did you never tell me?" Judith blurted out. "About James? About the child? James is deeply hurt and furious with you right now. I confess I've been pretty unhappy with you myself. And poor Helen is a walking emotional time bomb. Miriam, what on earth were you thinking?"

Miriam radiated sadness and regret. "I had to be true to my vision."

"Weren't there other ways to honor it without so much pain and sacrifice?"

"I couldn't think of any, Snoop. Maybe you will be wiser."

Judith was not so certain about that. She knew only that she needed and wanted to let go of her wrath and to forgive Miriam, for both of their sakes. She sorted through as many of her emotions as she could identify, feeling the anger finally dissolve. When it was gone, she knew she was able at last to forgive Miriam, deep within her heart as well as from her spirit. And with that release there came to Judith the strongest sense of peace and serenity that she could ever recall experiencing. It was utter bliss, profoundly healing, setting aside for the moment her new concerns about Helen and the danger from the Stoneslayer.

"If you need it, Miriam dear heart, you have my forgiveness," she whispered as the first rays of sunlight stole into the room.

Finally, Judith slept.

# CHAPTER THIRTY-SEVEN

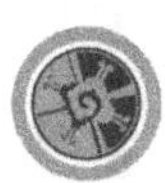

Like Judith, Helen could not sleep. She lay on her bed in her father's manor, her mind going strong despite her physical weariness.

Lord Matthew was the biggest concern keeping her awake, although she had many other fears gnawing at her, too. The skin grafts would not be enough for him to heal completely. There was an alternative hinted at in the medical literature, but even if she developed it into a procedure, her medical peers would regard it as experimental and might not grant her permission to do it. If she was forbidden to try it, how would he ever get better?

Frustrated, she bounced upright, massaged her temples, and rotated her shoulders, trying to unwind and relax. Her green stone appeared in her inner vision and she lowered her hands. Maybe it could help him. It helped her save Prince Harnak's life and Orlando's. Helen tapped her fingers against her chin, thinking. She needed to know fully what had happened. How did the stone work? What were its limitations, if any?

"No!" The eerie red glow flashed through her inner vision and then packed the chamber with rough, roiling energy. Helen's upper body slammed against the mattress. Horrible, crushing weight pressed down on her torso. She gasped, heaving her chest outward, trying to fill her lungs with air. She could not take in enough of it. The bed spun beneath her and black spots floated before her eyes.

"No!" The horrible menacing voice filled her head. "You have no right to use that stone! It is mine! Give it to me now! Or I will send you to the darkest hellish depths where you will despair forever."

Her body faded away so far, she almost lost her connection to it. Utter blackness enveloped her, shutting off all warmth. All light. All love. All support. All hope. She was pinned, alone, naked, and freezing before a beast so terrifying she struggled to avert her gaze but could not.

Horns arose from the top of what had to be a head. Fangs protruded obscenely from a frowning hole that must have been a mouth. Unsheathed claws threatened instant evisceration. Horrifying eyes. Two cesspits of black fury in which red flames churned like burning blood. They bore down on Helen, intensifying the pressure on her to the point of agony.

Inside her head a message played over and over. *You are helpless.* Helen's fragmented thoughts spun wildly. What to do? How to stop this nightmare?

The wretched voice roared again, like nails clashing against slate. "Give me the stone! Now!"

The fury hurled at her backfired. It ignited her own simmering rage against anyone and everyone trying to run her life. Can't give in! Won't give in! Evil! Evil! Resist! Resist! Resist!

A faint, distant pulse tapped her chest, right over her heart. Another one. And another one. The very softness and silence of the gesture captured her attention despite the malicious chaos in her mind and surrounding her.

The green stone! The gem was sending her a message. Act now or it would be too late! Sweating, panting, resisting with every ounce of strength left to her, she wriggled a finger and managed to brush the jewel. *Help! Help me!*

"Noooooo!"

The wretched voice screeched and shut off. The boulder weight crushing her dissolved. She gulped in deep breaths, once more fully in her body and lying on her back. She turned her head deliberately from side to side, astonished. The bed was in its proper place, the sheets and comforter barely disturbed. *Was it all in my mind? Was it real?*

She threw the comforter off her shoulders and launched her upper body upright into a seated position. She brought her legs close to her chest, and wrapped her arms around them, her chin resting on her nightgown-covered knees. Rocking backward and forward slowly, Helen tried to calm herself and get her racing heartbeat to slow down and return to normal.

*What just happened to me? What was that…that monster?*

The small hairs on the back of her neck ran riot. She reached out to the night table and flicked on a light-stick, scanning the bedchamber. The seemingly solid wall next to the bathroom entrance was rippling and curling while a filmy substance spilled from it into the room. Out of this mist-like essence a very tall, rail-thin form took shape before her.

Helen said nothing, did nothing. Gaping, she realized she was not so much terrified as alert, almost completely re-energized, and, finally, no longer panicked. Her breathing and heartbeat were steady, and somehow that mist-enshrouded being was responsible.

The change in her physical condition persuaded her that this was not just some fatigue-induced delusion or stress-based hallucination. It certainly was not anything like the attack — or whatever it was — she just experienced and barely survived.

The figure was obscured by a dark green cowl and shapeless dark garment. It floated in front of the wall. "Do not be alarmed, Stonehealer."

One of the figure's loose-fitting sleeves fanned out as it lifted its arm toward Helen. "I am not imaginary. I am Maguari. And I am not the being you just met — and defeated."

Helen could not respond. Why did she have no desire to scream for help like she did before? Perhaps it was because the being's voice, reedy and echoing, as though it came from a long distance, was nonetheless comforting. And familiar.

How utterly bizarre. Surely, she had never met this creature before. A million questions poured through her mind.

The cowl flopped to one side. "We last were together while you were still in the womb. That is why I seem both odd and not entirely a stranger. You know my energy."

Helen just gawped. The cowl flipped in the other direction; he/she/it was laughing. Maybe. It sounded like a strangled cackle.

"It might help to know that your mother's friend, Judith Altair, also finds me somewhat, shall we say, unsettling."

Helen looked from the wall, which seemed steady once more, to the gap between the floor and the bottom of the hovering garment. She licked her lips.

"Your voice. It was you. You told me to use the green stone on Prince Harnak! And on Colonel Orlando! I heard you so clearly inside my head. Did you just now somehow send me a message through my stone?"

"Yes, to all of those questions. I did. The stone you wear has many properties and potentials. But I also must ask you, as did your mother, not to let anyone know when or how you use it for healing."

Helen lowered her knees and took a cross-legged position on the bed, pulling the comforter closer to cover her lap fully. "Who are you?"

"The people of Southern Alta call me and my kind *Oonakim*, Mist-Weavers. It is a quaint description of what energy-mastery looks like to their uneducated eyes."

"There has to be more to it than that," she replied, thinking of her first uninvited visitor.

"There is. Mist-Weavers are interdimensional, among the first of the spirits the Creator called into being. Over vast stretches of what you perceive as time, a few of us have befriended spirits while they live a human existence."

Helen hiked an eyebrow. "I guess that makes sense. You surely are not a priest. I doubt any of the Brotherhood of Kronos knows how to perform the kinds of tricks that get you into a room through a wall instead of the door."

She could have sworn she heard an indignant sniff, as though the being were insulted. "These are not tricks." The voice was even more reverberating than before.

Helen squeezed her eyes shut briefly, chagrined. Would she ever learn to think before speaking? "My apologies, Master Maguari. I meant no insult to you or your kind. I had a rough time of it just now and I'm not thinking any too clearly."

Maguari seemed mollified, folding the lower part of his figure into a cross-legged seated position. Helen did find it disconcerting to watch him drift between the ceiling and the floor with no visible means of support.

She ventured a question. "What just happened to me?"

"You faced the Stoneslayer," the strange being answered. "Unlike many men whom the beast overwhelmed quickly, you did not give in, despite your terror and pain. Your inner strength and courage are precisely why it loathes you and craves you all at once."

Helen shook her head. "That is not much comfort, Master Maguari. "What is the Stoneslayer? Is the Stoneslayer a Mist-Weaver?"

"No," Maguari said, quickly and firmly. "The Stonelayer is one among the souls that chose to reject the Creator. In rejecting the Creator's love, such souls lose their own innate power and must find the power to be, to exist, from another source.

"All souls come into being with their own inherent power, and continue to exist because that power is constantly replenished with the endless flow of the Creator's unconditional love. Spirits that deny such love must feed off the energy of other souls — or some other power source like the green stone you wear."

Maguari's cowl swished from side to side. "You and yours have already crossed paths with the Stoneslayer many times, over many physical lifetimes, and you must be prepared to do so again — for the sake of all."

Helen let out a long breath, trembling anew. She stretched forward to grab an extra blanket from the foot of the bed, wrapped it around her shoulders, and sat upright again.

"Is that why you are here, Master Maguari? To warn me?"

He bobbed up and down, hovering midway between the wooden floor and the beamed ceiling. The Mist-Weaver version of yes, Helen supposed. She rubbed her face. She was spent, but she still had more questions. "Where is the Stoneslayer now?"

"The Stoneslayer possesses the body of a soul seeking ultimate power in Azgard," Maguari said. "It has an ally in the top ranks of the Temple."

The skin on the back of Helen's neck crawled in confirmation of the Mist-Weaver's words; she shuddered again and hugged the throw tighter around her upper body.

Maguari continued. "He still wants your green stone, and you must do whatever you can to keep him from obtaining it — despite the perils."

"But I feel so alone and powerless," Helen almost wailed. "What can *I* do against such evil?"

"You are hardly powerless," Maguari countered. "You did not give in to its coercion, and you have no idea how many supposedly strong men it has vanquished with merely a taste of what you endured just now."

Maguari sent her gentle pulses of calming and supporting love-energy. "Nor are you alone. You have many allies and helpers, including the Mist-Weavers. I promise to show you how to harness the green stone to keep yourself and others safe from the Stoneslayer — and anyone else who would harm you or those you love."

Helen let out a long breath. There was another message or warning in what the Mist-Weaver just said, but it was all too overwhelming to think about right now. Maybe not ever. She had no idea what to do about pretty much everything in her crazy mixed-up life as it was now. She unexpectedly felt drowsy. She shrugged off the small blanket and tossed it to the foot of the bed, then lay down again, pulling the comforter up to her shoulders.

"Sleep now," Maguari urged her softly. "Your physical body needs rest, and so do your heart, mind, and spirit."

Even before he finished speaking, Helen fell into a deep, dreamless slumber, leaving behind for another day the added dangers and challenges she now knew she faced.

# CHAPTER THIRTY-EIGHT (AFTERWORD)

Helen was so much braver than I. Had the Stoneslayer attacked me like he did her, or had Maguari warned me about the danger he posed, I would have run screaming and thrown myself into the deepest, darkest hole I could find. Ignorance was a form of bliss, I guess, until it wasn't.

The Stoneslayer was patient, playing the long game, slowly sapping the integrity of our most powerful institutions and leaders. And ever ready to kill off anyone who might get in the way of its relentless march toward chaos and annihilation.

After everything that has happened, I am still glad that I did not know and could not foresee what awaited us all. I don't think I could have made it through one night if I had.

END OF BOOK ONE

Did you enjoy Scandal? I hope so.

Please go to your favorite online bookseller or reading group and leave a review — even just a few words. Reviews go a long way to help indie authors like me. To be notified about new books in the Stoneslayer series, sign up for my very infrequent, no spam-no fluff newsletter at https://www.candacelynntalmadge.com

Family trees and a Glossary of people, places,
and things in Azgard are next.

# RULING HOUSE OF POSEIDON

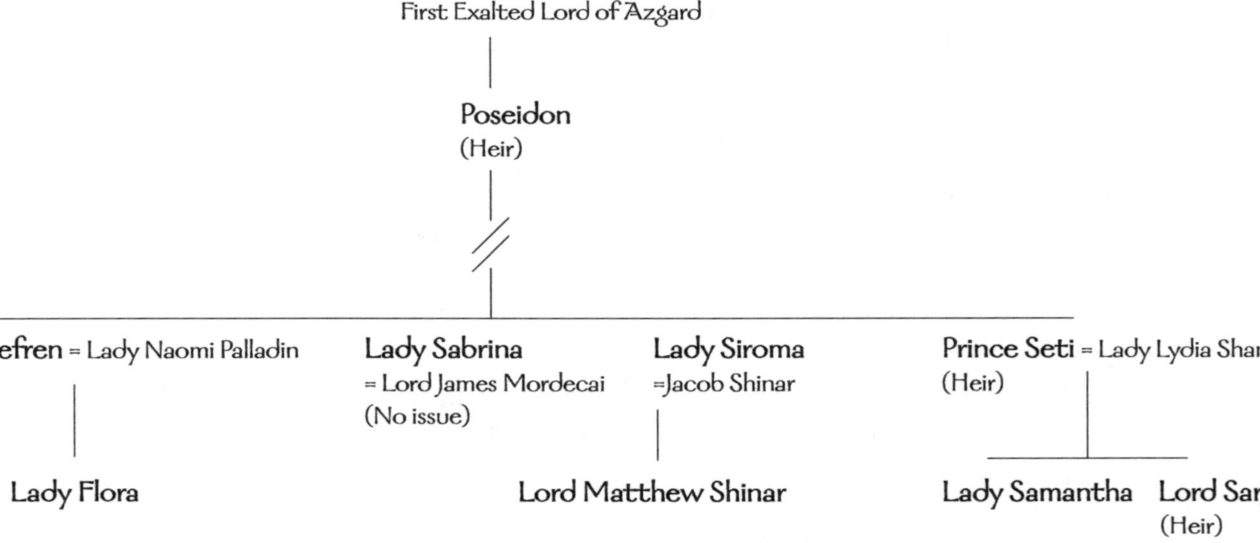

# ROYAL HOUSE OF ATLAS

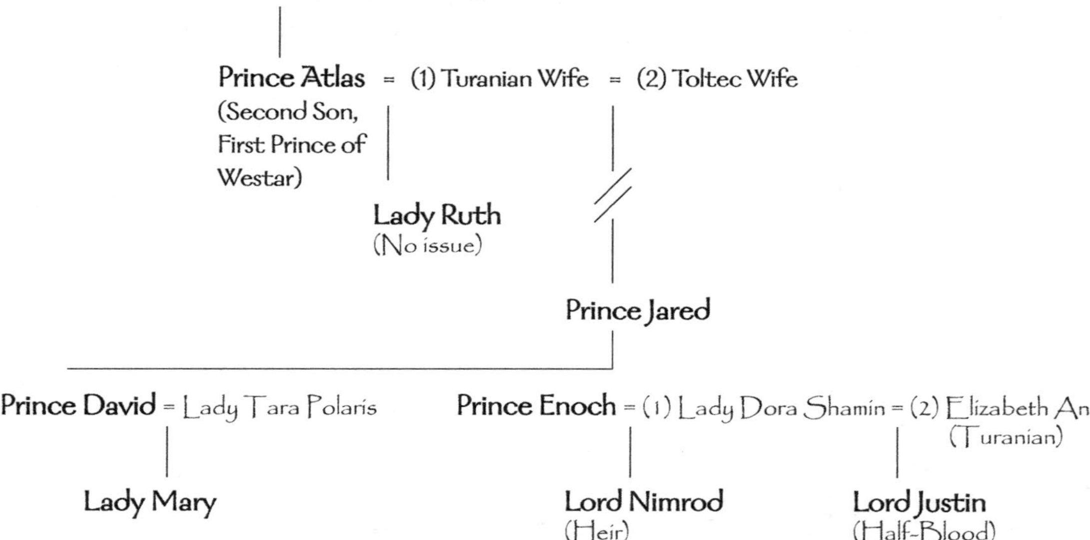

# HOUSE OF MORDECAI

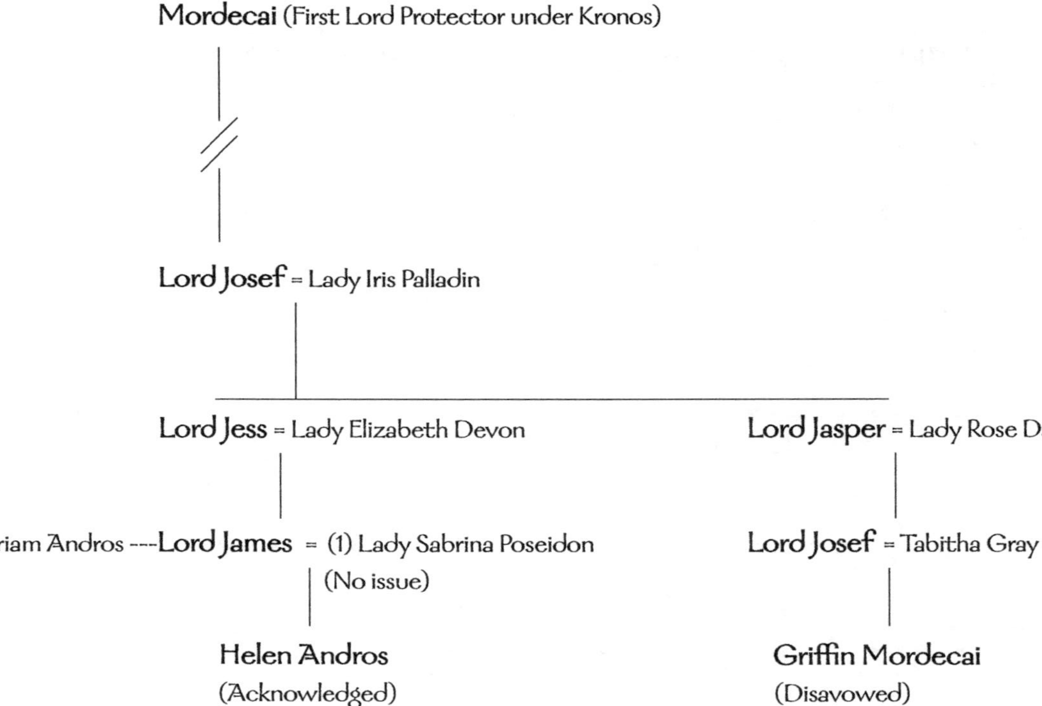

# ANDROS FAMILY

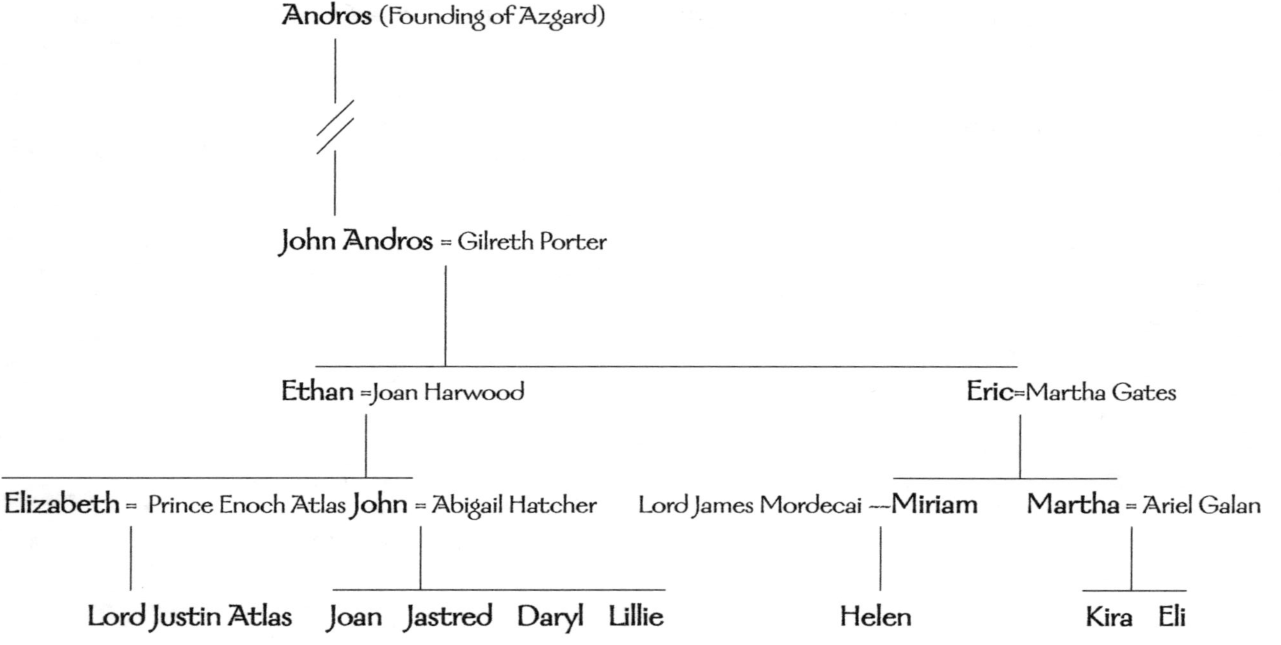

# GLOSSARY

**Akkad, Ibrihim**

One of Azgard's most wanted criminals, his real name, appearance, and background were shrouded in mystery. Out of nowhere he became an assassin-for-hire and was wanted in connection with many other brutal crimes, most notably the Lesser Shore building implosions that killed dozens and ensnared Helen's mother in trumped-up charges that led to her exile in Kamut.

**Altair Family**

An ancient family well known in Southern Alta Province, where the members owned and farmed land. The male head of the family was chief of Clan Altair.

**Altair, Judith**

Judith was born and brought up in the mountainous region of Southern Alta Province. At age twenty, she was taken by priests to the Sacred Academy of Kronos, where she studied religion and counseling and befriended a Turanian named Miriam Andros. Judith became an advisor to the rich and powerful. She was unusual as an unmarried woman of independent means and widespread connections.

**Altair, Loren**

Born Loren Orlando, she married Morgan Altair and had three children, the eldest of whom was a daughter, Judith.

**Ames, Sheridan**

A Turanian cloth merchant and a key member of the Consort's ultra-secret spy network.

**Andros Family**

Turanians who were prominent in far northern Westar Province, where they farmed extensive land just south of the Shiloh River.

**Andros, Abigail**

Born Abigail Hatcher, she was married to John Andros, head of the Andros family.

**Andros, Elizabeth**

Princess of Westar, second wife of Prince Enoch Atlas, and mother of Lord Justin Atlas. She was the elder sister of John Andros and cousin of Miriam Andros and Martha Galan.

**Andros, Ethan**

Head of the Andros family who preceded his only son, John, and father of Elizabeth. He threw Miriam Andros out of his house upon learning she was pregnant with a mixed-race child yet not wed to the child's father. He refused to allow Helen to visit the Andros farm after she arrived from Kamut.

**Andros, Eric**

Younger brother of Ethan. A blacksmith by trade, he was the father of Miriam Andros and Martha Galan.

**Andros, Helen**

Natural daughter of Miriam Andros and Lord James Mordecai. A top honors graduate of the Sacred Academy of Kronos in medical arts and science, she was a physician in the 163rd Regiment and, at age twenty-one, became an acknowledged daughter of the House of Mordecai. She was the holder of the green healing stone given to her by her mother.

**Andros, John**

Head of the Andros family and owner of the Andros holdings in far northern Westar Province. John was the younger brother of Elizabeth Andros and cousin of Martha Galan and Miriam Andros.

**Andros, Miriam**

Daughter of Eric Andros, cousin of Elizabeth and John Andros, and secret *lizun* of Lord James Mordecai. Miriam attended the Sacred Academy of Kronos, where she earned degrees in physical therapy and massage. There she befriended Judith

Altair. Prompted by a mysterious vision, Miriam conceived a mixed-race child out of wedlock with Lord James. She was exiled from Azgard after being wrongly accused in a series of building collapses. In Kamut she brought up her daughter and was believed to have died in the Second Nubian War after sending Helen back to Azgard. She received the green stone from Lord James.

## Agarthi

The name of the palace that was the official residence of the Exalted Lord. It was located on the northern shore of Lake *Shambhala*.

## Alta, City of

The capital city of Alta Province on the northwest coast.

## Alta, Dukedom of

Position held by the head of the House of Mordecai. It was a major political power base and bestowed great wealth on its holder.

## Alta Province

The richest of the four provinces, Alta Province formed the northwest quadrant of the island and was noted for its fishing fleets, its indigenous horses, and an abundance of precious minerals and gems. It came to the House of Mordecai after Kronos rewarded Mordecai with first choice among the provinces.

## *Arkana*

A collection of texts written over thousands of years by a variety of authors, mostly priests. The writings addressed a wide range of subjects. Helen studied the portions of the *Arkana* that dealt with medical topics to learn about the healing properties of herbs and how to prepare and use them. The sections covering highly sensitive religious and political topics were kept from the public by the Brotherhood of Kronos.

## Arkstone

A huge boulder that dropped onto earth in ancient times and amazingly did not disintegrate. It was multicolored and stored vast amounts of energy. Guided by the Mist-Weavers, a few Toltecs culled small pieces of the Arkstone and used their energies to power machines and devices without fuel or pollution. By Helen's lifetime, the existence of the Arkstone and its fragments were known only to a few. One of these was the Stoneslayer, who craved all remaining Arkstone pieces to gain enough power to be unstoppable.

## Atalan

The language of the Turanians, it was preferred for commerce and daily use. It was much simpler to learn and use and offered a more graceful speech pattern than the Toltecs' language. The Toltecs readily adopted it after the Battle of *Shambhala*.

## Atlanta, City of

The capital of Istar Province on the northeast coast. Heavily populated by Toltecs, it was a major manufacturing and export-import center.

## Atlanta, Dukedom of

Title held by the son of the Prince of Istar and a position of great wealth and influence. The Duke of Atlanta customarily was in line to inherit the Kingship.

## Atlas, House of

The junior branch of the Toltecs' Royal family. This Royal House descended directly from Prince Atlas, officially the younger son of Kronos. The lord of the House of Atlas held the title of Prince of Westar. His heir was known as the Duke of Avalon.

## Atlas, Prince David

Elder brother of Prince Enoch and father of Lady Mary, his only child. Died before fathering an heir in the unexplained crash of a *zefir*.

## Atlas, Prince Enoch

Second son of Prince Jared Atlas, younger brother of Prince David (deceased). By his first wife, Lady Dora Shamin, he had his heir. By his second wife he had a mixed-race second son.

## Atlas, Prince Jared

Father of Prince David and Prince Enoch, grandfather of Lord Nimrod and Lord Justin.

**Atlas, Lord Justin**

Second son of Prince Enoch and only child of Elizabeth Andros. Lord Justin attended the Sacred Academy of Kronos, studying mathematics and graduating with the highest academic record of any student up to his time. Mixed-race, he was a cousin of Lady Mary Atlas and second cousin of Helen.

**Atlas, Lady Mary**

Only child of Prince David and his wife, Lady Tara Polaris; niece of Prince Enoch Atlas and Lord Tarkon Polaris, Duke of Eden. Betrothed at birth to Lord Sargon Poseidon (second in line to the Kingship). Mentored as a young woman by the Consort, Lady Mary became a close friend of Helen despite the differences in their ranks and social standing. She was a cousin of Lord Nimrod and Lord Justin.

**Atlas, Lord Nimrod**

Elder and favored son of Prince Enoch, he was Duke of Avalon and heir to the Princedom of Westar. He trained in law at a specialized professional school since he did not meet the academic requirements to attend the Academy.

**Avalon, City of**

The capital city of Westar Province on the west coast of Azgard. It was also the seat of the only university on the island, the Sacred Academy of Kronos.

**Avalon, Dukedom of**

A position of considerable wealth and influence. This title was held by the heir of the Prince of Westar.

**Azgard**

An island the size of a continent ruled by a people known as the Toltecs, who conquered it thousands of years before the life of Helen. It was roughly three thousand miles across and five thousand miles north to south. It was divided into four provinces, each bordered by two of the four Sacred Rivers.

**Blood, The**

This was a term Toltecs used to signify membership (or lack thereof) in their race. It was a shortened version of the phrase, *Blood of the Kindred*. Only those of The Blood could receive most of the religious sacraments offered by the Temple of Kronos. Most government positions were also reserved only for those of The Blood.

**Blood-Oath**

Taken by candidates for membership in the Brotherhood of Kronos, these vows transformed them into priests.

**Brotherhood of Kronos**

Formal name of the priesthood that interpreted, followed, and enforced the state religion of the Toltecs.

**Dilmun**

The name for Azgard in the dialect of Kadosh spoken by several of the Twelve Tribes of the *Umarii* Federation, including the Kalmuk.

**Eden, Dukedom of**

Held by the head of the House of Polaris, this was another position of political influence and some wealth.

**Eden Province**

In the southeastern part of the island, this was the least affluent of the four provinces. Its main income sources were agricultural products that included wool and rice from the lowland marshes.

**Exalted Lord**

The Toltecs' formal title for their ruler, who was also referred to simply as the king or holder of the Kingship.

**Floater**

A part of the high technology of the earliest Toltecs, this self-powered device suspended matter above the ground and could raise or lower it. Floaters were used for elevators in multistory buildings. Smaller, personal versions could be used like crutches to support the physically challenged. During Helen's life, floaters had become rare and costly because no one knew any longer how to make or repair the energy generating mechanism.

**Galan, Ariel**

The uncle of Helen by marriage to her Aunt Martha, Ariel was a provisioner by trade. He and his wife owned a shop in the City of Avalon where they sold excess merchandise that he came across in his work purchasing goods for his various noble and business clients.

**Galan, Martha**

Born Martha Andros, she was Helen's aunt and the younger sister of Miriam Andros. She was married to Ariel Galan and had two children, Kira and Eli.

**Green Stone**

A fragment of the original Arkstone, this gem came to Miriam Andros from her secret lover, Lord James Mordecai, who received it from his mother. It was a unique combination of teal sapphire and other rocks that provided a powerful tool for healing and protection. It also had other properties and potentials that made it dangerous in the wrong hands.

**Grid**

The Toltecs' technology for short and long-distance communication and for storing and retrieving documents. Grid access was limited to Toltecs and certain Turanians, such as Ariel Galan, who were acting with permission from a Toltec master or client. Helen had Grid access based on her medical degree.

**Harnak, Prince**

A political hostage of the state of Azgard, Helen kept him from dying. He was the son and heir of the ruler of Kamut, a vassal state of Azgard.

**Holy One (Supreme Lord of the Temple of Kronos)**

The religious leader and final authority on doctrine within the Temple of Kronos. In the first part of the life of Helen, this office was filled by Ezekiel Malachi. It conferred a great deal of prestige and political power upon its holder.

**Impeller**

A motor that never needed fuel. These machines powered devices like floaters, skimmers, and *zefirs*. Impellers were energy-based technology imparted to the Toltecs during the life of Kronos by the Mist-Weavers. By the time of Helen, the Toltecs had forgotten how to fabricate impellers and the Mist-Weavers refused to share that knowledge with them again based on their abuse of the Turanians.

**Istar, Princedom of**

The position held by the heir to the Kingship, usually the eldest son of the Exalted Lord or, when the Exalted lord had no son, the Exalted Lord's younger brother. This was the case when Helen was a young woman because Kefren had no son. The title bestowed great wealth, power, and influence on its holder.

**Istar Province**

The province in the northeast of the island, ruled by its prince. It was highly industrialized and derived its wealth from manufacturing.

*Kaf*

A hot brewed drink like coffee and widely popular throughout Azgard.

**Kamut**

A desert country far to the east of Azgard. Its importance lay in its strategic position next to major waterways and trade routes for an entire hemisphere. Helen was born and spent the first ten years of her life in this country.

*Kazil*

A trial for a capital crime. This special body consisted of the members of the *Kinshazen* and the Host of the Faithful, the high-ranking priests who helped the Supreme Lord define and enforce matters of religious doctrine and practice. The Exalted Lord could attend a *Kazil* but did not have a vote. A *Kazil* was presided over by the Lord Steward.

*Kindlemaz*

A Toltec winter holiday adapted from the Turanian religious celebration.

**Kindling**

A Turanian religious festival based on the winter solstice. It lasted a week and consisted of parties during the evenings, with the initial ceremony the most important and known as the First Feast.

**Kindred**

Defined narrowly, this term referred to the five hundred-and-two eligible voting members of the *Kinshazen*. In a wider sense, it was another name for all Toltecs.

**Kindred House**

The building in the government administrative complex on the western shore of Lake *Shambhala* that housed the *Kinshazen*.

***Kinshazen***

The legislative body of the Kindred, comprising the heads of the five hundred noble houses, greater and lesser. The Houses of Poseidon and Atlas each had two voting positions in the *Kinshazen*. The *Kinshazen* usually rubber-stamped legislative proposals from the Exalted Lord, but not always. Proceedings were governed by the Lord Steward.

***Koji/Koja*** **(Koo-yee/Koo-yah)**

A physician, male or female, who took the Blood-Oath and served the Temple in some sort of medical capacity.

**Kronos**

The Toltecs' God-King and leader of the Kindred. The Toltecs believed it was Kronos who first led them to Azgard several thousand years before the life of Helen. Kronos was recorded as the first Exalted Lord of the Kindred in Azgard.

**Kronos, Father of**

The Toltecs' term for the Divine, or God.

***Kudik***

A Terzil word that figuratively meant powerless and literally, without male sex organs. It was a highly degrading slang term for anyone who was not Toltec and male. *Kudik* also was the only word in Terzil for a man who sexually desires other men. Same-gender sexual relations were banned by the government and the Temple and punishable by death. The word used in this manner was almost never mentioned in public.

### *Kufir*

A Terzil word for excrement. It was rarely used in public and considered very rude. It was also a highly insulting slang term for a Turanian.

### *Kura*

A Terzil word for the kind of subtle energy that could not be measured or perceived with any instrument available to scientists.

### Kadosh

The language spoken in Kamut. Dialects were used throughout the region.

### Lake *Shambhala*

The huge body of water around which the Sacred City was built. It was extremely deep and froze only during the coldest of winters.

### Link

Technology that enabled the Toltecs to tap into the Grid in order to communicate over short or long distances and retrieve documents.

### *Lizun*

The Toltecs' word for a woman who has sexual relations with a man not her husband and to whom she was not contractually bound, which would have made her a concubine instead.

### Mist-Weavers *(Oonakim)*

A multi-dimensional race of beings who wandered in the mountainous region of Southern Alta Province. Their leader called himself Maguari and tended to be the only one among them to interact directly with human beings. Mist-Weavers knew a great deal about *kura* and how to master and use it. They also were aware of the history of the Toltecs that had been destroyed or altered by the Temple and the role of the Arkstone in that history.

**Mordecai, House of**

The leading Great House. The lord of this House was the Duke of Alta as well as Lord Protector, a position handed to the original Mordecai by Kronos.

**Mordecai, Griffin**

The disavowed heir to Lord James Mordecai, Griffin was Lord James' cousin once removed and second cousin to Helen.

**Mordecai, Lord James**

Duke of Alta, father of Helen, and secret lover of Miriam Andros. He was the first Lord Protector for several hundred years to have a military background and actual command experience before assuming his title.

*Nahazi*

A Terzil word that literally meant "mixed." It was insulting slang for those of mixed-race parentage or for anyone of mixed racial descent. The plural form was *nahazim*.

**Nighthall**

A complex of administrative buildings and courts situated around a huge square on the western shore of Lake *Shambhala*. The government and military of Azgard operated from inside this complex. Chief among the buildings in Nighthall was Kindred House, next to the lake.

**Orlando, Jackson (Colonel)**

Helen's commanding officer as head of the 163rd Regiment. After Lord James acknowledged Helen, Jackson quit the army to become her bodyguard. Lord James made Jackson his personal aide. Among his many talents was investigation.

**Palladin, House of**

One of the Great Houses, the source of its wealth was in patents and trade rather than in land holdings.

**Palladin, Lord Andrew**

Head of this Great House, he was nephew of the Consort and rose to prominence during the final years of Kefren's rule.

**Palladin, Lady Naomi**

Wife of Kefren, she was Consort of Azgard and the real ruler, working behind the scenes to keep her husband and daughter safe from her power-hungry, unscrupulous brother-in-law.

**Polaris, House of**

One of the Great Houses. The head of this House also held the Dukedom of Eden.

**Polaris, Lady Tara**

Mother of Lady Mary Atlas, wife of Prince David Atlas, she died in an inexplicable crash of a *zefir*.

**Polaris, Lord Tarkon**

Duke of Eden, head of the House of Polaris and younger brother of Lady Tara. Lord Tarkon was unmarried for many years and a solid supporter of Prince Seti.

**Poseidon, House of**

The senior branch of the Toltecs' Royal family, believed to be descended from Poseidon, thought to be the elder son of Kronos. The head of this House also inherited the Kingship.

**Poseidon, Kefren**

Holder of the Kingship during the early part of the life of Helen. Kefren was far happier as a scholar than a ruler. He relied heavily on his wife, the Lord Protector, and the Lord Steward to keep him secure in his position.

**Poseidon, Lady Sabrina**

The elder and preferred of Kefren's younger sisters. She was married to Lord James Mordecai but lapsed into a coma and later died before producing any children. She was attended to by Miriam Andros.

**Poseidon, Lady Samantha**

Eldest child and daughter of Prince Seti and his wife. After Lady Sabrina's death, Kefren betrothed Lady Samantha to Lord James Mordecai over her father's strenuous objections.

**Poseidon, Lord Sargon**

Only son of Prince Seti and second in line for the Kingship after his father. He was also Duke of Atlanta and betrothed to Lady Mary.

**Poseidon, Prince Seti**

Younger brother of Kefren, the Exalted Lord, and his heir. He was born to the title of Prince of Istar since Kefren had no son.

**Poseidon, Lady Siroma**

The younger and least favorite of Kefren's sisters. She was married to Jacob Shinar, the Lord Steward, and was the mother of Lord Matthew Shinar.

**Protectorship**

The hereditary military position held by the lord of the House of Mordecai. Often it was little more than ceremonial. Lord James Mordecai was a notable exception to this rule, bringing years of military and command experience to the post.

**Rotor**

An aircraft primarily used for military transports, although the wealthy could and did keep these machines to traverse the island much faster than by land or sea. Unlike vehicles powered by impellers, rotors needed fuel to operate.

**Sacred Academy of Kronos**

The only institution of higher learning in Azgard. The Academy had rigorous standards and admitted few Turanians, even fewer mixed-race students. It offered scholarships to those who, like Helen, passed an extremely difficult entry examination.

**Sacred City (Shambhala)**

Located at the center of the island, this city was where the Exalted Lord lived and ruled. It was also home to the seat of government administration as well as estates of the Great Houses.

**Shamin, House of**

A Lesser House distinguished primarily through advantageous marital connections that resulted from providing its two daughters with enormous dowries.

**Shamin, Lady Lydia**

Wife of Prince Seti and Princess of Istar, mother of Lord Sargon and Lady Samantha, and younger sister of Lady Dora Shamin, the deceased first wife of Prince Enoch Atlas and mother of Lord Nimrod Atlas.

**Shinar, Jacob**

Father of Lord Matthew Shinar and married to Lady Siroma Poseidon, Jacob held the office of Lord Steward and was a staunch ally of Kefren against his younger brother, Prince Seti.

**Shinar, Lord Matthew**

Only child Of Jacob Shinar and Lady Siroma Poseidon. He and Helen developed a lifelong close friendship during their time together at the Sacred Academy of Kronos. Lord Matthew was secretly in love with Lord Justin Atlas, who returned his feelings.

**Silenas, Lucan**

The Holy Deputy during the younger years of Helen. He was amoral and power-obsessed and had a demonic ally.

***Sigra***

A cross between a cigar and a cigarette, it was a favorite smoke of Lord James Mordecai and other Toltecs.

**Skimmer**

Vehicles that glided very fast over water or land, using impeller engines to keep them elevated and moving. They did not need fuel to run so long as the impeller was intact.

**Slipskin**

A cheap, lightweight material that was waterproof and sturdy. Poorer people used it instead of leather for shoes, clothes, and other items.

**Stewardship**

One of the bases of power in Azgard. The holder of this lifelong office was generally but not always proposed by the Exalted Lord and confirmed by majority vote of the

Kindred. He presided over all sessions of the *Kinshazen* and was the leading civil and criminal magistrate.

**Stoneslayer**

A demonic entity that existed by possessing souls both in human and nonhuman form, feeding off their emotions, and stealing their power in order to survive. The Stoneslayer carried one of the Arkstone fragments and craved the gem Helen owned in order to magnify his power and make him unstoppable. The Stoneslayer pursued Helen and her family through the ages due to their ties to the Arkstone and its fragments.

**Sudras, Isaac (Grand Master)**

The Grand Master of the Sacred Academy of Kronos and a *koji*, Isaac Sudras was a staunch supporter of Helen during her years at the university and when she began practicing medicine. He was also a good friend of Judith Altair and did not hold extreme views about Toltec racial superiority.

*Sung-fei*

A Terzil word for an ancient Toltec sexual ritual that involved varying degrees of violence and bondage. It was believed to be necessary to conceive strong leaders and great warriors.

**Temple of Kronos**

The institution of the Toltecs' state religion, ruled by the absolute authority of the Supreme Lord. The Temple preached the political and social dominance of the Toltecs based on their presumed superiority over other peoples. By the life of Helen, the Temple also espoused racial purity and frowned on marriages or sexual relations between Toltecs and any other people.

**Terzil**

The language of the Toltecs. It was reserved for official documents and debate on the floor of Kindred House. It was a complex tongue with a guttural sound and cadence, not easy to learn or use.

**Toltecs**

A race of very tall strong people with coppery to dark red-brown skin, dark brown eyes, and thick, coarse black hair. They were more technologically advanced than other peoples of the world and some political factions wanted to control world events and other countries. They ruled Azgard and discriminated against anyone who was not Toltec. They lived far longer than other people.

**Turanians**

The conquered people of Azgard; they had light skin, blond, brown, or red hair with blue or green eyes. They had no power or influence, and could find work only in factories or as servants. A fortunate few managed to own and farm land or engage in humble occupations, such as blacksmith, farmer, or tailor/dressmaker.

**Westar, Princedom of**

The position held by the head of the House of Atlas, the junior Royal House descending from Prince Atlas. The title bestowed great wealth, power, and influence on its holder.

**Westar Province**

The domain of the House of Atlas, this province was in the southwestern portion of the island. Its wealth derived from a mix of trade and agriculture. The very popular liquor pepper brandy came from this province.

**Wordskin**

The Toltecs' version of paper, similar to parchment. During the life of Helen, wordskin was used primarily by Turanians because they were not allowed Grid access to store documents in nonphysical format.

***Zefir***

Airships built in the earliest days of the Toltecs' dominance in Azgard. Fast and silent, they required no fuel to stay airborne or move. Only the Royal Houses and Great Houses could afford them by the life of Helen. Most were reserved for military use during war.